# THERE LIES

# A HIDDEN

# SCORPION

Also by Takis and Judy Iakovou

*Go Close Against the Enemy*
*So Dear to Wicked Men*

Takis and Judy Iakovou

# THERE LIES

# A HIDDEN

# SCORPION

ST. MARTIN'S
MINOTAUR

St. Martin's Minotaur ❧ New York

Library of Congress Cataloging-in-Publication Data

Iakovou, Takis.
    There lies a hidden scorpion / Takis and Judy Iakovou. — 1st ed.
        p.      cm.
    ISBN 0-312-24200-X
    1. Greek Americans—Florida—Tarpon Springs Fiction. I. Iakovou, Judy. II. Title.
PS3559.A45T48    1999                                    99-34020
813'.54—dc21                                                  CIP

First Edition: November 1999

10   9   8   7   6   5   4   3   2   1

For
Cathy and Tim,
whose loving support
has so often sustained us

*Underneath every stone there lies a hidden scorpion, my friend.*
*Take care, or he will sting you. All concealment is treachery.*

—Anonymous Drinking Song,
Fourth Century B.C.

*Acknowledgments*

Any reader familiar with the city of Tarpon Springs, Florida, will recognize that the site of the *Mediterraneo* Hotel has usurped a prominent residential area. Our apologies to those people who were moved from their homes to suit our purposes.

We would like to gratefully acknowledge the assistance and support of many residents of Tarpon Springs, in particular Officer Robert Quinn of the Tarpon Springs Police Department for his assistance in police procedural matters; Ms. Mimi Chamberlain of the Tarpon Springs Fire Department for information about geography and water rescues in the area; Andreas and Rene Salivaras of Mykonos Restaurant for taking the time to acquaint us with the Tarpon Springs Greek community, the Epiphany celebration, and the area in general; and the many residents, shopkeepers, and restaurateurs who gave us a taste of life in their beautiful town.

Thanks also to Mr. Cecil Greek for his guidance in Florida law; to Mr. Peter Zoudis for instructing us in the art of iconography and precious metals; to Dr. Thomas Conahan for his steadfast willingness to give us medical guidance; to Father Michael Eaccarino for his guidance through Orthodox theology; and to Ms. Harriette Austin and her

Murder and Mayhem group for their valuable support and advice. Any errors in the book are strictly our own.

We are especially indebted to our agent, Joan Brandt, who will straighten us out yet; to our editor, Kelley Ragland, for her gentle guidance; and to our children, Angie, Mari, and now Andrew, who always go along with us, even when they'd rather not.

And finally, a special word of thanks to Beverly and Charles Connor, Diane Trap, Marie and Richard Davis, and Mike Swanson, all of whom were there in the eleventh hour. Thanks, guys!

THERE LIES

A HIDDEN

SCORPION

*Chapter One*

The Greeks called him Eros. The Romans called him Cupid. Today he'd probably make the rounds of all the television talk shows, hailed by the pop culture as a modern love guru. But the Eros of ancient times was no benign, beaming angel of cherubic proportions, wings and eyelashes all aflutter. Nor was he blind. On the contrary, a spoiled and headstrong lesser god, he knew exactly what he was doing. His quiver was chocked with arrows—half of them wrought in gold and half in lead—waiting for targets who were less the objects of tender goodwill than of spiteful pranks. It was a happy coincidence indeed when both the suitor and the object of his affections were struck by golden arrows. Too often, the suitor's sweetheart took the lead bolt—sure poison to any budding love affair.

According to legend, Eros sharpened his arrows on a grindstone wet with blood. And so it was for Kate and Alex, descendants of these noble Greeks. Their wedding invitation arrived two days after Thanksgiving.

Mr. and Mrs. Manolis Papavasilakis
request the honour of your presence
at the marriage of their daughter
Katerina Nicole
to
Mr. Alexandros Kyriakidis
on Saturday, January 8
at seven o'clock in the evening
St. Nicholas Greek Orthodox Cathedral
18 North Hibiscus St.
Tarpon Springs, Florida


Reception immediately following
The Mediterraneo Hotel
Consulate Room
The favour of a reply is requested

The first two hours of the trip to Tarpon Springs were as peaceful as could be expected with Jack, our Scottish terrier, bouncing between the front and back seats, barking at a disembodied voice that took our orders at a drive through window, and smudging the back window of the car with his wet little nose. Somewhere around Macon, I slipped him a doggie downer in the crust of an Egg Mc-Muffin. By the time we reached Valdosta, he was snoozing peacefully on the back window ledge and Nick and I had our first opportunity for rational conversation.

We'd been listening to *demotiki* music, that is, authentic folk-dance tunes, for a hundred and fifty miles. Nick had been trying to teach me some of the more difficult Greek dances for the last three weeks. He seemed to think that if I listened to the music long enough, I'd somehow absorb its rhythms into my genes, but Irish–American is not so easily transmuted to Greek. The only thing our music had in common was the occasional soulful wail of a bagpipe— Nick's of the goatskin rather than the tartan species. I popped the tape out and snapped in Vangelis's "Chariots of Fire," holding up a hand to stave off comment.

"Still Greek," I said.

When the invitation arrived, I never dreamed that we would be going to the wedding. But the students at Parnassus University had gone home on break, and no one else had the money to eat out after the holidays. Even the Buffaloes, our local businessmen's group, were usually too busy to continue their regular morning "meetings" at the Oracle, our café in Delphi. In their case, it wasn't a matter of money. They never spent any anyway. But they did go out of town for the holidays, or on hunting trips, or took cruises, or whatever people with an excess of time and money and a dearth of meaningful work did during the post-holiday season. So we hung a "Closed For Vacation" sign on the front door, pulled out a map and brought our suitcases down from the attic.

Our cook, Spiros, was Kate's godfather and had been asked to serve as the *koumbaros*—the equivalent of best man, but a position accorded considerably more stature among Greeks. When he invited his elderly neighbor, Miss Alma Rayburn, to be his date, she jumped at the opportunity, feeling that Tarpon Springs might be the closest she'd ever get to Greece. We saw them off, contentedly settled into the yawning interior of Spiros's vintage '69 Pontiac for nine hours of bobbing down the highway without the benefit of shock absorbers. It was now the next day and we were following the same route.

I was looking forward to the wedding, and to a vacation together. We hadn't been able to take one in several years. It was good to be getting away from Delphi, if only for a week or so. Still, as we got closer to Tarpon Springs, my mind filled with a nagging disquiet. I knew what was causing it, I just didn't know how to broach the subject to Nick. Somewhere near the outskirts of Tampa, I took a deep breath.

"Nick, I need you to promise me something."

"Anything, *koritsi mou*. Your wish is my . . . whatever."

"I want you to stay with me."

"I wasn't planning to leave you."

"No," I said. "I mean while we're in Tarpon. I want you to stay with me. Don't go off with Manolis and leave me with people I don't know."

He shot me a puzzled expression. "I don't understand."

Oh, how to explain this to a man who had lived away from his own country for ten years? We were going to be with Greeks—Americans, but people still very much entrenched in their ancestral culture—and I was already conscious of feeling out of place. I turned this over in my mind, trying to put my fears into words.

"I know you're excited about being with Manolis again."

"Well, you know Manolis and Georgia."

"Yes, I know them. But we're not close. And when everyone is speaking Greek, and telling jokes and laughing . . . I feel kind of left out. And it's awkward, you know? When they realize I'm not following, they get embarrassed and apologetic. Then I feel like I've put a damper on everything and . . . I just want you to stick with me. Somehow when you're around, it's not so bad. Do you understand?"

"Maybe better than you think," he answered quietly.

He didn't mean it as a rebuke, and yet it felt like one. Nick hadn't spoken English very well when we met. His English was much improved but far from perfect even now. Sometimes, I knew, he had a hard time following conversations. He hadn't even been sure he was going to stay in America until I came into his life. He'd made the adjustment seem easy, but I knew it wasn't. He was separated from his family and the country and traditions he loved. He'd made sacrifices for me. A week of feeling excluded was little enough to endure for him.

"Never mind," I said, patting his hand. "I want you to have a good time. That's all that really matters."

He reached up to stroke my cheek with the back of his hand. "Don't worry. I'll be right there with you. I promise."

I gazed down at the map as we crossed onto 275, by-passed Tampa and veered onto the bridge across Tampa Bay. I pulled out Georgia Papavasilakis's carefully written directions and pointed Nick onto Highway 19, which was not unlike entering the stock-car races. Flocks of snowbirds with out-of-state and Canadian license plates clogged the highway, turning the more intense commuters into Mr. Hydes of the road. I gripped the dashboard and held on as semis and sports cars tore around us on all sides.

"Okay, left on Klosterman Road. There!" I said, pointing to the sign. We followed it across to Alternate 19 and hung a right, leading us straight into downtown Tarpon Springs. My heart began hammering at the wall of my chest. This wasn't exactly in anticipation of the happy event. There was one thing I hadn't told Nick. I wasn't sure that the hotel accepted dogs.

I had planned to break this to him somewhere around Gainesville, but the opportunity hadn't presented itself. He hit the brakes in front of the cathedral, turned a hard right and slammed into the church parking lot.

"You what? You said you called them."

"No, actually what I said was that I *would* call them. Only, I . . . didn't. Look, I'm sure it will be fine. It's always easier to get forgiveness than permission. If they won't let him stay, there are bound to be kennels in Tarpon Springs. He'll be better off here than in Delphi—the weather's much warmer."

In fact, at that moment, it was positively scorching inside our little Honda. Nick's temperature had gone up—way up—and he radiated steam. The muscles in his jaw rippled. "I can't believe you did this." In retrospect, it didn't seem too prudent.

"Nick, I just couldn't leave him—" I stopped, realizing it was an empty justification. Jack had filled a need in my life when I'd miscarried late in my pregnancy. But, I reminded myself, he was still a dog. "I'm sorry."

Nick laid his forehead against the steering wheel and took several long, slow breaths. "We'll have to find a kennel. Manolis's family and mine have been friends for twenty-five years. I can't do anything that would embarrass him, Julia." We sat in silence, listening to Jack snore and snuffle in the back seat.

"I'm sorry," I said again, and truly I was. This was no way to begin our vacation. "I'll start calling kennels as soon as we get checked in."

"No," he said, putting the car back into gear. "Let's go find a phone and call one now."

The first two kennels I tried were booked through Epiphany. One took our number at the hotel in case an opening turned up after the New Year, when residents in the area started returning from holiday trips. The third kennel, The Coddled Canine—"Boarding Tampa Bay's Particular Pets"—wanted to know if Jack was AKC registered. I assured them he was. Their rates were high, but we really didn't have much choice. We left him still sleeping off his doggie downer.

"Please," I said, handing over the plaid pillow out of his basket bed. "Make sure he has his pillow." It wasn't as if he ever slept on it, but I thought the familiar smell might be a comfort to him when he woke up and found us gone. The Coddled Canine "hostess" greeted the idea with withering scorn.

"We'll have to spray it for fleas and ticks," she said. And of course there would be a separate charge.

"I thought you said you pampered the dogs you kept here," I pointed out, loading her arms with other necessities for Jack. She favored me with an atrophied smile. She took his toys, rawhide bones, and assorted sundries with a distaste registered by her two-fingered grasp, but declined his bag of kibble.

"We only serve our guests our own mix of dietetically balanced protein, vitamins, and minerals."

I nodded in hearty agreement. "Yum!" I returned to the car feeling like an intruder in the aristocratic world of the canine elite. I hoped the other dogs wouldn't snub him.

It had taken us longer to find Jack appropriate accommodations than we anticipated. I glanced at my watch as I climbed into the car. "You know, we're going to be late if we go to the hotel first," I said. "Why don't we just go on to the restaurant and call the hotel from there? They can hold the reservation for late arrival."

Nick agreed and headed the car toward the Sponge Docks area of town. There were no parking spaces directly on Dodecanese Boulevard. After making several passes up and down the street, we gave up on the idea of getting close to the restaurant and found a space at the end of the street, where it ends at the Anclote River and hooks a right angle into Island Drive. The street, at that end, was quiet, the silence broken only by the occasional plaintive cry of a gull. The evening was cool and damp, the air tangy with the odor of fish, which might have had something to do with the wholesale fish market across the street from our parking space. Still, I didn't find the smell unpleasant. In fact, it reminded me of our honeymoon, spent in the Greek islands. I said as much to Nick.

"Remember the first night on Hydra?"

Nick laughed and took my elbow, moving to the outside of the street as he guided me around the curve in the road. "What I remember about Hydra is you on that donkey."

"I don't want to talk about that. Anyway, it wasn't my fault."

"Yeah, but Julia, I tried to tell you—"

He never finished his sentence. A squeal of tires brought our heads up. Farther along Dodecanese Boulevard, pas-sersby screamed and dove inside the doorways of the little shops that lined the street. Nick shoved me sharply to the right as a car careened toward us, shot up over the sidewalk and thumped back onto the pavement, headed directly for us. He tackled me, propelling me onto a grassy verge next to a parking lot and covering me with his body. Before I hit the ground, I had a brief glimpse of a passenger wrestling with the steering wheel and a driver slumped over the wheel. Both of them were women and one wore an expression of utter horror. Even above the engine noise and the friction of rubber and pavement, a shrill scream flowed through a half-open window and left behind it a wake of terror.

Another screech of rubber as the car veered away from us, fishtailed, and slammed the driver's door against a streetlight. Glass shattered and metal shrieked and buckled, but the impact scarcely seemed to slow the car's momentum. By the time we were back on our feet, the car had catapulted off the seawall and the front end disappeared into the river.

## Chapter Two

"Get help!" Nick shouted over his shoulder.

He was already across the street and racing for the river. Farther up the block, other pedestrians froze to watch the car in alarm. One man sprinted past them, shouting into a cell phone. I knew he had the help call covered, so I took off after Nick, but by the time I reached the river, only his shoes, yanked off at the bank, were in sight. I stood at the edge of the seawall and watched the water swallow up the remainder of the car, praying, watching for any sign of my husband, and praying some more.

How deep was the water? Had the car reached the bottom, or was it still dropping slowly, inexorably? The water was dark and brackish—a mixture of fresh and salt water blackened further by the churning of boats in the shipping lane. Somewhere out of sight, out of reach, two young women were struggling for their lives, and Nick along with them. My God, the sheer panic those women must feel—unable to cry for help. Would they know that they had been seen? Would they realize that help was on the way? I shivered reflexively and dug my nails into the palms of my hands, willing them all to appear.

Suddenly Nick surfaced, but only long enough to gasp

for air and dive again. *Be careful,* I admonished him silently. To my left, another diver plunged into the river in a great spray of water. He'd left a trail of hat, glasses, and a package wrapped in white paper scattered across the dirt. Beside me, the man with the cell phone appeared, pulled off his jacket and began rolling up his sleeves. Some of the other pedestrians had reached the river.

"How long?" the man asked. "How long have they been in there, do you think?"

"I . . . I don't know. A minute or two, maybe a little more."

"How much help do they have?"

"Two divers—my husband—" Nick appeared on cue and disappeared again. "—and someone else."

"I've called for a rescue squad."

I nodded and turned back to the water.

Nick appeared again. This time, he had a body in tow. He pulled her toward the edge of the river, where willing hands brought her up onto the bank. Nick again stroked swiftly toward the place where the car had disappeared as the man with the cell phone pushed the crowd back.

"I'm a doctor," the man shouted. "Give me room to work." He dropped to his knees and after a cursory examination, pulled the girl upright and performed a Heimlich maneuver on her. He rolled her onto her back, threw his jacket over her and began mouth-to-mouth resuscitation. I turned back to the river, watching Nick for signs of fatigue.

A wail behind me, a car sharply braking, and the quick whoop of a siren dying. A police-band radio squawked and the murmuring of the crowd escalated. But I couldn't turn my gaze away from the dark water to look.

In the water, the other diver surfaced—a familiar-looking mustache dripping water, his gaze myopic without his thick glasses. Spiros. "*Ella,* Niko" he cried. "*Then boro na tin vgalo exo.*"

11

Nick swam to the left and dove again, joining Spiros under the water. A cop was past me and over the edge of the seawall, stroking in their direction. They reappeared at intervals, long enough to gasp deeply, get their bearings and dive again. Several bystanders joined them in the water.

I lost track of time. It could have been only minutes. It seemed like hours. Nightfall and dark water, men without light or diving equipment. And below them, a young woman who surely, now, had taken in deep lungfuls of water. Was she conscious? Did she know how hard these strangers were working to help her? Was she thinking about her family? Was she afraid to die?

Nick reappeared, swimming back to his right and disappearing under the surface again as the rest of us stood by watching helplessly. I could have gone in myself. I'm a fairly good swimmer. But Nick is far stronger in the water than I—his island upbringing is as ingrained as his accent—and I knew I would only be a distraction. Instead, I resumed my watch for my husband, praying that nothing unforeseen would happen in those dark waters, counting the seconds until his head emerged again.

Behind me, more pedestrians crowded the scene and a second siren wailed. "The ambulance"—whispered in hushed voices by the crowd. A retching, gurgling sound followed by murmurs of relief. The doctor had resuscitated the girl Nick had brought in. A clatter of metal—a gurney being pulled from the back of the ambulance—and another siren's wail and the heavy thrum of an engine. A rescue truck. Squawking radios and men shouting.

Nick's head appeared briefly on the surface. "We need a knife," he shouted.

A large pocketknife whistled past me. He snatched it out of the air and disappeared again as the other divers emerged to the right and went under once more. Finally, they all appeared and began straggling into shore.

The cop towed the young woman to the edge of the river, where the doctor and an EMT pulled her limp body up over the concrete ledge. Her face was deathly pale, her lips blue—a sharp contrast to the long, wet auburn hair that clung to her face like strings of seaweed.

"One, two, three . . ." They initiated CPR, sweating over the girl's body for what seemed like hours. The crowd was agonizingly quiet. I think we all knew there was no hope for her. Even if they could have raised a heartbeat, too much time without oxygen had elapsed. She would be irreparably brain-damaged—probably condemned to a future of life support. At length, the doctor sat back on his feet and shook his head. They had been too late.

I clutched Nick and drew him close, ignoring the water that ran off his face and body. "Are you all right? Oh, my God, Nick, are you okay?"

He shivered, gasped and pulled me into his arms. "I'm okay. We couldn't . . . her door was stuck. Belt jammed. Couldn't see, couldn't get to her. We just couldn't get her out." He tightened his grip around me and his chest heaved convulsively.

I knew what he was feeling. I felt it too. The elation of saving a life, the despair of losing another. The victims were young, probably in their early twenties. The one would live, but the other . . . well, somewhere there were parents to notify, maybe a husband. Someone might be expecting her home soon, even now looking at the clock and wondering what could be keeping her. Oh no, I thought, suppose she'd had children? I couldn't bear to think about it.

"How did Spiros—"

"I don't know. Where is he?"

I spotted him first. He was standing at the edge of the crowd, gazing at the car's passenger. He'd retrieved his hat and glasses, which he adjusted to get a better look at the girl. She was strapped to a gurney. An oxygen mask covered her nose and mouth. The two EMTs hoisted the litter and slid it into the back of the ambulance.

Spiros is our cook at the Oracle in Delphi. He came to us by way of Manolis, who is his cousin, at a time when we desperately needed to get Nick out of the kitchen. But more than an employee, Spiros is a dear friend—herculean of stature, tender of soul. He broke away from the crowd and loped toward us, shaking his head.

"Too sad, Zulia," he said.

"Where were you, Spiro?" I asked.

He pointed down the street. "Feesh mar-ket. *Kalamari.*" He walked over to the bank, returning with a bundle wrapped in white butcher's paper. His gaze traveled to the edge of the river, where a young woman's body lay carefully covered. I took his hand.

"You did everything you could. Both of you."

"Her door wouldn't open," Nick repeated. He seemed to be talking as much to himself as to me. "It was all smashed in."

"From the street lamp," I said. He only nodded.

"Her window was broken. We might have pulled her out, only the seat belt jammed. We had to cut her out of the belt, but we couldn't see. It was just too late."

I hugged my husband again. "At least you saved the other girl. I heard the EMT say she's going to be all right."

Nick nodded. I followed his gaze to the still body on the bank. She was covered by a paper sheet. Only her left hand hung limp, her curled fingers resting on the dirt. A small diamond on her fourth finger flashed in the arcing blue beam from the police light bar. An unexpected sob caught at the back of my throat.

Spiros took off his glasses and wiped his eyes with the back of his hand. He pulled a wet handkerchief out of his pocket and blew his nose softly. Behind us, a siren howled as the ambulance pulled out onto Dodecanese Boulevard. Spiros watched it recede in the distance and shook his head. He turned back to me.

"*To koritsi,* Zulia. Thees girl—I know her."


Our arrival at the hotel was not what I had imagined. I drove with Nick beside me, still wrapped in the blanket, and Spiros wedged into the back seat. Honda back seats are not made for the likes of Spiros.

We turned on Bath Street, following it about a block to a marble sign set on a pair of Doric columns. The drive was cobbled, winding, and lined with massive live-oak trees dripping Spanish moss in lacy webs that gave way to hedges of pittosporum. Beyond them, the hotel stood washed in late-day sunlight—four stories of simple, white-stucco exterior with bright blue shuttered windows, much like the hotels we'd stayed in on the Cycladic islands.

So this was the *Mediterraneo* hotel—a new inn on Spring Bayou, owned by Christos Kyriakidis, the father of the groom. Christos was not a resident of Tarpon Springs, but a hotelier originally from the Patras area of Greece. He now made his home in Athens, where he could conveniently travel to any of the chain of hotels that dotted the Aegean islands like an add-a-pearl necklace. His newest venture was a departure from the others only in location.

The merchants of Tarpon Springs, so Manolis had said, had been trying to attract a major hotel into the Sponge Docks area of town for some time. When none of the large American chains expressed interest, they turned to their compatriots across the Atlantic. Christos Kyriakidis was the first—but not the only—Greek hotelier to express interest in the project. His interest quickly turned into a buying spree as he picked up enough homes on the bayou, at top drachma prices, to not only construct a one-hundred-twenty-five-room hotel and Continental dining room, but to protect it on all sides with several acres of Mediterranean terraces and gardens. It was an edifice worthy of the Mediterranean coast, and its Grand Opening, by invitation only, would take place on New Year's Eve. Among the guests currently registered were members of the wedding party and a string of Christos's VIP business connections.

To the right of the hotel, a swimming pool lined with citrus trees sparkled in the exact blue of the Mediterranean. And rising from the center of it, a Venus de Milo surrounded by misty fountains invited us in for a quick dip. She was a beautiful thing, but Nick stared at her with a distracted expression. The gruesome parallel was not lost on me. I squeezed his hand gently as we continued on the drive, circling around to the main entrance to stop under a portico.

"I'll get us checked in," I said, "so you don't have to stand in the lobby wet like that. Be right back."

Inside, the hotel was far more elegant than its façade suggested. The walls were of white stucco, the floor made of lightly veined white Penteli marble; the lobby was as simple, in its way, as the plain, boxlike exterior. To the left of the main entrance was a glass-enclosed gift shop, and next to it, a small hairdresser's shop. The desk was off to the right, unobtrusively up to date, with three computer terminals spaced at even intervals over a dark oak countertop. I headed that way and gave the clerk our name.

"Do you have a reservation?" The girl behind the desk, whose badge read "Lucy Wharton", puckered her brow and tucked a lock of hair behind one ear.

"Yes, and if you don't mind, I'm in kind of a hurry." I pulled a scrap of paper out of my bag and read her our confirmation number.

She tapped at the keys on the computer in counterpoint to my fingers drumming on the desk. At length, she blew a sigh that ruffled the wispy bangs on her forehead.

"Just a minute, please," she said, disappearing through a door behind the desk. In a second, she was back with another desk clerk in tow—a young man whose starched collar, Greek-key tie, and navy blazer did not disguise his youth. He checked the reservation number, took his turn tapping the keyboard and hit "Print."

"Lucy," he said, "you're going to have to learn your way around this program." He presented her with a sour smile, picked up a clipboard and turned back to the door, stopping short as a woman, armed with a leather binder, marched out of the inner office. "I have a new Greek Key Club list. Can you sign off on it?" he asked her.

The woman reached for the clipboard, stopping short before actually taking it from his hand. "No. That's Mr. Kyriakidis's—Mr. Alex's—project. He'll have to go over it."

She shifted the binder from one arm to the other. "There are too many interruptions here," she said. She pushed open the Dutch door of the desk and clicked across the lobby on two-inch, all-business heels. "I have to get this seating chart done before I leave. I'll be working in my apartment," she called over her shoulder. "And I don't want to be disturbed for any reason. You should be able to handle anything that comes up." She executed a right face and disappeared down a corridor off the lobby.

The clerk ducked his head, cleared his throat, and slipped through the door to the inner office. That left me with the girl with the bangs, who blew them again and pushed the printout across the desk for me to sign.

"That was close. If she had any idea of how much trouble I was having with this system, she'd have me cleaning *toilets*," Lucy said, giving the word a French spin.

"Who was that?"

"Ms. Paradissis," she said with a little smirk. "The guys in the kitchen call her 'The Baked Alaska'—you know, hot on the outside, but . . ." Lucy thumped her chest ". . . frozen in here."

Despite a few questioning glances in our direction, the bellboy was too polite to ask about Nick's bedraggled appearance. We followed him along the same path Lucy's boss had taken, across the lobby and down the hall to the right of the desk, stopping at the ninth room from the lobby. He stepped back to allow us to enter.

The first thing I noticed about the room was the set of French doors leading out onto a flagstone terrace bordered by pots of purple and carmine petunias and hedges of oleander and pittosporum. Beyond the terrace, the grounds of the hotel stretched all the way to Spring Street and the water of the bayou.

The room was spacious and decorated in much the same style as the lobby. The walls were a cool, white stucco, the floors a richly burnished hardwood. A huge rag rug accented oak furnishings stained a Mediterranean blue—a king-sized bed with delicately carved head and footboard and a matching blue chest. A soft, white flokati awaited our bare toes in front of a marble counter with a double sink, a small coffeemaker, and a compact microwave oven.

The bellboy disposed of our luggage and hung our clothing bag in an old-fashioned wardrobe chest of the same bright blue. He made the rounds of the room, checking the small bar judiciously hidden under the television stand, showing us the remote control and explaining the telephone system. When he was gone, I went to my husband, standing at the French doors, and wrapped my arms around him.

A last burst of sunlight twinkled on the dark bayou. It would have been a charming view two hours before, but now, the sight of that water was only a grim reminder of death.

## Chapter Three

"You need to get in a warm shower," I said, turning Nick around and pointing him toward the bathroom. "I'll get you some fresh clothes and call Manolis and Georgia."

On the dresser, a tissue-lined basket held two soft, real sponges, probably harvested by the spongers of Tarpon Springs. Wedged in between them was a selection of Godiva chocolates, a bottle of silky lotion, and an apothecary jar filled with bubble-bath powder. A white card had been stuck in the top of the basket.

Welcome to Tarpon Springs!
Thank you for being here to share our special day.
Love,
Kate and Alex

*How sweet*, I thought as I grabbed the basket and followed Nick to the bathroom. And what a bathroom it was. It held a second set of marble double sinks and, to give it a genuine European flavor, a bidet. Like the outer sinks, a backsplash of brightly colored, hand-painted tiles carried over into a border around the bathtub—a very large, square bathtub.

With a Jacuzzi. I started the water running and helped my husband peel off his wet clothes.

At any other time, I might have been tempted to climb into the tub with him, but it seemed a little frivolous at the moment. Instead, while he showered, I inspected the remainder of the room's appointments. A square game table stood in front of the window, a pair of ladder-back chairs on either side, just waiting for a game of *tavli* to begin. In fact, the designer had even been thoughtful enough to provide an inlaid backgammon board and a small drawer fitted with checkers and dice. I was sure Spiros and Nick would make good use of them.

I called the restaurant to let them know what had happened. Georgia understood. Everyone would be waiting for us whenever we could get there. It wasn't a wonderful way to begin a vacation.

A pall hung over the car as we pulled out of the hotel parking lot that night. "The girl," Spiros said, "and the other—the friend. At *O Kritikos*."

"When? Tonight?"

"Yes," he answered slowly. "Tonight. They sit . . ." He shrugged broadly and lapsed into Greek, explaining to Nick what was too difficult for him to say in English.

The girls had been to Manolis's restaurant—*O Kritikos*—early in the evening. They had stopped in briefly, had one or two drinks at the bar and left at the same time that Spiros had left for the fish market. Spiros had been gone only as long as it had taken to walk to the end of the street and pick up the *kalamari*, which had been ordered in advance by telephone. His estimate was not more than ten minutes, probably less.

"There must have been something wrong with the car," I said.

"Maybe," Nick agreed. "But it looked like the driver was passed out. Did you notice?"

I had. She had been slumped over. I hadn't even seen her hands on the steering wheel—only the poor girl next to her, frantically trying to get control of the car.

We pulled onto Dodecanese Boulevard, all three glances going inadvertently to the end of the street. Two police cars sat at the scene of the accident, but their lights were now turned off. Several officers were studying the dirt next to the seawall. A police photographer was taking pictures of the edge of the water where the car had plunged into the river. The crowd had dispersed. One look at Nick's face, etched with agony, told the story. He was feeling the loss much more than the win.

Earlier, the police had been eager to interview both Nick and Spiros, even me, as to what we had seen and done. The officer who was first on the scene had sat slumped-shouldered, wrapped in a blanket, staring over the seawall. Another officer had found several more blankets for Nick and Spiros and taken our statements. Nick had translated for Spiros, who had come out of the fish market just in time to see the car go off the seawall. Nick had beaten him to the scene by a matter of seconds. Could it have been only seconds? The car, the officer had said, would be brought out of the river and inspected in the morning.

The officer had tucked his pad and pen away in the pocket of his shirt. "I'm going over to the hospital next. See what the other one—the passenger—can tell me. If she can talk. We may have more questions for you later, Mr. Lambros. You'll be around?" Nick had told him how to reach us before we all piled back into the car, anxious to escape the crowd, and returned to the hotel.

Now Nick angled the car into a space across from the Sponge Docks, but none of us moved to get out. Spiros ticked his tongue and shook his head. *"Mikres kopeles."* he whispered. Little girls.

"Look," I said, "this has been very sad. But we're not being fair to Kate and Alex if we let it spoil their party tonight. They're over there waiting for us, worrying about us. We're going to have to put on happier faces than this for their sake. Come on." I climbed out of the car. "Let's put it behind us for tonight."

I glanced around the street, trying to see Tarpon Springs for the first time, as I might have seen it several hours earlier. Little white boats chocked the river, most of them trimmed in shades of blue and christened with the names of saints who would be expected to watch over them while at sea. Principal among them was St. Nicholas, patron saint of seafarers, for whom the cathedral was named.

Farther up the river, two husky tour boats waited for their passengers to board for dinner and an evening cruise. Long strings of white lights twinkled on the dark water. Somewhere on the roof of one of the boats, a band played a Miami Sound Machine tune. Nick grabbed my hand and sambaed me up the sidewalk. I went along with it, both of us pretending that our hearts were in it, knowing all the while that they weren't.

"Manolis's place is over there." He wrapped his arm around my waist and hurried me across the street, with Spiros bounding along behind.

Tarpon Springs has an unusually large Greek population. Divers from the Dodecanese islands were originally brought in to the area when sponge divers were needed to work the beds in the local waters. Although the diving trade has mainly passed into the hands of other groups, the Greeks have remained to raise their families and open other businesses.

We walked past a bakery, the fragrant smell of honey

and lemon wafting out the door, and on up Dodecanese Boulevard. As the clock ticked toward nine, the shopkeepers had began taking in the racks that lined the sidewalks with sponges, shells, and T-shirts, chattering to one another in Greek. I wished I had been more meticulous about studying Greek instead of relying on Nick to translate for me. I understood quite a lot, actually—more than I ever let Nick know—but I would have liked to exchange more than pleasant greetings with people.

We turned onto Athens Street, away from the central business area, passed *Dino's* and *Zorba's*. Bouzouki music filtered out the doors of the *tavernas*, wrapping around us and calling us in to dance. But we didn't stop, persisting on up the block to Manolis's café—*O Kritikos*—the Cretan.

"Niko! Thank God you are here safely," Manolis cried, coming through the dining room. "And you, *xadelphaki mou.*" He slapped Spiros heartily on the back. "We were worried about you."

"We're fine," Nick said.

"It was a dangerous thing you did, Niko *mou.* We've had customers who saw it all . . . it's all they're talking about. My cousin and my friend—heroes."

"Not really, Manolis." Nick frowned. "We weren't able to save the driver."

"But you saved the other girl," Georgia said, arriving at her husband's side. She hugged us warmly. I glanced over her shoulder and gave Nick an exaggerated smile—a reminder that this was supposed to be a happy occasion. He responded as best he could, given the circumstances.

I hadn't seen Georgia since our own wedding, over seven years before, when Manolis had served as Nick's *koumbaros.* She was unchanged. Her glossy-brown hair hung smoothly to her shoulders, with only an occasional silvery strand to mark the passing of the years.

"*Ella, ella koritsi mou.*" Spiros pushed a young woman to

the front of the group and stood behind her, his hands resting comfortably on her shoulders. He grinned happily. "*I nifi*, Zulia." The bride. And here those seven years caught up with me.

Kate Papavasilakis had been an awkward, predominantly knees-and-elbows fifteen-year-old with possibilities when Nick and I married. She had more than fulfilled her adolescent promise. Slender as her mother, the knees and elbows had turned into long, gracefully curved limbs. Kate had the classic beauty that hearkened back to her ancestors—a long, straight-sloping nose and gently curved full lips. Her hair, thick and chestnut-brown, gleamed with natural highlights of red and blue. Her laughter reminded me of wind chimes as she reached up to give Spiros's mustache a playful tug.

On Kate's heels stood a young man whose eyes never left her face. She pulled him around beside her. "And this is Alex," she said.

Alex took my hand and pumped it warmly. "Oh, never mind this," he said, his English only lightly traced with an accent. He pulled me into a hug, burying my face in a muscled shoulder that smelled of Lagerfeld cologne. Kate's prince was charming.

He stood a good six inches taller than Kate, putting him right around six feet, and every inch of it attractively packaged. His eyes were almost as black as his hair, and very round, giving him an alert and slightly amused expression. His nose, like his fiancée's, was classic Greek, but heavier boned and larger. Smoothly tanned olive skin glowed with a kind of Mediterranean exuberance. And a grin, equally matched to those mischievous eyes, split over even rows of marble-chip teeth. This was a face and body that belonged on a *Cosmo* calender.

"Come, come," Manolis said, shepherding us toward the dining room. "Everyone waits to meet you."

We followed him to a large table in the center of the dining room, where Miss Alma sat congenially chatting with Alex's family. She wore a soft lavender pantsuit that complemented her silver hair. Approximately thirty-five years Spiros's senior, she had been an isolated, frightened old woman when he came bounding into her life, moving into the house next door, irrepressibly eager to right the wrongs in the neighborhood. Until then, she'd been content to simply survive, but Spiros's attentions had energized and redefined her. I hugged her and took the seat next to her, one of the three remaining empty chairs at the table.

Manolis hovered down at the end of the table, directing waiters in rapid-fire Greek to bring more *mezethes*, wine, and bread. He was smaller than his six-foot cousin by a foot, a sinewy little man who seemed to have copper wiring where there should have been veins. What he lacked in stature he made up for in spirit, with the broad gestures and brisk movements of a man who was as quick to laugh as he was to quarrel. His skin was the same color and texture as Nick's old brown bedroom slippers, a visible reminder that he had come to Tarpon Springs as a sponge diver years ago.

Sponge diving can be a dangerous occupation, often taking its toll early in life. Manolis had given it up several years before, putting his hopes in the restaurant business, which, though difficult at best, was not as physically draining as diving. Still, though he was only fifteen years older than Nick, the ravages of sun, wind, and salt had added another fifteen.

Nick glanced around the dining room, which was filled to capacity. "Business seems to be good, Manoli," he said.

Manolis grinned, giving me a sparkling view of his gold inlays. "I keep my head above water."

It was an unfortunate joke under the circumstances—a

fact that was not lost on Georgia. She gave her husband a hard glare from the opposite end of the table.

"But now you must meet *ta sympetheriká*," Manolis added hastily. An interesting word, I reflected, characterizing the relationship between in-laws.

"This is Alexandros's father, Christos Kyriakidis."

A burly man with iron-gray curly hair rose and reached across the table to shake our hands. "It is a pleasure. My friend Manolis, here, had told us all about you, but we did not know that you are a hero. We have heard nothing but good reports."

"All exaggerated, I'm sure," Nick replied.

Where Alex was very American, in the style of Dockers and Calvin Klein, his father was strictly European. His hand, shooting out of a French cuff, felt surprisingly soft and smooth. He wore a heavy gold wedding band on his right hand and a TAG Heuer watch on his left wrist. His pleated trousers of soft gray flannel were strictly class and complemented a silvery crisp shirt, open at the neck to expose tufts of curling, wiry hair at the base of his throat. Some women would say he exuded sex appeal. I thought he radiated money and power.

"Your hotel is absolutely beautiful," I said, anxious to change the subject for Nick's sake. "Everything is perfect— very Greek, but with all the comforts Americans expect."

Christos smiled broadly with genuine warmth. "You could not have paid us a higher compliment. That is exactly what we were striving for."

"And this—" Manolis broke in, getting on with the introductions "—this is Alex's *yia-yia, I Kyria* Pagona Kyriakidis."

Pagona struggled to her feet and extended her hand, its cold skin as sheer and translucent as a sheet of phyllo pastry. Built along the same proportions as a mason jar, she was almost the same height standing as sitting. Her face reminded me of pilgrim glass, crackled with tiny wrinkles and fissures. She wore no makeup—not even the lightest touch of lipstick—nor did any hint of a smile grace her lips. Her thin hair was pulled back in a no-frills bun at her neck. Her plain black dress tagged her as a Greek widow.

Pagona's style was as unassuming as any island woman's but for her jewelry, which would have kept a peasant in widow's weeds for a decade. Several heavy red-gold chains dangled out from under her collar, the thickest bearing an elaborate gold-and-silver-filigree cross about the size of the pope's. But unlike any cleric I knew, the chain also held a large *mati*, a ceramic eye encased in a wide bezel of gold. It stared at me from across the table—a warning that sent a chill from the base of my spine to the roots of my hair.

I do not like superstition. I tolerate the strings of garlic in the kitchen and the rest of Spiros's ritualistic voodoo only because I don't take them seriously. But the blue *mati*, intended to protect the wearer from the evil eye, goes beyond tossing salt over the shoulder and avoiding ladders. It watched me with a sinister gleam.

I glanced around the table to find the other members of the wedding party paralyzed with anxiety. Kate bit her lower lip and twisted her engagement ring on her finger. Alex wore a solemnly unreadable face and gazed at his grandmother as though willing her to some action. Georgia toyed with her silverware, her cheeks flushed and her eyes averted from the rest of us. Christos towered over his mother, his hand resting on her shoulder with fingers curled so tightly they must have been pressing into her flesh.

"Hello," Pagona said in carefully enunciated English. Her son made the introductions to her in Greek, explaining that Nick was Manolis's friend, and I, Nick's wife.

"Oh, *neh? Neh?*" she said. Clearly, Pagona and I were not destined to long, intimate chats by the fireside.

Once we had been introduced, the peculiar disquiet at the table seemed to dissipate—breath was let out, fingers stopped fluttering, and expressions grew affable once more. Pagona turned her attention back to her plate, heaped with olives, feta and thick slabs of bread spread with *taramosalata*, but she didn't pick up her fork. Instead, she pursed her lips and grabbed at her cross, fingering it until she had clasped the *mati*. She looked up at the rest of the table, her glance moving suspiciously from one guest to the next as though sizing us up as potential purveyors of the evil eye.

Christos gestured to a young woman seated next to Pagona, across from me. "This is Miss Xanthe Saros," he said. "Miss Saros is my mother's nurse-companion. I am not able to spend as much time with my mother as I would like, but Miss Saros looks after her nicely."

Xanthe Saros stood up hesitantly, like a child called upon to recite in front of the class. She didn't offer her hand; instead, she patted her hair, which was unsuccessfully anchored in a French twist. It was coarse hair, spiraling out wildly from her hairpins as though it adamantly refused to be contained. Her eye contact was fleeting.

She wore a camel-colored jersey wrap dress—a revival of the Diane Von Furstenburg style so popular when I was a little girl. It was a good dress, well tailored and of an excellent quality of jersey. It just wasn't right for her. The jersey refused to meld to her shape—a build never envisioned by the designer. She was large-busted and thick in the waist, with such narrow hips that her torso was as square and bulky as a refrigerator. A telltale flash of chrome revealed that she had pinned the wrap at the bustline, but even then, the fabric gapped below the pin, throwing the line into a shapeless mass.

"I'm happy to meet you," she mumbled, ducked her head and dropped back in her chair. I smiled at her, but she stared into her empty plate. I passed her a platter of *tyropitakia* and was rewarded by a shy, fleeting smile.

With the introductions made, Alex, who stood at the other end of the table, snagged a bottle of *Achaia Clauss Retsina* and another of *Mavrodaphne* and began making the rounds.

"Dry or sweet?" he asked, holding up the two bottles to Miss Alma.

"Sweet, I suppose. But only half a glass for me," Miss Alma said.

"*Ohee, ohee!*" Pagona clucked her tongue and beckoned with her hand, insisting that Alex should fill the glass to the rim. Miss Alma smiled and agreed.

"Excellent choice," Christos exclaimed. "I am from Patras myself—the only place in the world where *Mavrodaphne* is produced."

Xanthe Saros had taken out a seven-day pillbox and was methodically arranging a rainbow of capsules on Pagona's plate when Alex appeared at her side. She stopped, staring so fixedly over my shoulder that I turned to look behind me. A bartender was serving drinks to a couple seated under the grape-arbor decor of the bar. Behind him, a busboy was drawing a soft drink from one of the taps.

"*Retsina*, Xanthe? *Neh?*" Alex asked.

"*Evharisto.*" Her hand shook as she held the glass out to him, and the tips of her ears turned crimson. I could almost hear the drumming of her heartbeat and wondered how this shy, awkward girl had managed to tumble into a job working for a man like Christos Kyriakidis.

"Ah, Ms. Paradissis, there you are!" Christos gestured to the empty chair beside him as The Baked Alaska hurried across the room. She still wore her office suit—a taupe skirt, sweater, and three-quarter jacket that implied it was Italian knit and had cost *molto lire*. Her warm brown hair had highlights that exactly matched her skin tones. It curved gracefully over her forehead before culminating in a smooth French twist. This, I realized sadly, was how Xanthe Saros wanted to look. Actually, so did I.

"You are just in time for a toast," Christos continued.

"I'm sorry I'm late," she said, glancing vaguely around the table. "I ran into a problem at the hotel. One of the guests apparently brought a hair dryer from Europe without a converter—"

"Enough," said Christos. "Tonight we do not talk business. But let me introduce you to our friends here." He turned to us.

"Mr. and Mrs. Lambros, my secre—"

"Executive assistant, Eva Paradissis," she said in flawless, unaccented English, offering us a willowy, long-fingered hand. There was nothing shy about Eva Paradissis. Her eyes—crystal blue and as hard as aquamarines—met mine evenly before turning, with interest, to my husband.

Christos laughed good-naturedly as she cut him off. "Yes, excuse me. Executive assistant. Ms. Paradissis is more fluent in English than I. She even knows the . . . how do you say it? Pop jargon?"

If his little gibe annoyed her, she gave no indication of it. Instead, she took the chair he offered. Nick grabbed the *Mavrodaphne* and reached for her glass.

"*Retsina, parakalo,*" she said, making a face at the dark wine. "I don't like sweet wines."

"It is one of her rare lapses in judgment," Christos said. "Our Ms. Paradissis is otherwise a most astute sec—executive assistant." The Baked Alaska smiled stiffly and handed her glass to Alex.

"To our new, good friends who will soon be almost like family," Christos said. "*Stin eyiamas!*"

We clinked our glasses in the manner of the Greeks— that is, each to each—which can become quite a procedure when there are more than two or three at the table. In this case, with Manolis and Georgia, Kate, Alex, Spiros, Miss Alma, Pagona, Xanthe, Christos, Eva, Nick, and me, we were a tangle of arms reaching, clinking, spilling wine on the *mezethes*, until the group dissolved in laughter.

"We Greeks," Christos said when we'd each taken our first sip, "believe that wine is meant to be enjoyed by all the senses." He held his glass aloft, so that the light cast a ruby glow over his features.

"We see its color, we smell its aroma. We hear it when we touch our glasses, and then, of course, we taste it." He followed this last with a sip, which he rolled on his tongue in a mocking pantomime of a wine taster.

"But you've left out one sense," I said. "How do you feel it?"

"Well," he said with a sly grin, "I feel it when it goes to my head!"

*Chapter Four*

The early part of the evening went smoothly. Three waiters attended our table, authentically dressed in stiff white shirts and Cretan *vrakes*—knee-length balloon pants tucked into the tops of black riding boots. Manolis and Georgia supervised them closely, apparently eager to make a good impression on Christos Kyriakidis. Christos, in his turn, was generous with accolades for the food and the atmosphere. Nevertheless, there was an underlying tension in the evening—a kind of background hum, as though an electric charge were running through the room. I glanced around the table, trying to find the source of this disturbing current, but apart from Pagona's reserved, wary gaze, everything seemed to be going well. I put it down, instead, to my own fatigue and the stress of the accident.

"I still have one more dress fitting," Kate explained to Miss Alma. "And Mama and I have to finish the *bonboniéres*."

"Those are the favors for the reception, aren't they? Maybe Julia and I could help you with those."

Kate nodded happily. "And I have to pick up the service booklets for the church and . . . oh, there are so many little details. I don't know how I'll ever get it all done!"

"Don't worry, we'll all help you. And now, I think it's

time for this," I said, producing a silver-and-white package. "I could have sent it ahead but I really wanted to be here when you opened it."

Kate smiled softly and handed the package to Alex to open. He did so with the glee of a toddler who's gotten hold of someone else's birthday present.

"Oh, Julia, how lovely," Kate exclaimed as Alex held a sparkling Waterford biscuit barrel up to the light. The remainder of our party murmured over it as it passed from hand to hand around the table.

"Wait, there is another one. It came today," Manolis said and hurried away from the table. In his absence, conversation turned to the wedding gifts.

"We have twelve full place settings of our china," Kate said happily. "And nine of our silver. But Alex's father gave us the most beautiful gift of all—an icon of the *Epiphánia*."

"I commissioned it especially for them," Christos explained, "from a craftsman in Athens. He does excellent work."

Kate agreed. "It's silver and gold. We've taken it to the church to leave it for the forty-day blessing."

"Here it is," Manolis said, returning to the table with a long, narrow box. It was wrapped in lacy white paper and topped with a pair of wedding bells centered in a fussy white bow.

"Pretty package," Kate murmured as she studied the card. "It just says 'To Kate and Alex.' Where did it come from?"

Manolis shrugged. "UPS. It came during the lunch rush. The box, it was addressed to the restaurant, so I opened it. The gift was inside."

Kate slapped at Alex's hands. "My turn. You got to open the last one. Daddy, I have to know who to thank," she said as she pulled off the paper and lifted the lid. "Did you keep the box? Maybe there's a return ad—oh!"

The box slipped from her fingers onto the cluttered tabletop. Her golden complexion had turned gray and her hand was clapped over her mouth. She shoved her chair back and staggered up. A vile odor arose around the table.

"Please excuse me," she said shakily. "I'm going to be sick." The bride had fled before any of us knew what was wrong. Alex and Georgia were close on her heels.

"What—"

*"I yiftisa! I yiftisa!"* Pagona shrieked and shook the box under her son's nose. She dropped it in front of him and began crossing herself.

*"Thio matia se matiásane . . ."*

*"Papse, Mana!"* As we watched, Christos put a handkerchief over his face, calmly lifted the box and peered inside before setting it back down. "It is a *maya*," he said quietly. I looked at Nick.

"A curse," he whispered, reaching across to pick up the box as the others recoiled in horror. I clenched my napkin over my nose and mouth, fearing that like Kate, the odor would send me reeling from the table.

Nick held the box with the tips of his fingers, cleared the space in front of him and gently set it down. Manolis and I peered over his shoulder, while Spiros paced behind.

A wad of cotton batting—the type used to cushion a silver fork or spoon—lay in the bottom of the box. But there was no sterling. No jewelry. Instead, there lay before us a monstrous collection of bewildering objects—a ratted tangle of black hair, a red thread tied into three knots, a scatter of fingernail clippings caught in the batting.

Next to the clippings lay a pile of feathers—or at least that's what it seemed to be. It was oozing a noxious fluid and clearly was the source of the odor. A rusty stain had clotted and dried into a hard crust on the cotton batting. I stared at the feathers and gasped—a black eye, glazed dull and glaring sightlessly at my husband, a yellow beak, and a pinkish fold of tissue, once red but now blanched. It was the severed head of a rooster that had already begun its decay.

Beside the rooster's head there lay a tiny fragment of white paper. Nick took his fork and gently teased it, turning it over on the batting. A piece of photograph had been carefully trimmed out of a larger picture. The face that looked up at us, its features much diminished, was smiling. I knew the smile—the even teeth brightly contrasted against smooth, olive skin. And I thought again that this was a face that belonged on a *Cosmo* calendar.

"Aris!" Manolis cried. "Aris has done this. It is time to take care of him for good." He stormed away from the table, with Spiros close on his heels. "*O Aris? Pios eine, o Aris?*"

The rest of us were left to deal with the horror of the *maya*. Eva and Xanthe had pushed their chairs back and were breathing heavily under napkins held close to their faces. I started to gag.

"Get rid of it, Nick. Please."

Nick carefully lowered the lid, holding the box at arm's length in front of him as he left the table. But the odor lingered on. Like Pandora's box, the evil, once escaping, could not be retrieved.

"A *maya*," Nick later explained to me as we returned to the hotel, "is a curse. Someone has put a curse on the marriage."

"You don't believe that, do you?"

Nick hesitated a beat before answering. "I'm not sure. You have to understand that I was brought up to believe in these things."

So was everyone else at the table, except for Miss Alma and me. We shared the opinion that it was a cruel, tasteless joke, probably conceived in the twisted mind of a jealous ex-boyfriend. The rest of them were not as sure. Georgia was Greek–American and had been raised in a more modern world than Manolis and Christos had been. She tried to be reassuring for Kate's sake.

"It's an ugly thing, but it can't really harm us," she said, her voice without conviction.

Pagona overrode her with a shrill cry. *"Ohee!"* She turned a shaking finger on Georgia and continued her diatribe. I understood enough Greek to know that she was roundly rebuking Georgia, returning again to the subject of a gypsy.

Kate stood beside her mother. Her face was still pale, and her lower lip trembled. Despite her noble effort to stay composed, it seemed to me that the facade could crack at any minute. I put my arm around her shoulder, gently leading her away from Pagona's tirade. "She seems to put a lot of stock in superstition," I said.

"She's just a frightened old woman, Julia. Alex is her life and she's terribly afraid of losing him." Oh, dear. So this was the tension I'd been sensing all evening.

Alex appeared at Nick's side carrying an eight-inch-square brown cardboard carton with a shipping label on the front. Nick whispered something to him and Alex nodded, handing him the carton before turning away to seek out his fiancée.

Manolis and Spiros returned to the table every bit as agitated as when they left. Manolis ran his hand through his hair, as though he didn't know what else to do. "Aris does not answer his telephone, but I know he is there waiting. He won't get away with this."

He moved around the table behind Georgia and gripped her shoulders with tense fingers while Pagona rattled on about black prophecies and tragic outcomes. I didn't know where the old bag was finding the wind to keep it up. Manolis shot her a warning glance.

"Christo," he said, the anger in his voice barely kept in check, "you must do something about her. Can't you see she's upsetting everyone? Please, take care of your mother or I will have to speak to her myself."

Christos responded at once. *"Stamata, Mana!"* Her jaws snapped shut like a clam.

"My mother," Christos explained to us all, "is not a worldly woman. She does not understand the way the universe works. She puts great belief in the cards and the cups."

"You will explain to her, Christo, *neh?* You have to make her understand. This threat—it is not real," Manolis said. "We will call Father Charles tomorrow. He will know what to do. And I will find Aris and put a stop to this."

Christos sighed. "I have told her. But I will try to tell her again."

*"Ella,"* Xanthe Saros said, pushing a pill toward Pagona. Christos joined Xanthe in exhorting his mother to take her medicine. Xanthe nibbled at her lip and stared down the table at Kate.

Eva Paradissis twirled her wineglass between her fingertips and studied the golden liquid in the bottom. Like Kate, her complexion had taken on a greenish tinge. She set her glass down and began nervously scraping the polish off one thumbnail with the other. The little pile of scarlet chips on the tablecloth reminded me of drops of blood.

Manolis patted Georgia's shoulder and continued to glare at Pagona. Georgia brushed her hair from her face with the back of her hand, reached up and fingered her earring. Alex had pulled a chair around to face Kate and they sat knee to knee, he whispering softly to her while she slowly nodded her head. Whatever he was saying, it had a calming effect on her. Once her lips even trembled in a tentative smile. Spiros grabbed an empty wine bottle and held it and two fingers up to a waiter. Miss Alma twisted her napkin in her lap.

"I think," I ventured carefully, "that maybe you should call the police."

The party broke up hastily after my suggestion. Kate and Alex excused themselves to walk along the Sponge Docks. It was apparent that they wanted to be alone, away from the tension that had crept into our little party. Christos, Pagona, Xanthe, and Eva left almost immediately, but not before Christos had shaken our hands all around and patted Manolis's shoulder reassuringly. He turned to Nick and me.

"I should take you all for a tour of the hotel. You would like to see the kitchen, eh? It is state of the art." He turned to Eva Paradissis. "Put it on my calendar, will you, Eva? You know what time I am free?"

She was ready with a quick response. "Not tomorrow, I'm afraid. But I think you might work it in on New Year's Eve."

"She is very efficient," Christos said, winking at me. We agreed upon a time in the afternoon and said good night. Before they left, Christos turned back to us, his gaze going to Georgia.

"Do not worry, Yiorgia," he said. "I will find out who did this to our children, and when I do, he will not go unpunished."

Nick opened the bar in our room and withdrew a bottle of ouzo—an indication that we were staying in a Greek hotel. He poured us each a little sip in a pair of balloon-shaped glasses, adding water until the liquid clouded in the glass like fog over the bayou. Although I don't usually care for ouzo, I reached for it greedily. Death and menace had converged upon us in one evening, and neither of us could shake them off lightly.

"Who is Aris?" I asked after taking a tentative sip that, thankfully, went straight to my head.

"Manolis's ex-partner."

"I didn't know he ever had a partner."

Nick nodded, taking a sip and savoring it before continuing. "It was when he first opened *O Kritikos*. Their partnership didn't last long. The breakup was pretty bitter."

"But why would Aris do such a hateful thing to Kate?"

Nick swirled the liquid in his glass and knocked back a big gulp. "To hurt Manolis, I guess."

I stared down at my glass. It reminded me of a crystal ball—the hazy, whitish liquid as mysteriously potent, in its way, as the superstitions that governed Pagona's life. But the glass held no answers for me. I wasn't sure there were any answers to the questions that hovered in my mind. Why would anyone inflict such cruel and senseless pain on Kate and Alex? They were too young to have made enemies. But Manolis was not and, I reminded myself, the sharpest blow to a man can always be delivered through his children.

"So why those things—all that nasty stuff?"

"It's part of the curse. It means that bad things are going to happen to Alex," Nick said. "You saw the picture. And the head of the rooster . . . well, the rooster is usually interpreted as a sign of death."

I gagged again at the recollection of that head—the glazed eye and the obscene odor leeching from the feathers and decaying flesh beneath—then grabbed for my glass and drank deeply. I let the ouzo slide down my throat, warming the pit of my stomach, which had turned decidedly sick and cold. "Okay, what about the hair and the nail clippings?"

"His. Or meant to look like they're his. The hair was the same color."

"And the thread?"

Nick picked up the ouzo bottle. His first shot of liqueur had disappeared a little quickly. "Do we have to talk about this, Julia?"

"Yes. I want to know what it means."

He sighed deeply and refilled his glass. "There is a belief that on the day of the wedding, at the moment when the priest blesses the couple, if their enemy holds a thread with three knots tied in it, the marriage is . . . how do I say this? It is possessed by the enemy. If no one unties the knots, the marriage will be cursed with bad fortune. Whoever sent the *maya* was warning Kate and Alex that their marriage would be . . ."

"Cursed. I got that. Go on."

"What bothers me most," Nick continued, "is that the thread was red."

"Yeah, and . . . ?"

Nick knocked back his second shot of ouzo in a single gulp. "Red, Julia, is the color of blood."

*Chapter Five*

As if the *maya* and the tension between the two families had not been enough, Manolis's troubles worsened that very evening when his head cook, Dimitri, walked out after the dinner rush without notice. This is not unusual in the food-service business. It probably doesn't occur often in upscale, three-star restaurants, but for most of us, it's an occupational hazard. It is also the reason that a restaurateur is usually a *chef patron*, able to step into the kitchen at a moment's notice. Unfortunately, Manolis was not an experienced cook. With Epiphany coming and the anticipation of hoards of tourists, as well as the pressures of the wedding, it was not a propitious time for a walkout. Spiros offered to step in and help until another cook could be found.

Nick turned the carton Alex had given him over in his hands, thoughtfully gazing at the bar-coded label. It was the box in which the *maya* had arrived, which Alex had retrieved from the kitchen garbage.

No one else felt that local law enforcement would take great interest in a prank of this sort, despite the fact that Nick perceived it as a serious threat. More to the point, I think, the superstitious nature of the thing made both Manolis and Christos reluctant to open themselves up to public ridicule. Only Spiros had no such qualms.

We'd stayed at the table with Miss Alma while our friends had seen Christos and his party to the door. "Ve-ry bahd theeng, Zulia. *Ta maya eine poli* den-ger-rous," Spiros had said. "*I Katerina,* ve-ry sahd. We feex, *neh?*"

As Kate's godfather, Spiros was entrusted with the young woman's spiritual welfare in a solemn compact made with God and her parents. It was a pledge he took very seriously. He'd pulled off his glasses and wiped them carefully with a napkin as if by cleaning them, he might get a clearer view of what was happening around us. Manolis, he'd said, had problems at the restaurant, and Christos was contending with both a new hotel and an old mother. We had both the time and, regrettably, the experience to track down the culprit. Spiros wanted us to trace the *maya*.

"It might be possible," Miss Alma had said. "There should be a receipt for it somewhere. If this Aris person is responsible, Manolis can take care of it. But if Manolis is wrong, you could be saving him from doing something rash."

Nick had agreed. He planned to call UPS first thing in the morning, before we set out to see the sights Tarpon Springs had to offer. I gently lifted the carton out of his hands and set it on the game table.

"Come on," I said, pulling him up. "We haven't even seen the hotel grounds. Let's go explore."

We stepped through the French doors and out onto the terrace. On either side of us, golden lights glowed behind curtained doors and dissipated over the grounds. Just past the courtyard, a flagstone path led into a garden. Orange vapor lights cast an eerie glow in the dark, creating elongated shadows that grabbed at our feet.

The hotel grounds were not unlike the National Gardens

in Athens—filled with citrus trees, pampas grass, and flowering shrubs, none of which I recognized, being a member of the Musewood Garden Club in name only. Beyond the garden, the path meandered between beds of creeping juniper and down to Spring Street. The hotel was built out on a point, the banks of the bayou curving back and out of sight on either side. Across the street, a deserted dock waited at the water's edge for the hotel's water taxi to return from the Sponge Docks. A fine mist had settled over the bayou. I could feel it dampening my hair and I shivered.

"Are you cold?" Nick asked, pulling me close into the crook of his shoulder.

"A little bit. Mostly, I guess I'm just spooked."

"You, too?" another voice asked. Nick's arm tightened about me defensively as we both spun around. I struggled to catch my breath, then forced a smile for Eva Paradissis.

I didn't recognize her at first. She had changed out of her suit into a pair of gray sweats, and her hair, free of its pins, curled softly around her shoulders. Despite her casual appearance, her posture was rigid. She plucked a leaf off a nearby oleander and stroked it with her fingers.

"Be careful," I said. "They're poisonous, you know." She dropped the leaf as though it had singed her, rubbing her hands on her thighs. "We don't want any more trouble," I added.

"No," she said. "We've got more than we can handle now." We drifted on toward the bayou together. Nick wandered over to the dock, while Eva and I stood at the water's edge.

"It's kind of late. Are you tucking the hotel in for the night?"

She shook her head. "We've got security for that."

"Well, then . . ."

"I couldn't sleep. You too, I guess."

"I think we just needed some fresh air. I can't seem to get that awful smell out of my nose," I said.

Eva rolled her shoulders, as though trying to ease the tension in them. "Yes. It was very nasty. I've been up at the gym," she said, pointing back in the direction of the hotel. "Sometimes working out helps. I ride the bicycle for a while, come out for a walk and cool down. I can usually relax after that. I have to be on my toes from the minute I get up. Christos expects it of me. But it's hard to wind down at the end of the day."

So, the charming Christos Kyriakidis was a hard taskmaster. It came as no surprise. Successful men usually are. "He obviously depends heavily on you," I said. "You seem to know his schedule better than he does."

"That's because I arrange it for him," Eva said, adding, "when he's here."

"Oh, I thought you traveled with him."

"Occasionally. But I've been here, in America, off and on for almost a year."

"Helping Alex get the hotel going?"

She nodded. "Bids. Contracts. Permits. I know how Christos likes to do things. Alex is . . ." Eva hesitated, looked out at the bayou and pulled her sweatshirt in close around her body, chafing her arms. In the distance, thunder rumbled and sheet lightning ignited the sky. A heavy drop of rain plopped onto my shoulder.

"You see, I lived in the United States for a while when I was growing up."

"Which explains your English," I said. "It's very good."

"The Chicago school system. I was ten when we moved here and sixteen when we moved back to Greece."

"Do you miss it? Greece, I mean, not the Chicago school system."

She laughed. "I miss my family—my father and my

brother. My mother is dead." The wind was starting to kick up. It blew a lock of hair across her face. She pulled it away from her mouth and pushed it behind her ear. "Have you been there?"

"Yes. Nick and I went to Greece for our honeymoon. I loved it."

"It's a beautiful country, in its own way. The islands. And the mountains."

"Are you from Patras too?"

Eva shook her head. "Salonika. But when we moved back, I went to Athens. I thought I would have a better chance there."

"A better chance?"

"For a good job. Women have come a long way in Greece, but not far enough. Do you know that during the war, the women always walked first—in front of the donkey, and behind it, the man."

I shook my head, pondering the non sequitur. Eva didn't hesitate to enlighten me. Her voice became bitter as she went on. "It was because of the German land mines. If one went off . . . well, you see, the farmer could not afford to lose his donkey, but the wife was expendable."

And that, I thought, explained a lot about Eva Paradissis and why she couldn't sleep. She worked for a difficult man, did her job capably and thoroughly, always careful to remain on her toes—because the one thing she would never allow herself to be was expendable.


I woke at dawn to my husband's gentle weeping. He had thrashed in the bed throughout the night, and now, with the release of sleep, the reality of the girl's death had overcome his inhibitions. I stroked his face softly.

"Nick, wake up. Nick, you're dreaming."

"Can't get her . . ." he mumbled.

"Nick, it's all right." He rolled over, swiped his nose with the back of his hand and slowly focused his eyes on me. "You were dreaming," I said.

"She died, Julia. I thought we were going to make it, but we didn't. She's dead."

I cradled his head against my shoulder. "I know."

He let out a long, ragged breath. "I've never seen water so dark—just shadows. The car was sinking. The other girl—she could help get herself out, you know? But the one—the driver—first we couldn't find her. She'd fallen over onto the seat, and the door was jammed. We could have gotten her out the window, but the belt was stuck. I don't know what was wrong—it just wouldn't release. She didn't even try to help herself. Why? I don't understand why." He squeezed his eyes closed, trying to dam tears that escaped anyway.

"It wasn't your fault, Nick. You know that, don't you? You didn't smash up the car. You didn't jam the belt or the door. All you did was try to save her. And you weren't alone. Spiros and the others couldn't get her out either."

"But maybe there was something else I could have—"

I put my finger over his lips. "There was nothing else you could have done. You tried everything. And let's not forget, you saved the other one—Rebecca?—what did the cop say her name was?"

"Seager. Rebecca Seager. I wonder how she's doing."

So did I. I wondered if she'd been told yet that her friend was dead. And I wondered if she remembered how she'd been rescued. And by whom. I hurt for her, but I hurt more for Nick. He needed to see her—to see that she was alive, to be reminded that he had saved her life.

"Nick, let's go see her at the hospital today."

"I don't know, Julia. She may not want to see me."

"Why wouldn't she want to see you? You saved her life."

"But I didn't—"

"We're going, Nick. You need to do this. You need to put some closure to it. We're supposed to pick up Miss Alma this morning to see the sights, then meet Manolis and Georgia for lunch, but this afternoon Miss Alma's going to want to rest. We'll go then."

We met Miss Alma at ten o'clock and pulled out our AAA guidebook to learn more about the community of Tarpon Springs. We started at the Cathedral of St. Nicholas—an exact, though considerably smaller, replica of St. Sophia in Istanbul. Since Nick was never likely to visit Turkey, the cathedral was probably the closest either of us would ever get to St. Sophia. But it was not so much the cathedral itself that drew me as the icon of St. Nicholas displayed in the vestibule.

To my untrained and non-Eastern eye, it was the most beautiful icon I had ever seen. Rendered in luminous pastel colors and gold leaf, it had none of the usual austere features and dark colors of other icons. The silver-bearded saint wore an alb of pale blue covered by a patterned chasuble of gold. He held the book of the Gospels crooked in his left arm and clasped in long, extended fingers. His right hand was poised in a blessing, the tip of his ring finger lightly touching his thumb.

His eyes—clear-rimmed and soft brown—shone with a deep compassion that was more than the careful rendering of a talented iconographer. This Nicholas had been a kind man. No wonder sailors turned to him in times of despair. But, I reminded myself, the icon was only a work of art. Or was it?

Although they are not unheard of in Orthodox churches, I had never seen a weeping icon until we entered the Cathedral of St. Nicholas that morning. But I had done my homework, reading everything about the icon that I could get my hands on, which was disappointingly little.

The first tears had appeared in December, 1969, disappearing again several hours after their discovery. The icon did not weep again until December, 1970. The crystal droplets did not come from the eyes of the painting, but appeared almost as beads of perspiration on the face and around the halo. It continued to weep throughout the month, even as church officials examined and tested it in a variety of settings and weather, puzzling over the phenomenon, at a loss to explain it. Thereafter it wept, but only during the Christmas season, until December 8, 1973. It never wept again.

I could see the tracks left by the tears, beginning on his forehead and coursing down over his cheeks, beard, and vestments to the bottom of the frame. The paint was undisturbed, and yet the traces were there, much like the white tracks of tears left to dry on the face of a child.

"Do you suppose it's really some sort of miracle?" I whispered to Miss Alma.

"I don't know, my dear. The world is full of miracles, you know. Even when there is a scientific explanation for an occurrence, it does not mean it is not miraculous. Nick's saving that girl's life, for instance. I'd call that a miracle."

She was probably right, I thought. But why did one girl deserve a miracle and the other one didn't? Of course, I wasn't the first person ever to ask the question. Somewhere close by, or maybe far away, the family of the dead girl was probably sharing my thoughts. Even St. Nicholas didn't offer any answers—just met my gaze with his mutely compassionate expression. Nick took Miss Alma's arm and my elbow and led us into the church.

The air was heavy with the sweet fragrance of incense that hung over our heads like the remainders of prayers.

Sunlit rays of ruby, blue, and gold poured through the stained-glass windows. We knelt in a pew and said quick prayers for Rebecca Seager's recovery and the soul of the dead girl before Nick began to explain the *iconostasion* and the significance of the Royal Gate to Miss Alma. But I couldn't focus on what he was saying.

As beautiful as the cathedral was, I couldn't tear my thoughts away from the icon of St. Nicholas and the whole matter of Eastern mysticism. I had seen, now, two sides of the question: the fear of lurking evil to be warded off with spells and charms, and the gentle, sad eyes of a weeping saint. And I did not know how much, if any, of this I actually believed.

Had the dead girl somehow been cursed? I shook off the thought as hysterical and melodramatic. There were no such things as curses—not real ones. Nevertheless, the *maya* had been real, and its intentions were decidedly evil.

## Chapter Six

Manolis met us at the door of *Mykonos* precisely on time. Like most restaurateurs, he enjoyed dining out in other restaurants far more than eating in his own. It's hard for a restaurateur to get a peaceful meal in his own place. There are always interruptions. Even between the lunch and dinner rushes, there are vendors to see, employees demanding schedule changes, phone calls to take, parties to book, and of course, the prep required for the next rush. Nick and I long ago determined that the only way to get a normal meal is to leave the Oracle.

Manolis had requested a large round table on a sunny, glassed-in porch overlooking Dodecanese Boulevard. The atmosphere was charming— white walls trimmed in Aegean blue with matching shutters that framed posters of the Greek islands. Georgia was already at the table.

"Good location," Manolis said to Nick. "Right here on the main street. Lots of walk-in traffic." The conversation switched to Greek as they launched into yet another analysis of the restaurant business as a whole and their own specifically. I turned to Georgia.

"Are Kate and Alex coming?"

"No," she said as she rearranged the silverware more to

her liking. "Alex is helping Christos with preparations for the party tomorrow night, and Kate . . . I think she needs some time to herself." Georgia shot her husband a wary look and lowered her voice. "She and Manolis are at each other's throats."

"But why?"

Georgia shrugged and divided her gaze between Miss Alma and me. "They're a lot alike, those two. I know it doesn't seem like it. Kate has more self-control than her father, but she's just as . . . what? High-strung, I guess, as he is. Anyway, he thinks this is all Pagona's fault—hers and Aris's. And he thinks Christos isn't doing enough to control his mother. But Kate doesn't want to upset the old woman any more than she already is. Personally, I'd like to deck her."

She opened the menu and abruptly closed it again. "Pagona wants Alex to cancel the wedding."

"Oh no, Georgia. Why?"

"Well, first there was this gypsy thing. Some gypsy in Athens predicted danger to someone she loved. She told Pagona that a celebration would end in disaster. Then there was the *maya* last night. The old woman is afraid."

I couldn't blame her. Although I don't believe in gypsies' dire omens or in horoscopes, these predictions were disquieting—especially when they seemed to be coming true.

"Now Manolis is talking about how maybe she's right and they should cancel the wedding. Kate's going to have to put up with Pagona for a long time. With all those pills, she could live to be a hundred. The old lady could make the next twenty years a living hell, and neither of us want that for our daughter. Anyway, Manolis has Kate so worked up she can't see straight."

Georgia massaged her temples. "I was up all night worrying about it until I can't think about it anymore. Let's try to enjoy our lunch." She opened her menu again and fixed her gaze on it, but I doubted that she was really reading it. Miss Alma and I followed her example.

There were too many good things to make an easy choice: shrimp, *kalamarakia*, moussaka, and roast leg of lamb. At last I decided on Chicken Sofia—a breast of chicken wrapped around a filling of spinach and cheese.

"I'll have *Garides Ellinikes*," Georgia said, handing off her menu before she turned to me. "Tell me about the hotel. It is comfortable?"

"Very. Our room looks out at—"

A prolonged squeal and a blaring horn turned all our heads around to the street. Nick leaped out of his chair, an involuntary reflex that was probably a result of the previous night's accident. A black Jeep, tires smoking, swerved to avoid a burgundy Taurus. The driver of the Taurus laid his forehead against the steering wheel, visibly shaken, even as the Jeep took the curb on two wheels before careening out of sight. Georgia shook her head.

"Father Charles. The man cannot drive. I don't know why the bishop allows him behind the wheel. Anyway, he'll be here in a minute, if he doesn't kill anyone first. I've asked him to meet us. I need to talk to him about Pagona. Maybe he can get through to her before everything falls apart."

I wanted to reassure Georgia, but there was nothing I could say. I was a *xeni*—a stranger among these people and their customs. Although I had tried, in almost eight years of marriage I had barely begun to understand their cultural identity. I had no idea of how much influence Alex's grandmother might have on him, and the effect of this *maya* had no place in my experience. Instead, I returned to the subject of the priest.

"Is he your pastor?"

"Oh no, no! Our pastor died suddenly of a heart attack just before Christmas. The diocese has sent us Father

Charles. We can't be without a priest during *Epiphánia*. He would have been coming anyway, for the services, so they sent him early. Oh, there he is."

Father Charles Millas stood in the doorway, a cigarette held toward his palm in the European manner. A portly man with a square face and ruddy complexion, his step was jaunty as he wound between the tables, stopping first to crush out his cigarette. Although his dark hair was only lightly silvered, worn brushed straight back from a receding widow's peak, his gray Vandyke beard bore witness to his age. He was probably in his mid-seventies.

"We heard you coming, Father," Manolis said.

"Eh? Oh, yes," he said vaguely. "You mean that little problem in the street. My fault, I suppose. But it was all right. No harm done."

His English was exact but softened by rolling Rs and lingual Gs. He waved his hand in circles. "As I tell the bishop, there is always a little angel sitting on the steering wheel . . ." I hoped she had her own air bag.

Georgia waited until he had ordered before raising the matter of the *maya* and Pagona. "Yes, I see," he said. He tapped a Winston out of its pack, paused to light it, drag deeply and exhale slowly.

"It is difficult, you know, with these old ones," he said with an apologetic glance at Miss Alma. I seriously doubted that Pagona had many years on him, but the point, of course, was less age than education and experience. For all that the Kyriakidis family had money, Pagona had never escaped her humble background.

"I will have to be very careful with her. There are still parts of Greece where the villagers believe that the priest is the worst sorcerer of all. And now, during *Epiphánia*, it is much worse. They expect the *exoticá*."

"The . . . what?" I asked.

*"Exoticá,"* Georgia repeated for me. "Fairies. Goblins.

They're supposed to come out between Christmas and Epiphany and work their mischief. For example, *Moírá* is fate. My grandmother believed that she came to the house when a child was born. She used to put out sweets so that *Moírá* would treat the child well."

"Are you serious?" I glanced from Georgia's face into the resigned expression of the priest. "I didn't know anyone still believed in . . . whatever they are. Demons, goblins."

"Few will admit to it," Father Charles said. "But many still believe. These forces help them to explain the tragedies and misfortunes in their lives."

So Pagona would be even more wary during the Epiphany season, fearing that the *maya* might be the work of a demon. Father Charles put out his cigarette and accepted the plate the waitress offered him.

"But supernatural forces do not use United Parcel Service to deliver their misery," he continued. "There is nothing mystical about this situation. We are dealing with a human being here."

"I called them this morning and gave them the tracking number," Nick said. "The package came out of Tampa. The local office will have the packing slip. I couldn't get a phone number for the office, though—they only have the one-eight-hundred line—but we'll go over there and try to find out who sent it."

Father Charles patted Georgia's hand. "You see? We'll find out who did it, and in the meantime, I will speak with the grandmother."

"I think you will not have to, Father." Manolis rose slowly from his chair, his black eyes gleaming as he stared across the room. His gaze never faltered as he folded his napkin deliberately and dropped it on the table. "I can take care of the problem myself."

"Manolis, no! Niko, go after him," Georgia cried as Manolis lunged around the table and strode across the room.

*"Ti?"*

"There," she said, pointing at a tall man who was taking a seat near the front door. "That is Aris!"

Aristotle Mavrakis stood almost as tall as Spiros, but had a slighter build. By the time Nick reached them, Manolis, with all the pluck and tenacity of a bantam rooster, had shoved Aris up against the wall next to the door of the restaurant. Nick herded them both out onto the street, away from the prying eyes of the patrons at *Mykonos* and the worried frown of its owner.

Father Charles, Georgia, and I clustered at the window and peered down onto the sidewalk, where the men had taken up their argument just below us. Aris's back was to us, the top of his head grazing the windowsill. Nick had maneuvered himself between the two men, but Manolis clambered over his shoulder to shake his fist in Aris's face. Aris dodged him, moving left as Nick darted sideways to keep them separated. Aris spoke in a calm voice and made placating gestures, all the while staying well behind Nick. Not so Manolis, who, as Aris kept a firm grip on reason, grew more voluble in his threats. Unable to go over Nick, he tried to duck under Nick's outstretched arm.

"Father, please," Georgia said. "His temper. Go try to talk some sense—"

The priest was gone before she finished her sentence. By the time Father Charles reached them, their positions had reversed and Aris faced us. He was fairer complected than either Nick or Manolis, with a long, equine face and light eyes. He glanced up at the window, his gaze meeting mine before flitting quickly to Georgia. He gestured broadly with his palms up, shoulders shrugged and lips clamped, as if to say he didn't understand what was going on. Georgia turned away.

I hadn't realized how large a man Father Charles was, but he towered a good ten inches over Manolis and was surprisingly strong. With his cigarette dangling from his lips, he looked like an aging bouncer in a clerical collar. He shoved Manolis backward against the wall, pinned him with outstretched arms and legs, spat the cigarette onto the ground and calmly blew the smoke in Manolis's face. Father Charles stepped back as Manolis coughed and doubled over.

Nick took his cue and steered Aris down the street before Manolis could catch his breath and push his way past the old priest. Aristotle Mavrakis went willingly, but not before he had turned back to the window once again to catch Georgia's eye. He smiled at her and shook his head sadly, then jammed his hands into his pockets and hunched his shoulders as he turned and hurried down Dodecanese Boulevard.

Becky Seager sat propped up in the hospital bed, her complexion as white as the pillowcase behind her head. She wore a bandage on her left hand, an indication of the recent removal of an IV. In the background, the television buzzed with the histrionics of an afternoon soap opera.

"I was planning to call you as soon as I got out of here," she said. Her voice was hoarse and raspy. I didn't remember whether they'd intubated her at the scene of the accident, but even if they hadn't, she'd probably done plenty of coughing in the ensuing twelve hours or so. "I wanted to thank you for saving my life."

Nick shifted from one foot to the other and glanced out the window. "I'm glad I was able to help you. I wish I could have—"

"Please," she said quickly. "Sit down." She gestured to a pair of chairs—one a vinyl-covered recliner, the other a hard, straight-metal affair. Nick pulled the straight chair close to the bed and pointed me into the recliner.

Becky toyed with her hair—dark, unruly curls that lay heavily against the pillow. "I know what you were going to say . . . about Eileen." Nick just nodded.

"Was that her name? Eileen . . ." I waited while she supplied the last.

"Reilly. Soon to be Simon."

"She was getting married?"

Becky picked up the remote and aimed it at the television, snapping it off. "In October. I was going to be a bridesmaid. Eileen and I work . . . worked together. We'd gotten to be good friends." A little sob broke through her calm facade. "I'm going to miss her a lot." She jerked a tissue out of the box on her bedside table and dabbed at her nose, staring out the window into a cloudless blue sky. Nick and I waited for her to collect herself.

"I remember you—at least a little bit. You were on the street just before . . . I was trying to steer the car."

"Do you want to talk about what happened?"

"No," she said sharply. "But I have to, don't I? That's what the grief counselors say, anyway. The last thing I want is to end up on a sticky vinyl couch with someone scrawling my dreams in a steno pad. So talk I must—get it all out, come to terms with it. Don't you just love that phrase? As if anyone could ever come to terms with death." She stopped to blow her nose heavily into the tissue, discarded it and yanked another one out of the box.

"I don't know what happened," she said. "It doesn't make any sense. First she was fine, and then we were in the river, and then she was dead."

"She looked like she'd passed out at the wheel," Nick said.

"She did! It was so . . . weird."

"She'd been all right during the day?"

Becky nodded vigorously. "The police keep asking me the same thing—implying that we'd been on a drunk—but we hadn't. Eileen's desk is right next to mine in the office. Insurance," she added. "We rode in to the office together yesterday, worked together all day, and stopped for a drink on our way home. We did that about once a week."

"How much did she have to drink?"

"That's what was so weird. We each had one drink at the bar at The Cretan. It's a Greek place on Dodecanese."

"Yes, we're—"

"We've been there," Nick said, shooting me a warning look. "Did you go anywhere else? Stop for another drink?"

"No. Absolutely not. We stopped at one of the bakeries to pick up a wedding-cake brochure. She was starting to act a little funny—stumbling over her words—but I didn't think anything about it. By the time we got in the car, she was acting drunk, but I thought she was just kidding around. We pulled out onto Dodecanese and . . . and she just keeled over, right there in the car. It was all I could do to reach the steering wheel and try to get control. We were moving so fast—I couldn't reach the brake—and we were all over the road. It happened so quickly and I . . . I just couldn't do anything. I've never been that scared in my whole life."

Becky laid her head back against the pillow and closed her eyes. Tears glistened through her dark lashes, spilled over and coursed down her cheeks. Before I realized what I was doing, I had taken her hand in mine.

"I'm sorry," she said.

"No, don't be. You have good reason to cry."

Nick stood up and wandered over to the window, staring down into the hospital parking lot. He wiped his eyes furtively before turning back to the girl. Her eyes were still closed. He motioned to me that it was time to leave, but Becky's fingers had curled around mine so tightly I couldn't pull away.

"Todd came to see me this morning," she whispered. "He was Eileen's fiancé." I waited for her to continue and at last her eyes fluttered open. "He was kind, but I know he must hate me."

"Why would he hate you, Becky?"

"Because I'm alive. Because Eileen is dead."

I knew she was right, and yet looking at her, feeling the agony she was suffering, and Nick's too, I didn't know how anyone could hate Becky Seager.

*Chapter Seven*

The phone woke us early the next morning. We'd planned to sleep late and relax around the hotel until it was time to meet Christos for our tour in the afternoon. I stared fuzzily at the clock, half listening to Nick's end of the conversation.

"*Neh, endaxi,*" he said and hung up the phone, turning to me. "Spiros. The police are at the restaurant questioning Manolis and Georgia. He thinks we should go down there."

"What's it about?" I asked, but knew the answer before the words left his lips. "The accident," we said in unison.

Spiros was waiting to let us in the front door when we reached *O Kritikos*. The restaurant would not open for several hours, but the kitchen staff was already at work prepping for the lunch rush and the bartender was taking inventory. Spiros's silent gaze went to the family table near the door to the dining room, where Georgia and Manolis were seated with a uniformed cop. Georgia's hands were carefully folded on the table in front of her, but Manolis's short fingers roved over the table, nervously picking at the place settings and rearranging the condiments.

Another officer stood at the bar questioning the bartender and making notes in a small, spiral notebook. I recognized him at once as the one who had taken our statements after the accident. At length, he passed a business card to the bartender and returned to the table. He was still standing, and met us before we could quite reach our friends.

"Can I help you, Mr. Lambros?"

"How is Becky Seager?"

"Improving. She'll probably be released today or tomorrow. She was able to tell us a little about the accident. That's why we're here."

"Is something wrong?"

The young cop looked uncertainly at the older officer at the table. Manolis leaped up and hurried to join us. "Please, they are our friends," he said. "I have nothing to say that cannot be said in front of them."

The two policemen seemed to come to silent agreement and nodded in the direction of the table. I took a seat next to Georgia and was shocked when her cold hand gripped mine.

"As I was explaining to Mr. Papavasilakis," said the officer we had met the night before, "the young lady in the hospital has told us that they stopped by here for a drink last night. She swears that they each had only a single drink, and yet her friend—the victim—began behaving strangely just after they left the restaurant."

"It is true, Niko," Manolis put in. "They each had one drink. I made them and served them myself."

Georgia's hand squeezed mine tightly. Nick's brow shot up and he ticked his tongue, trying to telegraph a message to Manolis to say no more. But Manolis, distraught, went on without noticing. "Vasilis—he is our bartender—he was off until six o'clock."

"So the bar was empty? They were the only ones there?"

"Well, no. I think there were one or two other people sitting at the bar. I can look at my tickets and tell you, because my register prints the time of sale on each ticket. Wait just a minute, please."

Manolis hurried away from the table, leaving the rest of us in awkward silence. Nick pulled his worry beads out of his pocket and began mechanically twirling them through his fingers. They don't call them worry beads for nothing. In a minute, Manolis was back and carefully spread five tickets on the table.

"Yes, I remember now. There was a couple—tourists, I think—at the end of the bar. They were drinking *Retsina*. And a man, next to the girls. The double Scotch is his. And this ticket—It belongs to the girls. One drank gin and tonic, and the other drank ouzo. I should have remembered that. It's very unusual, you see." He pushed the display of tickets toward the two officers. "This helps? Yes?"

The older officer—his name tag read "Jacobs"—stacked the tickets neatly. "Do you mind if we keep these, Mr. Papavasilakis?"

Manolis's confused glance went to Nick and back to the cop. "Why do you want them? Do they tell you something I don't see?"

Jacobs ignored the question. "Would you show me where everyone was sitting that night, please?"

Manolis rose slowly and led the men to the bar. Vasilis watched them curiously, as did several of the kitchen staff who passed through the bar to get soft drinks and lingered intrusively. Gossip in the kitchen would be rampant by dinner.

The couple had been sitting at the left end of the bar. Three stools away sat the man. There was another empty stool to his right, then the two girls. "The redhead, she sat here," he said, pointing to the first stool. "And the other one, on her right."

"And you were . . . ?"

"Behind the bar, of course."

"The whole time?"

"Well, no. Maybe not. I don't remember. Please, I don't understand what this is about. The girls had one drink only, no more."

Jacobs tucked the bar tickets inside a folder and snapped it shut decisively. "So Ms. Seager said. Mr. Papavasilakis, we're just trying to get to the bottom of the accident, so to speak. The car has been raised and a forensic team is still going over it, but it appears right now to be mechanically sound."

"What about the autopsy? They are doing an autopsy on Eileen Reilly, aren't they?" Nick asked.

Jacobs reopened his folder and rearranged the tickets. At length, he blew out a long sigh and turned to Nick. "We have some preliminary findings. Ms. Reilly did not have a heart attack. She was a young woman in good health. The toxicology reports probably won't be in until next week—the lab's short-staffed for the holidays. We may know something by Monday."

"What about blood alcohol? You must know that."

Jacobs shook his head. "That will come in with the toxicology report. I can tell you that Ms. Seager's blood alcohol was tested at the hospital and found to be under the legal limit—consistent with the one drink that she claims." He snapped his folder closed again and gave his partner a nod. They moved toward the door.

"But, wait!" Manolis cried, trailing them across the dining room. "You still haven't told me why you're keeping my tickets."

Jacobs paused at the door. "Just routine at this point, Mr. Papavasilakis. We'll be back in touch."

The door slammed behind the two officers as Manolis turned to the rest of us. "I don't like this, Niko *mou*. They are not telling me the truth. They couldn't think I had anything to do with this terrible thing—could they?"

Nick shoved his worry beads back in his pocket and patted his friend on the shoulder. "Manolis, you know the old saying—'It's the tailor's fault, but they beat the cook.' It was a terrible accident. They're looking for someone to blame. Don't worry. Whatever happened, you had nothing to do with it."

Christos was prompt, meeting us in the lobby at the stroke of four o'clock, as agreed, to conduct his tour of the hotel. Manolis had decided to close early on New Year's Eve. Normally, he would have been open for business, but his mandatory appearance at Christos's party made it too difficult to cover the restaurant on the heaviest drinking night of the year. Spiros had left the restaurant after the lunch rush and he joined us in the lobby. Christos took Miss Alma's hand and draped it over his arm, bowing to the rest of us.

"Now you will see that the hotel is shaped like a square C. The long back faces the drive, and the wings project toward the bayou. This part, of course, you have seen. The marble is from Pentelis, imported from Greece, as are the rugs, flokati, and artwork. The tables as well."

"Did you bring your own decorator?" Miss Alma asked.

Christos shook his head. "No. Alex convinced me that it would be better for our relations with the community to bring in a local decorator. You will probably meet her tonight at the party. She has done a fine job, eh?"

We agreed that she had. Two tall glass display cases divided the lobby from the check-in desk, each of them displaying a variety of pottery and sculpture. At the top of the case to the right sat a large amphora, a two-handled terracotta vase decorated with bands and chevrons in brown and deep red. A small sign below it read "Cypro–Geometric, ca 600 B.C."

"But this is real," Miss Alma cried. She reached toward the glass, almost as if to pluck the vase from its case.

Below the amphora was displayed the small figure of a woman, dating from the third century B.C. She stood only about six inches high, but the graceful curves of her arms and the deep folds of her drape gave her an appearance of life—as though she might step off her pedestal at any moment and walk away if her feet hadn't been missing.

"A bargain," Christos said with a wink.

The third shelf held several smaller pieces: an Attic geometric cup covered in Greek keys and delicate line art in beige, black, and brown, and a primitive statue of a horseman that reminded me of the pre-Columbian art of the Americas. The sign beneath it read "Boetia, 6th Century B.C." The second case was devoted to more contemporary crafts. There were painted tiles from several of the islands, and enameled metalwork.

Christos waved toward the corridor on the left. "These are guest rooms, and there are several utility closets and the laundry at the end of the wing. But come, we will go up to the kitchens. I know that is what Niko wants to see."

Christos led us across the lobby, past a flight of stairs with wrought-iron railings, to the elevator, which opened on the next floor to a smaller waiting area furnished much like the one below. Beyond it was the dining room—another wide expanse of marble that led to a wall of glass. The view was spectacular, evoking gasps of delight. Christos smiled broadly. "You like it, eh?"

The entire dining room faced out onto the terraced gardens and the bayou, where a water taxi was pulling into the dock. Four passengers disembarked, carrying bags of souvenirs and small white pastry boxes.

Spiros had wandered to one end of the dining room, where a crew of four men was putting together a portable dance floor. He took a spin on it, turning in a circle, his arms flung wide, hands drooping in the classic step of the *zeibekiko.* *"Kalo eine,"* he said to the astonished crew. "Is good. You fee-nish."

I glanced around the dining room. Along the walls, original water colors were shown off to good advantage by track lighting, and just below the ceiling, a hand-painted Greek-key border spanned the perimeter of the room. There were two more glass cases flanking the windows.

"Julia, look," Miss Alma said, pointing to a marble bust dated second century B.C. The tip of its nose was broken, and it was missing a chunk of beard, but even these faults could not disguise that this was the bust of a deity. There were more small vases and amphores, most of them in the black-figured Corinthian style and all quite beautiful, but nothing could rival the bust, until we moved on to the second case.

"Alexander," Miss Alma whispered, pointing to a small bronze statuette. Its left hand was upraised, as if in a blessing. It stared back at us through silver-inlaid eyes that shone only a little less than Miss Alma's. "How exquisite!"

I knew that Miss Alma had always wanted to go to Greece, but until I saw her face-to-face with Alexander, I'd never realized how much. We reluctantly followed the men away from the display cases.

"How many people can you seat?" Nick asked.

"Two hundred and fifty, two seventy-five if we crowd them."

The tables were set with heavy white linens and dazzling white china trimmed in a two-inch border of cobalt blue. The border was further enhanced by a gold Greek key that led to "The Mediterraneo Hotel" printed in quasi-Greek letters at the top of each plate. Nick picked up a fork, weighed it in his hand and whistled under his breath.

"Top of the line," he whispered. I gave him a shot with my elbow.

"And now, the kitchen!" Christos gestured toward a pair of swinging doors discreetly hidden behind a short wall in the far corner of the room.

We followed him into a wide corridor equipped with hand sinks, coffee machines, tray stands, and small wares. At one end, a white-jacketed busboy filled a bank of refrigerated cases with Greek pastries, napoleons, and tarts. Christos inspected them critically before giving the boy an approving nod.

"This way, this way," he called, beckoning us toward another pair of double doors. These were open, held back to allow the wait staff easy entrance and exit. We followed him into a room of stainless-steel paneling that was, as he had promised, state of the art. The aroma of lemon, garlic, and oregano permeated the kitchen.

There was a prematurely festive craziness about the kitchen as the staff, in gleaming white jackets, scurried in all directions. Vendors bringing in last-minute orders—the freshest of produce and seafood—directed their deliverymen, all the while keeping within view and earshot of Christos. A man pushing a hand truck loaded with cases of wine swerved around us and trundled briskly toward the back of the kitchen. I recognized some of the names—*Demestica, Roditis,* and *Retsina*—but many I did not.

"You will excuse this chaos, I hope," Christos said.

I glanced around the kitchen. Despite the frenetic activity, everything was well organized. A central island of four eight-foot stainless worktables, two each side back to back, constituted the focal point of the room. An enormous rack of stockpots, steamer baskets, skillets, and crepe pans floated overhead.

Two chefs hovered over the tables. One buttered narrow sheets of phyllo, his hands moving with a quick and fluid assurance as he centered a dollop of filling and flag-folded the pastry around it. The second chef worked at the table closest to the door. He was putting the finishing touches on an ice sculpture—Venus arising from the . . . punch? Christos stroked her back with his index finger, once again nodded his approval, and Venus was whisked away to the walk-in freezer to await her debut.

"We will be baking all our own breads," Christos said, pointing to a row of proofing cabinets along a side wall. "You see there? Those are the *vasilopites* for the party tonight." Even as he said it, a baker opened one of the cabinets and set a tray of small, round loaves inside to rise.

"Mr. Kyriakidis, I was just coming to look for you."

*Chapter Eight*

Eva Paradissis looked tired. Beneath the brutal exposure of fluorescent lighting, the crescent smudges under her eyes had a greenish cast. A shallow furrow began between her eyebrows and faded out in the middle of her forehead. Likewise, the beginnings of tiny lines were appearing around her eyes and mouth. But that's where the aging stopped. Although she was probably over thirty, her posture and slender figure were those of a teenager. She wore another business suit—this one black crepe with a fitted, hip-length jacket and narrowly gored skirt. The buttons, slash pockets, and collar were trimmed in velvet. Very pricey, even for an executive assistant.

"I need your final approval on the seating arrangement," she said, handing Christos a clipboard.

He studied it carefully. "No, no, Eva. You cannot put Rula in this corner. Move her to my table—no, over here. That will be better. And this is out of the question," he said, pointing to the chart. "I told you how Alex feels about him. Put him at the table with Rula. Move Georgia and Manolis to my table."

He made a few more changes, slashing through names with his Montblanc pen, drawing arrows from one table to the next, before handing it back to her. "There, that is better, eh?"

"I'm sure. Thank you," she said, pivoting briskly on her heel to exit the kitchen.

Christos rocked back on his heels and watched her for a moment before turning back to us. "One must use diplomacy in seating, eh? These guests—some are here for the wedding, like yourselves. But most are business associates. We all worked together to create this—" he said with a generalized sweep of his hand. "Now we will celebrate together, but—" he waved his index finger, as if in warning "—if we wish to do more business, we must, how do you say it? Walk on our toes. We cannot afford to give offense to anyone."

"Then you're planning to build more hotels," Miss Alma said.

"Yes, yes. We are looking for suitable properties in Miami and Tampa Bay. St. Augustine is in negotiation. *Siga, siga.* Slowly, slowly. Everything in its own time. And now, the ovens."

Three double-convection ovens—square, shiny, and stalwart—stood clustered under a ventilation hood behind the prep tables, ready to receive the *vasilopites*. Next to the bank of ovens, a six-eyed commercial range and charbroiler cozied up to a flat-top grill as big as the deck of an aircraft carrier. And, finally, there was a rotisserie large enough to broil Spiros, but loaded instead with legs of lamb waiting to begin their slow rotations over a low fire.

Nick sighed wistfully. "Oh, what I could do with a rotisserie like that. Julia—" I imagined us, with a trailer hitch on the back of the Honda, towing the thing up I-95 and hastily pulled him away to follow Christos past a colossal dish machine and racks of storage containers.

"This," Christos said, gesturing to an open door, "is our wine storage. Climate-controlled, of course." Inside, racks of bottles waited, resting comfortably on their sides. Behind the racks, additional shelves held cases stacked to the ceiling—modest wines, expensive wines, wines with musical names like *Saint-Emilion* and *Muffato della Sala*. A tall, slender man with a clipboard in his hand and a pen stuck behind his ear argued with a deliveryman.

"I ordered one case," he said, gesturing to a box of *Mavrodaphne*. "It's a dessert wine. Take the other case back." The deliveryman rolled his eyes and set the extra case back on his hand truck.

Christos pointed across the hall to another open door. "Dry storage," he said. "And back here, we have our prep-and-salad room." We followed him into a tiled room adjacent to the walk-in cooler. Another busboy worked there, this one boning chicken breasts. Christos clapped him on the back. "This is fresh, eh? Not frozen, eh, Tony?"

"No, sir. Fresh," Tony said, but Christos had already turned away.

"The walk-in was specially designed—" he said as he yanked open the cooler door. "Xanthe! What are you doing?"

"I was just getting . . ." Xanthe's face flushed as she stammered out a reply. "*I Kyria* Pagona wanted some fruit and there was none left in the apartment, so I thought—"

Her arms were loaded with fresh fruit. She reached up to push a strand of hair out of her face and an orange rolled from her grasp, bouncing on the cooler floor and through the door to stop at my feet. I picked it up and set it back in her arms.

"Thank you. Was it not all right? I mean, for me to come here for fruit?"

"Of course, of course. Take as much as you need." Christos grabbed a nearby bus tub. "Put it in here. If you drop it, it will bruise."

Xanthe gratefully dumped the fruit into the tub and took

it out of his hands. She glanced nervously at her watch and back at Christos. "It is almost time for her medicines. I must hurry. Excuse me, please." She edged past us and out the door of the prep room as Christos watched her pensively.

"She is a very competent nurse," he said, "but a shy young woman. I have wondered how she would behave in a crisis." He shrugged. "Nevertheless, she gets along well with my mother, which, between us, is not always an easy task. She seems to understand *Mana* very well. Now, as to the cooler . . ."

When we returned to the main kitchen, a tray of *vasilopites* was laid out on the center island. The baker gave us a thin smile when we stopped to watch him carefully brush the top of each loaf with egg white. I could only sympathize with the chefs, facing a debut that Christos would expect to be perfect. The last thing they needed was a demanding boss and a group of strangers under their feet. They must have been relieved when, at last, we left the kitchen.

From there, we proceeded up another floor to the gym and weight room, directly above the dining room. It was equipped like the best of spas, with exercise machines, sauna, and Jacuzzi. A masseuse was available between the hours of ten and three. The space occupied by the dining room and gym was, on the fourth floor, devoted to a conservatory and game room.

"So, what do you think, eh?" Christos asked, sending the elevator back to the first floor. We all agreed that he could be justifiably proud of his achievement.

As we stepped into the main lobby, Christos spread out his hands. "So that is it. You have seen the pool and the tennis courts, I imagine. The family quarters and manager's apartment are down there." He pointed to our wing.

"Will you be living here?" Miss Alma asked.

"No, no. I will return to Greece as soon as Kate and

73

Alex are back from their honeymoon. Alex will take over our American efforts," he said. "After we have been in operation for six months or so, he will be hiring a kitchen manager, and a general manager for the hotel, of course, since he will be busy with negotiations for new sites. I will keep my apartment here, as I'll be traveling back and forth from Europe frequently, but Alex will be in residence permanently."

"Here in the hotel?"

"No, no. I have purchased a small house for them in town. A new marriage is difficult enough without adding to the strain, eh?"

I certainly agreed.


Black is Nick's color, and it is never more evident than when he's wearing a tuxedo. The New Year's Eve party was to be a black-tie affair. I realized, while dressing, that I envied men. After all, black tie is black tie—no decisions required. I, on the other hand, had agonized for days over what I would wear to this party. Sequins? Not really my style. Short? Not with my legs. Black? Very in, very chic, and a very bad color on me.

I had hit every store in Delphi twice, tried on everything sparkling, spangled, baubled, shiny, and low-cut, only to decide that my style was none of the above. I knew what I wanted. It was a garment that didn't exist. In the end, I visited a dressmaker.

The result was exactly what I had designed myself—a long, burgundy-silk dress with a cowl neckline and three-quarter sleeves. The cowl was trimmed with dyed-to-match pearls and dipped almost to the waist in the back, baring skin that I had browned on my one and only trip to a tanning salon. The dress had a long, sleek line, and the low back hinted at the Jazz Age—something Zelda Fitzgerald might have worn. Still, I stood in front of the mirror tormented by another crisis of confidence. That is, until Nick, coming out of the bathroom, stopped to give a long and suggestive whistle. That's why I love him.

The party was to begin at nine o'clock. The Americans would already be there, but the Greeks would be late. Not fashionably late—just late. Greeks always are. The activity level at the hotel had picked up. In the lobby, late-arriving guests were still checking in as couples in formal dress passed on to the elevator for the ride upstairs to the dining room

"I'm a little nervous," I said as Nick closed the door to our room behind us.

"Why?"

I rearranged the cowl at my throat and switched my beaded bag from one hand to the other. "I don't know. Feeling out of place, I guess. You haven't forgotten your promise, have you?"

Nick took my hand and arranged it over his arm, leading me toward the elevator. "I haven't forgotten."

Christos stood at the door to the dining room greeting his guests when we stepped off the elevator. He might have just strolled off his yacht, or out of one of the casinos in Monte Carlo. He was not a handsome man, but so well-groomed and self-possessed that I knew women on the prowl would find him very attractive.

Alex stood beside his father, far more handsome and exuding the confidence of a young man born to the villa. He reached out surreptitiously to touch Kate's fingers—an unexpectedly vulnerable gesture from a man who had every reason to be entirely comfortable in his surroundings. And she, wrapped in a soft ecru gown, her hair piled in curls and tendrils, was an Aphrodite among mortals. I swallowed a lump of envy the size of Mt. Olympos, and hugged them both.

"Are your parents here?"

"Not yet," she said with a frown. "They should be on their way. They were just about ready when I left. I don't know what's keeping them."

A visit from the police might well have caused some anguish in the Papavasilakis household, but I didn't mention that to Kate. She was nervous enough. We snagged our place cards, which put us at table number three, and walked on into the dining room. Spiros and Miss Alma were already seated at the otherwise empty table.

I had expected Spiros to look a bit like a dancing bear in his tuxedo and was surprised to find that he wore it quite well, although I would have left off the Greek sailor's cap. Miss Alma wore a pale pink shantung suit—fitted jacket and long skirt. The high color in her cheeks matched her outfit.

"Isn't this fun? I haven't been to a New Year's Eve party in thirty years, maybe more," she said. Her glance strayed to the bandstand, where the musicians twanged their bouzoukis and made last-minute adjustments to the amplifiers. "Nick, will you teach me some of the Greek dances tonight?" He assured her that he would.

Greeks love to dance. Like poetry, it's a national art form that is taken very seriously. Good dancers are much admired. Nick is one of the best. He's built like a flamenco dancer and moves with the same virile grace. I, on the other hand . . . well, I do have an ear for rhythm. It's just that the rest of my body isn't always paying attention. The band swung into a Theodorakis melody—a light and easy *kalamatiano*—and Nick grabbed my hand.

"Nick, there's no one else on the dance floor. I don't want to be the center of attention."

He dropped my hand with an exasperated sigh and pulled Miss Alma to her feet. "Now's as good a time as any," he said. *"Ella."*

Miss Alma followed him eagerly, escorted by Spiros. They formed a line of three in front of the band as Nick began to count. "One, two three four, five six seven . . ."

My feet picked up the rhythm as the count silently ran through my head. To my surprise, some of the American couples joined them on the floor. They watched attentively as Nick slowly coached them through the twelve steps, gradually picking up the pace to keep time with the music. I had about decided to grab on to the end of the line when another guest joined me at the table.

"Is this three?"

I moved the centerpiece slightly so she could see the unobtrusively displayed number and invited her to take a seat. "I'm Rula Vassos," she said, shooting a businesslike hand across the table. I introduced myself and pointed Nick out to her. She gave him a lingering glance before turning back to me.

"I'm on my own tonight," she said. She set her bag on the table and arranged herself in her chair so that her legs were shown off to good advantage. "I thought about bringing a date, but I decided I'd rather take my chances on meeting someone interesting here." She glanced around the dining room, as though mining for same. I doubted that she ever had trouble meeting men.

She was a bit younger than I—maybe twenty-eight. Her shiny brown hair hung in layers to her shoulders, each strand perfectly arranged so that the overall effect was seductive—as if she were scantily draped in a black-satin sheet instead of her short black dress. A necklace, composed of two bands of gold intertwined in a figure-eight design, rested heavily just above a quite impressive cleavage. Tiny gold leaves and delicately curled tendrils were threaded through the bands to create a golden grapevine. It was her only accessory, but it was enough. Before I could comment on her stunning jewelry, a waiter appeared at the table in search of a cocktail order.

"Gin and tonic for me and a rum and Coke for my husband," I said.

Rula took her time deciding, voicing and rejecting several possibilities before settling on Chivas Regal on the rocks. Maybe that's what I should have done—ordered by brand name. I even practiced in my head—*Beefeater's, please. I wouldn't touch anything else*—the words uttered with a blasé yawn. But it's not as though I'd really know one gin from another, which only underscores the conclusion I reached years ago, that I am not cut out to travel in lofty social circles.

"So what do you think?" she asked. "I mean about the hotel. Do you like it?"

"It's beautiful."

"Tastefully done, isn't it?"

I agreed and was glad I did. "I designed the interior," she said with a little nod. She pulled a business card out of her bag and pushed it across the table to me. "Panache," it said.

"What do you do?"

"I'm a speech pathologist, but I only work part time—"

"Really," she said, turning away. I followed her gaze to the dance floor and Nick heading my way. Rula pulled her fingers through her hair and nibbled her lower lip.

"Okay, Julia, let's go." Nick had me by the hand, pulling me out of my seat and toward the once-again empty dance floor. I recognized the first few bars of *a pentozali*.

"Oh, no. Not this one."

"You've been practicing for weeks."

"But . . ." I snagged my gin and tonic and guzzled half the glass, willing the alcohol to go straight to my head and drown my inhibitions.

"Remember, start on your left foot. Now, one, two

hop . . ." Rula watched with a condescending little smile that did nothing to bolster my self-esteem.

We returned to the table breathless. "Don't, repeat *don't*, do that to me again!"

"You can do it to me any time," Rula said to Nick with a suggestive smile. And then to me, "Dance, that is." Hmm.

Eight of the ten chairs at the table were now full. Miss Alma introduced us to Paul and Helen Compton first. "Mr. Compton is a marble importer," she explained. "He's responsible for this beautiful floor. And this is—"

Before another introduction could be made, Manolis and Georgia joined us. They were to be seated at the head table but stopped to say hello. I hugged Georgia affectionately, noticing that like most mothers of the bride, she looked tired—slate-gray crescents under her eyes perfectly matched to the shade of her dress. But I suspected that the wedding was not responsible for the troubled expression on her face and my suspicion was not unfounded. Before she left the table, she whispered in my ear.

"I need to talk to you as soon as we can slip away. Manolis must not know, but Aris called me before we left tonight. I may need Nick's help."

## Chapter Nine

I set aside the troubling news about Aris Mavrakis and tried to pay attention as Miss Alma made the rounds of introductions once again. Paul and Helen Compton were already acquainted with Rula Vassos and the other guest at the table. I had scarcely noticed him, and as I turned to meet him, I wondered how I could have overlooked him. He was not an easy man to miss.

"Julia," Miss Alma said, "I'd like you to meet Mr. Lakis Plemenos."

"My friends call me Lucky," he said, taking my hand in his. It was not a handshake but a caress, and to my embarrassment, I felt my hand go limp in his.

Lucky Plemenos was not a handsome man in the classic sense, not like Alex, for example. His face was narrow, his nose bony, projecting from a strong brow ridge that receded into a high forehead. A straight lock of chestnut hair fell down over eyes so dark and shiny they reminded me of chunks of onyx. He had an unpredictable, roguish quality with a quick smile—fleeting before it fully registered—and his black eyes burned with intensity. I was, for the moment, the absolute focus of his gaze.

"I'm pleased to—" I stammered, and felt my voice catch.

I sensed Nick's eyes boring into me, but I couldn't seem to turn away from Lucky until, abruptly, he shifted his focus to my husband with a handshake and a business card. The cool reserve in Nick's greeting sent a chill up my bare back.

Miss Alma continued the introductions—to Spiros, who studied Lucky shrewdly, and finally to Rula Vassos, who, while fanning herself with her napkin, explained that they were already acquainted. But Lucky scarcely seemed to notice her and immediately turned his attention back to me. This was heady stuff. I'm not used to being noticed in preference to women like Rula. I felt Nick stiffen beside me.

"Is everyone having a good time here?" I tore myself away from Lucky's gaze to find Eva Paradissis standing over us. The men hopped to their feet, all but drooling on their starched shirts.

Eva had almost managed to eclipse Kate. She wore velvet as black as a midnight sky. A belt of winking rhinestones encircled her tiny waist, as though the stars had marshaled themselves for the purpose. The neckline of her dress plunged into a low V, a cap sleeve hugged the edge of her shoulders, and a snug bodice tapered into a narrow skirt. She wore black, elbow-length gloves. A sparkling diamond tennis bracelet set off her slender wrist. It was a Marilyn Monroe look, and it produced all the expected reactions. Beside her, Rula Vassos looked like a cheap knock-off, and I felt like a dowager queen.

"Yes, it's a lovely party," Miss Alma said. The men seemed to have been struck dumb, but every male eye was trained on Eva's swaying hips as she excused herself and moved on to the next table.

"As I was saying," Miss Alma continued, "Mr. Plemenos—that is, Lucky—is a wine importer. He deals in Greek wines."

"Also," Lucky added, "olives and tobacco." His voice was soft and husky—gentle, but decidedly male.

"I see. And what makes you so lucky?" I asked.

"Well," he said, the evanescent smile briefly returning, "the pleasure of your company, for one thing."

I like to dance. In fact, I love it almost as much as Nick does. But I am not Greek, and in the company of Greeks, who dance not merely for fun but because it is as instinctive as laughter or tears, I feel like an interloper and poseur. I can do the steps, I can keep the beat. But the music of minor keys and shifting rhythms isn't written on my DNA spiral. I don't feel it the way they do. And so I watched them wistfully as Nick and Rula led the line in one dance after the next.

Rula was a beautiful woman, in her own way. Said way was sexy—even erotic. She gazed into my husband's face with an expression of longing, her lips slightly parted and eyes smoky. While Nick and I are almost the same height, she stood a good four inches shorter than he, which made her petite and a perfect dancing partner for him. Her feet moved quickly and gracefully, attached to their shapely and much-exposed legs. Those legs led to curving hips and a narrow waist, and from there to breasts that I couldn't quite believe were hers. Silicone, I thought.

"Implants," Lucky whispered to me with an amused smile. I blushed, caught in the act of openly envying another woman. It was just the kind of thing that made ardent feminists writhe. "That one is not to be trusted," he said.

"Maybe not, but I trust Nick." Still, I wished he'd sit out one or two dances. Lucky excused himself and crossed the floor to speak to the bouzouki player. In a minute, he was back.

"Would you care to dance?"

The band had switched into a soft, mellow version of "*Al Di La.*" This was the kind of music I really enjoyed, cradled in the arms of my husband. Yet it wasn't Nick, but Lucky, who held out his hand and gently pulled me to my feet. His arms were strong, his abdomen flat, and the muscles in his back hard. His hold on me was in every way proper, but still felt indecently intimate. I glanced over his shoulder to find Nick, standing in the middle of the dance floor, watching us with a deepening scowl. His worry beads were spinning so fast they rocketed out of his hand and onto the edge of the carpet. I buried my face in Lucky's shoulder to hide a smile. When I looked up again, Rula had retrieved the beads and was taking Nick's hand.

"You move very well," Lucky said.

Gulp. And what should I say to that? If I'd ever known how to flirt with a handsome stranger, I'd long ago forgotten. And it had been a long time since I'd been so conscious of a man's hand on my back. The whorls of Lucky's fingertips seemed to sear their prints into my skin.

"Thank you. My husband is a good teacher . . . I mean, he taught me to dance and——" My face flamed at Lucky's hearty laughter.

Xanthe Saros danced passed us in Alex's arms. She wore heavy makeup and had chosen a dress of royal blue—pretty enough, and probably quite expensive—but it did nothing to complement her olive complexion. Her face flushed and her eyes sparkled as she gazed up at Alex, so that in spite of her garish makeup, she looked pretty and surprisingly animated. She had all the raw materials, and given good advice, could have been a heart-stopper. All she lacked was self-confidence, which, unfortunately, is not a commodity to be bought off a department-store rack. If anyone knew about that, it was me—at least in this situation.

Nick danced Rula in our direction. She looked up at him with shining eyes, laughed when he whirled her into a spin I thought he reserved only for me. A knot formed in my throat as I moved in closer to Lucky's chest.

"Are you here for the wedding?" Lucky turned us expertly, dancing us into the crowd and away from my husband and his adoring partner.

"Yes, Nick is a friend of the bride's family. We came early—for the party and Epiphany. Is this business for you?"

"No," he said. "I consider this evening strictly pleasure."

"I meant—"

"I know what you meant," he said, pulling back to gaze into my face. "And I'm sure you know what I meant."

Nick and I were on the dance floor when the clock struck twelve, engulfed in a cool, distant silence as we fox-trotted around the perimeter of the floor. But I believe in bringing things out into the open—a conviction that hasn't always served me well. "Are you having a good time?" I asked.

"Ye-es," he said cautiously. "Are you?"

"Sure. Lucky's an excellent dancer. Almost as good as you are."

"Watch out for that guy, Julia. I don't like him."

"He's very nice, Nick. Not that you've had time to notice—"

He spun me around and pulled me back against his chest. "Look, he's using you to get to me."

I didn't stomp on his toes, but I wanted to. "To get to you? Why would he want to get to you? I suppose you can't possibly believe that another man could find me attractive. Not non-Greek, slightly plump, and just-a-little-clumsy me." Hot tears stung behind my eyelids at this ultimate humiliation. Meanwhile, there was Rula, who watched us intently from the edge of the dance floor.

"No, Julia, it's just that I have a restaurant and he's a vendor and—"

The band stopped. *"Theca, enya, octo . . ."* They had begun the countdown toward midnight. I swiped at my eyes and tried to smile.

"I only meant—" he began.

I held up a silencing hand, not trusting myself to speak.

*"Efige o palios o chronos . . ."* Half of the people in the room were singing, while the other half looked slightly bewildered.

By the time the song ended, I had gotten a shaky hold on my emotions. I glanced around the dining room at the other perplexed American faces. "What happened to 'Auld Lang Syne'?" I asked.

As if in answer, the band swung into the more familiar tune. ". . . We'll take a cup of kindness yet . . ." I sang, thinking that kindness was very much missing from the occasion.

"And now, my friends," Christos said into the microphone, "it is time for the *vasilopita*. If you will please take your seats."

As soon as the last guest was seated, the kitchen door swung open and, led by Eva Paradissis, a battalion of chefs and waiters entered carrying the firm, golden loaves high above their heads. They set their trays on the cleared buffet tables, except for one, which was set at Christos's place.

"For the sake of our American guests," Christos said, "I would like to explain the tradition of the *vasilopita*. In Greece, it is customary to begin the New Year with the bread of St. Basil. Tradition says that when thieves stole the jewelry and valuables of the people of Caesarea, they were recovered and returned to the bishop—St. Basil—who was to restore them to the people. But no one could agree upon rightful ownership. St. Basil suggested that the women bake the coins and jewels inside a large pita. When he cut the bread, each owner miraculously received his own treasure. Today, we bake a coin into each loaf, and the one who receives the coin in his piece is assured good luck for the coming year."

Christos took the French knife that had been set before him and made the sign of the cross over the loaf. "The first piece," he said as he inserted the point of the knife, "is for the Christ Child." He took the piece and wrapped it in a napkin. "It will be placed in the *iconostasi* in my son's new home." The guests applauded as Alex took the piece from his father and handed it to Kate.

"The second piece is for the Virgin, and this one—" Christos set aside another slice "—is for St. Basil. The fourth is given to the poor." He laid the knife on the table.

"Now this one little loaf will not, of course, serve all these people. My name may be Christos, but I am not a miracle worker." The guests laughed politely.

"So," he continued, "we have prepared many loaves. If you will be patient, my staff will serve you shortly. And remember," he said, holding up his hand, "if you receive a coin in your piece of the loaf, you must call out. And now, dear friends, my family and my *sympetheriká*—" he nodded toward a table, where Manolis inclined his head in acknowledgment "—wish you all *chronia polla*—many years!"

The band began to play again and Nick grabbed my hand, pulling me onto the dance floor before either rival partner could interfere. Around us, the waiters scurried toward tables with plates of St. Basil's bread. Xanthe, Eva, Kate, and Alex were all pressed into service.

"Happy New Year," Nick whispered in my ear. "I'm sorry if I hurt your feelings."

There didn't seem to be much point in holding a grudge. "Maybe you'll get the coin this year," I said.

Nick pulled away from me, locking his eyes with mine. "I don't need a lucky coin. I already have you."

And inside my dyed-to-match, burgundy-satin pumps that pinched just a little on the heel, my toes curled.

When we returned from dancing, the last two seats at the table had been filled. Father Charles had joined the party late, having spent most of the evening making hospital visits. He had taken my seat next to Lucky Plemenos, who gave me an amused wink and tapped a cigarette out of his pack.

"I import them, Father. Here, have one." Lucky proffered a pack of *Palas* cigarettes and, as the priest lit one, laid the pack on the table with the invitation to help himself to more at any time.

Father Charles inhaled slowly and exhaled with a contented sigh. "I used to smoke them in Greece."

"Well, as of Monday, you'll be able to buy them in the gift shop, right downstairs. I'm importing them for the hotel."

From tobacco, their conversation veered to cars as Father Charles held forth on the merits of his Jeep Cherokee. The way he drove, it seemed to me that a Hummer with rollover bars and an open top for easy escape was the only vehicle quite equal to him. Lucky's tastes ran to the lower, leaner, and meaner. They conversed happily, which left the rest of us to make conversation with the newcomer at the table—a difficult task considering the events of the afternoon, for next to Rula Vassos sat the other late arrival—Aris Mavrakis.

*Chapter Ten*

So this was what Georgia had wanted to tell me. Aris must have called her to warn her that he would be at the party. I'm sure he'd approached the evening with some apprehension, and yet he was there, which implied that he had nothing to hide. I glanced over at Georgia's table to find her returning my look with a mute plea. Beside her, Manolis's glare would have melted Venus arising from the punch, had she had the misfortune to come between him and his ex-partner. Spiros sat with his arms folded, biceps bulging inside the sleeves of his tuxedo jacket. Not a muscle in his face twitched. He scarcely blinked, and his gaze never left Aris Mavrakis. Nick, on the other hand, was coolly cordial as he shook Aris's hand.

"Are you a friend of Christos's?"

Aris took a sip of his drink and leaned forward, elbowing the table in a familiar, confiding posture. "Business associate, actually. I'm in real estate," he said, producing the ubiquitous business card that seemed to be de rigueur for the occasion. Aris Mavrakis brokered commercial properties.

"Ah," I said. "You brokered the site for the hotel?"

Aris grinned, a toothy smile suited to Mr. Ed, and shrugged modestly. "It was a matter of timing. And a little

fast talking. Christos . . . well, I hate to put it quite this
way, but he made them an offer they couldn't refuse, if
you know what I mean." Aris rubbed his thumb against his
fingertips, a gesture that said Christos had been willing to
pay dearly for the properties he'd acquired. Aris Mavrakis
had probably profited nicely from the deal.

"And you're here for the wedding," he continued. "Manolis has told me all about you."

"He has?" I said incredulously, then wished I could take
it back.

Aris shifted uncomfortably in his chair. "Ah," he said. "I
see you've heard. But of course, you were at *Mykonos*."

He plucked a matchbook off the table and began turning
it, corner by corner. He had long fingers—fluttering fingers
that reminded me of a hummingbird hovering over the object of interest before making its decision to light. "He told
me about you before, when we were friends. As you saw
this afternoon, our relationship has deteriorated. Manolis has
gotten it into his head that I am trying to hurt his business.
But I'm his landlord. Why would I do that when I need the
rent from the restaurant? It doesn't make any sense."

In Delphi, where everyone seems to know everyone
else's affairs, Nick and I had seen partnerships break up. No
matter how good the friendship had been, no matter how
reasonable the motive for the breakup, no one ever came
out of it the same. It is not, I reflected, unlike a divorce.

"He is behaving very oddly. It could be the wedding, I
suppose," Aris continued.

Spiros leaned forward, his hand over his mouth, index
finger pressed to the bridge of his nose. He narrowed his
eyes as he concentrated on what Aris was saying. There was
nothing friendly in his disposition toward the broker.

Aris's glance shifted to Nick, then warily back to Spiros.
"This business of a *maya*—all silly superstition anyway—as
if I'd do anything like that. It must be the wedding. I'm

not married myself, but I'm told that it's hard for a man to lose his only daughter to another man."

*"I Katerina—"* Spiros loomed over the table, pointing, his finger grazing the lapel of Aris's jacket. "You stay away."

Aris's face went pale as he leaned back, away from Spiros's imposing form. His hand came up, palm to his chest in a mute protestation of innocence. "I would never hurt Kate. I've known her since she was a little *koritsaki.* Has everyone convicted me already?"

"Of course not, Mr. Mavrakis," Miss Alma said hastily. "I'm sure you understand that Kate's family is under a great deal of pressure."

She turned to Spiros, who was still glowering down at Mavrakis. "Please, my friend, I have a headache." She put her palms to her face in pantomime, then slipped her key into his hand. "Will you get me an aspirin? *Aspirini?"* She pronounced the word carefully, with a verifying glance at Nick.

Spiros backed off slowly. Although he didn't want to leave, he could never deny Miss Alma anything. *"Neh, neh, endaxi,"* he muttered, stalking away with a backward glance at Aris that left no doubt about his intention.

"It will take him a little time," Miss Alma said after Spiros left. "There's none in my room. He'll have to go to the gift shop. I don't like tricking him that way when he's always so good to me, but . . . let's talk of more pleasant things."

Father Charles agreed. "Manolis tells me that you are a soccer player," he said to Nick. That was all it took to spur the conversation along, and soon the men were arguing about the performance of the Greek team at the last Olympics, which left me to converse with Rula Vassos and Miss Alma.

"Now, as I understand it, you are responsible for finding all these lovely pieces. And Mr. Kyriakidis says they're authentic. How in the world did you get ahold of them?" Miss Alma asked, waving a hand toward the display case on the dining-room wall.

"Buying trips to Greece. Eva wanted everything done in authentic Greek furniture and art." Rula signaled for the waiter and held up her empty glass before continuing. "It took three trips—first to the islands. Then on another one, I concentrated on the Peloponnesus. I went back two months ago, spent some time with Christos, and then took a buying trip up north."

I gazed at Rula speculatively, wondering if she had something going with Christos Kyriakidis. Maybe that explained her interest in Nick. She might be trying to make Christos jealous. I didn't know whether it was working on him, but it certainly wasn't doing me any good.

"I thought it was illegal to buy antiquities," Miss Alma continued.

"Only certain things," Rula said. "Most of these were already in private collections. I located them, and Christos was willing to pay the price."

My thoughts began to explore a possible romance between Rula and Christos. Somehow, I'd expected better from him. I could hardly blame Rula for being interested. Christos was not a handsome man, but he was charismatic. I did not, however, envy Rula the battle she would face with Pagona if she were going to be a permanent part of Christos's life. Pagona Kyriakidis had choke holds on both her son and grandson. Now with Alex marrying, she was not apt to surrender Christos easily. Nor, I noted, was Rula the type of woman to wait for her man to call the shots. When the band struck up a rumba, she had Nick on the floor before I could say *"Arriba!"*

"I wonder how one would go about buying a piece," Miss Alma speculated to me.

I tried to pay attention to the conversations at the table

while my husband floated gracefully through my favorite dance with another woman. I watched them, wondering if there really was something to the seven-year itch. Tonight, anyway, Nick seemed to have broken out in a rash.

"And which olives do you import?"

"*Kalamata*, Father. Is there any other kind?"

"Precisely, my friend. We seem to have the same tastes." Father Charles helped himself to another of Lucky's cigarettes. "Have you thought about bringing in *tarama?*"

The band had switched from a rumba to a samba. Nick and Rula were now the only ones on the floor. Latin dances are so romantic, I thought. And ground my teeth.

"You have to be careful, Mrs. Rayburn. There are many reproductions out there," Aris said.

"Well, there's not anything really wrong with a reproduction, I suppose."

"Not," Aris replied, "if you know about it. I know a potter in Salonika whose work is so good, he always paints his name, Andreas, somewhere into the pattern—"

"We considered other marbles," Paul Compton said to Lucky. "But I convinced Christos that Penteli was the way to go. There is something so—"

The conversation whirled around me, but I couldn't focus on anything other than the dance floor. Nick knew I loved the Latin dances. Why didn't he suggest they sit this one out, then come and get me? That would send her a message—*I prefer to dance with my wife.* But apparently he didn't, because now the band moved on, still its in Latin suite, to a tango. Nick dipped her gracefully. *Drop her, drop her!*

"Your *vasilopita*, ma'am." The waiter stumbled over the word as he set the bread in front of me. Although the staff had obviously been coached on pronunciation, he was probably terribly self-conscious with Eva supervising beside him. He kept his back to her while he served until she, with a sigh for his incompetence, picked up a plate and slapped it down in front of Aris. I was beginning to understand why Lucy—of the *toilet*—was so apprehensive about her boss. They all seemed to be a little afraid of her.

"Good," Aris said. "Perhaps this will be my lucky year."

"I could use a little luck myself," I said with a glance to the dance floor. I probed my bread with the tines of my fork, but found nothing in it except dough. I mined Nick's too, since he was too engrossed in Rula's swiveling hips to worry about coins. So much for the Lambros luck.

All around us, other guests called out in pleased surprise as coins were unearthed and held up triumphantly. "Ah," Aris said with a grin. "It seems I was right. A good omen." He dropped the coin into his pocket.

"Oh, may I see it?" If I couldn't get one in my own bread, maybe a little of Aris's luck would rub off on me.

He brought the coin back out, passing it across the table to me. It was brass—about the size of a quarter—in a two-drachma denomination. The obverse side featured a figure-head—one George Karaïskakis, a hero of the Greek War of Independence. I rubbed the coin between my fingers, wondering at my desire to believe in luck when I was struggling so hard with superstition. It didn't seem to be presenting a moral dilemma to anyone else in the room, though. The good luck was spread far and wide, and everyone was enjoying it thoroughly. That is, until the crash at the head table.


Three people at our table found coins in their slices that night: Aris, Helen Compton—and Rula, who didn't need any luck as far as I could tell. But by then, all the joy had gone out of the evening. With a strangled cry, Kate had unexpectedly lunged backward, away from the table and into a waiter delivering a tray of *vasilopites*. The tray crashed to the floor, calling our attention to the head table in time to see Kate, a quivering hand over her mouth, pointing at her bread. The gesture left no doubt in anyone's mind that something was very wrong.

Alex whisked the plate from her place and rushed into the kitchen, followed by Christos, Eva, and Nick. Spiros stepped off the elevator just in time to see Kate's parents hurrying to their daughter's side, and he joined them there. By the time I reached them, Kate's face was as white as her gown. Once he was sure that she was not physically harmed, Manolis hastened to the kitchen, leaving the girl in her mother's care.

Pagona elbowed her way between them *"Ti eine? Ti eine?"* No one answered her, but despite Xanthe's best efforts to pull her away, the old girl persisted loudly. *"Ti eine?"*

Georgia, flushed with rage, grabbed my arm and shook it. "I have to get Kate out of here, away from that old witch. What am I going to do?"

I fished around in my bag and pulled out my room key, shoving it into her palm. "Take her down to our room. I'll be along in a minute. Don't let anyone else in, especially—" My gaze went to Pagona, still ranting and raving in Kate's face, while Xanthe nervously wrung her hands.

Ever respectful of the elderly, Spiros had stood by and watched Pagona as long as he could bear it. But when the old lady tried to twist the engagement ring off Kate's finger, he'd had enough. He picked her up under the arms and swung her away from the table, holding her in midair while Georgia pulled Kate out of her chair and hurried her toward the elevator.

I rushed back to our table and Father Charles. "Please, Father," I said, pointing toward Spiros and Pagona, "please try to reason with her. She's gone berserk."

He was already out of his chair. By the time he was halfway across the dining room, Miss Alma had grabbed her bag and followed me to the kitchen, leaving Aris, Lucky, and Rula in bewildered silence.

The kitchen was practically empty. Eva had gathered up the staff and herded them to the prep room at the back, the better to question them about who could have tampered with the *vasilopita*.

"What's going on?" I asked Nick.

He nodded toward the work island, where Christos, tongs in hand, carefully probed the *vasilopita*. As the rest of us looked on, he extracted a long, heavy needle from the bread. It was the type of needle used for bargello and crewel embroidery—too large to present a serious danger, but perfect as an implied threat. This wasn't just superstition. This was black magic.

Alex turned on his heel and stalked toward the prep room. "Eva? Don't let anyone leave!"

Manolis ran a hand through his hair. "How could this happen, Christos? In your own kitchen?" Christos stared at the needle, saying nothing. He didn't even seem to hear Manolis.

"Answer me, dammit. This is my daughter's life we're talking about. How could you let this happen?"

Christos's face was a mask of anguish. At length, he turned to Manolis. "I do not know, *agori mou*. I wish I did."

Manolis slammed his hand down on the worktable. "Wishing is not good enough! Maybe your mother is right. Maybe there should be no wedding. My daughter is not some . . . some vestal virgin to be sacrificed for your son. If you and Alekos cannot take better care of her than this—"

I shot Nick a worried glance as he stepped between the fathers of the bride and groom. *"Ohee, agori mou,"* Nick said reasonably. "You know how restaurant kitchens are. Anyone might have had access—"

"Even the kitchen of the great Christos Kyriakidis, Niko?"

Manolis curled his fists belligerently, swaying unsteadily on his feet.

Christos ignored Manolis's taunting. "Niko, please, take him to the dining room and get him some coffee. I must question my staff."

But Alex was already taking care of that, in a manner of speaking. His angry voice echoed from the tiled prep room. "Kate's life, my life, at stake here . . . the reputation of this hotel! I want an accounting from all of you. Do not plan to leave . . ."

For the second time that day, Manolis tried to get by Nick. "I don't want coffee. I want answers, Christo!"

Christos slammed the tongs and the needle down on the table. "I don't have any answers!" He picked up an aluminum stockpot from the worktable and hurled it against the wall. "By God, I wish I did!"

*Chapter Eleven*

Christos's show of temper had its effect. Paralyzed with shock, we all stared at the stream of chicken stock that ran down the wall and pooled on the tile at the base. Christos took a deep breath and turned back to Nick. "Manolis has had too much to drink, Niko. Please, take him to the dining room and sober him up. Alex and I will come shortly."

At the back of the kitchen, Eva shrieked "No! Alex, don't . . . *Christo, ella. Grigora!*"

"Oh, dear lord," Miss Alma murmured. "That poor boy."

Christos skirted the table and flew toward the prep room. Manolis would have followed, but Nick forcibly turned him toward the door, shoving him back into the dining room. Miss Alma and I straggled along behind, wanting to escape the shouting and scuffling in the prep room.

In the dining room, Pagona sat back in her chair at the head table, arms folded over her breasts, her black eyes staring straight ahead. Spiros stood glowering over her, his hands on his hips, while Father Charles, squatting next to her, spoke quietly. Miss Alma joined him, drawing up a chair next to the old woman. Xanthe hovered uncertainly in the background. The last of the guests were crowded onto the elevator. At the back, Aris peered over the heads of the others, his brows drawn together in a worried frown.

I left Nick pouring coffee and sympathy down Manolis's throat in approximately equal measure and took the stairs to the first floor. Georgia let me into our room only after I had identified myself. Kate was lying on the bed with a damp washcloth over her eyes. She sat up when she heard me come in and pulled the cloth off. She'd been crying.

Georgia took the washcloth from her and ran it under a stream of cold water at the sink, wringing it out as though it were Pagona's neck. "What's happening upstairs?"

I dropped my bag on the bed, sat down, took off my shoes and rubbed my feet. Stalling. "Christos has the needle. I don't know what he's going to do with it. Spiros has Pagona under control for the moment."

Georgia muttered an epithet under her breath. "Where's Manolis?"

"He's . . . um . . . Nick's got him in the dining room. There was . . . sort of an argument in the kitchen."

"Oh, Mama, now what?" Kate swung her legs over the side of the bed as if to get up. "I've got to stop Daddy before he does something awful—"

"It's okay," I assured her. "Nick's with him. He won't let anything happen. Besides, Christos wasn't exactly a model of propriety himself. Everyone's under pressure up there. Alex was . . . uh, questioning the cooks when I left."

Georgia sighed and sat down next to Kate, pushed her daughter back against the pillows and clapped the wet cloth back on her eyes. "Manolis has had too much to drink."

"Please, Mama." Kate squeezed her mother's arm tightly. "You're the only one who can deal with him. Go upstairs and make him come down here before he cancels the wedding himself."

Georgia looked at me. "Go ahead," I said. "I'll stay with Kate."

When the door closed behind her, Kate pulled off the cloth and pushed herself up on the bed. She winced and clasped her hands to her head.

"What can I get you?"

"A couple of aspirins," she said. I went straight for my cosmetic bag, returning with the pills and a glass of water. "And a new life. A new father. Maybe even a new fiancé." She grimaced. "No, I don't mean that. Marrying Alex is the only good thing about this wedding."

I took the glass out of her hand and returned it to the counter in the dressing area. "He is a charmer."

She smiled, even through her headache. "A real sweetie. Good thing, too, because some of his baggage isn't so wonderful. His *yia-yia*, for instance."

"She's a tough one to understand," I said, striving to be fair. "All this nonsense about curses and gypsies—"

Kate leaned her head back against the headboard and closed her eyes. "It isn't nonsense, Julia. At least not to her. I think even Mama and Daddy are a little frightened by it—not that they'd admit it, you understand." She chafed her hands against her bare arms and shoulders. I grabbed my robe, threw it over her shoulders and sat down beside her.

"I'm afraid too," she said quietly. She opened her eyes and looked at me. "For Alex. It's not the superstitions. I don't believe in all that stuff. But whoever's doing this must be crazy, and I'm afraid they might be dangerous. I can't admit it to Mama. That would just make everything worse. And heaven knows, I can't say anything to Daddy. He's already about to blow a gasket."

She swallowed hard, blinking back incipient tears. "What am I going to do? If the threats don't stop, one of them—

Pagona, Daddy—one of them is going to insist we cancel the wedding."

"Oh, Kate, surely not. Christos and your parents are reasonable people."

She shot me a doubtful glance. "Most of the time, maybe, but this has everyone spooked." She brushed the back of her hand over her eyes and pulled herself up higher on the bed. "Well, I'll tell you one thing, Julia. None of it's going to keep me from marrying Alex. If we have to elope, we will, but we're going to get married. To hell with the rest of them."


Another hour passed before Nick and I were alone again in our room. Miss Alma came by to check on the girl before returning to her own quarters. Spiros arrived shortly thereafter, followed by Nick, Georgia, and a much subdued Manolis. Kate shooed them all out as quickly as she could.

"Alex will bring me home, Daddy. We need to talk."

"But, *koritsi mou*, I don't think you should be alone. These threats, first to him, now to you. I'll wait—"

Kate sent her mother a warning look and set her jaw stubbornly. "No, Daddy. Alex is going to be my husband. He will bring me home."

Georgia pushed Manolis out the door before he could protest further, dragging Spiros along behind her. By the time Alex arrived, Kate had managed to pull herself together and met him with a smile. Nick closed the door behind them, leaned against it and blew an exhausted sigh.

"They can't take much more of this."

He pushed away from the door and fell heavily onto the bed, reaching down to untie his shoes. I slid my dress down over my hips and slipped it onto a hanger, then shoved it into the wardrobe.

"I know. I just wish we could do something to help.

Kate's threatening to run away with Alex. I don't think she really means it, but—"

He shook his head. "I hope not. That would break Manolis's heart, and Spiros . . ."

Nick was right. Spiros would be the most devastated of all. He'd been looking forward to this wedding for so long. And he loved Kate as dearly as if she were his own daughter.

"Well, at least you managed to get Manolis calmed down."

Nick tugged at the knot in his bow tie. "Not really. Father Charles did that. Can you help me with this thing?"

I worked at the knot while Nick trailed his fingers up and down my bare back until I shivered. "What about Christos?"

"He and Alex were still with the kitchen staff when we left. Christos has brought in hotel security, but to tell you the truth, I wasn't too impressed."

He leaned over to nibble on my earlobe. "Did I mention how much I liked you in that dress?"

"No," I said, thinking he had been too busy admiring Rula.

"Almost," he said, breathing onto the back of my neck, "as much as out of it."

Well, maybe I should let bygones be bygones.


Nick and I have our own New Year's tradition, which seemed especially poignant to me that night. All the turmoil of the evening had given us both a reason to reflect on the fragility of happiness. I, for one, had made strengthening my marriage my first resolution for the year, and toward that end, we exercised vigorously. We were up quite late and slept in the next morning.

We were planning to attend the late service at the church. It's a nice way to begin the year, and under the circumstances, both Nick and I felt a strong need to connect with a higher good. Although there was no question that the needle in Kate's *vasilopita* had been put there by a human hand, there remained a sick and pervasive shadow of evil over the previous night.

I was trying to tame my hair, gone wild in the humid coastal air, when the phone rang. It was Georgia, calling to confirm dinner after church.

"How's Kate this morning?"

"Better. Alex and Christos have brought in more security, and Father Charles managed to get Pagona settled down. But I'm still a mess, and Manolis had too much *Retsina* at the party to be any good to me this morning. While you and Nick were dancing, before everything else happened, he invited everyone at your table over to the house for New Year's Day dinner. Except Aris, of course, which was probably the point—to insult him."

"Oh dear."

"Worse yet, they all accepted. So our dinner party has gone from twelve to something over twenty people. I'm a wreck."

"Not to worry, you can count on us. We'll meet you at church."

We were just starting out the door—early, for once—when the phone rang again. "Mrs. Lambros, this is Colette at The Coddled Canine. I'm afraid I have some bad news."

Nick tore a check off his checkbook and passed it across the counter to Colette. "Dogs are like children," she said. "Some of them just aren't ready to be left with a stranger. And some of them take their aggressions out on others," she continued, with a meaningful glance at Jack. "I don't think he slept much last night. He's barked himself hoarse."

Poor Jack. He was sulking in the waiting room, his back turned to the rest of us, but I saw him cut his eyes around. He knew we were talking about him and his antisocial behavior.

"This covers everything, right?" Nick growled. "Including the bill for the other dog?"

Colette nodded, gave us a facsimile of a smile and handed me a plastic grocery bag with the handles tied tightly together. "Don't forget his bed," she said. "Or what's left of it."

I peered into the open edge of the bag. Foam—lots of little shreds of foam rubber compressed into a mass. Through the bag, I could see the remnants of his plaid cushion.

"Don't open it!" Colette cried. "It'll go everywhere. The stuff expands. It took me over two hours to sweep it all up and clean the other dogs' cages."

We gathered our errant Scottie and slunk out of The Coddled Canine in disgrace. In the background, howls, snarls, and yips followed us to the car—probably the other dogs jeering at us. It didn't seem to bother Jack, who happily trotted along beside us.

"You know, German shepherds are big dogs," I said to Nick when we'd gotten back in the car. "He was probably intimidated by—what was the other dog's name?"

"Woden."

"Well, no wonder he was scared. He probably had to defend himself."

"If Jock had been defending himself, he'd be the one wearing the bandage now. No, I think he was definitely the aggressor."

"Well, he was upset."

"Not as upset as I am."

We slipped Jack into the hotel through the terrace entrance to our room. I had wrapped him up like a baby using a blanket from the car.

"That doesn't look too bad," I said, carrying him to the mirror. We were reflected back—I, dressed for church in a flowing challis dress with an empire line, Jack, cradled in my arms. Madonna and . . . dog.

"Black hair, square jaw. He could be yours. I think we could get away with it—for a while, at least," I told Nick.

"Right. I might as well start packing."

I tried several kennels in and around Tarpon Springs as soon as we got back to the hotel, but without success. Two of them were not answering. The third was booked. Word had probably gotten out that a deranged Scottish terrier had blown into town looking for digs.

"He's going to have to stay here," I said, hanging up the phone. "There's nowhere else to take him." Nick—a master of the wordless rebuke—glared at me. "I'll give him a downer and he'll sleep all day," I hastily added.

"No! He's had enough drugs. We'll have to take our chances." I smiled to myself as Nick squatted down to Jack's eye level and grasped the dog under his muzzle. "You're going to be a good boy, aren't you, Jock?" He scratched behind Jack's ears softly, patted the dog's head and offered him a rawhide bone. I snapped on the bedside radio and turned the volume up a little.

"Maybe it'll drown out the hotel noise," I said. "Besides, she said he's barked so much that he's hoarse. Probably no one would hear him anyway."

"We can hope."

When we left, after firmly hanging the "Do Not Disturb" sign on the door, Jack had happily drifted off to sleep on Nick's side of the bed. I pulled the door closed behind me, silently praying that our little dog would still be there when we got back. Not to mention our clothing, suitcases, and personal effects.

"For our deliverance from all affliction, wrath, danger, and distress, let us pray to the Lord," Father Charles sang out.

*"Kyrie eleison,"* responded the choir. Lord have mercy.

The Orthodox Divine Liturgy is the oldest service in Christendom, and the petition for protection from danger and distress seemed especially appropriate for there was, without question, distress in the Papavasilakis family. And if Nick was right, possibly danger too.

"Pagona has a lot of influence over Alex," Nick had said the night before. "She raised him after his mother died. He listens to her. If Pagona wants to cancel the wedding—"

"Alex will be caught between a rock and a hard place."

Nick nodded solemnly. "Scylla and Charibdis."

Georgia had told me a bit about Christos Kyriakidis and his family. Their first hotel was built on Rhodes by Christos's father, for whom, in keeping with Greek tradition, Alex had been named. When the elder Alexandros died, Christos took over the family business and shortly thereafter took a wife. Eleni Kyriakidis bore Christos one child before discovering, when her son was four, that she had uterine cancer. It was detected too late to save her. Eleni died two weeks after Alex's fifth birthday.

"Alex has refused to cancel the wedding," Nick had continued. "But that needle has just fueled Pagona's fears that the marriage is cursed."

*"Tas thiras, tas thiras!"* The doors, the doors! We were entering the part of the Liturgy when the worshipers recited the Creed in testimony to their beliefs. In ancient times, the doors of the room would be closed and guarded, pre-

venting nonbelievers from participating in the most solemn part of the service.

"I believe in God, the Father, the Almighty, Creator of heaven and earth, and of all things, visible and invisible . . ."

*Visible and invisible.* The words resonated in my mind. I couldn't shake off the feeling that the visible—the *maya,* the needle—were only a fraction of some larger, invisible evil. Despite the warmth in the church, I shivered convulsively.

". . . let us worthily give thanks to the Lord." Father Charles had just returned to the altar after distributing Communion. The choir responded, *Kyrie eleison,* as he moved into the next petition.

"Help us, save us, have mercy upon us and protect us—" the chant stopped abruptly, followed by several seconds of silence before it began again "—O God, by Your grace."

The remainder of the service went on smoothly, but when Father Charles turned to face the congregation for the dismissal, it was with a face as white as the church's marble columns. Nick reached for my hand as Georgia glanced from Manolis to me.

"My children," the old priest said, stopping to clear his throat, "we have an extraordinary situation here. I must ask you to remain at the conclusion of the Liturgy for a special prayer service." He returned to the altar and brought out a large, ornate silver-and-gold icon.

"This icon," he said, "is weeping."

*Chapter Twelve*

Father Charles held the icon at waist level as each of
the worshipers came forward to reverence it with a kiss on
the corner of the glass. Christos and Pagona preceded us,
Pagona loudly keening as she crossed herself continuously.
Encouraged by Nick, I eased toward it, my stomach
clenched and churning with apprehension. As much as I had
wanted to see the weeping icon of St. Nicholas, I could not
feel the same anticipation for Alex and Kate's icon of the
*Epiphánia*. It was, for me, just one more bizarre event in a
nightmarish litany of pranks. I reluctantly stepped forward
to take my turn.

The icon was a bas-relief, wrought in silver and with a
halo of gold. The only painting on it was the face of Jesus,
rendered on a small piece of canvas inset into the metal.
And there, on that face, were two large crystal tears.
Smaller droplets gathered around the edges of the gold. I
backed away from it reflexively, telling myself that it was
a tasteless and frightening joke. The tears were fake—put
there by a clever prankster to serve his own dark purposes.

"Go ahead, my dear," Father Charles said. "You have
nothing to fear here in the church."

The glass felt cold against my lips. I caught my breath as

the tears became dislodged and trickled onto the silver. I glanced around, as though something in the church might explain how it had been done—what sleight of hand had created the illusion. But when I looked back, another droplet had formed at the edge of the halo. I stepped away, turned and hurried down the aisle to the vestibule, breathed deeply and leaned against the wall.

The tears were real. I had watched as they formed on the halo and spilled over the face. Evil. The word insinuated itself into my mind, as clear as if it had been spoken, while from the *proskenetarion* against the wall, the compassionate eyes of St. Nicholas gazed up at me in mute warning.

"Come on, let's get to work," I said, leading Georgia into her kitchen. Spiros and Miss Alma were already there and busy—she peeling potatoes while he basted a turkey about the size of a small emu. I had resolved not to think about the icon and had adopted a pretense of calm. I could not, would not, dwell on the supernatural.

The kitchen looked as though Georgia had pulled out the entire contents of her pantry and was hastily throwing them together to feed the five thousand. She had sent Manolis over to *O Kritikos* for more wine and some *souvlaki* she could throw on the grill. While Nick buttered and layered phyllo for *tyropita,* I tossed together a salad in a bowl the size of a bathtub.

Among Greeks, *philoxenia*—hospitality—is a most important virtue. With both Christos's and Manolis's only children marrying, they'd pulled out all the stops for the wedding—Christos magnanimously offering hotel rooms to close friends and his dining room for the reception, while Manolis and Georgia entertained us all both in their home and at their restaurant. By the time she was finished, not an inch of Georgia's mahogany dining table would be visible around the platters of food she'd have set out for her guests.

"Did you see Father Charles's face? Even he was frightened by it. And Pagona—well, this probably finishes it for her."

I cut tomatoes into big chunks and dropped them into the salad bowl, capitulating to Georgia's need to discuss the morning. "Why?"

"Because a weeping icon is a bad omen." Georgia stuck her head in the fridge and rustled around. In a minute, she reappeared and grabbed the wall phone. "I'm almost out of feta. I hope I can catch Manolis before he starts back."

She did, giving him explicit instructions to get the feta and head home. He was not, she said sharply, to stop for any reason, then slammed the phone back into the cradle. The tension was starting to get to her.

"Well, what about the St. Nicholas icon, then?" I asked. "Did anything terrible happen after it started weeping?"

Georgia shook her head and began crumbling the remaining feta over the salad. "No. But it wasn't really weeping," she said. "The tears formed on the brow, not around the eyes. It was more like . . . sweating. As if he was working very hard."

This seemed like a minor distinction to me, but it gave me a toehold. "Okay. Well, did you look closely at Kate's icon? The drops were around the halo, not the eyes, so how do you interpret that?"

"I don't know," Georgia said as she rinsed her hands at the sink and stared thoughtfully out the window into the backyard. She dried her hands on her apron. "I wish Manolis would hurry up and get here."

"Just how many people are you expecting, Georgia?"

She ticked them off on her fingers. "Father Charles, the Comptons, Rula . . . I'm not sure who else Manolis invited. He was all over the dining room last night. Including us, something like twenty-five." They began to arrive just as she finished her estimate.

Being Americans, the Comptons were the first to appear. Rula Vassos came right behind them, flanked by two other couples I didn't know. I did recognize one of them, the happy recipients of a lucky coin. They were introduced as Mr. and Mrs. Larry Fisk, of Fisk's Fine Fruits and Vegetables. The other couple was obviously Greek—Mr. and Mrs. Makris, of Chicago. Both were vendors Manolis dealt with and had recommended to Christos.

Out on the street, a low purr advised us that another guest had arrived. It was followed by a squeal of brakes and a sickening crunch. By the time I got to the window, Father Charles was out of his Jeep and standing with Lucky Plemenos. Both of them were staring at the sleek, black Lotus Esprit hugging the curb in front of Georgia's house—the Esprit with the major rear-end damage.

"It's all right, Father," Lucky said as they came through the front door. "You have insurance, don't you?"

"Yes, yes. The diocese—" Father Charles's face turned ashen. "The bishop will not be very happy about this. If it had been a Ford, or even a Chrysler. But a Lotus! I'm sorry, my friend. I am not myself today."

Lucky clapped the old priest on the back and laughed. "I will smooth it out with the bishop. A small contribution to his favorite fund, eh? *Then pirazi*, Father. Do not worry."

I swiftly excused myself and headed back to the kitchen, but not before I'd noticed three things. First, Lucky looked just as attractive in casual black slacks and a gray heather turtleneck as he had in a tuxedo. Second, even as he greeted Georgia, his glance moved about the room until it came to rest on the object of his search—me. And third, it did not escape Nick's notice.

"You're looking very fresh this morning."

I didn't have to turn around to recognize Lucky's voice. I almost dropped the turkey baster. I took a deep breath.

"Thank you. I don't recommend mixing gin and *Retsina* with champagne, though. It certainly didn't do me any good." I turned around to face him. He cocked his head right, then left.

"I don't know. Your cheeks are quite pink. You know, I much prefer the northern European coloring to the darker Mediterranean. There is something more . . . enigmatic, perhaps, about the appearance of such women. Mediterranean women wear their sexuality too openly, I think—"

This time, the baster went, splattering all over the kitchen floor. We almost bumped heads as we bent to retrieve it. Too close. I could smell his cologne—not overbearing, just a hint of something I didn't recognize and that Nick probably couldn't afford. We straightened up together. He wrapped his hand over mine as I wrestled the baster from his grasp and that was how Nick found us when, at that exact moment, he came through the kitchen door.

"I dropped the baster. What a mess," I said by way of quick explanation, hastily jerking a wad of paper towels off the roll. Lucky grabbed them and mopped at the floor while I washed the baster at the sink. When he finished, he stuffed them into the trash and quietly left the kitchen. Nick scowled at me silently before turning on his heel and stalking after Lucky. By the time the Kyriakidis family arrived, I was already pretty rattled. They did nothing to improve things.

Christos propelled his conspicuously silent mother gently but forcibly through the door, with Xanthe Saros in close proximity and Eva right behind her. As the two women danced attendance on Pagona, Christos pulled Father Charles and Georgia toward the kitchen. As if for support, Georgia grabbed me along the way.

I tried to busy myself, again basting the turkey, but I couldn't ignore their conversation. From what I got of the Greek, Pagona was more convinced than ever that the wedding should be canceled, citing the will of God, which I thought was a bit presumptuous of her.

"I have called the bishop about this and I am waiting on his instructions," Father Charles said. "Besides, we do not yet know whether the tears are genuine. There are, of course, certain scientific possibilities to be considered."

"But my mother will not believe them," Christos said ruefully. "To her, science is as strange as these superstitions are to the rest of us." In a moment, he brightened. "However, I am sure, Father, that you will be able to find a way to reassure her."

Father Charles sighed deeply. "It was hard enough last night, convincing her that the needle did not necessarily mean another curse. A weeping icon will be considerably more difficult to explain. All I can do is try, I suppose. Your mother is a very tenacious woman, my friend . . ." His voice trailed away as he followed Christos from the kitchen.

"Kate," I said, "I don't think I thanked you for the basket in our hotel room. I've already eaten the chocolate." I handed her a cup of coffee, passing another one to Alex, and one to Eva, sitting next to him.

"Spiros gave me his bath powder," Miss Alma admitted. "I don't suppose he takes many bubble baths. I'm saving it until I get home. It will be such a pleasant reminder of our trip."

Kate looked at us without comprehension, but Alex was quick to explain. "The Greek Key Club. I told you about it."

"Oh, yes. I'm sorry, Julia. My mind was somewhere else—pre-wedding jitters, I guess." Who could blame her under the circumstances? Apparently, Manolis had the same thought—but with a slightly different twist.

"*Katerina mou*, if you have any doubts—"

"I don't, Daddy."

"But—"

"I'd really like to see your wedding dress," I said hastily. She shot me a grateful glance. "I'm afraid it's still at the shop. We were waiting for the *flouria*. Which reminds me," she said, turning to Christos, "I'll have to get it from you tomorrow. My final fitting is first thing Monday morning."

"What, may I ask, is a flour—"

"*Flou-ree-ah,*" Kate pronounced slowly for Miss Alma. "It's Alex's family jewelry—a coin necklace. Christos made a gift of it to me at the engagement party. It's been in his mother's family for over a hundred years."

Manolis poured Christos a shot from the bottle of Scotch he'd been wagging around the room. "The father of the groom," he said, smiling, "has been kind enough also to provide the *proika.*" He clinked his glass to Christos's and knocked back his shot. Kate glared at her father.

Christos stiffened. "The *flouria* is not a dowry, Manolis. It is a tradition in our family, that is all." He set the glass down on a nearby table and stalked away. Manolis followed his back with an angry scowl.

"Daddy, how could you?"

"*Katerina mou*, I think perhaps the Papavasilakis family is not good enough to marry into—" Before he could finish, Spiros grabbed his cousin's arm and propelled him toward the kitchen.

Miss Alma took Kate's hand, preventing her from following her father. "Oh, Kate, I'd love to see it—the jewelry, I mean," she said.

Kate turned back to us hesitantly, her gaze following the men. "Yes, well, I'll be picking it up in the morning, if you'd like to come along."

We set a time to meet before I turned away to look for

Nick. A girlish giggle fluted up from the other side of the room. Rula, laughing at one of Nick's jokes as if he were the funniest man on earth, which I knew, for a fact, he was not. Beside me, a warm male presence appeared.

"In Greece, we have a saying," Lucky said softly. " 'A man who is covered with flies is touchy.' "

"You think your precious hotel is more important than my daughter's safety?" Manolis shouted.

"Of course not! I'm only saying that I don't think it's necessary to bring in the police when my own security people can handle it, Manoli."

The respective fathers were in the living room, and judging by the decibel level of the conversation, they were not sharing golf stories. Manolis was in no condition to confer reasonably with anyone. He had been drinking heavily all afternoon. Fortunately, most of the guests had already left by the time the trouble broke out. Eva, Xanthe, Pagona, Spiros, and Miss Alma had returned to the hotel. Georgia and I had just gone to the kitchen to start cleaning up. By the time we reached the living-room door, Manolis was brandishing his fist in Christos's face.

"Hah! Clowns. If they had been doing their jobs, it would not have happened in the first place."

"We don't know that. We don't know when the needle was put in the bread. I have questioned every member of my staff. I have no reason to think that any of them want to harm Kate, or Alex either. And don't forget, Manoli, the *maya* appeared in your restaurant, not mine. And the threat was to my son, not to your daughter."

Manolis flushed angrily. "What are you saying?"

"Nothing. Just that it has happened to both our families. It is obviously someone outside—"

"Unless, of course, you're trying to get your son out of this marriage, Christo. Is that it? My Kate is not good enough for him?"

"Manoli, please." Christos spread his hands apart in a placating gesture. "I love her as though she were my own daugh—"

"But she is not your daughter, Christo. She is mine, and if I decide there will be no marriage, there will be no marriage, Do you understand?"

"No, Daddy," Kate said calmly. She walked across the room, took the bottle of Scotch out of his hand and passed it to her mother. "Whether or not there's a wedding, there will be a marriage."

Alex came to her side, wrapping his arm around her slender waist and turning them in a half circle. His dark eyes took them all in—Manolis, Georgia, and Christos—with a sweeping gaze. His voice and manner were every bit as authoritative as his father's.

"I would like to remind all of you that this is a new age and that these are our lives, not yours. We don't need your blessing—any of you. I don't need your job, *Baba*. I can find work elsewhere. And," he continued, facing Manolis, "the days of the *proika* and the father's permission are long gone, *petheré*. Kate and I will be married with or without you."

He took his fiancée's hand. "Come on, Kate. Let's get out of here."

*Chapter Thirteen*

Georgia watched from the front door as the couple climbed into Alex's little Miata and peeled away from the curb, leaving enough rubber for a bicycle tire. She closed the door and stepped into the arch leading into the living room.

"I warned you, Manoli. This isn't some remote mountain village, and Kate is not a possession to be controlled. She's your daughter. Now are you satisfied? You've chased them away. God knows whether we'll see them again."

Manolis clapped his hand to his chest. "I? I chased them away? What about Pagona? She's been opposed to the marriage almost from the start." He wheeled on Christos. "Maybe you've decided she's right. Maybe you thought you could frighten my Kate away."

"My mother," Christos said icily, "is an old woman with little understanding of the world, Manoli. You should know better."

Manolis advanced on him angrily. "Of course, you know everything. You are Christos Kyriakidis—a Midas—successful, rich, powerful. How can you allow your son to marry beneath himself?"

"Is that what this is all about, Manoli? My money? I

thought we were talking about our children. Your daughter. Whatever you may think of me and my success, I would never, ever, hurt Kate. I love her, and if you love her, you will sit down and try to work this out." He paused, frowning at Manolis. "Well?"

Georgia folded her arms across her breast and glared at her husband. Manolis's gaze traveled from her to Nick. At length, he dropped into a chair and gestured to another seat for Christos. Nick and I eased toward the door.

"No, please," Christos said. "Stay." His lips twitched in a half-smile. "We may require mediation."

Manolis sat on the edge of his chair, head hanging as he stared at the backs of his hands. Christos waited for the rest of us to take our seats before beginning.

"The events of the last few days have been stressful, my friend, and we are all upset," he said reasonably. "But if we begin fighting among ourselves, we are playing right into the hands of whoever is doing these terrible things."

We all looked at Manolis, waiting for him to agree. He remained obdurately silent. Christos shrugged and went on.

"I do not want to call in the police at this time. I have security people at the hotel who can look into the matter. If the police are brought in, it will damage the reputation of the hotel."

Manolis shifted back in his chair. "Which is all you care about," he muttered.

Christos gazed at him evenly. "It is what we must all care about," he said. "You seem to forget that your daughter's future rests on the success of the hotel. Believe me, my friend, I will not put our children at risk. As soon as my people turn up anything of substance, we will turn the evidence over to the police. In the meantime, I will make sure that an extra security detail is on duty at all times. Do you agree?"

Manolis turned to stare out the window as though he

were expecting Kate to return at any second. But outside, the street remained quiet. Georgia stood up and walked over to his chair, placing a gentle hand on his shoulder.

"Manoli?"

He sighed. "Yes, all right. I agree. But if anything else happens, you must bring in the police."

Christos stalled for a minute before agreeing. "All right."

He stood up and offered his hand to Manolis, who, prodded by Georgia, returned the handshake. "I am meeting with my chief of security in the morning. I'll be asking him to look into Mavrakis's background first."

Manolis looked thoughtful. "Aris, yes. Do that."

Georgia walked Christos out to his car, eager, I imagine, to apologize for her husband's behavior. It wasn't an auspicious beginning to a lifelong relationship. As soon as they had left the room, Manolis pulled Nick and me into the kitchen.

"I don't trust him," he said. "He may want to use his security people to cover up the facts. He has money, and money can buy anything. Aris had a business deal with him. They may be in this together."

Nick shook his head. "Manoli—"

"No, Niko, it is possible. Christos and Alex needed local contacts. I introduced them to vendors and contractors. Even to Aris—because then we were still in business—don't you see?"

Manolis's voice had taken on a strident urgency. He had Nick by the shoulders. The odor of Scotch still permeated his breath. "Now that the hotel is built, he doesn't need me anymore, and now Kate is not good enough for his son. And Aris—well, I know he is involved in this, Niko. If Christos refuses to bring in the police, there is nothing I can do. But you can help. You must help me, *agori mou.*"

Nick frowned at me over Manolis's shoulder. "What can I do?"

"You are there, in the hotel. You can watch for me. Spiros told me—you are good at . . . *erévna* . . . how do you call it?"

"Investigation. But, Manoli, you realize that Julia and I just fell into—" The front door closed and Georgia's footsteps sounded in the foyer.

Manolis glanced toward the door and back to Nick. His eyes gleamed. "You must help me, Niko. Kate—my *Katerina*—could be in danger. I'm your *koumbaros,* Niko. Promise me. Promise me you'll help."

Nick sighed. "All right, my friend. I promise."


Georgia and I sat at the kitchen table nursing lukewarm cups of coffee before tackling the dishes. "I don't know, Julia," she said wearily. "I'm beginning to wonder if Pagona's right, that we're cursed. We're a very superstitious people, you know. Women like Pagona live by these old ways."

"But you're a well-educated woman, Georgia."

"Raised by a mother and a grandmother just like Pagona. My head knows that it's all superstitious nonsense, but . . ." She clasped her arms over her stomach. "I still feel it here, you know?" She got up and took an empty glass from the cabinet, filled it with water and set it down on the table before going to her pantry.

"What are you doing?"

"I have to find out," she said, bringing out a bottle of olive oil. "There's a way of testing for the evil eye."

I watched, mystified, as she carefully poured three drops of oil into the water, waited for a moment, crossed herself then peeked into the glass. I, too, peered over the rim at the three drops, watching as they moved together to form a glistening, golden pool on top of the water. At length, Georgia sighed with obvious relief.

"*Kala eine*. It's all right." She snatched the glass and dumped the contents into the sink. "If the oil had dispersed into the water," she continued, "it would have meant that someone had cast the evil eye upon the family. But you saw for yourself that it didn't."

I nodded, wondering what three drops in Pagona's glass would do. Georgia returned to the table with two fresh cups of coffee—Greek for her, American for me.

"Tell me," I said, "about Aris."

According to Georgia, Aris Mavrakis was congenial and well-liked in the community. He was already a successful real-estate broker when he and Manolis decided to partner *O Kritikos*. Aris owned the building and was willing to take out loans for equipment and opening costs. In return, Manolis would work as the managing partner. Their agreement had been that Manolis would be paid well enough to gradually buy a half-interest in the assets of the business. In the meantime, he would still have equal influence in the decision-making at the restaurant. Or so he thought.

Like all new restaurants, *O Kritikos* had enjoyed an initial honeymoon with the community, a flurry of business as everyone in town rushed to try out the new place. And, like all new restaurants, the honeymoon had ended when, curiosity satisfied, people resumed their usual habits. The most critical period of a restaurant is at the end of the honeymoon, when its staying power is tested. Manolis understood this, but Aris, believing Manolis had failed him, was worried about his investment. He tried to take control of the business—opposing Manolis's decisions to advertise and make menu changes. He would not allow Manolis access to the books.

Georgia rinsed the last plate, stuck it into the dishwasher and dumped Cascade into the detergent cup. "Meanwhile,

Manolis was working open-to-close seven days a week. 'Sweat equity,' they call it. Aris came in to help when it suited him, which was not very often. Mainly, Aris wanted a place to bring his girlfriends—you know, to act like a big-shot restaurateur."

I smiled. Most people in the business will agree that there is no more humbling experience than cleaning out a clogged grease trap or jerry-rigging a broken ice machine. The restaurant business is nothing if not hands-on. I dumped the remainder of the salad into a plastic container and handed her the bowl.

"There was not a thing Manolis could do about it. He couldn't go back to diving— his health wasn't good enough. And he's not trained to do anything else."

I pulled a dishtowel off a hook inside a cabinet door and plucked the salad bowl out of the dish drainer. "Didn't they have any agreement? Anything in writing? Couldn't Manolis force his hand?"

Georgia stared at the bottom of the roasting pan, covered in grease, with a grimace of distaste that might not have been related to the pan. "We trusted him, Julia. Perhaps you have to know him to understand. He is so . . . easy-going. So friendly. But then he panicked—claimed he was losing his shirt. He still had a note on the building to pay, and equipment leases and loans. I don't have to tell you, it's very expensive to set up a restaurant." She picked up a steel wool pad and began to work on the bottom of the pan.

No. She didn't have to tell me. That's why Nick is always on the alert for used equipment. And the independent restaurant business being what it is, there's usually plenty of it around at auctions and bankruptcy sales. Our basement is decorated in early Hobart and vintage Vulcan.

"So—" I prompted her.

"So they were fighting all the time. They were already

in a lot of debt, but business was picking up. We had some lucky breaks. A TV station in Tampa featured us on a travel program and it brought in a lot of customers. Things were getting better."

Georgia turned to me, her hand on her hip. "By then, we knew that Aris was keeping most of the money. Vendors were complaining that they weren't getting paid. They started refusing to deliver to the restaurant except on a cash basis. Manolis was embarrassed and ashamed, but there was nothing he could do. Aris was taking all the money out of the business." She went back to the pan, scrubbing it with such vengeance I thought she might take the enamel coating off.

"Then one day Aris told Manolis that he had filed for Chapter Seven bankruptcy and was closing the place. He had nothing to lose personally, because the restaurant was a separate corporation and he had recouped all or most of his investment by withholding payments. It didn't matter at all that Manolis had no job to go to. They had been in business only six months."

"Oh, Georgia." My heart went out to her, and even more to Manolis. I knew all about sweat equity—about working day and night to make a business succeed, and about being threatened from the outside by things you couldn't control. But somehow, Manolis had managed to hang on.

"We mortgaged the house," Georgia continued, turning the roaster over into the dish rack. "We'd just finished paying it off the year before, but we had to mortgage it again. There was no choice. Manolis didn't have a job and you know, at his age, how hard it would be for him to start over doing something else."

"So you bought Aris out?"

"Yes, sort of. We stopped the bankruptcy, paid off the vendors and the loans. But Aris wanted the moon for the business. He knew he had Manolis by his tomatoes. Manolis has a few more payments on the business. He was going to try to buy the building from Aris, but now——"

Georgia picked up her scrubber and savagely attacked the top of the stove, unable to go on. She didn't need to finish. I understood. After all that had happened between them, Aris would make Manolis pay dearly for the building, if he agreed to sell it at all.

"You see what's happening here, don't you, Julia? Manolis has been badly burned once—by Aris. He's afraid it's going to happen again, only this time it won't be his business, it'll be something infinitely more precious."

"Kate."

She nodded. "He adores her. Aris made Manolis feel like . . . like a freeloader. Aris isn't in Christos's financial class by a lot—nor does he have Christos's class—but he still managed to make Manolis feel beholden to him. Now there's Christos—wealthy, powerful—giving them a big wedding and a new house. Manolis and I could never have afforded to put on this wedding without his help. Manolis thinks he's trying to take away his daughter, just like Aris tried to take away his business. He's afraid of losing Kate not once, but twice—to Alex, of course, but also to Alex's father. I've never seen him so frightened."

It made sense, and it explained why Manolis was behaving so oddly—even believing that Christos and Aris might be in league in a plot to undermine him. "I don't understand, though, why Manolis thinks Aris is behind all these tricks, Georgia."

Georgia tossed the scrubber back into the sink and guided me to the kitchen table. Our cups waited there—mine empty and hers full of dregs. She turned hers over with a thin smile. "Force of habit," she said. "The last thing we need is more dire predictions."

She picked up the cup and carried it to the sink without looking inside. There would be no reading of the cup—no predictions deciphered from the dregs on the ceramic. I was just as glad. I'd had just about enough of the metaphysical. Georgia dropped back into her seat and swiped at the table as though it were covered in crumbs, though not a one was in sight.

"Manolis thinks Aris wants to hurt him. You see, word gets around very fast in a little town like this. Everyone knew that Aris had filed for Chapter Seven. He never accused Manolis outright that I know of, but people seemed to have the idea that it was Manolis's fault that the place was failing. There were rumors that Manolis tricked him into starting it in the first place, which I know for a fact is not true. Aris came to him with the idea." Georgia's voice trailed off, as though she were trying to decide whether to confide something else. Her decision made, she went on.

"There were times when they were partners that I agreed with Aris. You saw how Manolis behaved this afternoon. He can be impulsive, not to mention stubborn. Aris is an easy man to get along with and sometimes I was . . . well, I took his side. You see what position that puts me in, don't you?"

I saw too well. Aris could claim that Manolis's own wife agreed with him, which she couldn't completely deny. It gave Aris more credibility in the community, and it must have made for considerable tension between Georgia and her husband.

"But to be fair, I've never heard him say a bad thing about Manolis, and no one has ever quoted him to me. I'm not sure where the rumors started. In the kitchen, maybe."

"Tell me, Georgia," I said, "do you think Manolis is right about Aris?"

"I don't know." She placed her hands flat on the tabletop, pressing her fingertips against the wood as though willing them to be still. "Aris and I . . . well, he's always very nice to me. In fact, sometimes he's too nice, if you understand what I mean. He treats me a little too kindly, as if he feels sorry for me, being married to Manolis. Pity is almost a harder thing to swallow than cruelty, you know."

If I followed Manolis's reasoning, Aris Mavrakis wanted to save face. Manolis's success at *O Kritikos* would show Aris up for a liar—even make him look stupid for having panicked and given up the restaurant. Therefore, Aris would still like to see the restaurant fail. Furthermore, if the business collapsed before Manolis had finished paying off the remainder of the sale, Aris could take it over and bring in a new manager. It was possible that Aris envied Manolis his success.

All of this, however, did not explain the tricks—the *maya*, the needle in the *vasilopita*. But if the wedding was canceled, Kate would be humiliated. There would be gossip about her marrying above herself. The business might not be affected, but Manolis would be hurt through his daughter. Maybe that was enough for Aris Mavrakis.


"There's nothing like a bath to ease tension," I said, pouring bubble bath into the tub. When it didn't bubble up, I added more and turned on the Jacuzzi. "Nick?"

"Hmm?"

I started back into the bedroom, tripping over Jack, who had ignored his water bowl in favor of the blue water of the *toilet*. "Did you hear me? I'm going to take a bubble bath. There's room for two."

He sat on the bed, staring at the weather forecast on television. I knew he really wasn't thinking about the barometric pressure, not when the other pressures of the day were still very much with him. I knelt behind him and tickled his ear. "Bath," I said. "A long, warm soak in the tub—maybe a glass of wine and—"

Jack gave a yelp in the bathroom and tore around the

corner, catapulting himself onto the bed. "Julia, have you tried any more ken—Stop that, Jock!"

He was chasing his tail, turning dizzying circles on the bed. He stopped abruptly, catching sight of himself in the full-length mirror next to the television, lunged off the bed and back onto it, barking wildly.

"Jock, be quiet! What's the matter with him?"

"He's been cooped up here all day," I said. "I guess he just needs to run off a little energy." We watched as he flew off the bed again, turned circles at Nick's feet before grabbing hold of one of his pants legs.

"Jock! He won't let go. Jock, stop—" Nick's voice rose, but not loud enough to disguise the rip of fabric. "My pants! Julia, he tore my pants!"

Jack shook the piece of fabric in his mouth, as though it were a prey he'd been stalking, and with a happy wag of his tail, deposited it at my feet. He turned back toward Nick's leg with a menacing growl. Nick clambered up on the bed. "What's wrong with him?"

"I'll bet they gave him a couple of downers at that kennel and they're just now wearing off," I said. "That's why I don't want to put him in another kennel, Nick."

Nick glared at me and eased himself back onto the bed. "He'll probably calm down in a minute," I assured him.

But Jack was determined to make a liar of me. He'd lost interest in Nick's clothing and returned to the dog in the mirror. The low growl in his throat escalated to frenzied barking as he charged the glass and threw his weight against it, falling back with a yip and a thump.

"We'd better get him out, Nick. Someone's going to hear him and—"

Too late. A sharp knock interrupted me. Jack tore across the room, growling and scratching at the door. Nick was after him in a beat, clamping his hand around the little dog's snout as he hoisted him under his arm. We exchanged glances—his said *I told you this would happen,* mine said *I'm sorry.* I inched past him to the door. Behind it stood Eva Paradissis.

## Chapter Fourteen

"I guess this means the jig is up," I said.

Eva's gaze went from me to Nick, to Jack, whose little legs were whirling in the air, and back to me. I gave her an abashed smile. "You win some, you lose some," I added, confronted by her uneasy expression.

For the first time, I realized what an awkward situation this was for all of us. Eva didn't want to be the one to throw Manolis's friends out of the hotel on their ear, and we didn't want to presume on the friendship and hospitality of her boss. What a mess I'd made of everything.

"We didn't mean to break your rules. We had him in a kennel, but they . . . well, they couldn't keep him and we had nowhere else to take him. I'm still looking. I've called all the kennels in the area and I'm sure one of them is going to have a vacancy—"

"It's all right, Julia." Eva stepped into the room and pushed the door closed behind her.

She reached over to scratch Jack under the chin. He was less than polite.

"Nick, why don't you get him out? Take him for—"

"We do allow pets, Julia. Normally, we require a pet

deposit, but Christos wouldn't want you to be charged anyway," she said.

Jack was squirming in Nick's arms and setting up such a racket that I thought we might well be the beginning of a new pet policy in the hotel. "Nick, please," I said. "Try taking him out for a walk."

Eva glanced doubtfully at me. "Do you think he can handle him alone?"

Good point. Jack was going to need a good long run to get the energy out of his system.

"Right," I said. "Well, maybe I'll just go with him."

I snagged Jack's leash and clipped it to his collar while Nick wrestled to keep the dog from leaping out of his arms. Eva eased back toward the door. "You might want to take him out that way," she said, pointing at the French doors. "I'm not sure he can handle the hotel lobby."

"Right. Let's go, Nick. You know, he's not usually quite this wild, but——" I opened the door for Nick while he deposited Jack on the floor. The lead grew taught and the two of them flew past me onto the terrace. I started to follow, but hastily turned back. "Oh my gosh, the tub!"

"I'll get it," Eva assured me, gazing incredulously at the empty doorway. "I think you'd better go after them."

By the time we got back, both Nick and I were sorely in need of a bath. Jack had run, and run, and then run some more. It was all we could do to keep up with the spinning of his six-inch legs.

"I just don't see how we can put him back in a kennel after this, Nick. Look at what they did to him."

I poured new bubble bath into the tub, which Eva, rightly figuring we would not be back before the water grew cold, had thoughtfully drained. She'd even brought us a new jar of bubble bath. I left the water running and stepped back into the bedroom. Nick was hunched over Jack, who lay on his back enjoying the sleep of the just—the just exhausted, that is.

"I guess you're right. Poor little guy."

I smiled to myself. Another crisis averted.

Kate arrived at the hotel promptly at ten o'clock the next morning. She didn't say anything about where she and Alex had gone the night before, nor what had happened when she went home. If she went home. I didn't ask. It was enough that they hadn't run away, leaving their parents feeling guilty and distraught.

I'd repeated my conversation with Georgia to Nick as we returned to the hotel the previous night. "I know," he said. "Manolis told me. He thinks that Aris is responsible for the cook walking out, too. Spiros and I are very worried about Manolis. In all the years we've been friends, I've never known him to drink like that."

"He probably needs to get away from the restaurant."

"Well, I want to talk to you about that. I hope you don't mind. Manolis and I are taking his old boat out for a while tomorrow. I'm sorry. I guess I should have checked with you. I know I promised I wouldn't—"

"It's fine, Nick—as long as you're not planning to take Rula along with you," I added. He didn't smile, and I decided not to push my luck any further.

So Nick and Manolis had left early in the morning to go fishing, or whatever it was they were going to do out there on that boat—male bonding *a la Grecque*. Miss Alma and I were looking forward to an afternoon of shopping down on the Sponge Docks.

"Now, tell us more about the necklace," I said as Kate shepherded us down the hall. We passed a door that Kate identified as Eva's apartment and went on to a pair of wide, carved-oak doors marked "Private." Kate gave them a rap before turning back to Miss Alma and me.

"Since Alex is the only heir, the *flouria* is passed to him for our children. I'm going to wear it for the wedding. Something old and borrowed, you know. I had to put off the final fitting until tomorrow because the neckline of my dress may have to be adjusted—"

Xanthe Saros stood in the open door. She silently pulled it back and ushered us in, rather like a housekeeper in a British gothic movie.

"*Kalimera*, Xanthe." Kate led us into a large living room, tastefully decorated in a surprisingly contemporary motif. Pagona awaited us, seated on a dark green leather couch with a half-finished needlepoint canvas in her lap. Kate crossed the room to peck her on the cheek.

"Ah, good. You are right on time." Christos stood in a doorway. Behind him, an enormous desk covered most of the far wall. Light from a green banker's lamp pooled on a stack of papers.

"I will get the necklace and be with you in a moment," he said, retreating into the room and closing the door.

Kate picked up Pagona's needlework and admired it, showing it to Miss Alma and me and translating our compliments for the old woman. Pagona looked pleased in spite of herself and had launched into an explanation of the folk-art pattern when Christos returned, carrying a large black leather-covered box. He led us to a table in front of a picture window that looked out onto the hotel terrace.

"Let me show you," he said, "how the clasp works." He lifted a small brass latch and raised the cover of the box. Chills scurried up my backbone.

I had seen photographs of coin necklaces before, but never a real one until then. More than just a necklace, it was an exquisite display of heritage and tradition. It lay on a bed of black velvet, the gold chains and coral inlay reminding me of a pirate's treasure. It tinkled like wind chimes when Christos lifted it carefully from the box and held the necklace in the light—four chains of gleaming gold, heavy with gold and silver coins set in twenty-four-karat bezels. "It is customary for the bride to wear the *flouria*. Of course, in many cases, it is her dowry—usually it belongs to the bride's own family."

Kate shifted uncomfortably. Her uneasiness was not lost on Christos, who hastened to amend his point. "But that is a very old custom, rarely kept these days, when young people are more independent. Nevertheless, it is a nice custom, and since I have no daughters of my own . . ."

Christos reached over to brush Kate's cheek affectionately. "But I soon will. *Katerina* will be like a daughter in the family." Kate glowed as she put her arm around him and gently stroked his back. I couldn't help but think about Manolis and how he would feel about it.

Miss Alma adjusted her glasses and reached out tentatively to touch the necklace. Christos passed it to her to examine more closely. "There are quite a few different dies represented here," Miss Alma said.

Christos agreed. "Generally in modern jewelry, you will find mainly reproduction coins—although still gold—on these necklaces. The Constantine coins such as these—" He pointed to a row of coins strung on the uppermost chain. "The head of Constantine was considered a talisman—a good-luck charm, if you will. Therefore, it is the most popular charm to reproduce. These Constantines, however, are genuine. There are also drachmas, which have been electroplated, and silver staters," he said, pointing out each coin.

"But in our family, there is a talisman of another kind. Do you see this one?" Christos pointed to a bright gold disk encased in a wide bezel. Although the casing was twenty-four karat, it paled next to the coin. Larger than the rest, it hung from the top chain.

"It's lovely. What is it?"

"It is our own special charm—the half-stater of Rhodes. When my father was preparing to build his first hotel, which was on Rhodes, he purchased a plot of land outside of Mandraki Harbor. The builders, of course, had to clear the land in order to build. One evening my father was walking through the site. The moon was full and the sky very clear. *Baba* saw something gleaming in the darkness and when he reached to pick it up, he found this and two others."

Christos took in our surprised faces and shrugged.

"It is a more common occurrence than you might imagine. Dig anywhere in Greece and you will find something ancient. But still, my father took the appearance of coins as a sign that the site of his hotel would be full of riches—which has proven to be . . . well . . ." Christos dropped his eyes modestly. "It has been a good investment for us.

"But to continue, my father took the coins to an antiquities dealer and discovered that they had some value. He sold two of them, which gave him the money to open a second hotel shortly, but he kept this one as a charm for good luck. He gave it to *Mana* as a wedding gift. The *flouria* was part of her dowry, but my father added the Helios before the wedding. She has worn it on her necklace since the day they married. It is fitting, eh? That we should open the *Mediterraneo* as we pass the *flouria* on to Alex and Kate? And now, about the clasp," he said.

Miss Alma reluctantly passed the necklace back to Christos. "Who," she asked, "is the figure on the coin?" I peered over Christos's shoulder to get a better look at the figurehead.

Christos cradled the charm in his hand. "It is Helios, the sun god. The coin dates to the first century B.C. Here . . ." He pointed to the crowned head of the god and the lines that radiated around it in relief from the gold disk. "You can see the rays—"

Christos moved closer to the light of the window. He examined the charm at length, turned it over to study the reverse and returned again to the obverse image. His gaze shifted quickly to his mother and back to the necklace.

"*Ti ipes?*" Pagona asked. A rapid burst of Greek followed, and although I am unable to repeat it, I understood most of it. Something was wrong with the coin. Christos asked his mother who had handled the necklace last. Her only answer was a quick turn on her heel to glare across the living room at a very white, very frightened Xanthe Saros.


We sat in the living room in silence, waiting for Alex to appear in response to Christos's terse summons. No one spoke. Xanthe, curled in a ball in the corner of the couch, would not meet anyone's gaze. She seemed to have withdrawn into herself like a traumatized child. I knew that Miss Alma and I should probably leave but when we stirred to go, Kate stopped me with a tight grip on my arm.

"Please stay," was all she said, but her fingers dug into my flesh with an urgency belied by her words. Miss Alma and I returned to our seats, reacting instinctively to the apprehension etched in Kate's face.

Alex arrived, taking a seat on the arm of Kate's chair as though he knew that disaster loomed. With Pagona's threats and pleas constantly hanging over them, he could hardly have thought otherwise.

Christos spoke to his son as though the rest of us were not in the room. "We have here a serious—very serious—situation. We must get to the bottom of it immediately. The Helios is missing."

Alex bolted across the room to snatch the necklace from

his father's hand. He confirmed the presence of the coin with a quick glance and turned an anxious face to his father.

"It is a fake," Christos said. "Gold, but not the real Helios. Someone has switched them."

"*I Xanthe eine!*" Pagona descended upon the girl, her hand raised as if she might strike her nurse. Xanthe reflexively raised her arms to shield her face, but Alex pulled his grandmother away, sternly forcing her into a chair.

"Where has the necklace been?" he asked calmly.

Christos jutted his chin toward the room where I had seen the desk. "In the office safe."

"And before that?"

"In the safe in our apartment *stin Athena*. It has not left the safe since it was returned from the jeweler."

"And who took it to the jeweler?"

Christos turned back to his mother, who was eyeing Xanthe with such malevolence that I thought she might have to be restrained again. No one needed to hear the name.

"No!" Xanthe cried out, turning from one of us to the next. "I did just as *I Kyria* Pagona asked. I took it to the jeweler for cleaning and to make certain that all the catches and links were secure. I did not touch it. I returned it just—"

"Which jeweler?"

"Kontalis. In Omonia."

Alex turned to his father, who shook his head decisively. "I have known Panos Kontalis for many years. His ethics are above question, but even if they were not, he would not be so stupid as to try to substitute a bad fake. You see?" he said, showing the coin to his son. "The rays of light on the head of Helios are not positioned correctly. The center ray should protrude exactly from the crown's center. This is offset slightly to the right. It is a fake, and not even a very good one." No one argued with him, although I privately wondered whether he could be wrong.

"It will be confirmed by a numismatist and you will see that I am right. The coin is a copy."

He turned upon Xanthe, his voice so icy and his stance so rigid that for the first time, I glimpsed the hard businessman who had built an empire. "Now," he said, "you will explain to me what you have done and where the real coin is."

"I don't know! You must believe me, I had nothing to do with it. You do believe me, don't you?" Her gaze shifted from one solemn face to the next. "Oh please, no—" she stammered, and began to cry.

An hour later, Xanthe's story had not changed. She had left the necklace with Kontalis Jewelers in Omonia, who had received strict instructions from Pagona. They were to clean the charms, check the chains for weak links, and make sure the clasp was secure. Three days later, Kontalis had called to say the *flouria* was ready to be picked up.

"It was the day I went shopping with Eva. You can ask her yourself. Please, call her. Eva will tell you."

Christos summoned Eva to the apartment, but the result was not exactly what Xanthe had expected. "I didn't go to the jeweler with you," Eva said. Her voice firm and even, she made it clear she would not be drawn into complicity.

"No, you met me at the boutique afterward. I had the box in my bag. We shopped. I bought the dress—"

"Yes, I remember." Eva turned to Christos. "It was the fifteenth of November. I went shopping with Xanthe, then Petros picked me up and brought me to the theater to meet you in the evening. We took Mr. and Mrs. Makris to Dora Stratou Theater that night." Christos nodded as Eva turned back to Xanthe. "But I left you in the American bar in Omonia. What did you do then?"

Xanthe shook her head, her eyes very wide and frightened. "I was so happy," she said. "I bought the dress—it was so beautiful. For the New Year's Eve party. We went to the American bar and then Eva left. I was not finished with my drink."

"Where did you go?" Alex asked Eva.

"Directly to the theater. I met your father and his guests."

"What time did Eva leave you?" he asked, turning back to Xanthe.

Xanthe frowned. "It was already dark. Near seven o'clock, I think."

"And you still had the necklace?"

Xanthe nodded miserably. "I never let go of my bag. It has to be Kontalis. He must have switched  "

"Why didn't you bring the necklace back to our apartment before you went shopping?" Christos demanded. "You were carrying a very valuable piece of jewelry."

"I . . . yes, I know. But Eva had only a little time for me. She was working until four o'clock and then she was meeting you—"

"We thought about that," Eva explained. "But there wasn't time to return it and no one knew she was carrying it. We thought it would be perfectly safe."

Alex eyed Eva skeptically as she made her explanation, then turned back to Xanthe.

"What did you do after Eva left?"

Xanthe lowered her head, as though she could not face anyone in the room. "I don't remember," she said in the small voice of a guilty child.

"You don't remember!" Christos thundered. "You expect us to believe you don't remember what you did next?"

Xanthe looked up, her face as white as the stucco walls. She sobbed and shook her head.

"I can't . . . I don't remember!"

Christos threw up his hands in exasperation, but Xanthe didn't notice it. She stared into the middle distance, hiccuping sobs. "I remember," she said slowly, "that I drank *Metaxa* with Eva. She suggested that we celebrate the new dress."

"I wanted her to enjoy it," Eva explained to Christos. "She's had little enough to celebrate in her life."

"I had not quite finished my brandy when Eva had to leave. There was music and dancing there in the bar, and I wanted to stay for a while." She turned a confused and tear-stained face to Christos.

"The next thing I remember, I woke up in my bed in your apartment. I was frightened because I couldn't remember coming home. But the box was still there in my purse as I had left it, and I checked—the *flouria* was right there. Safe."

"How did you get home? Who were you with? Were you by yourself? Did you take a bus or a taxi?" Christos fired his questions at her.

Xanthe's body jerked convulsively, as if she'd been hit with a bullet instead of a question. "I don't remember! Please, you must believe me. I cannot remember any of it. I woke the next morning in my room, that is all."

Christos shook his head, his disbelief apparent, his disgust palpable. He rubbed his face briskly and took a deep breath. "Had you been injured? Hurt in any way?"

Although she was calmer, Xanthe wore a perplexed expression. "No. I felt all right. I dressed and delivered the necklace to *I Kyria* Pagona. She accepted it from me, checked it, and took it to the safe."

All eyes went to Pagona. She muttered something at the girl, crossed herself and fingered the *mati* at her neck. Christos questioned his mother softly. No, she had not noticed that the coin had been exchanged. How could she, with cataracts as big as—She held out a fist, turned and shook it at the wary girl.

"*Esei! Esei eise i kleptra!*"

*"Ohee!"* Xanthe cried out, huddling back into the corner of the couch. At length, Eva moved across the room to sit with her, taking Xanthe's hand in hers. She waited until Xanthe's tears had subsided before lifting the girl's chin and turning her face. She pushed a lock of hair back from Xanthe's forehead.

"Are you all right?" she asked softly.

*"Then katalavaino,* Eva," Xanthe said. "I don't understand."

*"Esei eise!"* Pagona would not be quieted. As well as I could follow, her accusations began to take an ugly form. Xanthe, Pagona claimed, was in love with Alex. From the corner of my eye, I saw Kate's hand grasp Alex's as the old woman went on. She pointed to her filmy eyes, and rattled in Greek, "You think I do not see how you look at my grandson? How your eyes follow him everywhere? You think I am a fool?"

"No, I—" Xanthe's gaze shifted to Alex's doubtful face before turning to the rest of us.

"He's been very kind to me. I would never do anything to hurt him."

"No, of course not," Eva agreed. But her voice betrayed doubt.

## Chapter Fifteen

By the time the police arrived, Xanthe had worn herself out. She had stopped crying but was shivering uncontrollably. The officer took down the information and impounded the coin necklace, but he refused to take Xanthe in for questioning until the forgery had been confirmed and Kontalis Jewelers in Athens contacted. "I assume, sir, that you have insurance."

Christos's brows knotted over his nose as he nodded. "Of course. But insurance companies do not indemnify luck, and ancient coins are not easily replaced." The officer did not press the issue.

"What do you estimate the value of this coin to be?" he asked.

Christos walked over to the window, leaned on the sill and fingered his lower lip. "To me, its value is immeasurable." He turned back to the officer with a shrug. "But to a coin collector, maybe fifteen, twenty thousand dollars."

I'm sure Xanthe must have gasped, but I couldn't hear her over my own sharp intake of breath. "No," she whispered. "So much?" No one answered, but she had the policeman's attention again.

"You speak English?"

Xanthe nodded miserably.

"Don't leave Tarpon Springs without letting us know about it." He returned to Christos. "I'll get back with you late this afternoon or tomorrow. Gotta find someone who can confirm that this coin is a fake. Someone in Tampa maybe . . ." he mused.

"Miss Saros will not be staying with us," Christos said. "I'm afraid that my mother—"

Pagona shifted heavily in her chair. Miss Alma had drawn a seat up next to her to comfort, and restrain, the old woman with a firm hand.

"My mother will not want her to remain with us. I'll find her a place to stay and make certain you have the address."

By the time the officer left, Christos was already on the phone to the front desk. "Find Miss Saros a room in Tarpon Springs and call me back." He hung up and turned to Xanthe, his eyes gleaming angrily and his jaw thrusting forward.

"I want the coin back, Miss Saros. I will pay for it, if I must."

"I don't have the coin. I have told you that."

Christos paced the room, opening and closing his right hand spasmodically. "It will bring you disaster, Xanthe. Stolen, it will bring you only bad luck. Return the coin to me and I will not press charges against you. I must have that coin!"

Xanthe set her jaw and brought up her chin. "I do not have it," she said evenly.

Christos threw his hand up. "All right! If you must persist in this ridiculous story, you leave me no choice. I would like to examine your things before you leave."

Xanthe's eyes grew wide, her glance flitting around the room wildly. "But they're mine. I do not have—"

"If I may suggest something . . ." Eva left Xanthe's side and drew her employer away from the rest of us. "She doesn't have to allow you to search . . ."

When Christos turned back to us, he had himself under better control, and he had reconsidered his demand. Apparently Eva had suggested that to force a search upon the girl might violate her rights and jeopardize any case he might bring against her later.

He turned a stony face to the girl. "Go. Pack your things. Someone will drive you to another hotel."

Xanthe hung her head and crossed the room, stopping only when she came level with Alex. She put her hand out in a tentative gesture, not touching him but close enough that she must have felt the warmth of his skin.

"I would never—" But Alex spun away from her, and Kate lowered her eyes. "I am sorry," Xanthe whispered.

When Xanthe had left the room, Christos turned to his son. "We must find that coin, Aleko." He grabbed Alex's shoulders, gripping them with such force that Alex winced and pulled away from his father's grasp.

"*Baba*, please. It's a piece of metal, for heaven's sake."

"*Ohee*, Aleko. It is much more!" Christos glanced at his mother, who nodded solemnly, and then at Eva. "Get security down here at once," he said.

Eva made the necessary call, hanging up just as Xanthe came into the room, dropped a suitcase on the floor and withdrew again. Christos rubbed his palm over his eyes. "This changes everything. The Helios is—"

"The Helios is a symbol, *Baba*, that's all." Alex's embarrassed gaze went to Eva, who averted her eyes.

"I should get back to my work," Eva said. "I don't think I can do any more to help here."

"Yes, go," Christos said, waving her away. "Watch over things closely, Eva. Very closely."

Xanthe huddled down in the passenger's seat of the car, her knees drawn up and her arms wrapped across her chest. Her eyes floated in large, glistening pools of tears that threatened to spill over their lids.

Kate had offered to drive Xanthe to the motel, but although I knew Kate intended the girl no harm, it didn't seem prudent to send them off together. Besides, Pagona had begun fretting again about a curse upon the family, and Christos himself was more agitated than I had ever seen him. It would take cool voices and level heads to reason with the Kyriakidis elders, and among all of them, the only composed people in the room were the bride and groom. And Miss Alma, of course.

While Christos briefed security, Alex's first priority had been to provide another companion for his grandmother. He made several calls to local home health-care and temporary agencies, only to learn that they were short-staffed during the holidays and could not provide him help on such short notice. Even so, I was surprised when Miss Alma offered to take Xanthe's place.

"I'm not a nurse, of course, but if it's only a matter of dispensing her medication—" Alex accepted her offer almost before it left her mouth.

I agreed to take the girl to her motel and see that she got settled into her room. I started the car and glanced over at Xanthe. "Are you sure you got everything?" I asked, checking the back seat.

Two unmatched suitcases stood on the floor—both of cheap plastic but in decent condition—a large one that might hold a week's clothing, and a smaller, overnight bag. It didn't seem like much for a month's stay. Xanthe nodded and turned her face to the window. I saw her hand go up to her eyes before she tucked it back under her armpit and shivered. We covered the first several blocks in silence.

"Xanthe," I said at length, "if you tell them where the coin is, they won't prosecute you. Christos will probably even pay your way back to Greece and you can start afresh."

She turned her head slowly, gazing at me through eyes so red and swollen that she must have had a headache. "I cannot tell what I do not know. And who will hire me when I have been dismissed by the Kyriakidis family? Who will hire a thief?"

"You really don't remember what you did with it?"

"I remember nothing about that evening. Why will no one believe me?"

"Because people just don't lose twelve or fifteen hours out of their day. Has anything like this ever happened to you before?"

"Never."

"Since that night?"

She shook her head. "No. Only that one night."

"All right," I said. "What's the last thing you remember?"

Slowly, thoughtfully, she unwrapped her arms and folded her hands in her lap. "Eva and I had a drink in the American bar. I was enjoying it—watching the couples dance, listening to the music. They were playing American rock and roll. Petros—he is the chauffeur—he came to pick Eva up to go to Dora Stratou. I had not finished my drink. Eva left with him and I stayed on to listen to the music." Xanthe's voice trailed away. She stared out the window while her fingers twisted her skirt into a knot.

"And then what?"

Xanthe gazed down at her rumpled skirt, pried her fingers apart and returned to crossing her arms. "I do not remember anything after that. You must believe me—I tried. I tried to remember!" A note of hysteria crept into her voice. "It is frightening to me not to remember! But I am afraid, also, to remember. It must be something very bad."

The While Away Inn, on the outskirts of Tarpon Springs, might have been a nice family accommodation when it was built in the 1950s. Forty years later, the caliber of clientele had dropped to hourly users, and its general appearance defined the word "shabby." It was, Lucy at the *Mediterraneo* had explained, the only motel in the area not fully booked for the holidays and Epiphany. Nevertheless, I thought that if Christos could see it, he would never have agreed to confine Xanthe between its peeling walls despite his animosity toward her. He was a demanding man, but I didn't think he was cruel.

I rattled the handle of the toilet but it wouldn't stop running. The mattress was old and limp—it had probably seen some pretty vigorous use. I pulled back a threadbare brown bedspread to be sure the sheets were clean. They were, but so thin that I could have written a musical score on the striped mattress ticking. Fleas clustered around my ankles. Obviously, The While Away allowed pets. It was good to know, in case the *Mediterraneo*'s policy changed, thanks to Jack, I thought despondently. I heaved Xanthe's suitcase onto the bed.

"I'll help you unpack," I said, yanking on the top drawer of the single battered chest in the room.

Xanthe said nothing, but took a little key to the lock of the larger case. She whacked it with her fist and the lid sprang open, a heap of clothes tumbling out onto the bed. She had not stopped to fold them. I could imagine her tearing them off their hangers and wadding them into the case, as eager to leave as the Kyriakidis family had been to get rid of her. There were only three hangers on the rack next to the bathroom. I began a shopping list. Hangers. Flea spray.

Xanthe Saros had not accumulated a lot of worldly goods. Her clothes were serviceable—plain skirts in solid colors that could be mixed and matched with her three blouses of white, pink, and a bilious chartreuse. I hung up her royal-blue party dress and the wrap dress she'd worn the night we met, reserving the last hanger for as many folded skirts as it would hold. At the bottom of the larger suitcase lay a photograph album. I flipped curiously through the pages, hoping to find some key to understanding this strange girl.

A picture of a couple—Xanthe's parents, I supposed— occupied the front page of the album. The color had been badly retouched so that the woman's lips were redder than any cosmetic might have made them. The man looked considerably older than his wife and despite his smile, appeared tired and beaten. The next pages were peppered with snapshots of this same couple and an elderly woman, generally featured in the same modest apartment. At the back of the album were more-recent pictures—a few of Pagona and Christos, but far more of Alex. My heart sank. It looked as if Pagona might have been right. I set the album aside and studied the girl as she listlessly folded her blouses and stuffed them into the top drawer of the chest. There were, I noticed, no white nursing uniforms.

"Where did you nurse before you went to work for Christos?" I asked. Xanthe glanced at me in the mirror before quickly turning away.

"In Athens."

"In a hospital, or were you a private-duty nurse?"

She hesitated for a moment before replying. "I worked in a hospital in Athens. Why?"

I shrugged. "You don't have any uniforms."

"No. *I Kyria* Pagona did not want me to wear a uniform."

"Didn't you like nursing in the hospital?"

Xanthe tossed the slip she was folding onto the bed and dropped down beside it. Her chin came up defiantly. "You do not believe that I was a nurse, is that it?"

"No. I only wondered . . . I was just trying to make conversation."

The rebellious expression left her face as quickly as it had appeared. "Well, all right. You are right. I did work in a hospital but . . . I was only an aide. I suppose now you will think I am a liar too, as well as a thief. But I needed this job and I was suited for it. I had nursed my *yia-yia*, who was much like *i Kyria* Pagona."

I picked up the slip and laid it out on the bed, taking elaborate care to fold it neatly. A poor quality of nylon, it was coming loose from the elastic. "Did you live with your grandmother?"

Xanthe nodded. "In Lavrion. My father was a miner. He was killed in an explosion when I was nine. They closed the mines soon after he died. The only work my mother could find was in *sto ergostasion*—how do you say it? The manufactory."

"Factory," I said, correcting her as automatically as I did Nick. "Doing what?"

"Putting together the little parts of . . ." Xanthe shrugged. "I do not know how to say it in English."

"It's not important," I assured her. Her mother had worked on an assembly line while Xanthe had stayed at home to nurse her grandmother. There couldn't have been much money in the household, and if Xanthe's *yia-yia* had been as difficult as Pagona, there probably wasn't much joy, either.

The silence between us deepened. I went back to the suitcase and pulled out a yellowed, much-thumbed Greek–English dictionary. "You speak English very well, Xanthe."

147

A phantom smile crossed her lips. "I was the first student in English in my high school, but I was not able to complete my education. There were expenses. *Yia-yia* became ill."

"But Greece has socialized medicine."

"Yes, but for an old lady, it is not enough. If you want more than the doctors are willing to give——" She rubbed her thumb against her four clustered fingers and let the gesture speak for itself. Money. Xanthe sighed.

"I went to work in the hospital to be near her and when they sent her to a nursing home, I followed her there and got a job. She died two years ago this month. At the nursing home, I heard about the job with the Kyriakidis family and applied. I was the fourth one he hired. The others didn't get on so well with his mother." No surprise there.

Xanthe stood up, took the slip off my lap and shoved it into the dresser drawer. "So now you can tell them," she said, gazing at me in the mirror, "that I lied. I do not have a nursing degree. I needed the job."

She turned to face me, and again a spark of defiance lit her eyes. "And I wanted it. *I Kyria* Pagona is not as difficult as you might think. She is like *yia-yia*, like all old women in my country. Her son—and her grandson—are everything to her. She thinks I have harmed the family. I do not blame them for dismissing me."

*Chapter Sixteen*

Xanthe picked at her *souvlaki* at lunch while I wrestled a *gyro* so thick and succulent that *tzaziki* dripped down to my elbows. We were seated on the porch at *Mykonos* with a clear view of Dodecanese Boulevard outside our window. The streets were filled with tourists vacationing during the holidays.

Aris Mavrakis sat with another man at a two-top—a two-person table—near the door. He looked up at us and nodded absently as we passed. "We need to throw him some business, Stellios," he said to his companion. "In a community like this, we all have to pull together. What hurts one, hurts all." I didn't hear his companion's reply.

I had hoped that lunch in a pleasant place might cheer Xanthe up some and make her open up to me about the coin. I couldn't have left her in the room anyway, since, after a quick trip to the store, I had started several flea foggers and fully expected that fleas were not the only vermin they would flush out. Some of the guests looked like good candidates for extermination as well.

Out on the docks, a few small boats were anchored next to a larger ship advertising dinner and sightseeing cruises. Nick and I hadn't made much headway in seeing the sights.

Events surrounding the wedding were careening toward disaster, and both he and I felt an obligation to our friends to try to help. My first job now was to see if I could coax information out of Xanthe Saros.

"You need to eat," I urged her. "I'll have them make up a plate for you to take back to the room so you'll have something for supper. You can relax in your room, try to get a little rest. Maybe something will come back—"

But Xanthe was not listening to me. Instead, she leaned toward the window, watching the crowd intently. She pressed her cheek against the glass as if following the progress of someone moving eastward along the street beyond the restaurant, until whoever it was had moved completely out of her line of vision.

"Xanthe? What is it?"

She turned away from the window and studied her plate with a perplexed frown. "I don't know. Just someone I thought . . ." Her voice trailed away as I glanced up at the window and Alex crossed my line of vision.

"Xanthe, about Alex—"

"Even I could not have planned this better," a voice behind me said. I glanced up to find Lucky Plemenos smiling down at me. "You see, there's a reason I am called Lucky."

He took my hand, turned it over and kissed my palm. From anyone else, the gesture would have been banal, but Lucky managed to pull it off so smoothly that my knees turned to egg yolk and slid down to my feet.

In a more objective moment, I might have wondered exactly what attraction he held for me. He was not classically handsome, nor was he a stimulating conversationalist. He did exude money and power, but neither of those qualities have ever touched deep places in me. This, however, was not an objective moment, and the answer to the question was as clear as the stupefaction on Xanthe's face. This was raw, sexual attraction, and it left me feeling confused and vulnerable.

"Um . . . are you here for lunch?"

Lucky's eyes never left my face. "Business. Now that I have the *Mediterraneo* account, I might as well open up the whole territory."

What was it he did? For a moment, I couldn't remember, captivated as I was by his intense, dark gaze. Olives. That was it—Greek olives and wines. By the look of him, business was going very well. I glanced over at Xanthe, found her watching me with a measuring gaze.

"Well, isn't that . . . um . . . nice! Xanthe, we really do need to finish our lunch," I said, and gulped down my iced tea. "I'm afraid we have to be going." I signaled the waitress and asked her to bring us a box for Xanthe's lunch and a take-out order of a large Greek salad and pita bread.

"Mr. Plemenos," the waitress said, "Andreas says he can give you a few minutes now."

"Ah, I must speak to him about his timing. Excuse me, ladies." Lucky winked at me and followed the woman through the kitchen door. I sighed with relief and turned back to Xanthe.

"About Alex," I said carefully.

Xanthe folded her napkin, dabbed it to her lips and dropped it onto the table, leaving her *souvlaki* uneaten. She continued to stare at the kitchen door as a blush crept up her neck and into her cheeks.

"He was kind to me. He seemed to notice me. *I Kyria* Pagona wants only what she wants, and her son cares only that she is kept happy. But Alekos . . ." The affectionate nickname was not lost on me.

"Alex," she continued, her eyes coming around to meet my gaze. "Alex is different. He treated me kindly. *I Kyria* Pagona accused me of being in love with him. Would that be so wrong? To care for someone who is kind to me? I would never do anything to hurt him."

Could she really have believed that she could entice Alex away from Kate? It was possible. Love makes dreamers of us all.

"But canceling the wedding would hurt Alex deeply. He loves Kate," I reminded her.

"The way your husband loves you?"

"Well . . . yes. Why do you—"

"In Greece, we have a saying," she said, her glance going back to the kitchen door. " 'The healer of others is himself full of wounds.' "

I was starting to get sick of old Greek sayings.

When we had left *Mykonos* and were driving back to The While Away, I broached the subject of the coin again. "Are you sure it wasn't taken before the necklace went to the jeweler?"

She thought about the question for a moment before answering. "I don't see how it could have been," she said. "*O Kyrios* Christos removed it from the safe himself and gave it to his mother. I'm sure he looked at it then. I know she did, but her eyes are not so good anymore. But the jeweler should have noticed it. Even a very good counterfeit would not be aged in the same way. And it would probably not be so dirty."

I glanced at her, sitting across the seat from me, her brow puckered in bewilderment. She had already been sifting through the possibilities. "Did Eva handle the necklace at all after you picked it up?"

Xanthe shook her head firmly. "I have told you already, it never left my purse. I met her to shop, we went to the bar, and then Petros picked her up. I had my purse with me the whole time. She could not have touched it. Besides, Eva would not do that to me. Why would she?"

I pulled into the parking lot of The While Away Inn, turned into a space in front of Xanthe's door and cut the engine. The mid-afternoon sun beamed down on drooping gutters and curling shingles. "And you remember nothing after that?"

Xanthe hesitated, examining her hands, folded in her lap. "I do not drink," she said. "Only a little wine now and then. That night, I had *Metaxa* at the American bar—two drinks, perhaps even three. I do not remember."

She took hold of the door handle, ready to get out, but released it again. "Eva knew where to shop—where to find the right thing for the party. I did not want to embarrass the family with my poor clothes and taste. It was a happy night for me. I must have had too much to drink. I cannot remember."

"You only remember waking the next morning?"

She nodded. "I must have come in very late. If *i Kyria* Pagona had been awake, I would have given her the *flouria* then. But Eva left me around seven o'clock, and after that . . ." Xanthe rubbed her hand over her forehead and eyes.

If Xanthe had gone home drunk to the apartment and passed out on her bed, she wouldn't have heard anyone come into her room. Anyone in the household might have had access to the necklace and plenty of time to remove the coin and replace it with a fake. Xanthe shook her head. "No. I always lock my door."

"But if you don't remember that night—"

Again, the same response. "It was locked that night, too. When I got up in the morning, I was frightened. I couldn't remember coming home, and I was still in my clothes. I checked my door, but it was locked, with the key in the door as I always leave it, so no one could have brought me home and put me to bed."

Xanthe rustled in her purse and brought out a key ring. She selected a dark old key and held it out in the palm of her open hand. "You see? It requires a key."

She fingered the remaining keys on the ring like a rosary. "I must have done it myself. But if I cannot remember, then perhaps I cannot remember taking the coin either. But maybe I did it, as they say."

"Well, if you did take it, what would you have done with it?"

"Nothing. I don't know. It is not in my things," she said. "I have checked them."

Xanthe doubted herself. Otherwise, why would she have searched through her own possessions? No one, she claimed, could have had access to the necklace, even in her room. Of course, there could be other keys to her room. I played out that scenario in my mind.

After Xanthe had gone to bed, someone had opened the door with another key, taken the necklace and replaced the coin with the fake. They had then gone to the door, inserted Xanthe's key in the lock and left, locking the door from the outside. There was just one problem with this scenario. I hadn't seen the room or the door, but I had seen the key and could imagine what the lock was like—old-fashioned, with the kind of keyhole Pagona might peek through. If the key had been in the lock and someone had tried to lock the door from the outside, wouldn't they have pushed the key out onto the floor in the room?

Without being able to test my theory, I couldn't know for sure. But I was betting that whatever had happened, it had occurred during the hours that were missing from Xanthe's memory—a realization that came as a shock to me. It meant that I believed Xanthe Saros after all.

―――――

I hated to leave Xanthe alone in that place, but it was getting late and Nick probably wondered where I was. I gave her my room number at the hotel and told her to call me if she needed anything. When I got back to the *Mediterraneo*, Nick was waiting in our room. He had a *tavli* game set up and was playing both sides of the table. He had already heard about the necklace, the coin, and Xanthe's abrupt dismissal.

He scattered the dice on the table with a little more force than necessary. "What were you thinking?"

I dropped into the chair across from him. "Nothing. What's the matter?"

"That girl could be dangerous, Julia. She must be nuts—sending the *maya* and putting that needle in Kate's bread."

I picked up the dice, rolled them and moved the checkers on my side of the table. "She's not dangerous, Nick. She's pathetic. Besides, I'm not absolutely convinced she's done anything wrong. She just isn't the criminal type."

Nick stated his opinion eloquently in a single raised eyebrow. He doesn't have much faith in my ability to judge character. "Have they found the coin?"

"No. And it's not in her things. I helped her unpack. She doesn't have much. If it had been there, I would have seen it." I handed him the dice. "It's your turn. I really do believe her. I don't think she's capable of stealing that coin. She used to take care of her grandmother," I said, as though that would justify my faith in her. Nick's silence was full of skepticism.

"All right," I went on defensively. "If you're so sure she took the coin, where is it?"

"It could be in one of a million places, Julia. Somewhere in Christos's apartment maybe. Or she might have given it to someone else. She's a very strange girl, or hadn't you noticed? Do you remember how nervous she was that day

155

in the kitchen? She acted like Christos had caught her doing something wrong."

He rolled the dice and mechanically moved the checkers. I took my turn with the dice, but stared at them without thinking. Nick reached across the table and impatiently moved my checkers for me, going on to his turn. "She's intimidated by Christos," I said. "And by just about everybody else, except Pagona." Which, I thought, was pretty amazing. Pagona certainly intimidated me.

Nick didn't bother handing the dice back to me. He knew I really wasn't interested in playing, since I'd probably lose anyway. He's a much better player than I am. I left him at the table and went to pour myself a cup of the morning's leftover coffee. I nuked it, dumped in some cream and returned to the table.

"Okay, let's say for the moment that she did take the coin. That still doesn't connect her to the *maya* and the needle."

"We'll have to wait until tomorrow to find out about the *maya*, but I've been thinking about the needle," Nick said. "That day—in the walk-in—she was so nervous. It was New Year's Eve. They were baking the *vasilopites,* remember? She had access to them. She might have put the needle in then."

"There were dozens of loaves, Nick. Even if she did do that, how would she know which loaf?"

"She might have marked it. I'm not saying it would be easy, but it could be done."

He was right, of course. It could have been done, but I didn't think that Xanthe had done it. Nevertheless, Nick had promised Manolis that we'd try to help put an end to these veiled threats.

"Then I suppose we have to find out whether anyone saw her near it."

## Chapter Seventeen

The pastry chef rolled, turned and folded puff pastry on a marble slab. He popped it into a reach-in cooler to chill, wiped his hands on a bar mop and turned to us.

"I can't say I remember. It was crazy up here—well, you saw how it was. There were people in and out all over the kitchen. Depending on the time, she'd have had to get into the proofing cabinet, and I don't see how she could do it without someone seeing her. But maybe." He shrugged, palms up in the air. "You could ask some of the others."

We stayed there in the kitchen for a minute, trying to decide what to do next. Who would have seen the most likely person to have seen Xanthe, if it was Xanthe, slip a needle into the bread? I mentally replayed the scene in the kitchen that afternoon and found, to my dismay, that the pastry chef was right. There had been cooks and vendors everywhere, all probably too busy to take note of Xanthe Saros. My thoughts were interrupted by Eva's voice, coming toward us from the back of the kitchen.

She stopped at a steel table and turned to the cook who had followed her from the prep room. "I don't make the schedule in the kitchen, Jimmy. That's up to Renaud. You want to work here, you do what he tells you. It's that simple."

The cook called Jimmy was a heavyset man with a bull neck. His whites were stained with marinara, and in place of a chef's hat, he wore a baseball cap with silver duct tape wrapped around the band at the back to extend it. "But we agreed—"

Eva shot him a withering glance. "Take it or leave it, Jimmy. I really don't care which."

He glared at her for a moment before lumbering away toward the back of the kitchen. She watched him until he had turned into the prep room, then fixed her attention on me. "Did you get Xanthe settled in?"

"Yes. But that motel is a dump. We need to find her a better place."

"I hardly think that Christos will be concerned with her comfort under the circumstances, do you?"

"Well," I said, "she may be innocent, you know. The police haven't even verified yet that the coin is a fake."

Eva rolled her eyes at me in exasperation. "Look, I like Xanthe. And I feel sorry for her. But she was the only person with access to the necklace and the coin. The coin is a fake—ergo, she stole the original and replaced it. She just didn't expect Christos to recognize the switch. I think it's time we realized that she's not the poor, naive little waif we all thought she was. And now, if you'll excuse me, I have work to do. Our computers are down this morning. I've got a programmer in my office trying to recover the data, and a boss who's driving me crazy."

I listened to the tattoo of her heels on the tile floor as she stalked out the door and reluctantly acknowledged that I was going to have to reconsider my point of view. There had been plenty of evidence that Pagona was right and Xanthe really was in love with Alex. Women in love could do reckless, foolish things. Here was a girl who had made the best of not completing her education, of caring for a sick grandmother and giving up most of the pleasures in life. She reminded me of a pack animal. She would never be delicate and graceful, never fleet of foot. She would never be admired for her pedigree as Alex was, and Kate by his reflection. Instead, she seemed doomed to lower her head and bear the load.

And yet, she had lied to get the job with Christos Kyriakidis, which meant that somewhere deep inside her there still burned a spark of ambition. Would she really jeopardize it in an improbable ploy to stop Alex's wedding?

We decided to take a casino cruise that night. I had looked forward to it—having Nick all to myself, dancing in the moonlight, playing roulette and pretending we were in Monte Carlo. We reached the dock too early to board.

"Come on," Nick said, grabbing my hand and guiding me across the street. "Let's get a drink at *O Kritikos*—see how Manolis and Georgia are holding up over this coin thing." When we got there, we discovered that the coin was the least of their worries.

Despite the incipient dinner rush, they were seated at the family table talking with a florid-complected man in a subdued glen-plaid sports jacket. Manolis shook his head and gesticulated with his hands until Georgia caught hold of them and brought them firmly down to the table. I caught Georgia's eye and nodded that we would be at the bar.

"Vasili," Nick said to the bartender, pointing toward the table with his chin. *"Pou eine?"*

*"I astinomia."*

The police. I glanced back over my shoulder. They were rising. The man in plaid nodded at Georgia and strode out of the dining room. She watched as he cleared the front door, but Manolis headed directly for us.

"Niko!" Manolis grabbed Nick's arm and pulled him off the barstool. *"Ella, grigora."* We followed him back to the family table.

"The police—they think I killed the girl."

"Wait, Manoli—what are you talking about? What girl?" Nick demanded.

"In the car! They think I killed her."

Georgia clapped a hand on her husband's shoulder. "Manoli, that's not what he said. They're just asking questions."

"What happened to the other officer—Jacobs, wasn't it?" I said to her. "Who was that?"

"A detective. His name is Fallon."

"A detective? On an accident case?"

I glanced at their faces and felt my heart squish into my shoes. Georgia crossed herself three times and turned to me. "It wasn't an accident, Julia. The girl was drugged."

"Drugged? Why?"

Manolis rocked back in his chair and forward again, setting it down with a thump. He ran a hand through his hair. "We don't know. They think I did it—put the drug in her drink."

"Manoli, they didn't—"

"I know they did not say it, Yiorgia, but that is what they are thinking. I served her the drink. There was no one else there but the other—what did he say her name is?"

"Seager. Becky Seager," I supplied. To their questioning glances, I explained that Nick and I had visited the girl in the hospital. Georgia grabbed my hand. "Could she have done it?"

"I suppose so, but it would have been suicide to get in the car with Eileen Reilly after drugging her drink. Nick?"

"No. I can't believe she did it. Maybe Eileen took the drug herself . . . maybe before they ever got here."

Manolis slammed his hand on the table. "Of course!

These kids today—always looking for more drugs to pour into their bodies."

"No." Georgia shook her head. "Whatever it was, the detective said it dissolves in alcohol and it works very fast. He's sure it happened here."

"But they haven't arrested you," I pointed out to Manolis. "If they thought you really did it, they would have arrested you."

"Not without evidence, Julia," Nick reminded me. "Manolis could be their prime suspect, but without any evidence, there's nothing they can do. Yet."

A heavy silence fell over the table. For me, it was accompanied by a rush of painful memories—another murder victim in a restaurant, another couple threatened. Nick took my hand and squeezed it gently, as if to reassure me that it would not happen again. I wanted to believe him.


"It's good to get away from it for a while," Nick said. We had missed the casino cruise after all, but decided to escape the tension at *O Kritikos*, if only for a little while, by wandering the streets of Tarpon Springs. By eight o'clock we were hungry and stopped for dinner at *Zorba's*, a restaurant and nightclub where we could blend in with the tourists who were filtering into town for Epiphany. I glanced around the dining room and noticed that all the other tables were filled with Americans.

The Greeks would not come out until later, after they'd closed their shops and grabbed a late bite to eat. The band was setting up to play. On the wall behind them, a huge mural of Anthony Quinn as Zorba smiled upon us, a visible reminder to live every day as though we would never die.

Nick was determined to have a nice evening, without another thought for either the Papavasilakis or Kyriakidis families. Still, as I studied him across the table and saw worry lines carved into the corners of his mouth, I realized that we were probably not going to succeed in forgetting about our friends.

Nick had promised Manolis that we'd be his moles in the *Mediterraneo*, but neither of us really believed there was a need for it, especially now that the police had been called in about the coin. Come to think of it, Christos hadn't mentioned either the *maya* or the needle during his interview with the police officer, which seemed rather odd. I said as much to Nick.

"I think he's embarrassed, Julia. People play practical jokes on each other all the time and many of them are nasty. It doesn't mean that they're serious death threats."

"But you've thought all along that the *maya* was serious."

Nick set his menu down and picked up the wine list, tapping the table as he made his points. "I think so. Manolis thinks so. Christos does, too. Because we're Greeks and we take that kind of thing seriously. That doesn't mean that American policemen will. Christos doesn't want to look like an ignorant green . . . foot."

"Horn. Greenhorn. Tender*foot*, green*horn*."

"Right. And now that Xanthe's been exposed, the police don't have to know about the other things she's done. They'll get her for the coin and that will be that."

"I still think she's been set up."

"Well," he said, returning to his study of the menu, "you just let the police handle it." When I didn't answer, he looked at me over the top of his menu. "All right? Julia?"

I sighed. "Okay. I just feel so sorry for her, Nick. She's had a pretty hard life. She needs someone in her corner."

Nick reached across the table to take my hand. "Julia, if anyone needs you in her corner, it's Kate. She and Alex are the real victims here. Now, what do you want to eat?"

We started with *saganaki*, a flambé cheese dish that's one

of my favorites, and followed it up with a *horiatiki*—a Greek salad of cucumbers, tomatoes, onions, feta, peppers—and fried shrimp. We listened to the band for a while, caught up in the happy notes of "*Samiotissa*" and our own thoughts.

It seemed strange to be out dining and dancing, knowing that our friends' lives were in turmoil. But Nick was right. It was our vacation and we were entitled to enjoy at least a little of it. Besides, for a Greek, dance isn't just an entertainment, it's a catharsis. Zorba himself had said it— "There's a devil in me who shouts, and I do what he says. Whenever I am choking with some emotion, he says: 'Dance!' and I dance."

The guys in the band must have been reading my mind. When they began "*Mana Then Phitepsamai,*" Nick rose and strode onto the dance floor alone. A hush fell over the dining room, muting the tinkle of crystal and the clatter of silver, as the singer lamented the loss of his mother. "We never finished our song," he sang.

On the dance floor, Nick raised his arms and slowly pivoted on his heel, beginning the slow, poignant steps of the *zeibekiko*. His right hand, palm out and fingers splayed, covered his face in a universally tragic gesture. Nick's mother had died shortly after we were married—a heart attack that while quick and merciful for the victim, had left her son with relentless regret. By the time he reached Greece, she was already in the ground. The song could have been written for him.

The Greeks had begun coming in, stopping at the door to watch Nick spin gracefully across the dance floor. He had finished his dance and stopped to speak to the band when a party of four men and two women took a table adjacent to ours. One of them was Rula. As Nick returned to our table, they stopped him.

"*Oreo,*" I heard one of the men say to him. "Beautiful."

Once the Greeks began arriving, the dance floor filled up

quickly. Rula Vassos openly gestured to Nick from the floor, an invitation he answered a little too eagerly for me. As I watched them, he leading the line as she quick-stepped next to him, I wondered what, exactly, bothered me about her. She was pretty, and petite. She could wear outrageous clothes. She was decidedly sexy—even kittenish, smiling up into his face, eyes wide with interest. But I knew Nick loved me, and I trusted him.

It might have been my inability to find a niche for myself there, in a room full of Greeks and American tourists. As the American wife of a Greek man, I was neither fish nor fowl. Had I been strictly another American tourist in an ethnic restaurant, the Greeks would have made every effort to see that I had a good time—to coach me in the dance steps and teach me a few words of the language—because Greeks are the most hospitable people on earth. But I wasn't strictly another tourist, I was a non-Greek spouse— not a member of the group, and not exactly an observer. More like a Greek groupie.

And yet, that wasn't entirely the problem either. For the first time in my experience, I couldn't establish any kind of relationship with another woman. To Rula, I simply didn't exist. I was the invisible wife, and Nick didn't even notice what was happening. Rula was a Circe, and she was turning him into a swine.

## Chapter Eighteen

I was saved from sinking into a quagmire of self-pity by the arrival of Aris Mavrakis. He didn't see me, and I didn't call attention to myself, but as he joined the party next to us, he gave me something else to think about besides my husband and "the other woman."

Manolis hated Aris Mavrakis, and Georgia seemed ambivalent about him. From what I'd seen of him, he was a personable man with an easy humor and a sincere manner. Could there be any truth to Manolis's claims, or was this just another case of ex-partner rancor?

The others at the table seemed delighted to see Aris. He ordered a drink, elbowed the table and picked up another matchbook, toying with it as he had the night of the New Year's Eve party. He grinned at the rest of the table and made an announcement, the substance of which I couldn't understand, but it drew the attention of everyone else. All other conversation at the table stopped as Aris went on. I leaned a little farther in their direction, concentrated on ignoring the music and focusing on his words, but I still couldn't pick up what he was saying. When he finished, the table dissolved in laughter.

One of the men clapped Aris on the back. He had their

complete attention now and he took full advantage of it. His expression became solemn and he spoke to them earnestly, punctuating his words with an occasional shake of his head or tick of his tongue. I would very much have liked to know what he was saying to elicit such somber expressions in his companions, but at length he stood up, grabbed his drink and with a little bow, excused himself to join a couple at another table.

"Whew," Nick said, dropping into the chair across from me. He took his napkin and mopped beads of sweat off his brow. "I haven't danced that much in a long time."

"Mmm," I said coolly. "Don't let her wear you out."

Nick ignored the jab. "Look, there's Aris."

"I saw him. I was just wondering if we shouldn't go over and speak to him—maybe try to find out if he's up to something."

"He's not going to admit anything to us."

"But you promised Manolis—"

"I know what I promised Manolis, Julia," Nick said impatiently. "I just don't see what we can do here."

I sighed deeply, then brightened. "You can dance."

"Huh?"

"You're right, Nick. We should enjoy our vacation. Isn't that a *pontiako?* You love that dance." Nick raised a skeptical eyebrow at me. "It's okay, go ahead," I said, grabbing my purse. "I'm going to the rest room anyway."

I didn't mention that the ladies' room was right around a corner from the table where Aris Mavrakis was now seated. With Nick's hand firmly settled on Rula's shoulder, he'd never even notice where I'd gone.

I passed the table, grateful that Aris didn't look up, and stepped around the corner into the ladies' room, pulled out my lipstick and ran my fingers through my hair in a vain effort to control the curls. "It was an interesting New Year's

Eve," he had said as I passed the table. And he was speaking English.

I studied my face in the mirror. Did I look like someone who would listen at keyholes? Could I live with myself if I stood behind that corner and eavesdropped on Aris's conversation? I thought of Kate, whose wedding plans were turning into a classic Greek tragedy, of Manolis, whose future might hang in the balance, and of vulnerable, frightened Xanthe. Could I live with myself if I didn't do everything I could to help them all? I eased open the door of the ladies' room, edged up to the corner, opened my bag and dumped its contents on the floor.

"I thought you knew," he was saying as I carefully crouched behind the wall and slowly retrieved my lipstick. I dropped it into the bag and leaned forward again.

"But you would have heard about it eventually. There are a lot of rumors circulating, but they're just not true. Manolis had nothing to do with it. He wasn't responsible. It's happening everywhere. Tampa. Ft. Lauderdale. Surely you heard about the girl on that gambling ship out of St. Pete?"

A muffled response came from the other side of the table just as a pair of black loafers appeared under my nose. I followed them up, past a pair of soft, black, pleated pants, white shirt and black vest, up to the curious face of our waiter.

"Here, let me help you with that," he said, squatting to grab my wallet and hand it to me.

"So clumsy," I said. "My shoe caught on the carpet and I dropped my bag."

The waiter shrugged as though it was a common occurrence, finding restaurant patrons clambering around on their knees. A breath of spearmint chewing gum washed over me. "You're not hurt?"

"Oh, no. I didn't fall. I just dropped the bag when I reached out to steady myself."

"Ah," he said, pausing to hand me my keys before continuing. "Your husband is driving tonight?"

Of all the nerve! He assumed that I'd been drinking. I was eavesdropping! I raised an eyebrow a la Lauren Bacall.

"We have to be careful, you know," he went on hastily. "If a customer drinks too much and has an accident on the way home, we might be held responsible. There is a case pending right now . . ."

A rustle at the table and Aris's voice eclipsed the waiter's explanations. "I've got to go back to my table. They'll be wondering what has happened to me," he said.

I leaped up, startling the waiter before he could quite finish justifying himself. "I understand, and I can assure you there's nothing to worry about. I'm perfectly fine. Now, if you'll excuse me—"

He bowed as I rounded the corner in time to see Aris standing, drink in hand, gazing down at two somber faces. "Really," he said, "*O Kritikos* is perfectly safe."

I was right. Nick never noticed my absence. He was too busy dancing with Rula. They were doing *tsifteteli,* a modified belly dance in which the couple face one another, arms extended as they shake, shimmy, and grind. Do I need to mention how I feel about this dance? My throat constricted as I watched them.

Rula smiled up at him—innocently seductive—her gaze focused only on him. What more could a man ask for? Even then, she was probably thinking about the next notch she was going to put in her garter belt. Hips swiveled and torsos shook, she charming and beguiling him as they slowly pivoted on the dance floor. But when his back turned to me, she broke off her sleepy gaze into his eyes to meet mine. Her insolent smile lingered just long enough to wire me a message—*I can have him any time I want.*

Somewhere, sometime, somehow, I was going to get even with Rula Vassos.


The phone call came early the next morning. I rolled over to find Nick already gone. But gone where? Tampa, I remembered hazily. He had wanted to get an early start for Tampa and the UPS office. Spiros was working the late shift at *O Kritikos* and wanted to go with him. As Kate's godfather, he felt it was his business to avenge her—a fact that caused me considerable worry.

I hadn't really wanted to go anyway. I was still smarting over Rula. I knew that if Nick and I got ourselves closed up in a car for any length of time, I'd end up picking a fight with him. Another one, that is, since the previous evening had ended on a somewhat strident note. In spite of my determination to act as though nothing was wrong, I hadn't been able to resist just one little jab.

"I guess I didn't realize, when we made our agreement, that you'd put Rula on as a rider."

"What are you talking about?"

I'd explained. In explicit detail. He hadn't liked it. We'd gone to bed wrapped in chilly silence, with Jack lying between us. Nick hadn't even awakened me before leaving. And the fact that he was gone meant that he would not be answering the insistent ringing of the phone. I glanced at the clock on the bedside table. Ten minutes of seven.

"Julia?" whispered a vaguely familiar voice.

"Speak up. I can't hear you. Who is this?"

"Xanthe. Julia, I need your help. The police—they're outside, knocking on my door. What should I do?"

I sat up in bed and rubbed my eyes. "You'll have to answer it, Xanthe. Don't hang up. Put down the phone and go to the door. See what they want."

She did as I instructed. Muffled voices—one male, one female—filtered through the receiver. I couldn't understand what they were saying, but there was no mistaking the all-business tone of their voices. In a minute, Xanthe returned to the line.

"Julia? Julia, they say I have to go with them. They're going to search my—yes, all right. Just a minute—What should I do?"

"Ask the officer in charge to come to the phone." I listened, unable to make out more than an occasional word. At length, a male voice came on the line.

"This is Detective Michael Fallon."

The man in plaid really got around. "Detective Fallon, I'm a fr—an acquaintance of Ms. Saros. She's very confused."

"Your name?"

I gave him my name, waited while he spelled it out, thinking that maybe it was a good thing Nick wasn't there after all. He wouldn't like this.

"Are you Ms. Saros's attorney, Ms. Lambros?"

"No, I—"

"I'm sorry then. I can't tell you anything."

"But—"

"Ms. Saros is under arrest. If you're a friend, perhaps you'd better start looking for an attorney."

"Officer Fallon, what exactly is the ch—" Click. Dial tone. I sat for a moment, too stunned to move. Somehow, I hadn't believed that anyone really thought Xanthe was guilty. Obviously, I'd been wrong. And now what?

I clambered out of bed and staggered to the little hospitality coffeemaker in the dressing area, trying to make sense of what had just happened. The officers had arrived with a search warrant and a warrant for Xanthe's arrest. I didn't think there was much point in calling back. They weren't going to let me talk to her, and it would only antagonize them. Nick had gone and I had no idea of when he'd be back. I turned on the shower, knowing that whatever I was going to do next—and I wasn't sure what that was—I would have to be dressed to do it.

Christos was probably not the way to go, I reflected as I shampooed my hair. Although I had felt from the beginning that he regretted having to fire Xanthe, he was the victim and not likely to be too sympathetic to her plight. Manolis and Georgia would have little pity for the person they believed was persecuting their daughter. Besides, they were already under too much strain. But I didn't know any attorneys in Tarpon Springs. By the time I'd dressed, I had decided there was only one choice.

I took Jack for a brisk walk, got him settled with a rawhide bone and the radio and locked the door behind me. At eight forty-five, I stood in front of Eva Paradissis's door.

"Eva?" I pounded on the door insistently, having not received an answer the two previous times. "Eva, are you there?"

I glanced up and down the hall, reluctant to disturb anyone in the family quarters. I wasn't eager to face Christos Kyriakidis, to try to explain why I was going to the aid of his adversary. Christos was not a man who would take his enemies lightly.

I could hear a clock radio blaring inside. She couldn't possibly be sleeping through the noise. Maybe she was in the shower. I pounded again. "Come on," I whispered under my breath. "Answer the door."

As if responding to my entreaty, I heard her fumbling with the safety catch. Finally, the door opened.

"Eva?"

Behind her, the room was dark, the radio blasting out a Tampa traffic update. A thin slice of sunlight cut through the draperies on the French doors. Eva blinked, as though she were having trouble holding her eyes open. She rubbed them with the backs of her hands, shook her head and peered out at me. "Yes?"

"Eva, I'm sorry to wake you—"

"What time is it?"

"Uh, almost nine o'clock."

"Nine o'clock! Oh, no. Not again!"

"Did you oversleep?"

She turned away from me and staggered across the room, pausing to turn down the radio before switching on the bedside lamp and stumbling toward the bathroom. I crept into the apartment, wondering what to do next. This was hardly the briskly efficient administrative assistant I had seen in action for the last four days. Through the bathroom door, I could hear water gushing into the sink, intermittently interrupted by splashing. In a minute, the door opened and she came out, pressing a hand towel to her cheeks. When she finally looked up, her eyes were clearer, brighter.

"I'm sorry—" I began.

"No, it's a good thing you woke me. I might have slept on for hours. Sometimes, when I have trouble sleeping—" She stopped, suddenly realizing that my early morning presence in her apartment was not the norm. "Is something wrong?"

"It's Xanthe," I said. "She's been arrested."

Eva gestured me to a tub chair and walked to the little kitchenette next to the bathroom. "Coffee," she said. "I think I'm going to need coffee."

I sat down and took advantage of the moment to check out her apartment. It was an efficiency—fairly small but attractively decorated in the same style as the guest rooms.

The bed apparently slid into a recessed area in the wall, thus forming a couch for daytime use. Track lighting eliminated the need for lamps, except for the single one on the side table. There were two tub chairs, a coffee table, which would be put back to place when the bed was made, a chest of drawers, and a small desk. In place of a wardrobe chest, Eva had a large closet. Through an arched doorway, I could see a galley-style kitchen. She spooned coffee into the basket of a Mr. Coffee. "Go ahead with your story."

"She called me early this morning. The police were there."

By the time Eva returned with two mugs of coffee, I had told her what little I knew about Xanthe's arrest. "Do you know an attorney I can call?"

Eva took a sip of her drink, closed her eyes and sighed while the caffeine headed for her veins. I knew the feeling. "No. I mean, I know attorneys but they're not in criminal law. I suppose I can call one and get a name, but who's going to pay for his services?"

Ah, good question. I had no way of knowing whether Xanthe could pay an attorney. Nick and I couldn't afford to take on the expense, and no one else involved with this girl was likely to be willing to pay for her defense. I finished the last of my drink and set the mug down. "I don't know what to do."

"Well, to begin with, you need to find out what the charges are," Eva said, her brisk professional persona returning. "I suppose the only way to do that is to go down to the police station."

"Alone?"

Eva rose, took my mug and her own and carried them to the sink. She did not offer me another cup of coffee. "I'm sorry, Julia, but I can't go with you. I'd be jeopardizing my job."

"But Xanthe thinks you're her friend."

"I'm as close to a friend as Xanthe has, but not so close that I can lose my job over this."

"But surely Christos would understand."

"No, he probably would not. And anyway, I can't risk it. Maybe you can find someone else to go with you."

No wonder they called her The Baked Alaska. I tried to understand her point of view, but friendship has always occupied a high priority with me—higher, apparently, than it did with Eva. Xanthe needed help, though, and I needed to find someone who would actually care what happened to the girl. By the time I returned to our room, I knew who to call.

*Chapter Nineteen*

"I will pick you up in an hour," Father Charles said.

"I could pick you up," I ventured, scrambling for an excuse. "It's on the way, and—" But of course Nick had probably taken the Honda, and I didn't have access to Spiros's Pontiac keys. I also don't have a pilot's license.

"Forgive me, my dear, but you do not know your way around Tarpon Springs and I do. Besides, I feel more comfortable behind the wheel myself. Indulge an old man."

Nick wasn't going to like this. I didn't like it much myself, since I wasn't in possession of a crash helmet. Still, I had no choice but to meet him at the entrance to the hotel at the designated time. I picked up the phone to call Miss Alma.

"I'm leaving Nick a note in the room, and if I get held up for some reason, I'll check back with him during the day. I just wanted to let you know where I was going."

We agreed that it would be best not to mention my mission to Christos and Pagona. The old lady was proving to be an easier charge for Miss Alma than either of us had at first thought. "She watches a lot of television," Miss Alma explained. "And she's perfectly capable of keeping track of her own medication. I think her biggest problem is loneliness. I'm teaching her to play whist, and she seems to be enjoying that."

I hung up the phone feeling that Miss Alma might be as much a prisoner as Xanthe was. But at least her sentence was going to be short.


We arrived at the Tarpon Springs police station at about ten o'clock. I climbed out of Father Charles's Jeep suppressing the urge to fall on my knees and thank God we had made it without incident. It had been an interesting ride.

"Now, my dear," Father Charles said, grasping my elbow and guiding me toward the door of a low, plain brick building, "perhaps I should do the talking." He straightened his white clerical collar and arranged the gold cross on his broad chest. I agreed that it was probably best. After all, Detective Fallon had made it quite clear that he had nothing to say to me.

I followed Father Charles through the door and stopped abruptly behind him. I don't know what I had expected, but there was no receptionist, no desk sergeant like on television. I surveyed the small waiting room in front of me—white walls and gray industrial carpet. Fluorescent lighting. A forlorn spider plant dangled from the ceiling near a display case of police patches from jurisdictions all over North America. To the right, a door with a window provided a view of a filing room. The sign above it read "Police Records." No one seemed to be in.

On the far wall, a black glass window glared at me like a cyclopean eye. I had the feeling that someone was back there, watching us and waiting to know our business. A telephone to the left of the window would connect us with a communications officer. Father Charles pointed me to a row of chairs against the left wall and strode across the room to the phone. In a moment, a door to the left of the phone opened at the hand of Michael Fallon.

Fallon was an attractive man—hair so black it accentuated the occasional streak of silver, eyes of sapphire blue framed by tiny laugh lines. His complexion was fair, with ruddy patches over cheekbones hidden by a comfort layer that repeated itself under the chin. "Father?" he said. "You wanted to see me? Come in." He opened the door wider and Father Charles was admitted to the recesses of the building without a backward glance for me.

There were no magazines in the waiting room. The Herculon seat of the chair scratched my legs and I shifted, unsure of whether my discomfort was physical or emotional. Police stations do not conjure up happy memories for me. I tried to concentrate on a poster of Tarpon Springs, displayed in a gold-tone metal frame. A sponge diver, a boat, St. Nicholas Cathedral, and the archbishop holding up a cross—a nice collage of images of the community. And the police patches: Milwaukee, Miami, Winnipeg . . .

"Come along, Julia. We have to go to Clearwater."

"What?"

"She's not here. They've taken her to the Pinellas county jail. They don't have a holding facility here."

"Will we be able to see her?"

Father Charles shrugged. "I don't know. She's scheduled for an advisory hearing at one. We can be there for that." He guided me back out into the brightly sun-spotted parking lot and held open the door of the Jeep. I stared uneasily at the waiting seat. Clearwater was what, twenty minutes away?

I clambered back into the Jeep, a mute prayer running through my mind as I fastened my seat belt. "What did you find out?"

"Well," Father Charles said as we squealed out of the parking lot and hung a careening left, "Detective Fallon is a nice Irish boy. A good Catholic. He'd like to see more communication between our churches."

"About Xanthe, Father Charles?"

"Yes, I'm coming to that. I had to establish some rapport with him first, you see. We discussed the church for a few minutes . . ."

A mental picture of Detective Michael Fallon floated before my eyes. Black Irish. He would have been brought up to respect a priest.

". . . she was booked there, at the police station. They didn't uncover the coin in their search."

That was a relief. Although I had bragged to Nick that I would have found the coin among her things, I knew that really wasn't true. For all I knew, she could have had it in her shoe. But the police had not found it either, which meant that she probably didn't have it—at least not with her. That was one point in her favor.

Father Charles leaned over me to pull a map out of the door pocket and tossed it in my lap. He righted the Jeep, which had veered crazily into the oncoming lane, and shook his head at the receding noise of a blaring horn.

"Florida drivers are not very polite. Yesterday," he continued, "they established that the coin in the necklace is counterfeit. They contacted the jeweler in Athens, and he verified that Mr. Kyriakidis's claim is correct. The original coin in the necklace was an authentic Helios, very rare. Worth something over fifteen thousand dollars."

"But that doesn't mean that—"

"He also verified that the girl had it in her possession when she left the store. That, coupled with the testimony of Christos, his mother, and his secretary, was enough to merit a warrant. She's being held for grand theft. A felony. Other charges may be pending."

He reached into the pocket of his pants and pulled out

a business card, handing it to me. Detective Michael Fallon. Tarpon Springs Police Department. "On the back."

I turned the card over. An address had been written on it in thick black felt-tip pen: "Criminal Justice Building, 49th Street South, Clearwater."

"That's where we're going. Can you find it on the map?"

I unfolded the map and held it up in front of my face, happy to have it to shield my view of the road. We were on Highway 19, a heavily traveled, fast-moving thoroughfare with a series of abrupt stop lights. By the time I'd decided exactly where we were, and where we were going, Father Charles had hit the fast lane, doing at least twenty miles over the limit. I swallowed the scream that rose in my throat.

"We've got plenty of time, Father. There's no need to rush. If the hearing isn't until—watch out!" The driver of a semi sat on his horn, following it up with a series of thoughtless gestures and some colorful suggestions.

Father Charles ticked his tongue. "I like to have plenty of time to find where I'm going." He glanced over at me and must have noticed my white-knuckled grip on the dashboard. He patted the steering wheel.

"The little angel, remember? She always rides right there. I was a driver during World War Two, you know. Before I entered the seminary. I suppose that's why I prefer a Jeep." He pulled out a pack of cigarettes from his shirt pocket, lit one and tossed the pack on the dash.

We stayed on 19 to Ulmerton Road, turned left, and left again on Forty-ninth Street, finally pulling up in front of the enormous Pinellas County Criminal Justice Center. Twenty-foot palm trees lined the walkway like tall, skinny sentries from a Dr. Seuss book.

"Wow, it looks like a resort hotel! Maybe being arrested isn't such a bad thing here," I said.

Father Charles zipped into the parking lot in front of the building and killed the engine. "This is not the jail. That's behind the building. I doubt that it's quite this nice."

Nice, however, did not describe the Criminal Justice Center. It was fabulous—a modern structure of pinkish beige and brown marble and heavy, tinted glass. Father Charles and I walked through the main doorway, craning our necks at the vaulted ceiling and glass wall of the lobby.

"Can I help you?" A Pinellas county sheriff's deputy, gray-haired and friendly, came forward to meet us.

"We would like to visit a . . . a prisoner," I said.

"Are you family?"

"Well, no . . ."

He shook his head. "No can do. Only family. Besides, it's not a visiting day."

Father Charles cleared his throat and looked meaningfully at me. I stepped back, casually walking toward the building's directory. In a few minutes, the priest and deputy joined me.

"It's quite fascinating, Julia," Father Charles said. "They have a very modern system here." He went on to explain that while we could not actually visit Xanthe, we could sit in on the advisory hearing and that possibly the judge might allow us to communicate with her. The entire proceeding would take place via closed-circuit television. The deputy directed us to Courtroom 17, on the third floor, and shook hands with Father Charles.

"Episcopalian," Father Charles murmured as we passed through the security checkpoint and stepped onto the escalator. "Isn't happy with the changes going on in his church. I encouraged him to visit us at the cathedral." He gave me a cheerful wink.

We found Courtroom 17 easily, halfway down a wide, airy, glass-and-marble hallway. We had just taken seats in the rear of the courtroom when another sheriff's deputy advised us to "All rise."

Judge Lisa Bostwick was an attractive woman. She appeared to be in her mid-thirties, with long chestnut hair and a serenely intelligent face. She took her place on the bench, in front of a seal of the Sixth Judicial Circuit, Pinellas County, Florida, which was anchored to a marble wall diagonally across the right-hand corner of the room. On the wall directly in front of us, a big-screen television displayed two rows of male prisoners in identical blue scrub suits. No women were in view. I nudged Father Charles and pointed to the screen.

"I saw," he whispered. "Poor devils."

While Judge Bostwick arranged her papers and prepared to begin the hearings, I took in the rest of the room. It was a surprisingly pleasant place, with light oak block paneling and desks. To the left, a jury box held twelve empty seats upholstered in burgundy fabric. They actually looked quite inviting. In front of the jury box, a wide desk was occupied by a tall young blond man.

"The DA," Father Charles mouthed at me.

"In the detention center, can you hear me?" the judge said into her mike. The prisoners answered with a variety of listless "Yeahs" and nodding heads. "Please rise to be sworn in."

"Where is Xanthe?" I whispered to Father Charles. "These are all men."

Father Charles shrugged. "I'll see what I can find out." He stepped up to the deputy, conversed quietly for minute and returned to his seat as the deputy went to speak to the clerk.

"She's on the docket," Father Charles said.

The court clerk handed a paper to Judge Bostwick, who looked it over before turning back to the screen. "Now, I must advise all of you as to the purpose of this hearing. It is called an 'advisory hearing,' and it is meant to advise you of the charges against you and of your rights, and to set bond for those charges. Do you all understand?" Judge Bostwick waited as the prisoners indicated that they did.

Once advised, the hearings went fairly quickly—each case more depressing than the last. Men and women, old and young, black and white, paraded before Judge Bostwick in a litany of charges: domestic aggravated battery, forgery, obtaining prescription by fraud. Worried family members stood at the microphone pleading the case of the defendant, or pleading that he be locked up. Judge Bostwick listened to them all, calm and unfailingly polite to both the prisoners and their loved ones.

"May I have Xanthe Saros next?" Judge Bostwick asked. Father Charles rose and went to the podium.

"Your honor," said the deputy, "this is Father Charles Millas. He's not a member of the defendant's family, but he's concerned that she may not understand these proceedings. He'd like to interpret them for the defendant."

"I'll have to swear you in, Father." Father Charles raised his right hand obediently. When it was done, Xanthe stepped up to the microphone.

Like the other women defendants, she wore a peach-colored scrub suit. But unlike most of them, there was no belligerence about her, nor any smug familiarity with the proceedings. Xanthe was frightened. Her face was pale, her limbs drawn into her torso protectively, and every muscle in her body seemed to twitch. She clutched her hands together, fingers interlaced, and pressed them against her stomach. She licked her lips repeatedly, as though she were trying to avoid vomiting.

As I watched her, I was carried back to another courtroom, another bond hearing, and another very frightened young woman. Xanthe would be feeling hot now, flushed as if with a fever, and trapped in some surreal nightmare. Her ears would be roaring so that she had to strain to hear the judge, and her throat would ache so that she wondered if she would be able to speak. She would remember that three days ago, she had been happy, try to remember how happiness had felt, and wonder if she would ever feel it again. I knew what she was feeling, because that other young woman had been me.

## Chapter Twenty

"We have to get her out of there, Father," I said as we returned to the Jeep. "But I don't know how we're going to do it."

"I'm sure we'll find a way, my dear. I have a few ideas." But he did not share them with me. Xanthe's bond had been set at fifty thousand dollars. I could only hope that Father Charles would be able to find someone willing to put up the necessary five thousand to bail her out.

"Do you think she's guilty?" he asked.

The question surprised me. "No! Do you?"

Father Charles tapped a cigarette out of his pack, lit it and squinted as the smoke drifted into his eyes. "I don't know. You must resign yourself to the possibility that she may have taken the coin, Julia. If I have learned anything as a priest, it is that the evil eye is a very powerful thing."

I stared at him, stunned. His rough beard twitched and the lips hiding behind it curved into a little smile. "You're surprised at that, my dear?"

"Um . . . yes. You mean you believe that a person can call down a curse on someone's head?"

"In a manner of speaking, yes. Let me ask you this—do you believe in a basic evil force in the world?"

I answered truthfully. "I don't know."

The old priest smiled. "It is a difficult question. I can only tell you, from my own experience, that there are forces moving in the world that are not of human making." We pulled out of the driveway, headed back toward Tarpon Springs. I was too distracted to worry much about the trip.

"You see," he went on, "the church teaches that there are only two forces outside of the world. There is the force of God, which is pure good, and the force of . . . whatever you may call it—the Devil, Satan, Lucifer—which is pure evil. Do you remember that Georgia mentioned the *exoticá?*"

"Demons. Goblins."

"Yes, exactly. They are imagined to be mischievous but occasionally good creatures. People who believe in them practice ways of appeasing or placating them. The idea," Father Charles continued, "is that these creatures can be turned either way—to do good or to do evil. But within the theology of the church, that ambiguous sort of creature cannot exist. That is why the church disapproves of this superstition."

"But doesn't that same ambiguity exist within people?"

Father Charles stubbed out his cigarette and lit another one. "It is the inclination toward sin that exists in man. You must understand that this is different from sin itself. It is a weakness, a frailty requiring protection. Of course, without the help of God, man will give in to this weakness and allow himself to be exploited by evil."

"I'm not sure I understand," I said.

Father Charles nodded. "Let me try to clarify it for you. You will agree that God has power over all things, including evil?"

I agreed.

"Evil exists only because God allows it. Evil forces are never, and will never be, as powerful as God. Therefore, to appeal to them—or to attempt to placate them, which is the case with the *exotica*—is pointless, because they have no final power. That resides only within God. Therefore, all rites of demonology, witchcraft, astrology, and sorcery are fruitless."

"But," I said, "the church makes an exception for the evil eye?"

"No," Father Charles stated flatly. "They are not the same thing."

"Okay, now I'm lost."

"Let us go back for a minute to the discussion of good and evil. Evil can overtake man's soul only when he is unbelieving and indifferent. As long as man has faith, the presence of God exists within him to fight evil. But indifference to God, or loss of faith, creates a vacuum in the soul. Corruption can and will fill that vacuum, making immorality seem normal and acceptable. This is extremely insidious.

"Now, the root of the evil eye is envy, which, as we know, is one of the deadliest of sins. It breeds the desire to harm, or at least to take away the blessings of another. It rebukes the Almighty. Let me give you an example. God has chosen to give one woman beauty, but not another, so to envy that woman for her beauty is also to question the judgment of the Almighty in bestowing His gifts. It is, therefore, evil. The true work of the evil eye is the effect is has upon the person who envies—not upon the one who is envied."

"Then what about the *mati?*"

"A folkway. However, the Christian may protect himself from evil by calling upon God for help. Therefore, prayers said to repulse the evil eye—or envy—are nothing more than petitions for God's protection, and thus acceptable within the church. Does that clarify anything for you?"

Not really. Or perhaps I just didn't want to understand what he was telling me—that if Xanthe envied Kate her relationship with Alex, then she might also be capable of doing terrible things. She might actually be behind the *maya*, which was as diabolical a threat as I could imagine. Perhaps there was something to this evil-eye business after all.

And that was the thought occupying both of us as we turned north on Highway 19, which, in my case, was better than dwelling on the drive back to Tarpon Springs. Father Charles hugged the bumper of the car in front of us so closely I could practically hear the driver's radio. The car was a red Porsche.

"Father, how would the bishop feel if you hit another sports "

"Oh, the bishop!" he cried, slapping his forehead. "He'll be here the day after tomorrow, and I'll have to give him a damage estimate."

"Yes, well . . . look out!"

In front of the Porsche, a huge semi careened wildly onto the esplanade, back onto the road and into the middle lane, where prudent drivers hit their brakes to make room for it. Smoke billowed off the Porsche's tires, and the odor of burning rubber invaded the Jeep. The Porsche shot into the middle lane behind the semi, leaving us hurtling toward the cause of the problem—a stalled car at the traffic light at Klosterman Road. Father Charles rammed the Jeep onto the esplanade, narrowly missing both the car and its appalled driver, shot through the orange light and spun a hard left.

"Are you all right, my dear?"

I gasped and nodded, unable to find my voice.

By the time we reached Alternate 19, the adrenaline rush had subsided. My heavy breathing was making me dizzy— a pleasantly relaxing sensation actually, which might only have been improved by a stiff shot of Scotch.

"Look, there! We must go back, my dear."

And so we did, via a narrow U-turn in the middle of Alternate 19, followed by a rattling, teeth-jarring trip over three speed bumps in a warehouse complex. When we finally stopped, three inches short of a brick wall, it was next to a black Lotus with a fractured bumper. Beside the Lotus, there were three other cars—a white Toyota pickup, a Chrysler New Yorker of about the same vintage as Spiros's Pontiac but in markedly poorer condition, and a rusting green Chevy Nova that might have had two years on the Chrysler.

"I have to have that damage estimate when the bishop gets here, my dear. Do you mind? It will take only a minute." He was out of the Jeep before I could voice any objection.

I reluctantly followed him up to a heavy steel door under a sign that read "Plemenos and Co., Import/Export Olives, Fine Wines and Tobacco Products." Two smaller signs affixed to the door read, "Please Ring Bell" and "By Appointment Only."

I pointed this out to Father Charles, who pushed on the bell, unfazed, and adjusted his clerical collar. "No one turns a priest away, my dear." We waited for a moment before he gave the bell another sharp stab.

"Yeah?" The man who answered the door was a near contender for Mr. Universe. The sleeves of his Grateful Dead T-shirt were full of biceps the size of basketballs. He had long, brown, sun-streaked hair pulled back in a ponytail, and eyebrows like frayed rope that drew together in a knot as he looked us over, his gaze mainly fixed on Father Charles's clerical collar.

"I would like to speak to Mr. Plemenos, please. I am Father Charles Millas and this is—"

"C'mon in," the man said, pushing the door open.

We followed him into a dark cavern of a room. There was no office. No receptionist. Just a quarter-mile of gray steel shelving set on a shiny concrete floor. The room seemed dark although, high above us, industrial lighting hung from steel rafters at twenty-foot intervals. The mysterious gloom, I decided, was caused by the aisles of shelves that stretched, one after the other, for what seemed like miles. The place was huge.

"Yo, Lucky! Visitors!" Mr. Universe cried out in an accent I recognized as Newark or its environs. "Right back there," he said to us, pointing vaguely toward the rear of the warehouse. "In the office, down this aisle and to the left."

"Thank you," Father Charles said, but the man had already headed for a small forklift and a stack of cardboard cartons. "This way, I think," he continued to me.

We passed through a row of shelving about fifteen feet high, dodged a rolling stepladder and squeezed around three cases of *Roditis* sitting in the middle of the aisle. At the end of the aisle, we turned left, headed toward a pool of light and eventually came to a glass-enclosed office.

Lucky Plemenos sat at a large steel desk, tapping on a laptop computer. He didn't look up until Father Charles knocked on the half-opened door.

"Father, what a nice surprise." His gaze traveled beyond Father Charles to me. "And even better," he said softly. My stomach fluttered.

"Please, come in. Have a seat."

Lucky stood up and came around the desk, gesturing to two steel armchairs covered in mossy-green plastic cushions. Father Charles waited until I was seated before taking the other chair. Lucky returned to his place behind the desk and pushed the laptop aside. "This is indeed a surprise," he said.

"Yes, well, we were coming back from Clearwater and I noticed your car in the lot out there. I'm going to have to have a damage estimate on it for the bishop. Has the adjuster seen it yet?"

Lucky shook his head, an amused smile trembling at the

corners of his mouth. "As a matter of fact, she's coming this afternoon. I should have it for you tomorrow. Do you have a fax machine at the church?"

Father Charles admitted that he did. "I have a little trouble operating it, but I suppose someone will know——"

"Just make sure it's turned on, Father." Lucky pulled open the bottom drawer of his desk and took out a box of cigars, passing them across the desk to Father Charles. They were locally made cigars—a product of the industry in Tampa—the box elaborately decorated with the name *Tampafino Maestros*. "Perhaps these will ease your way with the bishop."

Father Charles took the box smoothly. "I'm afraid that the bishop does not really appreciate fine tobacco the way you and I do. But I will enjoy them, you may be sure." He caressed the box lovingly and set it on the desk.

"Let me write down my fax number." He took a card out of his pocket and patted around for a pen. Lucky plucked one off his desk, handed it to the priest and turned to me.

"So you've been to Clearwater, eh?"

"Yes, I'm afraid we've been at the jail."

Lucky raised an eyebrow at me. "Someone I know?"

I thought everyone had probably heard the story of Xanthe Saros's arrest. It surprised me that Lucky was unaware of it, but Father Charles soon rectified the matter.

"I had no idea," Lucky said. "Well, I'm sorry for her. It seems like a very foolish risk to me. She was bound to be found out. I've done quite a bit of business with Christos Kyriakidis." His headshake completed the thought. One would not want the hotelier as an enemy.

"Well," Lucky continued, "since you're here, let me show you around."

I would rather have gone straight back to the hotel—preferably by some other means of transportation—but Father

Charles seemed eager to see Lucky's operation. Instead, I asked to use the phone.

"I'm very concerned about the girl . . ." Father Charles said as their voices receded into the cavernous warehouse.

"I was starting to wonder," Nick said. His voice resonated with irritation.

"I'm sorry. They didn't have her at the police station. We had to go to Clearwater." I explained about the advisory hearing and told Nick about the bond.

"I thought you promised me that you were going to stay out of it."

"I'm not in it. She didn't have anyone else to call, Nick."

"Father Charles could have gone alone. Jail visits are one of the things priests do."

"All right. Look, I'll be back at the hotel soon. We can talk about it then."

"Where are you now?"

I hesitated, twisting the phone cord between my fingers. "We stopped at Lucky's warehouse."

Nick's voice was chillingly soft. "What are you doing there?"

"Father Charles needed to talk to him about the damage to his car."

"I don't like it, Julia."

"Nick, it wasn't my idea." Silence on the other end of the line. "Nick?"

"What?"

"I said, it wasn't my idea."

"You could have waited in the car."

"That would have been rude."

"Mmm."

"Okay, fine. I could have waited in the car, but I didn't want to. I was hoping for a quick liaison. I'll see you when I get back to the hotel," I said and slammed the phone into the cradle so hard I thought I'd cracked the plastic.

When, exactly, had all this friction started? It had been building, I realized, since we'd arrived in Tarpon Springs. Nick had promised me that he wouldn't leave me stranded by myself while he cavorted with his Greek friends, but I felt he'd broken that promise several times over. Like the previous night at *Zorbra's*, for instance, when he'd danced the night away with a woman who wasn't his wife.

Now I'd broken my promise to him—not intentionally, but I had to admit that Father Charles could have gone to see Xanthe without me. I just felt so sorry for her. She was one of the disenfranchised, and I knew how she felt. And that, I realized, was the root of the problem between Nick and me.

Neither Rula nor Lucky had improved the situation. Rula was gleefully hammering a wedge between us, doing everything she could to make me feel even more the outsider. Lucky, in his gentle and charming way, was trying to make me feel that I belonged, which should have been my husband's job. And Nick wasn't doing anything at all.

Since the day we'd married, I'd never looked twice at another man—well, not seriously—and I'd certainly never shimmied and undulated on a dance floor with one. So what right did he have to question my motives? None, I decided, and I was going to tell him so, first chance I got. I grabbed my bag and left the office, nearly colliding with Mr. Universe as he came out a door next to Lucky's office. He was pushing a hand truck loaded with cardboard crates labeled *Poura* and started when I crossed his path.

"Um, I'm looking for Mr. Plemenos and Father Charles." He pointed me toward the aisle of crates we'd come through earlier, turned abruptly and disappeared down another aisle.

"On this side," Lucky said, gesturing to a shelf on the right stacked high with tubs of olives, "are the imports. Here, as you see, are *kalamata* olives. Two aisles over, we have cigarettes, and the rest of this aisle and the next are our Greek wines." He handed Father Charles a bottle of *Vin Santo.* "It makes the best altar wine," he explained.

Father Charles agreed. "I will save it for *Epiphánia.* The bishop will be pleased. I hope," he added with a troubled frown.

"And for your personal use, Father," Lucky said, handing the priest a bottle of *Roditis* before turning to me. "And for Julia . . ." He pulled open a case labeled *Sta. Helena,* withdrew a bottle and pressed it into my hands. "Think of me when you drink it," he said softly. I blushed, wondering how I would explain it to Nick.

"Over here," he continued, pointing in the direction Mr. Universe had gone, "are the exports to Greece. American cigars and cigarettes, and I am thinking about adding blue jeans. You know, Greeks love American products."

I had to stop playing emotional games with Nick. I wasn't at all sure I could win, and I certainly had a lot to lose. Many women found Nick attractive—particularly when he took to the dance floor—but few were as blatantly obvious about it as Rula. And none that I could recall had ever challenged me, silently or otherwise, to hold on to my husband. But the smile she'd given me at *Zorba's* was as good as a glove thrown down on the dueling ground of my marriage. Rula made me feel inferior, and I was beginning to believe she was right.

"Don't you think so, my dear?"

"I'm sorry, what?"

"I said it's quite an impressive operation." Father Charles nodded at the cases lining the aisle. I could hear the whir of the forklift moving into position. Behind me, Lucky's breath tickled the back of my neck.

"Yes," I stammered, too uncomfortable to think clearly. I stepped sideways, closer to the door, keeping my back to Lucky. "Father, I really think we need to be going."

I wasn't anxious to get back into that Jeep, but I couldn't stay there, three feet from an attractive man who thought I was desirable, at a time when my self-esteem was around my ankles like a pair of cheap pantyhose. Lucky might want to help me pull it up, and I just might want to let him.

We were almost back on the road to safety when Father Charles threw the Jeep in reverse and hurtled us backward over the speed bumps. "I forgot the cigars. Julia, my dear—"

"Um, you want me to go back in?"

"If you wouldn't mind. They're still on the desk in the office."

"Oh, Father, do I have to?"

*Chapter Twenty-One*

I rang the bell, but the door hadn't fully caught behind us, so I went in unannounced. The forklift was still on the move somewhere down one of those dark passages, where Mr. Universe couldn't hear the ring over the machine's droning engine. My heart raced just a little bit and my knees felt like I'd spent the last month on roller skates, sure signs that I should not be walking in the direction of Lucky's office, his cologne and lingering gazes.

What was it about Lucky Plemenos that made my stomach cannonball to my feet? The answer was simple. He was very good for my ego. It wasn't Lucky himself, I realized, although he had all the right chemical elements to detonate an explosion. It was the fact that he made me feel attractive and desirable. But didn't Nick make me feel the same way? The answer was "No." Most of the time, Nick made me feel loved. And feeling loved, I thought, was the most important thing. But it wasn't the only thing.

At first I was shocked by Lucky's interest in me, knowing very well that I had sent him no sexual signals. But after Rula entered the equation with her messages of contempt for me and my ability to hang on to my husband, something had subtly changed. Lucky's attentions became less undesirable and more comforting. It was a dangerous spot to be in.

What I needed was some reassurance from Nick. I needed to recapture the solidarity that had always been the foundation of our marriage. Instead, we were allowing two strangers with their own agendas to interfere in the most intimate relationship in our lives. It couldn't continue.

I stopped short of Lucky's office, where he sat once again tapping on his laptop. He'd taken off his jacket and loosened his tie. His silk shirt hugged his broad shoulders like another skin. His fingers were sure and quick on the keyboard—very strong, very masculine hands. No, I definitely could not go in there. I'm good at making resolutions, I'm not as good at keeping them. I snagged a box of cigars from an open carton and backtracked down the aisle.

I had come face-to-face with a serious flaw in my character—one I'd never suspected—and it shook me to the core. Nick was right. I wasn't a very good judge of character, not even of my own. Physical attraction can be a very dangerous thing. Xanthe was attracted to Alex. Maybe, I thought sadly, she was guilty after all.

Nick stood at the French doors, staring out into the courtyard, his shoulders slumped and his back firmly turned to me. "It didn't occur to me to wait in the Jeep. There's nothing going on between me and Lucky."

"How do I know that?"

"Because I'm telling you."

"You mean, the way I've told you that Rula is nothing more than a woman who likes to dance?"

"Yes," I said. "Like that. Oh, Nick, I don't want to fight anymore. Can't we just make up and forget about both of them?"

He turned to gaze into my eyes—measuring, I thought, my sincerity. At length, he pulled my head against his shoulder. "I love you," he said. "And there's something I want to explain to you, but I don't know how."

"Try."

"Promise me you'll listen and not get angry." I agreed and he went on. "There are men who . . . who never have enough. If you have a good business, they want it. If you have a nice house, they want it. If you have . . ."

"A good wife?"

"I have the best, Julia. Lucky Plemenos is that kind of man. He always wants more—more money, more power. More of what the other guy has. He wants you until he gets you—until he succeeds in taking you away. Then, when he finds out you have a few flaws—"

I pulled away to look into his eyes. They were twinkling. "Just a few," he added. "Then the next guy's wife will start looking good. If he's so charming and attractive, why haven't we seen him with a woman?"

"I don't know."

"Because he hasn't found the perfect one yet. The only perfect woman is always married to someone else. Right now, she's you. Do you understand what I'm trying to say?"

"I think so. The thrill of conquest, I guess. But how do you know that about him? You haven't even talked to him—"

"I don't have to talk to him. It's . . . what do you call it? In . . ."

"Instinct."

"Yeah, that. I can see it in his eyes. He's like a panther, moving in on his prey—always watching for a moment to strike. And here's the point, Julia. He moves when you're . . . *trotós*. I don't know the word in English. Weak."

"Vulnerable," I supplied.

"Yes, that's it. A man like that will do anything to get what, or who, he wants. That's why he's dangerous. Please, I want you to stay away from him."

There was something in what he said. I knew he was right. Lucky might have been attracted to me, but it was for the wrong reasons. It didn't matter. What did matter was that Nick loved me, and loved me for the right ones.

"Let's go out by ourselves tonight," I said. "Let's take that dinner cruise. It could be so romantic."

"We can't," he said regretfully. "I promised Manolis we'd meet them at the restaurant for dinner. I've got to tell them what Spiros and I found out at UPS."

I had completely forgotten about his trip to Tampa. "Oh, did they track the box?"

He pulled a folded sheet of paper out of his pocket and handed it to me. It was a photocopy of the packing slip. The handwriting was almost illegible—a tight, pointed script that required some study before I could make out a name. When I finally did, I looked at Nick and blinked.

"Oh, come on."


"The clerk remembered him—sort of. The box was sent by a man. She thought he might have been young, but she wasn't sure. She remembered commenting on the name. He laughed and said he had the name, he just wished he had the money. That was all she remembered."

Manolis maintained a cold silence toward Christos, watching him suspiciously as Nick produced the packing slip. Christos studied the handwriting carefully. "A joker. Aristotle Onassis, indeed. Mavrakis, I suppose." He laid the slip on the table and turned to Manolis. "You've said all along that he's to blame."

"Yes," Manolis acknowledged. "But he may not have

acted alone." If Christos caught the innuendo, he didn't dignify it with a response.

Georgia was skeptical. "Aris is too clever for this. Even if he did it, he wouldn't put his own first name on it."

"Have a look at the handwriting," Nick suggested. "Does it look familiar?"

Georgia puzzled over it for a minute. "Well, it doesn't look like Aris's, I'm sure of that."

She excused herself and went to the office, returning in a minute with a folder full of invoices. Some of them went back to the opening weeks of the restaurant when Aris himself had signed in the orders. His signature, being a broad, aquarish style, was nothing like the handwriting of the other Aristotle.

"Which proves absolutely nothing," Georgia said, setting the folder aside, "except that we can't conclusively prove anything."

"Well, there's nothing more to be done about it tonight," Christos said, picking up the photocopy. "I will take this to my security people tomorrow. Now at least they will have something to work with."

"Of course," Manolis said, reaching for the slip of paper, "it was not your people who discovered it, Christo. Maybe they're not so efficient as you say, eh? I'll just keep this and make you another copy."

Christos shrugged. "As you wish," he said stiffly. He turned to the rest of us at the table. "Now, tell me what you have seen and done since you've been here. Have you been out to the beach?" Regrettably, we had to admit that we had not. With everything else going on, there hadn't been time.

"I feel terrible that my family's problems have usurped your vacation this way," Christos said. "You haven't had a chance to see any of the sights. Tomorrow night is the

Sponge Festival down here on the docks. You must plan to go. There will be live music and I'm told it's quite pleasant. Besides, I believe we are now close to solving these puzzles. Obviously, Miss Saros has an accomplice. He sent the *maya*, and she stole the coin. It is now only a matter of finding out who helped her and what they did with the Helios."

"Will you be able to get it back?" Miss Alma asked.

Christos stroked his chin. "I don't know. They may already have disposed of it."

"Couldn't the coin still be in Greece?" I wondered.

Christos shook his head doubtfully. "I don't think so. The laws regarding antiquities sales are very strict in Greece. Any dealer—legitimate or not—would view the sale of such a coin as a very high risk. Its monetary value is not that high . . ."

I gulped. Fifteen thousand dollars seemed like a hefty wad of cash to me.

"What makes it so risky is that it is exceptionally rare," he continued. "You must understand that while ancient clay amphoras, for example, are quite valuable, they are not particularly scarce. A dealer might consider handling one if he knew it was going overseas. But a coin like the Helios raises the stakes quite a bit because of its rarity. With so few around, any sale is likely to raise eyebrows, even if it is claimed to be part of a private collection."

Christos thought that Xanthe had smuggled the coin out of Greece, possibly with the help of her accomplice. He had brought the necklace through customs himself, but had not checked it when he presented it to the customs agent.

"Then you don't know that it wasn't stolen after you got here."

Christos raised an eyebrow and Nick pinched my thigh under the table. I met Christos's gaze evenly and waited for an answer.

"I carried the necklace directly from the airport to the

safe in my apartment at the hotel. Absolutely no one handled it along the way. The switch was made in Greece."


"Nick," I said after we'd returned to the hotel, "do you think the coin might have been over-insured?"

My loving husband's reflection glared at me from the bathroom mirror. He'd had little to say on the way back, I realized, but I'd been too preoccupied to notice at the time. He spat a glob of toothpaste into the sink, rinsed his mouth and dried his face on a hand towel.

"Julia, couldn't you see your questions were making Christos uncomfortable?"

"Why should he be uncomfortable, unless he's hiding something? Manolis certainly thinks he is."

"He wanted you out of the hotel. That's why he suggested the Sponge Festival," Manolis had said to us after Christos left. "Did you see the way he wanted to keep that copy? He may have been planning to destroy it."

"Or," Georgia had said sarcastically, "he may just think we're all on the same side."

"Manoli, you're overreacting. Christos figures we ought to let professionals handle the investigation," Nick had replied. "And I think he's right. But," he'd continued in answer to Manolis's worried frown, "we agreed to help and we'll do whatever we can. I'm just not sure of how much help we can be."

"I'm counting on you, Niko. I know you won't let me down."

I pulled back the covers and was climbing into bed when I noticed that the message light on the phone was blinking. "My dear," Father Charles's voice said, "I wanted you to know that I have bailed out Miss Saros. She is back at that appalling motel. Perhaps you could call her tomorrow and cheer her up."

Nick was not delighted to hear the news. "We're supposed to be helping Manolis. If you're so anxious to fit in, why are you helping Xanthe when you know very well she's guilty? I think it's time you decided whose side you're on—Xanthe's or everyone else's."

I glared at him, keeping my voice even. "I'm sorry, I didn't realize they were mutually exclusive."

"Right," he said, rolling back over. "Let's just drop the subject."

I tossed in bed for a long time that night, puzzling over the tension in our relationship. When I didn't come up with any answers, I turned over and tackled the problem of the coin and the other incidents. In view of the hostility Manolis had radiated, I actually thought Christos was remarkably patient about answering my questions. Pagona had not changed. She was still wary, fingering her *mati* and treating us all to a megadose of suspicion. Why, I wondered, if she really believed her nurse was guilty, was she so suspicious of the rest of us?

I pounded my pillow and stuck my feet out from under the cover. If Pagona didn't want Alex to marry Kate, she might try to break it up. She could be responsible for the *maya* and the needle, and she'd certainly had access to the necklace. Nick was going to hate this idea.

"Having trouble sleeping?"

"Mmm. Nick, suppose you found out that someone you liked was responsible for all the trouble? Could you handle it?"

"*Neh.* Of course." But his voice, in the dark, wasn't as sure as his words. At length, I heard him take a breath. "I guess I really haven't been handling all this very well, have I?"

*Tread softly.* I reached for his hand. "You're in a tough position, Nick. I know that. You don't want to see anyone get hurt, and you're trying to be careful of everyone's feelings."

"Except yours?"

I couldn't answer, but he didn't give me a chance to anyway. "I'm sorry. I guess," he added reluctantly, "I was a little flattered by Rula's attention. I don't know why."

"Try thinking of her as the female version of Lucky Plemenos, Nick. She's been sending me messages all along telling me that I can't hang on to my husband. Well, I'm serving you—and her—notice right now that I'm hanging on for dear life."

He rolled onto his elbow and looked down into my face. Even in the dark, I could see he was grinning. "What part of me . . . exactly . . . did you want to hang on to?"

## Chapter Twenty-Two

The subconscious is a marvelous thing, sorting, filing, and grouping even as we do other things, such as sleep. I awoke the next morning with an idea tickling the back of my brain. Fortunately, Nick was more amenable to listening than he had been the night before.

We were out on the grounds of the hotel, down near the bayou and off to the left in a little copse of trees. After sleeping most of the previous day, Jack had returned to his normal self—alert, chipper, and only marginally crazy. As we waited for him to mark his territory, I explained my thinking to Nick.

"I really think I've got something here. In fact, it even fits into Manolis's theory about Christos hiding something— in a way—because Christos would want to protect his mother. Maybe the security people have already figured it out.

"Listen to this. Pagona has every reason to want to see the wedding canceled, right? She had the means and the opportunity to do it all. She was sitting at the head table at the New Year's Eve party, so she could easily have slipped the needle into Kate's bread. In fact, it was the kind of needle she uses all the time for her needlework. She certainly had access to the coin. She could have hidden it anywhere—either in the apartment in Athens or the apartment here. She knows how to open both safes."

"And the *maya?*"

Oh. That did present a bit more of a problem. The package was delivered by UPS. Would Pagona even know that UPS exists? And who was the man who had mailed it? It might have been Christos. I considered the possibility of an insurance scam and rejected it quickly. If Christos Kyriakidis needed money, that fifteen thousand dollars would be nowhere near enough.

Of course, Manolis could be right—Christos might not want Alex to marry out of his class. But even as I thought it, I knew it didn't fit. Christos was many things—tough, powerful, demanding—but he wasn't a snob.

Nick stroked my cheek softly. "It just doesn't work, Julia." I knew he was right.

When we got back to the room, I decided to have another go at it. "If Christos is right, the coin is here in the U.S., since it's too risky to try to sell it in Greece. But it's not in Xanthe's things, and it didn't turn up during the customs search."

"Which only means that it was well hidden."

"I'm not so sure, Nick. Don't they routinely x-ray baggage these days?"

The question gave him pause. If they x-rayed the bags, surely a little metal disk such as a coin would have appeared somewhere. And presumably it would be hidden somewhere inconspicuous, such as in the lining of a suitcase, which would be enough for the customs authorities to be suspicious. They would search carefully until they located it. Which meant to me that the coin had not been in the luggage. Nick had to agree.

"Unless it was hidden in something metal, something that disguised it," he said thoughtfully.

I picked up the phone and dialed, catching Miss Alma about to leave to sit with Pagona. "Just keep your eyes open in the apartment," I said after explaining to her what Nick and I were now both thinking. "Look for metal things like . . . I don't know really . . . a locket, maybe. Something gold."

A coin could be hidden in a locket, and if that locket were gold, I didn't think it would show up as a separate object in the X-ray. Nick, who had been listening to my end of the conversation, put his hand on my arm, as though he had just thought of something.

I hastily finished my conversation and hung up the phone. "What?"

"I think I know where the coin is hidden."


Father Charles was at his desk, wreathed in a cloud of smoke, when we arrived at the church. He tugged his beard absently. "The bishop," he said, "will be arriving this afternoon. I don't think there is much we can do before he gets here. This issue will be a high priority with him."

"On the other hand, Father, if there is something fishy about it, it might be a good thing for you to uncover it first, don't you think? Especially after the accident to Lucky's car." I held my breath. I wanted to know if Nick was right, and I didn't want to wait for the arrival of the bishop to find out. It seemed to me that at this point, with the wedding only four days off, every minute mattered.

At length, he stubbed out his cigar, laying it carefully in the ashtray, and pushed his chair away from the desk. "All right," he said. "Let's go."

We followed him out of the parish building and across the street to the cathedral. "Did you get my message about the girl? We really must find her somewhere else to stay."

"It was very good news," I said. "Who put up the bond?"

"I'm afraid I can't tell you that, my dear. Ms. Saros's benefactor does not want it known." Oh, well. I tried.

We entered the cathedral, pausing to reverence the icon of St. Nicholas, and again I was struck by the deep compassion in the saint's eyes. It was easy to understand how the legends had grown up around this man. And it was easy to believe that this icon, with its white tracks of tears, was somehow special.

"Father, has the church ever declared the weeping a miracle?"

"Our church is not in the business of declaring miracles," he said. "We try to ascertain that there is no trickery involved—a publicity stunt, for example—but once that is established, we can only accept that this is an occurrence for which there is no apparent earthly explanation. Come along."

We followed Father Charles through the nave and waited in the front pew while he disappeared behind the *iconostasion*. In a minute, he was back, carrying the icon of the Epiphany—Christos's gift to Alex and Kate. He sat down between us on the bench and pulled a magnifying glass out of his pocket.

"I'm not so young, you know," he said by way of explanation. "I find it useful at times."

The morning sun beamed into the church and onto the silver repoussé picture. Father Charles turned it over first, examining the back of the frame for indications of tampering. "Hmm," he said, scrutinizing it carefully. "Yes, it has been opened. But of course I couldn't say when. I don't recall looking at the back of it when it was first brought to the church."

"May I, Father?" Nick asked, reaching for the glass. After a moment, he passed the icon to me.

The frame had indeed been opened. There were gouges along the edge of the wood where the nails had been pried loose. They had been hammered back into place, but not expertly enough to be seated in exactly the same grooves. In fact, most of them lay at an odd angles—as if the job had been done very quickly, with little effort to disguise the break-in. I turned the icon over and scanned it with the magnifying glass before handing it back to Nick.

"I don't see anything, do you?"

Nick took his time before answering. He methodically scanned the metal, closing in with more care on the gold halo around the head of Jesus. "There," he said. "Do you see?"

There was still a bead of moisture on the halo, and even as we watched, it grew larger before coursing down over the painting of the face. A second bead began in its place.

"There's a hole in the metal—right there," Nick said, moving the magnifying glass closer to the icon. "Do you see it?"

I did. It was not so much a hole as a crack where the metal had been bent and the strain had caused a minute fracture. The tears were seeping from a cleft in the joint between the gold and the silver.

"I think," Father Charles said somewhat sadly, "that we have our explanation here."

"But what's the moisture?" I asked.

"Condensation, Julia. We're in a humid area here along the coast. Moisture is building up on the inside of the icon and causing it to sweat."

"But how's it getting in there? Through that tiny little crack?"

"No, I doubt it," Nick said, turning the icon over in his hands. "Father, now that we know that it's been tampered with, is it all right if I open it?"

"It has already been done. Yes, go ahead. We are into this now. I would like to be able to tell the bishop something conclusive."

Nick took out a pocketknife and pried back the nails that held a solid wood backing in place. He removed the wood, exposing a layer of soft foam that had been packed into the hollow back of the metal. One side of the foam was loose, where it had been pulled away from the icon. Nick peeled it back, exposing a deep imprint in the foam that replicated the icon itself. But there was no coin.

"There," he said, pointing to a circular depression in the foam. "Right behind the halo."

So that was how it had been done. The icon had been violated, and the coin had been laid directly behind the one gold section where an X-ray would not reveal its presence.

"The icon didn't begin weeping until New Year's Day, is that right?" Nick asked. Father Charles agreed that it was.

"So the coin was probably removed before then," Nick continued. "Whoever took it peeled the foam back, which broke the seal. The coin itself cracked the metal, probably at some time during the shipping. When the seal was broken, the humidity caused moisture to build up and then seep out of the crack."

"I wonder how long that would take," I said. "Would it happen right away?"

"I doubt it. It would take a little time for moisture to condense in there. The more humid the weather, the quicker it would happen. It rained the first night we were here, remember? That may be when it happened."

"Well," Father Charles said, "there's only one thing to be done, I'm afraid."

He called Detective Fallon from his office. Nick didn't bother to return the icon's backing to its place. In fact, from that time forward, both he and Father Charles handled the icon as little as possible. The police would want to take fingerprints. There might even be some process to determine that the Helios actually had been secreted behind the halo. It had not left a distinct print of the sun god, but maybe they would be able to find something. In any event, Father Charles knew that he had no miracle on his hands. What he had was another crime.

Detective Fallon asked Father Charles to do two things—to lock up the cathedral, because it was probably a crime scene, and after carefully wrapping the icon and touching it as little as possible, to bring it to the hotel.

"It will be easier for him if everyone is in one place," Father Charles explained.

We followed Father Charles's erratic progress in our own car, arriving together at Christos's apartment. Neither the detective nor Father Charles had called ahead, so we were fortunate to find Christos there and not off somewhere on business.

"Come in," he called from his study. "I'll be out in a minute."

Pagona eyed us with her usual suspicious scowl, as Miss Alma turned off the television and gathered up the playing cards. Maybe Pagona just didn't like her game interrupted, I thought. Or maybe she realized that her little game was up.

Christos joined us quickly, a subtle question on his smiling face. "And what have you brought me, Father?" he asked, gesturing to the bundle Father Charles had wrapped in an old *St. Petersburg Times*. Pagona gasped and crossed herself, and Christos's smile faded as the priest peeled the paper back.

"I don't understand. What have you done to my icon?" Christos reached for the frame, but Father Charles pushed his hand away.

"We know how the coin was brought into the country," Nick said, pointing to the icon. "The problem is, it's still missing."

Father Charles took over the explanation then, including Pagona as he described the morning's events in brisk Greek. I gave Miss Alma a rough translation, all the while keeping an eye on Pagona. She seemed as shocked as her son did.

Nick went straight to the point. "Who had contact with the icon, Christos?"

"Why, only me! I commissioned it, and I picked it up myself from the artist."

"Was it ready to be shipped?"

"No. I had that done. Eva took it . . ." Christos laid his hand on the back of a nearby chair. His jaws came together, and his lips pressed into a thin line. "Eva," he whispered under his breath. He strode into his study and picked up the telephone, punched a single number and waited, tapping impatiently on the top of his desk.

## Chapter Twenty-Three

"Find her," Christos said and slammed the phone back into its cradle. He rubbed his face with his broad hand, rapped once on the desk and stalked back to us.

"Eva took the icon to be crated for shipment. She offered to do it. I would have sent Xanthe with it, but Eva said she was going that way. She and I were the only ones who touched it."

When the phone rang, we all jumped. "Did you try her apartment? No, never mind. I'll go over there myself." He slammed the phone down again and returned to the living room.

"Ms. Paradissis has not been seen this morning, but her phone is busy. Sometimes she works out of her apartment. I'm going to go get her."

"Wait," Miss Alma said hurriedly and turned to me. "Julia, why don't you go get Eva? I imagine Mr. Kyriakidis has questions he'd like to ask Father Charles—and the detective, when he arrives. He's very upset," she added sotto voce. "Heaven knows what he might do. Take Nick with you, in case she tries something."

Eva did not answer her door. Inside, her clock radio blared, just as it had the morning before. I glanced at my watch. It was 11:45. "Surely she's not still asleep," I said to Nick.

"With all that noise? How could she be?" We knocked—in fact, we pounded—on the door again. "Eva? *Anixe tin porta, se parakalo*," Nick said. "Open the door."

No answer was forthcoming. We stood there for a moment, trying to decide what to do. Nick pushed on the door and quickly determined that TV detectives notwithstanding, he could not kick it in.

"You know, if she's not in there, we'd have a chance to search for the coin," I said.

"Let the police do that, Julia."

"But the police will have to get a warrant. In the meantime, she'll move it. It's not like moving a piano or something. She'll just put it in her purse and walk out with it. By the time the cops have a warrant, that coin will be long gone."

It made sense. Even Nick had to agree with that. But it didn't make getting the door open any easier.

"I suppose one of us will have to go back to Christos's apartment and have him call security," Nick said reluctantly. I knew he was thinking about the promise he'd made to Manolis. If security got there first, he could never swear that Christos hadn't engineered a cover-up.

"There may be another way," I said.

"What?"

I pointed over Nick's shoulder. Lucy Wharton was coming down the hall, her face downcast. She blew on her bangs and squared her shoulders, stopping in front of Eva's door.

"How are things going, Lucy?" I asked. "Still having trouble with the computer?"

At that, tears welled up in her eyes. "She thinks it was my fault. They've already told me—she's going to give me the axe today."

"I'm sorry?"

Lucy jutted her chin toward Eva's door. "Ms. Paradissis. It wasn't my fault. I was just checking in a guest and suddenly the screen went blank. The programmer spent all day trying to retrieve the data. He thinks my terminal caused it. We had a nine o'clock appointment, but she didn't show."

Ah, what was that knocking I heard? Could it be opportunity? "I don't think you have to worry about Ms. Paradissis, Lucy. She's going to be too busy trying to hold onto her own job to think about yours. That is, if you just go back to the desk and wait."

Interest quickened on the girl's face. "Really? Are you sure?"

I smiled. "Very sure."

"Oh, thank you! That's the best news I've had all . . . well, in a long time. I didn't know what I was going to do—getting fired from my first job. How was that going to look on my resume?" She rocked up on her toes and down again. "Thank you so much for telling me. I'm not even going to go in there. I'm going to go back to the desk—"

Lucy stopped, tugged at her suit jacket, trying to assume a more managerial demeanor. "Is your room comfortable? Can I do anything for you?"

"As a matter of fact, there is something you could do to help us. You see, I left something in her apartment last night . . ."

We waited until Lucy had hurried away down the hall, tucking her master key back into her pocket, before Nick pushed the door open, grabbed my hand and pulled me inside. The bedroom was cold, the air conditioning turned way too high for my comfort. And it was dark. It took my eyes a minute to adjust.

"*Panaghia mou,*" Nick said.

"What?"

He pointed wordlessly at the body of Eva Paradissis, draped diagonally across her bed.

At first I thought she'd just overslept, like the day before. I reached for her wrist, gasped and dropped her cold, stiff hand.

"Don't touch anything," Nick said. He snagged a tissue from a box on the bedside table, picked up the telephone, which dangled off the cradle, and tapped the button a couple of times. When he had a dial tone, he punched in the hotel operator. In a minute, he had Christos on the line. Detective Fallon had not yet arrived.

"I imagine he's already on the way, but you'd better call, just in case," he said. "Eva is dead."

She still wore work clothes—a navy-blue knit dress, topped by a matching short jacket, and low-heeled, navy-leather pumps. She'd never changed for bed, I realized. She hadn't even taken her shoes off.

She'd had such a lovely golden complexion in life. Now her skin was bluish white. Her features were composed as if in sleep, but her eyes seemed oddly flat. A large, empty wineglass lay on the floor beside her bed. I couldn't see a stain on the carpet. She must have finished off the wine, become sleepy and dropped the glass.

Christos was at the door almost before Nick could hang up the phone. "How?" he demanded.

Nick pointed to a bottle of *Mavrodaphne* on the table and a small, flat box with a prescription label taped to the top of it. "It looks like suicide."

"*Ohee.* Not Eva. Never."

I eased around the bed to get a better look at the box. The prescription was in Greek. "Nick, what does this say?"

He studied the box, leaning over close to read the label without handling it. "It's a sleeping pill. It says to take for sleeplessness as needed."

Eva had intimated that she sometimes took sleep aids, which explained why it had been so hard to wake her up the morning before. She'd been drugged. And this time, I wasn't able to wake her up at all. "What's the pharmaceutical name?"

Nick translated it as best he could. It was nothing I'd ever heard of, but whatever it was, it was strong, and apparently deadly when mixed with alcohol.

"Where is she?" Father Charles gasped and leaned against the door jamb. His stole dangled from his arm, and he held a prayer book in his hand. He must have run back to the Jeep before coming to the apartment. The exertion was almost too much for the old man.

"Slow down, Father. There isn't anything you can do for her now anyway." Nick pointed to the body. "She's been dead for a while."

Father Charles moved slowly across the room, his hand on his chest as if to still his overworked heart. He dropped his stole over his shoulders, blessed himself, and began to intone the *Trisagion* for the dead. We crossed ourselves and stood respectfully by while the priest completed the rite.

"Mr. Kyriakidis?" Detective Fallon stood in the doorway to the hall. Behind him waited a uniformed cop. "I'll need all of you to step back out into the hall. Try to follow the same route you came in, please."

We tiptoed back across the carpeting, as if we could really follow our own invisible tracks. When we got to the hall, the uniformed officer pulled the door closed behind us and took up a sentry's stance.

"Let's go back to your apartment, Mr. Kyriakidis," Fallon continued, ushering us down the corridor toward the family quarters. "I've radioed for the crime-scene team and the medical examiner. Did any of you touch anything?"

Nick explained that he had touched the telephone, using a tissue, and that I had touched the dead woman's wrist to take a pulse. Fallon turned to me expectantly. I shook my head.

"She's pretty cold. And her arm is . . . stiff. I think she committed suicide, or maybe it was an accident."

"Why?"

"Because there's an empty bottle of wine on the table in there, and a sleeping-pill prescription. I know she took the pills. I don't know how regularly."

"Did you handle the box?" We each shook our heads. "Did you say the phone was off the hook?"

As a matter of fact, it was. Odd, I thought. Who had Eva been calling? Had she reached them? She might have realized what she'd done and been calling someone for help. How sad to have come so close.

"I think," Nick said, "You might want to tell your people to be watching for a gold coin when they go through her things."

By the time we got to the family quarters, Christos had explained that only he and Eva had had access to the icon. "I'm afraid she was in league with Miss Saros all along."

Fallon grabbed the phone and ordered someone to pick up Xanthe at the motel and bring her to us, then returned to Eva's apartment to wait for the crime-scene team. Poor Xanthe, I thought. She'd just gotten out of jail and now this—her only friend dead. And in spite of the fact that it was now obvious to me that Eva had set her up, Xanthe would probably remember only that Eva had helped her pick out her clothes and taken her out for a drink.

———

Before the uniformed officer showed up with Xanthe, we'd all been over our stories with Detective Fallon several times, interviewed independently in Christos's study. When Xanthe arrived, her face was puffy and tear-stained. She cast me a desperate, frightened glance before she was escorted into Christos's study and the door closed firmly behind her.

"Shouldn't they call an attorney?" I said to Nick.

But before he could answer, the uniformed cop intervened. "It's routine questioning, ma'am. The detective will call one if she asks him to, but it's not really necessary at this point."

I wasn't so sure about that, but other than Nick and Miss Alma, I had no allies in the room when it came to Xanthe. And even Nick was in question. Father Charles had been interrogated and permitted to leave so that he could meet the bishop's plane. Christos had accompanied his mother to her bedroom, insisting that she rest after the shock of Eva's death, although I didn't think she seemed particularly upset by it. He had not yet returned. Alex had seen the crime-scene van and the legion of police cars and had come hurrying down to the apartment. Stunned by the news, he shook his head grimly.

"Eva and I didn't always agree about how to run our American operation, but I'm sorry to hear about this. I've never understood what would drive a person to take his own life. She didn't seem depressed."

"But she did have trouble sleeping," I said. "She told me so herself."

Alex poked his hands into his pockets and pursed his lips. "Eva was a complex person. She was very good at her job. In spite of the fact that my father calls her his secretary, she was much more than that. She did a lot of the advance work for the hotel. She was a woman with great drive."

"Did she have anyone special in her life?" I asked.

"Not that I know of. She dated occasionally, I think. But

it was always hard to tell if Eva's dates were . . . dates, or whether she had some sort of business agenda. And she was a private person. All business with me."

There was so much about her we didn't know. Even Christos and Alex seemed unaware of her private life. There could have been an unhappy love affair, I thought, and no one would have known about it. But if that were the case, there might have been signs of depression.

"None that I noticed," Alex said, "but we didn't spend that much time together. She was a liaison of sorts—between the operation here and in Greece. She traveled back and forth quite a bit."

And yet, the personnel in the hotel knew her quite well and were afraid of her. I'd seen her in the kitchen on New Year's Eve consulting with the chefs, and again, several days later, talking to a cook. It didn't seem like liaison work. It seemed more like hotel management, which was, as I understood it, basically Alex's job.

"Yes, she had a way of involving herself in hotel matters," he admitted. "It was a source of friction between us at times. My father's plan is to hire a general manager for the hotel so that I can move on to run the American operation as it grows. I don't know, maybe she was hoping for the job, although it doesn't much seem like her style, getting into the gritty, hands-on side of management. Eva liked to handle the bigger things—financial transactions, real estate, and vendor contracts. And I have to admit that she was pretty good."

My picture of Eva Paradissis was beginning to come into focus around the edges. I doubted very much that she fit the profile of a suicide—she was too intelligent, competent, and ambitious for that. Which left us with accidental death.

"What do you think she wanted with the coin?" Nick asked Alex. "Did she need money?"

"I don't think so. She made a good . . . in fact, a very

good salary. Her travel was paid for by the company, and her living expenses in Greece were much lower than they would have been here. Besides, she had her apartment here in the hotel as a fringe benefit of the job. Unless she was spending lavishly, she couldn't have needed money."

"Unless she was a collector," I said. "Of antiquities, I mean. That would explain the coin, don't you think? Maybe she saw it and just had to have it. Collectors can be like that, you know." Still, it didn't fit my profile of Eva. I shrugged. "Maybe Xanthe will know more."

Unfortunately, she did not. She slumped into a chair in the living room. "I do not remember the name of the law-yer—the one the judge gave me. It is written down in my motel room, but I did not think to bring it."

"Did Detective Fallon ask you many questions?"

"Only about Eva. What I knew about her. He said he would want to question me again, but I would have to call the lawyer first. He says he he is waiting until they finish with her . . . with her body and her rooms. I am to wait out here."

In the background, a phone rang once, picked up sharply before it could ring again. Christos rejoined us in the living room with only a curt nod for Xanthe. In a moment, De-tective Fallon appeared in the doorway.

"I can give you a little information now," Fallon said. "That call was from the medical examiner's office. As you said, Mr. Lambros, the prescription was for a sleep aid. A local pharmacist—a Greek—translated it for us. The drug was . . ."

Fallon broke off, glancing down at a scrap of paper in his hand. "Flu-ni-tra-ze-pam," he pronounced carefully. "That's the generic. The trade name is Rohypnol." He looked up at each of us, studying our reaction to the name. At length, he continued. "We have someone checking with the doctor in Greece now, validating the prescription."

"Can you tell us something about this drug?" Christos asked. "Could it have killed her?"

"In large doses, or mixed with alcohol, yes. Rohypnol is not legal in the United States. It's a Schedule Three drug with the DEA, but it's being reevaluated because of recent abuses. It's brought in from Mexico and sold on the streets to enhance other drug and alcohol highs. It is legal in Europe, however.

"Ms. Paradissis obviously brought the drug in from Greece for her personal use. She must not have been aware of the dangers of mixing it with alcohol. The wine bottle was empty, suggesting that she consumed quite a lot. The ME has given us a preliminary fix on the time of death—somewhere shortly after midnight. We won't know if she actually took the drug until the toxicology report comes in, but we'll be able to rule out other causes after a full autopsy. For the moment, we're treating it as an accidental death.

"Her death does not, however, solve the theft of the coin," Fallon reminded us, his gaze going directly to Xanthe. "It has not been found in the apartment. But," he continued, turning to Christos, "there are some other personal effects I'd like you to look at. An officer will bring them down. We're going to seal the apartment until the results of the inquest are final."

"I understand," Christos said.

It must have been disconcerting for him—his beautiful new hotel marred by police seals—but it could have been much worse. At least the family quarters and Eva's apartment were on a closed wing, with secluded, private entrances. His guests would not be constantly reminded of the cloud of death that hovered over the place.

It wasn't long before a uniformed officer appeared at the door. He carried a brown suede briefcase in one hand and a slightly smaller cosmetic case in the other. "Some of her personal effects, sir."

Fallon nodded and brought the cases into the room, dismissing the officer to return to the apartment. He set the briefcase on the table in the dining area and motioned for Christos to join him. Together, they opened the briefcase.

"Nick, Julia," Miss Alma whispered. "Have you heard of that drug? Rohypnol?"

"No," I said hesitantly. "I don't think so. Why?"

"Because they featured it on one of those news magazine shows—*Dateline,* or *Twenty/Twenty.* I saw the program. I'm sure it's the same one. That's the drug they call the 'date-rape' drug. There's been a lot of publicity about it lately."

Nick snapped his fingers. "Yes, I—"

"What are these?" Christos asked in a perplexed voice. "Alex, come here, please." He shoved a folder of papers at his son. "Have you ever seen these?"

Alex thumbed though the folder. "No. Where did they come from?"

"They were in the briefcase," Christos said. "They're some kind of aerial photographs of the coastline. Look," he said, pointing at one of the pictures. "Do you recognize that?"

"It looks like the causeway to Clearwater, maybe."

Fallon peered over his shoulder and nodded, indicating a spot on the photograph. "Yes. That's the Bay Bridge there. You see, here's the airport, just to the south."

"Is this something you're working on?" Christos asked his son.

"No. I don't know where these came from."

There were, apparently, other aerial photographs in the file. Alex couldn't identify them, but Fallon recognized at least one as just south of Panama City.

"Port St. Joe?" Alex suggested. "We did some preliminary research there, but it's one of the last on our development schedule. St. Augustine, Miami, and Key West are at the top. But Eva thought they were overbuilt. She was pushing for the panhandle."

"So you didn't commission these photographs, Mr. Kyriakidis?" Each man shook his head.

Fallon pulled a bundle of documents out of the briefcase, thumbed them quickly and handed them to Alex. "Site surveys. Same areas, looks like. I suppose you didn't commission these either?

"Eva must have done this independently," Alex said, shaking his head. "I wonder why."

*Chapter Twenty-Four*

Eva's effects did not include her clothing, which would take more time to search. Fallon's immediate concern was locating her next of kin, but the remaining papers in her briefcase revealed nothing, and the cosmetic case was filled with drugs from her medicine cabinet, makeup, and a few personal bills. If Fallon learned anything from them, he didn't share it with us.

"I'm afraid I do not know very much about Eva's family," Christos said. "She came from Salonika. I suppose we should begin trying to find the family there. Perhaps Miss Saros knows more?"

Xanthe did not. Christos agreed to undertake the search and called his Athens office to put someone on it right away. Detective Fallon packed up the remaining effects and, after setting them aside, turned to Xanthe.

"Ms. Saros, I would like you to contact your attorney immediately. I will want to see you, with your lawyer, in my office at nine o'clock tomorrow morning for further questioning."

Xanthe calmly agreed to be there, but her glance to me suggested that she was barely holding on. I took her hand and squeezed it gently.

"I may have additional questions for the rest of you," Fallon said. "You'll need to stay available. Please don't leave Pinellas County without contacting my office first."

Once we were dismissed, Nick, Miss Alma, Xanthe, and I returned to our room. We were greeted by a muffled woof—Jack, slaking his thirst in the bidet. I made coffee while Nick called room service and ordered sandwiches. It was mid-afternoon. I hadn't realized how hungry I was.

Xanthe sat on the floor playing ball with Jack. She laughed out loud as he spat his ball in her lap, lunged onto her knees and covered her face with kisses. How nice to hear the girl laugh. When she'd been in the company of Pagona, I'd seen only an occasional bittersweet smile, and there had been nothing for her to laugh about in the last few days. She needed the release.

When the sandwiches arrived, we spread out a picnic of sorts on the bed. Spiros came in soon afterward. Word of Eva's death had already reached *O Kritikos*.

"*Po, po, po,*" he said, circling his hand in the air. "Ve-ry bad. Too much bad."

"I have an idea," I said. "I know that we've had an upsetting morning and we're all feeling pretty low, but there's nothing we can do for Eva, and probably nothing we could have done to prevent her death. The Sponge Festival is down on the docks tonight. I think we should all go. We need a lift."

"Oh, I don't know," Xanthe said. "It does not seem right."

Miss Alma reached over to pat the girl's hand. "Julia's right, my dear. None of us could have prevented what happened to Eva. It was a tragic accident. I know she was your friend—"

"I am not so sure of that anymore," Xanthe said quietly.

"I thought Eva was my friend, but . . . I think now she was using me. She must have taken the coin from me that night, but how?"

"Rohypnol," Nick said quietly. He turned to Miss Alma. "You said they call it the 'date-rape' drug?"

"Yes. When it's dropped into alcohol, it increases the effects. But the worst thing about it is—oh, Nick, I see what you're getting at."

"What?" I asked. "I'm not sure I understand."

"I've been reading about it in the trade magazines. The DEA is cautioning bartenders and restaurateurs to be careful. The drug," Nick explained to us, "not only increases the effects of the alcohol, but it also creates an amnesia effect. That's why it's used for date rapes. The man drops it in the woman's drink. Not only does she get very drunk, but she can't remember much, if anything after that. The effects last a long time—all night and into the next day."

"Which explains why Xanthe can't remember what happened to her that night."

"Exactly."

"And Nick, it probably explains what happened to Eileen Reilly! Someone dropped a—"

"Roofie," Miss Alma supplied with a little shrug. "That's the street name. I heard it on television."

"Okay, a roofie. Someone dropped one in her drink at *O Kritikos*. You said it makes the effects of alcohol worse. That's why she passed out. Nick, do you think we should call Detective Fallon?"

Nick popped the remainder of his sandwich in his mouth and chewed thoughtfully. "No. I think he already knows," he said. "He's just not telling us."

It took little convincing after that to get Xanthe to agree to go to the Sponge Festival with us. Spiros and Miss Alma took her back to The While Away so she could call her attorney and try to arrange the meeting in Fallon's office, while we went on to *O Kritikos* to fill our friends in on what we knew about Eva's death.

Georgia met us at the door of the restaurant. "The police have already been here," she said.

"About Eva?"

Georgia nodded, glanced around and lowered her voice. "They wanted to know—they wanted to know where Manolis was last night. He was at home with me, asleep, of course. But I'm his wife. I don't know if they believed me."

Suspicion confirmed. It was the same drug that had killed Eileen Reilly, and Detective Fallon knew it. And apparently he suspected that Eva's death was not from natural causes.

"Where is Manolis now?" Nick asked.

"He went into Tampa this afternoon to pick up some equipment." A thin smile tightened her lips. "The ice machine's down. We're using bag ice until he gets back with a new compressor. Come, let's sit down." She led us to the family table.

"Was he here when the police came?"

"No. Thank heaven he'd already left. I don't know what he'll do when he finds out they were asking questions about him. He's already falling apart."

I tried to reassure her that Fallon's questions were strictly routine, reminding her that they would have to have physical evidence or a witness to put Manolis in Eva's apartment. But Georgia was not a stupid woman. Both she and I knew that even the rumor could hurt her husband irreparably. Nevertheless, she pretended right along with me.

"Georgia," Nick said, "Manolis said that on the night that Eileen Reilly was killed, there was a man sitting next to her at the bar, and a couple nearby. Could the woman have been Eva?"

Georgia smoothed an imaginary wrinkle in the tablecloth,

studying the fibers as though trying to determine the warp from the woof. "I don't think so. Manolis would have recognized her and mentioned it. He would have remembered, I'm sure."

"Did he know her that well?"

"She came in here every once in a while," Georgia said. "Sometimes just for a drink, sometimes for dinner."

"Did you talk?" I asked. "Did she seem depressed or anything?"

"No. But we didn't talk much. She didn't encourage it. Polite conversation—that's about all."

So Georgia had little to add to our picture of Eva. But there were questions that nagged at us persistently. If Eva had drugged Xanthe, as Nick and I were now sure she had, then she did know about mixing alcohol with flunitrazepam. Georgia could have been wrong. Manolis might not have remembered that she was in the bar that night. If Eva had been sitting near Eileen Reilly, she could have easily dropped a pill in the girl's drink. In fact, I was sure she had. But why?

And why would she commit suicide? And who had she tried to call? And what had she wanted with the coin? And where was the coin now? And if she had drugged Xanthe and taken the coin, how was it that she'd managed to get to the theater on time? And where was Xanthe all the time that Eva was entertaining Christos's business associates and attending the theater? And . . . and . . . and . . . I rubbed my forehead with frustration. Too many questions. And the only one who had the answers was dead.

By the time we met the rest of our group at the Sponge Docks, Xanthe seemed considerably cheered. She had changed into her wrap dress and brushed her thick hair out around her shoulders. It was quite a pretty effect.

"Her attorney seems like a nice young man," Miss Alma said. "I spoke to him myself. It was easier for me to explain everything that's happened than for her. He's meeting her in the morning at Detective Fallon's office. I think some of us should go with her, though, just to give her moral support."

I agreed. With the bishop in town, Father Charles would not be available to help her, which left only us. Xanthe's spirits were better, but I knew it would take little to send them plunging again. The case against her was by no means closed. In fact, unless we could prove our theory about Eva, it might actually be worse. Xanthe had been bonded out before Eva died.

Miss Alma and Spiros guided Xanthe along the street, pointing out the little boats anchored at the docks and the strings of sponges waiting to be cleaned. Spiros regaled them with a story—half in Greek and half in broken English—of his days as a merchant seaman. Xanthe giggled, her laughter tinkling like a glass bell.

Nick and I followed them, hand in hand. "What's bothering me is what happened after she was drugged," I said. "Christos says that Eva met him at Dora Stratou as scheduled. His chauffeur picked her up and delivered her. Of course, Xanthe could have gotten the time wrong. There might have been time for Eva to get the coin."

"But she didn't do that in the bar, Julia. Too many witnesses."

"Well, maybe she did it in the limo. It should be easy enough to find out from the driver whether Xanthe was in the limo with Eva."

"Right. I doubt if Christos is going to be willing to check up on it, but maybe Xanthe's attorney can find out. If he can reach the driver, that is."

We agreed that we would have to go with her in the morning and decided to set the matter aside until then.

There was no point in belaboring it and ruining everyone's evening.

A band had set up on a portable stage, with the little harbor as a backdrop. We stopped to buy *souvlaki* and baklava, then found an empty bench on the sidewalk. Xanthe, Miss Alma, and I crowded onto it, while Nick and Spiros squatted at our feet. The band struck up its first song—"Sittin' on the Dock of the Bay"—which sounded refreshingly American. They launched into a series of oldies—fifties', sixties', and seventies' tunes—while we listened, contentedly licking honey off our fingers.

"I like American music," Xanthe said. "That is why we went to the American bar that night. To listen to the music and watch the dancers. Some of them were very good. There was one—" She stopped and frowned, staring off into the middle distance.

"What is it, Xanthe?" I asked.

"I . . . I'm not sure. A little picture in my mind. A man. He was dancing, and then . . ." She shrugged. "I don't know. Oh, let's not think anymore about it tonight. I'm having so much fun."

"*Ella*, Xanthe. *Pame*," Spiros said, pulling her to her feet. "We dance."

In spite of the fact that no one else was dancing, Xanthe allowed herself to be wrapped in Spiros's muscular arms and whirled around the docks to "Wake Up, Little Susie." Spiros is not an especially accomplished dancer, but he makes up for it with tremendous enthusiasm and soon had her doubled over laughing.

Miss Alma smiled at him affectionately before turning to us with a nod. "Go on, you two," she said. "Show them how it's done." Which was all the encouragement Nick needed.

"The movie wasn't so hot. It didn't have much of a plot . . ."

Nick swung me across the sidewalk and twirled me under his arm. By the time the music ended, Xanthe and I were breathless. "Whew! I need to sit—"

A hand clamped over my arm. Beside me, Xanthe seemed to sway, rubbed her forehead and glanced back up at the spectators. "Xanthe?" I said. "Are you all—"

"The song . . . wake up . . . that man," she whispered, pointing into the audience. "He . . . he was there that night in Athens. He spoke to me."

"Which man? Who?"

"That one. Look, he's leaving. Wait!" she cried, staggering into the crowd.

Reacting to the urgency in Xanthe's voice, Nick and Spiros tore out after them. "What is it?" Miss Alma asked, scrambling up from the bench.

"I'm not sure. Something about a man in the audience." I watched Nick's back, torn between trying to follow him and staying with Miss Alma.

"You go. I'll catch up later," she said.

By the time I broke through the crowd, Nick and Spiros were in hot pursuit of a tall slender man in a black leather jacket. Xanthe had stopped in the street to catch her breath. I ran up beside her. After the dancing, neither of us could keep pace with the men.

"Xanthe, what's going on?"

"That man . . . the American bar . . . I danced with him to that same song. I remember now. The black jacket."

There must be millions of black leather jackets in the world, I thought. James Dean and Elvis are still cultural icons. What were the chances that the same man would be here, halfway across the world from Athens, in Tarpon Springs? Unless he was here for a reason, like to collect a coin.

"Come on," I said, grabbing Xanthe's hand. "Let's go."

Nick and Spiros wound in and out of the crowds on the

street. I could barely see the crown of Spiros's black fisherman's cap as his tall frame receded in the distance. Nick was lost to view completely. Xanthe and I stumbled along in their general direction until we reached the end of Dodecanese Boulevard. Ahead of us stretched the river, but there was no sign of Nick or Spiros. We stood there panting, trying to catch our breath and decide which way to turn. Finally, we chose the shorter street, to our right, and ran head-on into the men.

Spiros had the young man's right arm in a hammerlock. Nick flanked them on the left, his hand squeezing the trapezius muscle in the young man's shoulder. The man was twenty-five at most—tall and slender, his narrow frame emphasized by the tapering waist of his jacket. His legs stretched as long as Spiros's, but they were thinner, and heightened by a pair of black boots with a stout heel. He tried once to squirm away but crumpled in pain as both men increased the pressure under their hands. Xanthe stopped in the middle of the street, staring at him as though she was trying to bring his face into focus.

"Is that him?" I asked her as Nick and Spiros propelled him forward.

"Yes. That is him," she said quietly. "His name . . . I remember it now. It is Theo." Theo said nothing.

"*Eise o Theos?*" Nick asked him. He didn't answer.

"*Endaxi,*" Nick said. "We can play that game if you want to." He patted down the young man's body, jerked up one leg of his jeans and extracted a vicious looking knife in a leather sheath from the top of Theo's boot.

"Ugly," Nick said, passing the knife to Spiros. A further search revealed no other weapons.

"Now, let's find out who you are." Nick peeled back the lapels of the jacket and reached inside. "Kind of hot for leather, isn't it? Ah, here we are."

He produced two small booklets, opening the first with

a snap before passing it on to me. It was an American passport, the photo a much younger version of the man before us. His name, it said, was Theodore Paras, of Chicago, Illinois.

The second booklet had a blue cover embossed in gold. Nick studied the seal on the front. "Right country," he said, leafing through it. When he handed me the passport, his eyes were twinkling.

The picture was a good likeness—leather jacket and a white T-shirt showing at the neck. His jaw was strong and prominent, thrust slightly forward. His eyes were as black as puddles of motorcycle oil, and a lock of black hair draped artfully over his forehead. The name was written in Greek, but I had no trouble deciphering it.

Theodoros Paradissis.

*Chapter Twenty-Five*

Miss Alma joined us just as we were escorting Theo Paradissis down to the river, to the privacy of an abandoned bait shack. I upended a wooden crate for her and another for Theo. Nick shoved one box under a broken window, where the halogen lamps along the harbor spilled orange light into the shack.

Spiros pushed Theo down on the box and withdrew the knife from its sheath, holding it an inch from the young man's jugular vein. Not for nothing had Spiros survived as a merchant seaman. He reminded me of the ancient volcano of Thera—his rage on the brink of eruption. The knife shook in his hand, causing the blade to graze the young man's neck. Theo edged away, glancing nervously over his shoulder. Spiros clapped his big hand on Theo's shoulder and pulled him back. Miss Alma moved her crate next to Spiros and placed a restraining hand on his arm.

"Please," she said. "It will be all right, my friend." Spiros loosened his grip and pulled back a fraction, nodding his head at Nick.

"All right, Theo," Nick said in Greek. "We know you were at the American bar in Athens the night that this young lady——" he gestured to Xanthe, who studied the young man closely "——was there. You danced with her."

"I don't remember. I dance with a lot of girls."

"I'm sure you do," I said in English. "They probably like that macho American look."

"Why were you there?" Nick asked.

Theo shrugged a la James Dean. "To drink. To dance. To have a good time."

"To help your sister steal the Helios coin," Nick added.

"My sister?"

"Eva Paradissis."

"I don't have a sister," Spiros moved the point of the knife an iota closer to Theo's neck. "I don't have a sister," Theo repeated.

"Then I don't suppose it will matter to you."

"*Ti?*" Theo said sullenly.

"What has happened to Eva."

His head came up sharply, his dark glance moving from one face to another. Then he smiled, as though he were on to Nick's trick. "I told you before, I don't have a sister."

Theo stubbornly clung to his story, even with the knife blade perilously close to the four-o'clock shadow on his jaw. He was at the bar dancing. He didn't have a sister. He didn't remember Xanthe. He didn't believe that Eva was dead, in spite of the fact that Nick's description of her demise was straightforward, if not brutal. Nothing moved him, until Miss Alma took over.

"Theodore," Miss Alma said in her teacher voice, "I want you to listen to me. This young woman is in trouble, and her friends are going to rescue her, no matter what they have to do to you." She cast a meaningful glance at Spiros.

"I don't know what this is all about," Theo said in lightly accented English.

"Yes you do. And I'm afraid they're telling you the truth.

Your sister is dead. She ingested a drug—the same drug she put in Xanthe's drink the night you stole the coin—and she drank too much wine. Her heart stopped. She was found this morning in her apartment."

Silence.

"Eva tried to call someone last night. She must have realized what had happened—that she'd taken too many sleeping pills—but it was too late. The hotel keeps records of phone calls. There will be records of your number, of other calls she made to you." The silence stretched on, broken only by the creak of his leather jacket as he slumped on the crate.

"Was she frightened, Theo? Was she worried? You knew her better than anyone else. Why would she take her own life?"

"She wouldn't!" He jumped up, pushing away the knife and overturning the crate, and paced the dirt floor of the shack. "I don't believe you. Eva would never commit suicide!"

"I'm sorry, Theo, but she did take her own life. She knew she couldn't mix those pills with wine, but she did it anyway. Why?"

"Eva isn't dead." He swallowed back a sob. "I don't believe you." But even as he said it, we knew that he finally did. We were not trying to trick him. Something had gone terribly wrong. Theo Paradissis began to cry.

We escorted Theo back to the *Mediterraneo*, where we could talk comfortably. When we'd gathered in our room, Nick poured him a stiff ouzo, hoping to oil his tongue. There were still so many unanswered questions.

"We had set it up that I would meet them at the American bar. Eva knew that she liked it." Theo gestured at Xanthe, who dropped her head. He sat forward, elbowing his knees. Spiros had put the knife away. We didn't think Theo would need any further coaxing.

"Eva would signal me when it was time to ask her to dance. She put a pill—maybe two—in the girl's brandy and waited a little while. Then she got up and went to the rest room. That was the signal. While she was gone, I asked the girl to dance. She was already getting drunk, but I guess it was a little too soon, because she wasn't supposed to remember me at all."

"And then?"

"I took the girl back to the table. Eva said she had to go. I waited a few minutes after Eva left and then I got her up to dance again. By that time, she was pretty far gone. She left with me."

"Where did you go?"

"I took her to my apartment. She fell asleep there while I replaced the coin. I put the necklace back in her purse, called a cab and took her home. I made sure she got into the apartment, and then I left."

"So what have you done with the coin?"

"Nothing. I gave it to my sister. She was going to smuggle it into the U.S. She knew someone who was going to fence it for her. I came here to collect the money. Eva was afraid to carry it, and she didn't want to wire-transfer and leave a paper trail."

I found myself leaning forward as Nick moved in on what we really wanted to know. "Who was going to fence it?"

Theo looked at us blankly. "I don't know."

Spiros retrieved the knife and returned it to its original position. Theo pressed his hand to his chest. "I'm telling you the truth."

"But why? Why did she want the coin in the first place?" I asked.

Theo's expression clouded over like the liquor in his glass. "You would have to understand my sister." He swallowed a sip of ouzo, closed his eyes and laid his head back against the chair. "We moved here, to Chicago, from Salonika when I was four. Eva was about ten, I suppose. Her adjustment was much harder than mine. Our clothes were different, and we didn't speak the language. Eva came home from school crying every day. I guess the other girls made fun of her."

What a traumatic time to move, I thought. Middle-school girls have all the sensitivity of serial killers. I could only begin to imagine how Eva might have been treated.

"My father had come to America with money to open his own business. He was a plumber, and very good at his job, but he was no businessman. He didn't understand American ways of business—unions and contracts."

Theo laughed bitterly and shook his head. "He thought Chicago was all Greek! He lasted a little while—long enough to get citizenship. He even changed our name, to make it more American. By the time he had lost all his money, and our house, Eva had finally found a way to fit in. She baby-sat and saved every penny. She bought the right clothes and learned to speak English perfectly. For me, it didn't matter so much, but for Eva, fitting in was everything."

Theo rose, took the ouzo bottle off the table and poured himself another shot. We watched as he went to the sink and topped it off with water, returned to his chair and knocked back a large gulp.

"She was bitter. My father had lost everything. She was in high school by then, and everyone knew about his failure. They either ignored her or made cracks about her. In the end, we had to go back to Salonika. I have thought about it all many times," Theo said. "My father's failure left a deep scar on Eva."

Eva's background explained a lot—her impeccable taste in clothes, her perfect English. It even explained her business sense—as if she could somehow vindicate her father, or herself, by becoming a tough, successful businesswoman. No wonder she didn't want to be referred to as a secretary.

"Eva had one goal in life—to succeed," Theo said. "She wanted money, of course. But she made a good salary—enough to buy expensive clothes and shoes, and to make a few investments. She had promised me money from the sale of the coin if I'd help her."

"But why would she jeopardize her job by stealing the coin?"

Theo smiled, acknowledging the cunning of his sister's plan. "Eva wanted to run the American operation of the Kyriakidis hotels."

"Ah, but that's Alex's job," Nick said, filling in the rest of the story. "So she thought that if she broke up the engagement, Alex would go back to Greece. Right?"

Theo nodded. "Eva was sure that Alex was moving in the wrong direction—going into the places that were already developed instead of buying cheaply and building up a resort area. She couldn't make him see that, and he'd refused to deal with the broker who could make it happen."

Nick's head snapped around to stare at me. We were on the same train of thought, and it was an express.

"So your sister was responsible for the other things too, then," Miss Alma said. "The needle in the bread, and that horrid gift—"

Theo nipped at a hangnail with his teeth and spat it off his tongue. "Eva didn't believe in all that stuff, but she knew the old lady did. She paid off a gypsy in Athens to scare her, and when that didn't work, she thought of the coin. It was supposed to be more bad luck, and she thought that even Christos might take it seriously. She was trying to apply pressure from all sides."

"Would that include Manolis's business? *O Kritikos?*" I asked.

Theo looked away. "I don't know anything about that. I just know she wanted to scare the old lady."

"So you were helping her," Nick said. "And you are the famous Aristotle Onassis."

"I don't know what you're talking about."

"The UPS clerk will be able to identify you, Theo. You'd be better off to tell us the truth now."

Theo plucked at his sleeves, sat forward and shot the cuffs of his leather jacket. "Yeah, okay, I mailed it. I killed the bird for her and we put the *maya* together in my motel room. It's no big deal—just a lot of superstitious voodoo."

"But a fifteen-thousand-dollar coin in a very big deal," Nick said. "This hasn't proven to be too profitable for you, has it? You come all the way over here to collect your cash and now you don't know who has the coin? Somehow, Theo, I just don't believe that."

"I swear it's true. Eva was handling it, and she was always very careful. She didn't think I needed to know, and I didn't care as long as I got my part."

Theo got up and paced in front of the French doors. He opened and closed his fists, as if ready to lash out at someone. I didn't want that someone to be Nick. Spiros stood up too, moving over to the bar to lean against the wall, within striking distance of Theo. He poured a little more ouzo into Theo's empty glass and handed it to him.

"Eva dead," Theo said. "How will I tell my father? He never forgave himself for what she went through as a kid. It wasn't his fault. He didn't know any better. But he never got over it."

"Suicide makes people feel so guilty," I offered.

Theo smacked his glass down on the table, sloshing the liqueur all over the backgammon board. "Don't you understand? Eva would not commit suicide! She was a fighter, not a quitter." He threw himself back in the chair and chewed on a knuckle. "You don't understand her at all."

But I thought we did—every one of us. We just didn't want to give voice to the unspeakable. If it wasn't an accident, and if it wasn't suicide, then Eva's death had to have been murder.

## Chapter Twenty-Six

Theo spent the night in Spiros's room, with the big cook sitting guard at the door. Theo was, after all, an accessory to the theft and although he had promised to spill the whole story to Detective Fallon in the morning, we couldn't take the chance that he'd have a change of heart in the night and disappear. He was the only person who could clear Xanthe's name. After they'd left, the four of us relaxed and savored our our relief.

"I didn't know you could have two passports," I commented to Nick.

"Greece recognizes dual citizenship, Julia. When . . . if . . . I become an American citizen, Greece won't revoke my citizenship. If Greece should go to war, I'll still be responsible to serve for my country." A disquieting piece of information, with the Balkans in turmoil.

"But why would he want to be an American citizen if he lives in Greece?"

"There could be many reasons. In case he ever comes back and wants work here, maybe."

"Yes!" Xanthe sat forward, her expression bright but somehow distant. "That's it. He has a job—here, in Tarpon Springs. I knew I'd seen him before. He works . . . he's a busboy at *O Kritikos*. I saw him the night I met you. He came out to the bar to get a drink."

Nick, Miss Alma, and I stared at the girl. So much had been locked inside her head, and the key to opening it had been a song, "Wake Up, Little Susie." The irony was not lost on me.

"What should we do?" I asked.

Nick stroked Jack's ears thoughtfully. "We can't let him know that we know or he might not admit anything to Fallon tomorrow. We wait, and when he's told his story, we'll confront him with the rest." We all agreed that it seemed like the best plan. Then Nick moved on to the next topic of conversation.

"So Eva was dealing with Aris. Alex didn't want to do business with him, because of his relationship with Manolis. But if Alex left, Eva would have had the freedom to deal openly with Aris Mavrakis."

"And it would be in Aris's best interests to help her in any way he could," I said, following Nick's logic. "Like, for example, fencing the coin."

"You know," Miss Alma said, "he knows more about antiquities than you might think. We discussed them at length on New Year's Eve. He was very knowledgeable. He might have wanted the coin for himself, or he might know a buyer."

Nick didn't think that Aris would keep the coin himself. "He's a coward. He's been operating a very clever smear campaign against Manolis—acting as if he was trying to discredit rumors about *O Kritikos*, when all he was really doing was starting the rumors himself. He probably had Eva drug Eileen Reilly. He wouldn't keep the coin now, knowing it's tied to a murder."

"How would he know it was murder, unless he killed Eva himself?"

Nick frowned. "Good point. But why would he do that? She was his trip to success."

242

"His ticket."

"Whatever. But I do think he has the coin."

"Well, okay. How did he get it? Wouldn't they be careful not to be seen together?"

"I think that's rather obvious," Miss Alma said. "She put it in his bread."

"Of course," I said. "The *vasilopita*."

It wasn't the first time we'd been in possession of information that the police needed and had been reluctant to give it to them. If we told Detective Fallon about Aris, he would have to get a search warrant, which meant he would have to prove probable cause. But we had no proof whatever that Aris was involved in this scheme—just a set of logical assumptions that might or might not add up for a judge.

And even if Fallon did succeed in getting the warrant, it didn't guarantee they'd find the coin. But it did guarantee that Aris would be tipped off. The coin would disappear. Aris didn't need the money, and he didn't need to be linked to a murder. He'd drop it in the bayou before he'd risk getting caught with it in his possession. The only way to get that coin was to force Aris to reveal himself. But how?

"I believe I know a way," Miss Alma said, and astonished us all as she laid out her plan.


At eight forty-five the next morning, the six of us were sitting in the waiting room of the Tarpon Springs police department. The door to the left of the communications officer's window opened. Detective Fallon scanned the waiting room and, seeing every chair occupied, rolled his eyes.

"I asked to see Ms. Saros and her attorney. Alone. What's going on?"

We dove into our stories, everyone talking at once. Fallon shook his head. "I don't know what this is all about, but I suppose I'm going to have to find out. Let me see if the conference room is free."

He returned in a minute to lead us through the door and down a short hallway remarkable only for its fluorescent glare and its stark cinder-block walls painted a noncommittal yellow. We took our seats around an oval maple table— Xanthe, Miss Alma, and me on one side, and facing us, Nick and Spiros, who flanked Theo in a clear message that he wasn't going anywhere until he told the truth. And maybe not then, I silently added.

Detective Fallon dropped a folder on the table, switched on a tape recorder and fell heavily into a chair. "Miss Saros, I thought I told you to appear with your attorney."

"He is coming, I think," she said. "He should be here soon."

"Don't say a word until he arrives, please. Now," he said, turning to the rest of us, "I would like one of you—*one* of you—to tell me what is going on."

Our glances shifted around the table, all going to Nick. "We know who stole the coin," he said. "And we know where it is. But you're going to need our help to catch the thief with it."

Detective Fallon smirked. "Oh, really?"

Five heads around the table nodded in unison. "Really."


Theo Paradissis told his story with a wary eye on Spiros, who had suggested that there be no alterations or permutations. It was only when he reached the part about removing the coin himself that Fallon sat forward and began to pay close attention. "Wait a minute," he said, pulling a card out of his pocket. "I need to read you your rights. You have the right to remain silent . . ."

I glanced across the table at Nick. "Too late," he mouthed silently. I thought he was probably right. If Theo were to be charged with the theft, a good defense attorney could probably get the case thrown out of court.

When Theo had finished his story—describing how Xanthe had been drugged and the coin replaced with the forgery—Fallon rubbed his face with his hands briskly and stared at his file. "My mother wanted me to be a priest," he muttered.

He picked up the folder, tapped it on the table and laid it back down again. "So you're telling me that your sister delivered the coin to an unknown fence who was going to sell it for her, and you came to Tarpon to pick up your share of the money? Which would have been . . . ?"

Theo shrugged. "Twelve, maybe fourteen thousand."

"And you claim you don't know who the buyer or the fence is?"

"I do not know who they are."

Fallon sat back in his chair, eyeing Theo skeptically. "All right. Assuming for the moment that you're telling me the truth, why have you come forward with this? Why not just get on a plane, or a boat, or a jet ski and get the hell out?"

Theo's expression had all the intensity of his rebel role models. His dark eyes glittered and his lips tightened. "Because," he said, "my sister was murdered."

Fallon picked up his folder and thumbed through it, looking not at the papers inside but at a distant point on the table. At length, he said, "I'll have a statement typed up for you to sign, and you'll be detained until I talk to the DA about jurisdiction. They may just deport you."

"There's something else you might want to discuss with the DA," Nick said. He rested his arm on the back of Theo's chair. "Tell him, Theo. Tell him where you work."

Theo made a move to rise, but Spiros forced him back

in the chair. "What do you mean? What's that got to do with anything?"

"I believe you know very well, Theo. The night Eileen Reilly died, you came out of the kitchen to get a drink from the bar. And while you were there, you doctored hers. Eileen Reilly wasn't supposed to die, was she? You couldn't have known she'd be driving a car when she passed out. You thought she'd just get very drunk, like Xanthe, and make trouble for Manolis, didn't you? That's what Eva told you, wasn't it?"

Theo said nothing, just dropped his head into his hands. It was enough.


Xanthe's attorney arrived half an hour late—just in time to see that the charges against his client were dropped. He conferred quietly with Detective Fallon and gave Theo his card. "Call me when they charge you," he said. Theo's expression remained unreadable.

After the attorney left, Fallon returned to us, looking as if he'd rather be anywhere else. "Now, about the coin."

Miss Alma set her handbag on the floor and leaned toward the table, her teacher persona rivaling him in authority. "I believe you will find, Detective, that our help will make things infinitely easier. You see, I am the only one in a position to suspect that Mr. Mavrakis has the coin. We discussed antiquities at length, and he is aware of my considerable interest in the subject. I believe I can make myself very credible with him."

"Mrs. Rayburn, let me explain something to you. We do not—let me repeat that—we do *not* use civilians in undercover investigations."

"Perhaps not, Detective Fallon, but there is no feasible way for an undercover officer to do this work. Mr. Mavrakis is not, I believe, in the business of selling stolen antiquities.

The indications are that he agreed to dispose of the coin in return for other favors from Ms. Paradissis—specifically that if she were successful in breaking up the engagement and taking over Alex's position within the company, she would deal exclusively with him. He would find appropriate real estate and she would recommend its purchase. He took part in the scheme because he had a long-range goal."

Fallon grinned, enjoying matching wits with Alma Rayburn, who, though eighty-something, missed nothing going on around her. "Do you really think, Mrs. Rayburn, that he's going to believe that—forgive me—a little old lady like yourself—"

"Detective Fallon, you're from Florida. Have you never heard of Ma Barker? Young thieves and grifters live to be old thieves and grifters. I'll bet you've got a few octogenarians right down there in that prison in Clearwater. Age does not guarantee integrity."

To his credit, Fallon was unfailingly polite, despite the fact that he knew he was dealing with rank amateurs. "I understand that, Mrs. Rayburn. But the man may be a killer," he said. "Preliminary lab reports indicate that there was a residue of the drug, mixed with the wine, in Eva Paradissis's glass and the wine bottle. Suicides and accidents don't usually mix their drugs to take them. They swallow a handful of pills and then decide to ease the way with a little shot of something, or in this case, with a bottle of wine. If what you're telling me is true, he's not just a thief. He's a killer."

Miss Alma agreed. "Which is why we have come to you. I would like police protection—you call it 'a wire,' I believe? But let me make my position perfectly clear. I have watched this young lady suffer the cruelties of ambitious people. I have seen my young friends, Alex and Kate, kept in agony at a time that should be the happiest in their lives. I have watched their parents suffer right along with them, and I am tired of it. I am going to do what I can to put an end to all this misery." Had she been wearing kid gloves, she might well have slowly removed them and defiantly tossed them onto the table.

"With, or without, your help," she added, just in case he'd missed the point.

The bug was installed on the phone in Miss Alma's room shortly before noon. Fallon sent Peter Haas, an electronic technician with the Tarpon Springs police department, back to the hotel with us. He would tape the call, which was to be made from her room in case Aris had caller ID on his telephones, and if necessary, he would also fit Miss Alma with a wire. There was, of course, the possibility that Aris would not take the bait.

When the equipment had been set up and tested, Miss Alma picked up the phone and took a deep breath. The rest of us held ours. "Mr. Mavrakis, please. This is Alma Rayburn calling."

When Aris answered, they exchanged a few pleasantries before the mention of Eva's death—which by then had made the papers—gave Miss Alma the opening she was looking for.

"Yes, things have been very tense. I've been helping out with Pagona, you know, and she's very upset. The papers are calling it an accident, but of course the police suspect murder."

A lengthy pause ensued, during which Aris must have been collecting himself. His little suicide ruse had not worked, and that put a whole new face on possession of the coin.

"No, I think we're all perfectly safe here," Miss Alma went on. "I'm not concerned. Ms. Paradissis was into some illegal activities apparently. We know that it was she who stole the Helios coin from the necklace. And you know,

Mr. Mavrakis, I've been giving that quite a lot of thought . . ."

"He didn't admit to having it," she said after she'd hung up. "But I didn't expect him to. He asked me if I'd ever seen the luminaries on Spring Bayou. I gather he plans to be there around seven o'clock tonight."

The technician replayed the tape and verified the time before calling Detective Fallon. At length, he set the phone back in its cradle. "We're going ahead with it," he said, turning to the rest of us. "But Fallon says he doesn't want any of you near the place. You got that?"

"Definitely."

"Neh."

"Wouldn't think of it."

As if we were going to send Miss Alma out there alone.

At five forty-seven, the last glimmer of daylight faded from the water and the luminaries came to life in a burst of sparkling lights as far as the eye could see. "Oh, Nick, how beautiful!"

We strolled together along the path in the park, he leaning on an old cane we'd found in a resale shop. He'd left his black sailor's cap in the hotel and streaked his hair with white shoe polish. He shuffled as if he might have a case of untreated gout. In front of me, Jack trotted along the walk-way around the bayou, pulling on his lead and darting off the path in search of new territory to conquer.

"We need an older dog," I said. "He's too spry for a pair of old folks like us." I adjusted the sock I'd stuffed with tissues and carefully pinned in my clothes to give me a more mature aspect, and wished I'd stuck with my own shoes. Miss Alma's feet were a size smaller than mine and despite the name—"WonderWalkers"—I was finding them very uncomfortable indeed. They did, however, have a rubber sole, which gave me the advantages of being both quiet and sure-footed.

We had walked down to the bayou from the hotel to be in place well before Miss Alma arrived. Now, with an hour or so to kill, we were taking the path slowly, cognizant of the need to be in just the right place when Aris and Miss Alma made their connection. On the street near the wharf, a white van with a "Public Works Department" sign on it sat, seemingly empty. Detective Fallon would be inside, waiting.

"Look at that one," I said, pointing to one of the white bags glowing with candlelight. The message said "Happy Holidays to Miss Shore, the Best Fourth-grade Teacher in the World." Attached to the bag was a flat red bow that some nine-year-old had colored with great care.

The luminaries along the bayou are a fairly recent addition to the Epiphany traditions of Tarpon Springs. For a small fee, families and businesses all over town purchase white bags on which they write Christmas and holiday wishes to other members of the community or their families. On the night before Epiphany—which is also known as the "Festival of Lights"—the banks of Spring Bayou are lined with these charming greetings. The bags are weighted with sand and the candles inside are lit. There must have been thousands of them glowing in the night and twinkling in reflection on the black waters of the bayou. No string of Christmas lights, no matter how elaborate, could ever match their placid beauty.

We walked on toward the park entrance at the foot of Tarpon Avenue, where a dais had been constructed on the wharf. The street entrance was marked by an arch of red Christmas lights and, above it, an illuminated cross. After services on the morning of Epiphany, the archbishop would lead a procession down to the bayou. There he would throw a white cross into the water and Greek Orthodox boys would dive to retrieve it. The one to find it would be blessed with good fortune for the year. A string of tiny boats waited, tied in a circle beneath the wharf, for the divers who would come on the morrow.

"Oh, Nick, look," I said. Small blue-paper crosses decorated the luminaries surrounding the wharf. These lanterns were in memory of the dead. I paused to read one, my throat tightening. "We miss you, Daddy" it read.

At the foot of the dais, a pile of unused bags and a box of candles waited to be returned to the committee. "Do you suppose it would be all right?" I asked. Nick stuffed a five into the box and handed me a felt-tip pen.

When I had finished, he set the bag in front of a blooming poinsettia. He took a lighter to the candle and the message was illuminated for everyone to see. "To Baby Lambros. Rest in peace."

"Look," Nick whispered, his hand tightening on my arm.

Across the bayou, in the lights of the park, we could see Spiros loping along beside Miss Alma. Detective Fallon had agreed that she would need an escort from the hotel, and in the end, he had allowed Spiros to get her safely there. Once within sight of the van, he was to break away from her.

Spiros's cover was the *glendi*, the festival to be held in the park after the cross diving. While Nick and I, and scores of other walkers, enjoyed a stroll along the bayou, members of St. Nicholas parish were industriously working on the other side of the park, setting up tables and tents for the next day. Spiros trotted off in their direction, leaving Miss Alma to reach the path along the water's edge alone.

"Let's go," Nick said, guiding me in Miss Alma's direction.

I grabbed his arm before his youthful stride could betray us. "We've grown old together, remember?"

Behind us, quick footsteps descended the stairs from Tarpon Avenue into the park.

## Chapter Twenty-Seven

We followed Aris as closely as we dared, stopping to admire the luminaries when he joined Miss Alma on the path. Our plan, undisclosed to Detective Fallon, had been for her to lead him in the direction of the old library, away from the path and the wharf. Spiros waited there, secreted in the shrubbery where he could keep an eye on the situation. We intended to slip around the library from the street side and move in as close as possible, where we could hear what was being said and be within striking distance should anything go wrong. It didn't quite work out that way.

Aris shook his head and gestured to a bench near the war memorial, out in the open in the middle of the park. There was only one place for us to hide, behind a lighted wire Christmas display, which would offer little or no cover. Nevertheless, with Miss Alma's safety our primary concern, we ambled in that direction. Half a block away, the van door opened and a man dressed in a public-works uniform climbed out, purposefully striding across the lawn, headed directly for us. I recognized him—Peter Haas, the technician who had tapped Miss Alma's phone.

"Excuse me," he said. "I'm new on the job here and I'm

looking for an address." He carried a folded map, which he opened and spread in front of our faces.

"Fallon says to get in the van right now," Haas whispered. "You know, the light's not very good here," he continued in a normal voice. "Would you mind coming over to my van? It's under a streetlight."

Nick scooped Jack up and we followed Haas back across the park. "When we get to the van," Haas said quietly, "we'll play this thing out—about the address on the map. Then walk around to the street side, as if you're walking up to the old library, and slip into the van. Got that?"


Detective Fallon sat on a bench seat perpendicular to the driver's seat in the back of the van. He had his hand over his mouth and squeezed his lips as if he were trying to keep them closed. His face was scarlet. He silently gestured to a place on the bench and gave Haas a nod. The van lurched away from the curb.

The opposite side of the van featured a wall of electronic equipment—tape recorders, amplifiers, and a tuner that looked like it might pick up radio stations in Singapore. A single small speaker was attached to the ceiling.

Fallon swallowed, peeled his fingers away from his mouth and articulated very slowly at first, but with gathering momentum, as if his words simply would not be held back. "We're going to have to move now. And we were in a great position. Just what the hell did you two think you were doing?"

"We only wanted to protect her," I said, trying to keep my tone of voice reasonable. Jack, who had been unceremoniously dumped at my feet, added a low snarl.

"Yeah, well, you may just have jeopardized the whole operation." He turned away from us with an expression of utter disgust. I wasn't feeling too good about things myself.

"There," he said, pointing to a space on the drive next to the old library. Haas pulled in and cut the engine in the van.

"You'd better hope Mavrakis wasn't paying attention. If he looks down here and sees us after that little caper in the park, we could be in real trouble," Fallon said to us. He clambered over Jack and our knees, squeezing between the front seats to fall into the passenger's seat. There he unfolded a map and laid it out across the lower window and dash, pulled a pair of binoculars out of the door pocket and held them to his eyes.

Peter Haas vaulted over the seat and into the back of the van. He began to adjust the tuner, and the speaker crackled to life, emitting a steady white noise. Behind the noise, there was an uneven hum. As Haas worked, the noise dissipated and Miss Alma's gentle voice came over the speaker.

"—told you, I've always been fascinated by the Hellenistic period. I taught World History for forty-five years, but I never got to go to Greece. And now it's too late for an old woman like me to be climbing over rocks and ruins. Too late," she added regretfully.

"I'm sorry," Aris said. "But I'm afraid I still don't understand what this has to do with me."

"Oh, Mr. Mavrakis, let's not kid ourselves," Miss Alma said wearily. "You know exactly what this has to do with you." Silence.

I glanced up at Fallon's back in the passenger seat. He still held the binoculars to his eyes. He sat completely rigid, his focus trained on the couple on the bench. But I could scarcely sit still. What could Aris be doing? If he pulled a gun, or a knife, could Fallon even see it from this distance?

"We've got to—"

"Shh!" Nick jerked his chin toward the roof speaker, where Aris's voice came across as smooth as if he'd dipped his tongue in olive oil.

"You seem to have the idea that I have something you want."

"Very badly. I want the Helios coin very badly, Mr. Mavrakis. If I'm never going to get to Greece, then I intend to own a little piece of its history. This is my opportunity."

"But there are other antiquities. I might be able to arrange something with a gallery—"

"Like your potter friend in Salonika? The one who makes perfect reproductions? No, thank you. I want to be sure I have the real thing, Mr. Mavrakis."

Aris laughed. "Well, if I had a Helios to deliver, how could you be sure it was real?"

"Because it belonged to Christos Kyriakidis, who would not own a counterfeit coin. And because you have not had time to procure a fake. And because, quite frankly, your time is running out."

"What do you mean, my time is running out?"

"There will be a murder investigation, Mr. Mavrakis. And the person with the coin in his possession will most certainly be a suspect. I happen to know that Eva Paradissis passed the coin to you in the *vasilopita*. I saw you make the exchange before you showed Julia your lucky coin—the one you supposedly found in your bread. You brought it with you and when the time came, simply switched it."

"If you're so sure of this, why haven't you told anyone else? Why didn't you tell Christos when they discovered the coin had been stolen?"

"Because I was waiting for my opportunity to get in touch with you. Murder moved the thing along a bit, wouldn't you agree?"

Again, Aris maintained his silence. Would he never implicate himself? So far, he had said nothing that could be construed as anything more than hypothetical. I wanted this over. I wanted Miss Alma out of there unharmed.

"Let's talk about money," she said, giving the conversation a little shove.

"I have heard that the Helios is worth fifteen thousand dollars."

"Yes, well . . . I've heard that too. Retired teachers, of course, do not have that kind of money lying around. I am prepared to give you six thousand for it."

I groaned inwardly. He'd never go for that. Why not just offer him the full fifteen thou? It wasn't as though she had to come up with the money, after all. Fallon dropped his binoculars and glanced back at the technician. He grinned broadly.

"Six thousand dollars? For a coin worth over twice that much?"

"As I see it, your choices are quite limited. You can hold out for more, which I will not pay you, and hope you find a buyer—a discreet buyer, of course—very soon. Or you can sell the coin to me now and be rid of it. Or, the least desirable of all solutions, you can be caught with the coin and probably arrested for murder. I think I have enough information to arouse official interest in you."

"I didn't kill Eva Paradissis. In fact, her death has been quite a blow to me."

"Perhaps. But a murder charge, even a false one, would do little to enhance your reputation in the community, Mr. Mavrakis. And I think you care very much about that."

Now that my ear was accustomed to listening to the speaker, I realized I could hear Miss Alma's breathing. It was regular, calm—not the least disrupted, even though at that moment, she was probably in the most dangerous situation of her life. Over the breathing, a rustle of fabric. Movement.

"He's standing up," Fallon said quietly. "Walking away from the bench, toward the bayou."

"If you're concerned about the money, Mr. Mavrakis,"

Miss Alma persisted, "I can assure you that I have it. In fact, I had my bank make a wire transfer early this morning. Six thousand dollars are just waiting to be picked up. Of course, if you refuse, I shall have to go to the authorities with what I know."

"He's turning around," Fallon said.

"Will you be coming to the Epiphany celebration tomorrow, Mrs. Rayburn?"

"Yes."

"Perhaps we will see each other there, then. At the *glendi*."

"I hadn't planned to stay for the festival."

"Oh, but I think you should. There will be souvenirs. You will want to come prepared. Souvenirs can be quite expensive."


"Have you ever considered police work, Mrs. Rayburn?" Detective Fallon asked with a grin. "You seem to have quite an aptitude for undercover investigation."

Miss Alma took the glass of *Mavrodaphne* I offered her and smiled. "Mr. Mavrakis is just frightened enough to want to believe that I would buy that coin."

"Well, the six thou you offered didn't hurt your cover any. You've got guts, Mrs. Rayburn, I'll give you that."

"I don't understand," I said. "Why didn't you just agree on the fifteen and get it over with?"

Miss Alma took a sip of her wine, set the glass down and turned her attention to me. "Julia, as far as he knows, I'm holding all the cards. I know he has the coin. He even thinks I saw him make the exchange, which was a bluff, of course. He knows I have him by the—well, you know— so why would I offer him full price for it? I offered him just enough to make it tempting, but not so much that he might be suspicious. A retired teacher might have six thousand to spend on a coin, but I don't know many who'd have fifteen."

We had returned by separate routes to the hotel. Spiros had watched them from his hiding place until Aris rose and strode back toward Tarpon Avenue. Miss Alma had remained on the bench until Mavrakis made the stairs. Then she'd casually stood and slowly traversed the park to the library complex. Spiros hailed her, as though they had just met, and escorted her back to the hotel. Only then were Nick and I allowed to slip out of the van and return to our room at the *Mediterraneo*. Meanwhile, Fallon and Haas took the van back to police headquarters, and the detective returned to the hotel in his own car. If Aris had had anyone watching the park, everything would have seemed normal. And now we were gathered in our room to make our plans for the next day, when Miss Alma would meet Aris at the *glendi*.

Detective Fallon's expressions of admiration for Miss Alma did not extend to us. In fact, he was downright curt. "So, you thought you could protect her better than trained officers could?" he demanded.

"Well, there were only two of you, and you were both in the van," I countered.

"On the contrary, Mrs. Lambros. There were four other officers in the park. You just didn't notice them—which is precisely the point. They weren't supposed to be noticed. I did, however, notice you. And more to the point, in trying to protect her, you could have put her in considerable jeopardy. This is why the police . . . discourage, shall we say . . . citizen involvement. You don't know what the hell you're doing."

He turned his gaze to Nick, his eyes narrowed in an unspoken threat. "There will be no repetition of this little escapade. I don't want to detain you at the station for interfering with an investigation, but I will. Let me repeat that," he said. "I . . . will . . . do . . . it . . . if . . . I . . . have . . . to."

This wasn't going according to plan. Our plan, that is. We'd put Miss Alma in this position and we weren't going to leave her hanging. Nick shook his head. "I'm afraid that won't work. Mavrakis will expect her to be at the cross-diving with us. We can't leave her out in that crowd alone—"

"She won't be alone. I'll have officers nearby."

"In a crowd of twenty thousand people? They'll have to be right there beside her. Aris Mavrakis lives in this town, Detective Fallon. He's active in the community. What makes you think he won't recognize police officers? And even if he doesn't, won't he wonder why she's surrounded by strangers instead of sitting with us?"

Fallon seemed to see the logic of Nick's argument. At any rate, he didn't have an answer for it on the tip of his tongue.

"Look," Nick continued. "I have another idea. It will take some setting up, but I think you—that is, we—can pull it off."

The next morning dawned gray and humid, with a dark, overhanging threat of rain. I stood at the French doors in our room and stared out past the terrace at the black waters of the bayou, silently praying that the rain would hold off until after the *glendi*. It was seven o'clock and we were expecting the technician at any minute.

"I wish you weren't doing this," Nick said. I turned to find him mopping shaving cream off his face.

"I don't think there's any real danger, Nick. I'm really just an observer."

"But there's always the chance that something will go wrong. I'd rather do it myself."

"You can't. He might be suspicious if you weren't danc-ing with everyone else. He knows I don't dance much, so I'll be free to move around. And I won't take any chances. I promise." A soft knock at the door announced the arrival of Peter Haas.

"We don't have much time," he said, coming through the door. "I was up half the night rigging this thing." The sagging pouches under his eyes and the lines of fatigue that tightened his mouth were proof enough. He handed me a compact video camera. "Be careful. Let me show you where the wire is."

Haas had attached a wireless mike to the side of the video camera, working into the wee hours to make sure that it functioned properly. Although Miss Alma was going in wired again, I would also be able to communicate with the van in case it was necessary. But I could scarcely walk around talking to myself without attracting notice. The video camera gave me two advantages—I could cover my face while I talked, and I could record, on videotape, the transaction between Aris and Miss Alma. If, that is, I could unobtrusively get into position, which was Fallon's chief concern.

"We'll have it all on tape anyway," he reminded me. "Don't get in a position where I have to protect both of you instead of just one."

## Chapter Twenty-Eight

We arrived at Spring Bayou at about nine o'clock that morning. The luminaries were gone—their dancing lights strictly a memory lingering in my mind like a dazzling, star-studded dream. In the gray, damp morning, it was hard to believe that they had been real.

The crowd was still small but people were arriving in a steady stream, carrying their lawn chairs and blankets along with steaming cups of coffee and bags filled with Egg McMuffins and doughnuts. The banks closest to the dais were already almost full. In the bayou, at the mouth of the basin, a few pleasure boats had dropped anchor to await the ceremony.

Miss Alma, Spiros, Nick, and I chose a spot on a sloping bank diagonally across the bayou from the dais. From there, we could see the steps from the park up to Tarpon Avenue, the wharf and the boats, and with the help of Nick's binoculars, we could watch the arriving spectators. The white public-works van was parked once again near the old library, some distance from the site of the diving but close to the branch of the park where the *glendi* would take place.

Christos had taken the morning off to bring his mother down to the diving ceremonies. To my surprise, Xanthe was with them, fussing over Pagona as she always had, and being treated by the old woman as though nothing had happened between them.

Although he knew that Xanthe had been cleared of the charges, Christos hadn't been told about Aris. Detective Fallon asked us to keep our plans quiet, which only made sense under the circumstances. If Manolis was right, that Christos was somehow involved, tipping him off could put Miss Alma in even greater danger.

I pointed them out to Miss Alma. "Yes," she said. "After Detective Fallon dropped the charges against her, he called Christos. I went to see Pagona yesterday afternoon, before we came down here to the park. I encouraged her to call the girl. It seems to have worked out."

Well, it had worked out fine for the old woman, but I wasn't sure it was such a good deal for Xanthe. Still, it seemed to be what she wanted. She was genuinely fond of Pagona. I wondered if the old girl would ever realize how lucky she was.

On the wharf, a boy stood staring down into the water. He wore a white T-shirt printed with a blue cross, neatly tucked into the top of navy-blue swim trunks. At length, he crossed himself and turned away to take the stairs two at a time up to Tarpon Avenue and from there, to the cathedral.

Police divers in black wet suits looked like seals, surfacing and diving inside the circle of little boats waiting for the cross divers. They appeared from the water with empty Coke cans and broken bottles, which they passed to waiting officers standing on the banks and the wharf. One diver even brought up a white cross intended, I suppose, to mislead the divers later in the morning. A cruel prank, meant to take the joy out of the occasion—an observation that took my thoughts back to Kate and Alex, to Eva and Theo, and finally to Miss Alma and Aris.

"Are you all right?" I asked Miss Alma.

She took my hand and patted it gently. "I'm fine. And I'll *be* fine. Now I want you to stop worrying about me and enjoy this ceremony. I know I'm going to."

"*Kyrie eleison*," the choir sang out. We had not tried to go to the cathedral for the service. This ceremony—the Liturgy, Blessing of the Waters, and Cross Diving—belongs to the parishioners of St. Nicholas Cathedral. It didn't seem right for us to deprive them of places in the very crowded church when they had worked and planned for the event all year. The cathedral helped to accommodate the crowd by broadcasting the services over speakers in the park. Helicopters from local television stations circled overhead, creating an annoying distraction, but we heard just enough to know when the archbishop delivered his sermon, when Communion began and when, finally, the procession moved to the water font outside the church.

"I'm afraid it's going to rain," Miss Alma said, frowning up at the dark clouds gathered overhead.

In front of us, a silver-haired man in a plaid sports shirt popped open a vinyl lawn chair, but turned to us before taking his seat. "It never rains on Epiphany," he said. "They predict it every year, and every year there are storm clouds. But I haven't missed an Epiphany in twenty years. Believe me, it will not rain."

Miss Alma and I smiled, but exchanged skeptical glances once the man was seated. The wind stirred in the Spanish moss that hung from the live oaks in the park like tinsel on a Christmas tree. The air smelled wet, and the water in the bayou was as black as India ink.

I pulled Nick's binoculars out of the bag and focused on the empty boats beneath the dais. They were variously named for islands and regions of Greece—Simi, Astipalea, Sparta, and Rodos—little blue-and-white boats that, though charming there in Tarpon Springs, still represented a very real way of life in Greece. I glanced at Nick and wondered, as I often did, whether he was homesick. In all the years we'd been married, he'd been home only twice, once for a late honeymoon and the opportunity to show me his island in the Cyclades, and again when his mother died. Even I, born and raised in the United States, felt a wistful tightening in my throat, brought on by the little boats. Nick gently took the binoculars from my hands and focused in on the crowd.

". . . for the rendering of this water, a gift of sanctification, a healing of soul and body . . . averting of every snare of enemies," said the deacon, "let us beseech the Lord."

The snare of enemies was very much with us. Even in that benign crowd, waiting eagerly for the culmination of this service in the cross diving, there lurked an enemy. As if in answer to my thoughts, Nick grasped my arm.

"He's here," he said. "Over there, near the dais." I peered through the glasses in the general direction of Nick's pointed finger. Aris had come down the bank to sit on the ground. Even as I watched, he fumbled in a bag and withdrew his own binoculars.

"Time to start filming," I said, thrusting the glasses beck to Nick. If Aris located us in the crowd, I needed to be seen with video camera in hand.

"In case you haven't noticed," I said into the mike on the camcorder, "our friend is here. He's on the south side of the bayou, near the wharf."

I have to admit, I felt a little foolish. I could imagine Detective Fallon in that van, rolling his eyes and calling me "Nancy Drew." But we were taking no chances with Miss Alma, which meant that someone needed to know where Aris Mavrakis was at all times. So let Fallon call me names if he wanted to.

As the service at the cathedral drew to a close, the park

filled up rapidly. Nick and I had begun our estimate of the crowd at several thousand. Now there were at least three times that—bright spots of color that looked like heaps of confetti on the banks across the bayou—and the numbers were climbing steadily. It would no longer be easy to track Aris's movements in the park.

We'd expected him to make contact with Miss Alma at the *glendi* and had agreed that she would stay highly visible, probably somewhere near the dance floor. Nick, Spiros, and I would be moving through the crowd, allowing Aris to approach her, but with our eyes constantly trained in her direction. I was beginning to understand why he had chosen the *glendi*—a perfectly natural place to run into tourists wanting to get a taste of the area. And he would be well protected by the crowd—a comfort to him, a serious concern to us. We had to stay near her, yet disappear among all the other sightseers. It was going to be a difficult task.

"Julia, listen!" Miss Alma rose from her chair and pulled me up off the bank. All around us, spectators hopped to their feet, pointing at the steps to Tarpon Avenue and smiling. "That must be the divers!"

The boys whooped and hollered like a tribe of primitives on the attack. The crowd lining Tarpon Avenue applauded and called out as the divers passed along the route of the procession. And then they appeared at the top of the stairs—clusters of young men in white T-shirts and dark swim trunks—barefoot boys with olive complexions and dark, wiry hair. Some were tall and lanky, others stocky, even running to fat. The universal they shared was youth, and an exuberance for the event that had been building the year long.

They came on like the runners of ancient Marathon—hurtling down the steps without pause, as though they had clambered over many a rocky cliff on bare soles hardened to leather. A rumble began in the crowd on the bank, escalating as the boys hit the wharf, split on both sides of the dais and dove for the water. A narrow shaft of sunlight speared the clouds and broadened to a bright ribbon over the divers. The man in front of us turned to us with a wide smile.

"You see?" he said. "God never sends rain on *Epiphánia.*"

The water churned up dark sediment as dozens of boys kicked and stroked toward the waiting boats. For one of them, today would be a day to remember his life long.

Behind the boys came a band in uniforms of maroon and gold, and representatives of other parishes carrying the banners of their churches. The archbishop, golden-robed and crowned, with crozier in hand, was followed by the Bishop of Atlanta, whose tall black hat, with its long veil streaming down his back, reminded me of the humble village priests of Greece. Father Charles stood at the bishop's elbow. I wondered whether he'd broken the bad news about Lucky's Lotus yet. It couldn't have been a happy reunion.

An entourage of priests and deacons, still in their vestments, climbed onto the dais, followed by a young woman in a dark green choir robe. She held her hands close to her body, cradling a snow-white bird as she took her place next to the archbishop.

"Wisdom," cried the archbishop. "Let us attend."

The Gospel of the day was from Mark. ". . . And immediately coming up out of the water, He saw the heavens opening, and the Spirit like a dove descending upon Him . . ."

How elegantly the dove soared into the sky, its glistening white body contrasted against a now blue sky. It smoothly circled once over the bayou, gracefully ascending over the boats anchored at the mouth of the basin before disappearing from view.

The boys stood poised in the little boats, waiting for the Gospel to be concluded. At length, the archbishop raised the white cross in his hands. The divers leaned forward, precariously rocking the boats. The cross flew end over end, its splash lost in the tumultuous churning of the bayou as the boys entered the water en masse. Ten seconds turned to twenty as divers surfaced, gasped, and dove again. My throat tightened as I thought of other divers, in the Anclote River, and Eileen Reilly dying below. Nick squeezed my hand.

And then it appeared. The square white cross broke through the water, clutched in the hand of a smiling diver. On the bank, the crowd roared. After kneeling to kiss the hand of the archbishop, the boy was carried off the dais on the shoulders of the other divers, a golden trophy held high in one hand and the precious cross in the other. For many of the divers, there would be other opportunities, but for the boy who won it that day, there would be no other. He was eighteen years old, and this was the last time he would be eligible for the dive.

"I am so glad that I was able to be here for this. Thank you," Miss Alma said, turning to Spiros. "Thank you for bringing me."

Spiros grinned, his big mustache quivering. "No problem, *Kyria* Alma."

The crowd dispersed quickly after the dive. Some turned toward town and home for private celebrations, but many, like us, turned toward the *glendi*. In the wake of the morning's clouds, the day had turned viciously hot and the sun burned our scalps and the backs of our necks. We tried to stay together, but the surge of the crowd toward the park inevitably separated us from Spiros and Miss Alma. We stopped to grab a soft drink at the first stand we passed. Throngs of people surrounded the Coke wagons, pushing toward the front with strident orders for drinks with plenty of ice. How quickly we lose the solemnity of the moment, I thought.

At the center of the park, a small curved band shelter sat like a giant turtle nestled among live-oak trees. The *glendi* committee had set up acres of tables around an asphalt patio at the base of the bandstand. Spiros managed to elbow through the crowd to procure a front-and-center seat for Miss Alma. He left her there and headed for the food tent. A bouzouki tinkled in the background as the band tuned up for its performance.

Nick ordered us plates of *kavourmá*, a rich, traditional meat dish favored by spongers because of its ease of storage, and found us seats to the left of the bandstand. Behind us, under the trees, a white-clothed table was reserved for the archbishop and his entourage. We could see Miss Alma clearly from our seats. Spiros brought her a plate like ours and took off for another Coke wagon on the right-hand side of the park. We had agreed that he would have to give her some space, finding excuses to leave her at frequent intervals. It would not do for him to stand guard over her for the entire afternoon. Music crackled through the speakers as the dancers from the church appeared.

The first line of dancers wore the costumes of Crete— men in black *vrakes* and women in their distinctive blue-velvet jackets, white skirts, and long white pantaloons. They had to have been hot—I was hot in a short-sleeved denim dress—but they danced as thought a cool zephyr blew down from the heavens just for them. I picked up the video cam and scanned the crowd, finding no sign of Aris.

"I'm going to move over there," I said to Nick, pointing to the center section of tables. "I want to get a better shot of the dancers."

The second line of dancers was comprised of little girls dressed in the white wool vests and sheer dresses of Arachova. Heavy *flouria* of fake gold coins jangled against their flat chests, and white tights bagged at their ankles, but they, too, danced on in the heat, because dancing is as much a part of their genetic makeup as the color of their hair and their eyes.

At length, a string of little boys in white *foustanellas* and equally baggy tights joined the girls for a quick-stepping *serviko*. I watched them wistfully, wondering whether someday I would be the mother wishing I had bought a smaller size of tights. I swallowed a hard lump at the back of my throat and reminded myself that there was work to be done. Somewhere in this crowd, Aris Mavrakis might be watching us all and waiting for his opportunity to connect with Miss Alma. I did not want this to be the last *glendi* she ever attended

An hour passed before Aris Mavrakis finally put in an appearance. Spiros had come and gone with drinks, pastries, and napkins several times. The dancers had finished their show and the band had taken its place on the stage, ready to begin. I had filmed—or pretended to film—everything of interest. Now what?

Aris handed the gatekeeper a dollar and entered the park, stopping to talk to other people in the crowd. He took a stick of chewing gum out of the pocket of his sports jacket and stuffed it in his mouth, waved affably to a server in the Coke wagon, and moved past the archbishop's waiting table. There he stopped and let his glance sweep over the crowd, lingering briefly in Miss Alma's direction. I wandered off to the left, toward the food tent, stopping to zoom in on smoking barbecue grills covered with *souvlaki*. "He's in the park," I whispered into the mike. "And he's seen her."

With nothing left to film, I returned to our place at the side of the stage. Nick had finished off the last of my *kavourmá*, keeping Miss Alma in sight all the while. The band swung into *kalamatiano*. "Time to get on the dance floor," Nick said with a quick jerk of his head.

Aris had taken Spiros's vacated seat and was talking with Miss Alma. Across the dance floor, Spiros stood with his arms crossed like Mr. Clean, his unwavering gaze drilling into the back of Aris's head.

"Right," I said.

There were already four or five dancers on the floor. Nick grabbed onto the end of the line, fell into step and tucked his hand behind his back. I angled around next to the bandstand, where Miss Alma and Aris would be visible, and held the viewer of the camcorder up to my eyes.

"He just sat down with her. They're talking. If he sees me, he'll think I'm filming Nick on the dance floor." I swung the camera a little to the right. Dancers were filling up the floor. Nick came into view. He'd moved to the front of the line to lead. And there, right next to him, was Rula.

Well, wasn't that just swell? Here we were in the middle of a sting operation and Nick was on the dance floor with the easiest virtue in western Florida. She wore a little nautical number—red miniskirt and white middie blouse, which in this case meant midriff length, with red stars on its wide sailor collar—straight off The Good Ship Lollipop. I pulled the camera away from my eyes and glared at my husband over the heads of bobbing, kicking Greeks and tipsy tourists. His eyes met mine and he shrugged, as if to say there was nothing he could do about it.

Rula coyly glanced back over her shoulder at me, tossed her hair and sent me a patronizing little smile. I smiled back. I think I even waved, all the while wishing that the five pounds in my hand was a product of Smith & Wesson's instead of Sony's. But revenge would have to wait. I was there to keep an eye on Miss Alma. I turned back to the table . . . and gave a little gasp.

Miss Alma and Aris were gone.

## Chapter Twenty-Nine

I whirled around just in time to see Aris take Miss Alma by the elbow as he guided her toward the gate. She moved slowly, while he glanced over his shoulder several times and seemed to tighten his grip on her.

Coming toward them was the archbishop, his entourage in tow. Aris and Miss Alma had no choice but to step off the path to allow the group to pass. *Now, now,* I whispered to myself. As if she had heard my silent exhortation, Miss Alma withdrew a thick envelope from her purse. They were standing behind the archbishop's table, perhaps twenty feet from me.

"Father Charles," I called, waving at the priest. He returned my wave, a cigar in one hand and a glass of wine in the other. I lifted the camera to my face and hit zoom to bring the exchange into focus.

"They're making the exchange near the gate. He's looking around. I think he plans to cut out as soon as it's done . . ." Aris looked up my way, pausing to focus in on me and my camera.

"Smile, Father!" I cried. Father Charles obliged, raising the wineglass in a mock toast. Aris turned his attention back to Miss Alma, drawing her farther away from the table and into the shade of a massive live oak. I sidestepped just enough to keep them in focus.

"Okay, he's opening a little box. She's nodding her head. He's got the envelope. He's looking inside. He's headed for the gate. He's got her with him. Oh, no. He's taking her— Move in now!"

But there was no sign of the police team. Instead, the gate and path were suddenly overrun with people. The winning diver had arrived, bringing with him the other boys and their friends and families. They came through the gates cheering and waving the trophy over their heads. The winner carried the cross and a silver tray, stopping to offer the cross to be reverenced as members of the community tossed a dollar or two onto the tray for good luck. Fallon's people would never get there in time.

Still, through it all, Aris made slow but inexorable progress toward the exit, with Miss Alma in tow. Why didn't she call out or pull away from his grasp? Did he have a weapon? And where was Spiros? He had disappeared. I turned back to Nick, who took it all in at a glance. He shot off the dance floor and past me, leaving a chagrined Rula to lead the line. I didn't have time to savor the moment, though. I was catching it all on film.

And so it was that I recorded Spiros reentering the park with the crowd. He seemed to be rocking, as though the throng of people was jostling him off balance. Just as he came parallel with Aris, who was moving in the other direction, Spiros reached out to steady himself, wildly clutching at Aris for support. He grabbed Aris's arms, yanking away his grasp of Miss Alma. Nick drew Miss Alma back to safety as the two men swayed and lurched before Spiros's great weight sent them both backward, out of the crowd and onto the ground.

"*Signome, agori mou, signome,*" Spiros cried, sitting squarely on top of Aris's chest.

Aris lay perfectly still, his features frozen into an expression of shock. I think that even then, he knew he'd been made. By the time Detective Fallon and his men appeared thirty seconds later, it was all over.

"Mrs. Rayburn," Aris said as they pulled him to his feet, "there must be some misunderstanding here."

"Indeed," she agreed. "I'm afraid you did misunderstand my intentions—rather like the Trojans misunderstood that big wooden horse."

They took Aris away quietly. Detective Fallon took possession of the Helios and passed it on to one of his men before joining Spiros, Miss Alma, and Nick. In a minute, they were headed my way.

"Julia! Up here, Julia!" The camera still in position, I turned back to look up at the archbishop's table. Father Charles set his wineglass on the table and moved in behind his superior. The archbishop waved and smiled beatifically into the camera.

"I really do not think I was in any danger," Miss Alma said. "He just wanted to talk to me about buying some other antiquities. Well, it's all on the tape, isn't it, Detective Fallon?"

Fallon allowed that it was indeed recorded on tape. He wasn't happy. Aris might have revealed other crimes or connections—fences and unscrupulous collectors—if we hadn't interfered. But with Miss Alma's safety our first priority, none of us had any apologies to offer him. We'd gotten what he wanted and the odds were that he had not only a thief, but a murderer, in custody. Nick and I thought we'd done a pretty good job, all in all.

I gave the camcorder to Fallon. "I tried to zoom in on the exchange," I said, "but I've never used one of these before, so I'm not sure how well it will turn out. I did my best."

"Well, we've got the audio tape and it's very clear, so this is just a backup anyway. The audio ought to be enough to get an indictment for receiving stolen property, accessory to grand theft and several other charges," Fallon said.

"So, what happens now?" Nick asked.

Fallon popped the video tape out of the camera and stuffed it into the pocket of his seersucker sports jacket. "He's being booked at the station. We'll question him before we send him on down to Clearwater. From there on out, it'll be up to the judge and the DA. We'll continue the murder investigation—try to tie him in."

"I'd like to sit in on the questioning," Nick said.

Fallon shook his head slowly and firmly. " 'Fraid not. This is police business."

"Yes," Miss Alma reminded him. "And catching him was police business, but you let us take part in that."

"That was dif—"

Nick shifted impatiently in his seat. "Look, Detective Fallon, there are still questions that need answers. Let us sit in on the questioning and we may be able to give you more information."

"If you're withholding anything—" Fallon said, his gaze taking in each of us in turn "—if any of you know something you haven't told me, you'd better spill it right now."

Miss Alma examined her fingernails. "I'd be happy to share anything I know, Detective, if you'd consider letting us hear what the man has to say for himself. It seems only right, in view of the fact that you put me at quite a risk."

"*I* put *you* at risk? *You* came to *me* with your little scheme."

"Detective Fallon, I am over eighty years of age. Some would say that I'm not in possession of my full faculties."

"Obviously you're in better possession of your faculties than I am," he muttered. "Look, ma'am, everything's gonna come out at the trial anyway. You can wait until then."

"Oh, the trial. Yes. By the way, I assume that the district attorney will want me to testify? Yes, well, I hope that will work out. I'm considering taking a trip to Greece. Possibly a very long trip, Detective. Of course, it could be postponed—in the interests of doing the right thing."

Fallon completed the thought for her. "If I let you sit in."

"Correct. There is a young woman out there, and her young man, who will be getting married in two days. I, for one, do not want them to begin their marriage under a dark cloud of suspicion. I would like to see this whole mess cleared up by then." Miss Alma's gaze sharpened. "I am confident that you are going to do the right thing, young man."

Michael Fallon shifted uncomfortably and sighed. "All right," he said. His gaze focused on Spiros, Nick, and me, pointedly ignoring Miss Alma. "I'll let you watch through an observation window, but that's it. And I want your agreement here and now that this is the conclusion of your involvement in this case. Do I make myself clear?"

"Of course."

"*Neh.*"

"Absolutely."


Spiros and Miss Alma had already followed Detective Fallon out of the park when Father Charles intercepted us. "The archbishop sent me," he explained. "He wants . . . now what does he want?" He giggled. "Oh, yes. A copy of your film."

"Oh, Father, I'm afraid I can't do that." I explained to him what I had really been doing with the camera, and how Christos's coin had finally been recovered.

Father Charles pulled out a pack of *Palas* cigarettes and lit one, raising his eyebrows as he listened to my story. "Ah, but

I'm sorry . . . to hear about our Mr. Mavrakis." Then he put a finger to his lips. "Shh. You must be very . . . shh . . . about this. Mavrakis put up the . . . money . . . for the girl. I went to see him. He has money . . . lots of . . . I knew it. We had a lit-tle glass of wine—" He pinched his fingers together, demonstrating how little said glass had been. Clearly, he'd had a bit more that afternoon.

Nick took the priest by the elbow and started walking him away from the archbishop's table and the scrutiny of the bishop as Father Charles continued solemnly: "—we talked about the girl. The jail . . . I made it sound very bad." Father Charles began to laugh. "But for the girl . . . wonderful news."

Nick and I exchanged worried glances. If Father Charles was drinking, it might account for his erratic navigation of the roads, and would certainly explain a lot about the accident to Lucky's Lotus. I asked how the bishop had taken that news.

"I am waiting," Father Charles said with a little giggle, "until he is in a receptive mood. Perhaps a glass of wine . . ." He gestured back at the table, where the a nearly empty bottle of *Roditis* sat at his place. The bishop scowled in our direction.

"I must go back," Father Charles added hastily. "They will be looking for me." He wove his way through the crowd, detouring near the bandstand long enough to dance a few steps of a *pentozali*.

Detective Fallon met us in the waiting room at the police station and escorted us into his office. He did not offer us seats.

"Let's get a few things straight," he said. "Whatever you may hear in there—and it may be nothing at all—his attorney's with him now, and heaven knows what he's going to advise him. Anyway, whatever you hear, you will keep in absolute confidence. There will be an officer in the room with you. You can send me messages through her."

We agreed to his terms without argument, after which he showed us into the observation room. A tall, blond uniformed officer took a seat at the back of the room. Miss Alma and I sat next to a window that looked into a small, bare room with shiny green walls and a dark oak table in its center. Nick and Spiros stood behind us.

After a few minutes, Aris Mavrakis and his attorney were shown into the examining room, followed by Detective Fallon, who was carrying a buff-colored file folder. A tape recorder was started and Aris confirmed that his rights had been read to him prior to his arrest. Fallon perused the folder at some length. If he was hoping to make Mavrakis squirm, the delay did not have the desired effect. Aris sat in his chair with his legs crossed at the knee in a prim posture, his hands neatly folded in his lap.

"Let's begin," said Detective Fallon, "with the Helios coin belonging to Mr. Christos Kyriakidis. You are aware that he is the rightful owner of the coin?"

"I don't know who owns the coin. I was asked by a friend to sell it for her. As far as I know, the coin belonged to her."

"Mr. Mavrakis, I would remind you that we have both video and audio recordings of your transaction with Mrs. Alma Rayburn. Would you care to reconsider your statement?"

"I have told you that a friend of mine asked me to find a buyer for her coin. Mrs. Rayburn was interested."

"And that friend would be Eva Paradissis?"

"Yes."

"Mr. Mavrakis, you do know that Eva Paradissis is dead, do you not?"

"I read about it in the newspaper, yes."

The substance of Aris Mavrakis's testimony was that he did not know exactly what Eva had been planning and he was in no way in league with her. He had not asked for proof that the coin was hers. He leaned over to brush the toe of one of his loafers. "Why would I? She was a friend, and I had no reason to think she would lie to me."

"In spite of the fact that you knew that a Helios coin had been stolen from Christos Kyriakidis?"

"But I didn't know about the coin. I no longer have a business relationship with the Kyriakidis family."

"And yet you posted bond for Miss Xanthe Saros, who had been arrested for grand theft of the Helios coin."

"I did not know what the charge against Ms. Saros was. Father Millas came to me and asked me to help the girl. He said only that she was in trouble. I asked no questions— for a priest, there are issues of confidentiality."

"So you just agreed to post five thousand dollars for Miss Saros's bond without asking for further information? Come on, Mavrakis, you don't expect us to believe that."

"You may believe it or not, as you like. Father Millas will tell you that I did not ask any questions. I did it as a favor to him. I knew the girl slightly, and I felt sorry for her. If you've met Pagona Kyriakidis, you will understand."

"What I understand, Mavrakis, is that you already knew why she had been arrested. You knew because Eva Paradissis was keeping you informed, and you wanted the girl free for other reasons."

Aris shook his head. "No, but I did know that Christos Kyriakidis had severed his relationship with her—Father Millas told me that much. And I knew what it was like to be cut off by Kyriakidis—promises made and then broken. I didn't have to know what she had done to feel some sympathy for her."

"Mr. Kyriakidis had also severed his business relationship with you, is that right?"

Aris shook his head sadly. I had seen this poignant expression before — the night of the party, when he was talking about Manolis. I had been taken in by it then, but I would not be taken in again.

"To my great regret, the son, Alexander, has made it clear that he is not interested in continuing our relationship."

"And why is that, Mr. Mavrakis?"

"I was at one time in business with his future father-in-law—Manolis Papavasilakis. Our partnership did not end well. Alex's position is understandable, of course."

"Then how did you happen to be invited to the New Year's Eve party? Isn't it true that you were invited by Eva Paradissis for the sole purpose of taking possession of the coin?"

"No, it is not true. I received an invitation that came, as far as I know, from Christos Kyriakidis. I had been instrumental in making the *Mediterraneo* a reality. The party was to celebrate the Grand Opening of the hotel. I think it was only reasonable that I was invited."

"All right. However, it is true that you received the coin at the party, is it not?"

"It is not. Ms. Paradissis had given me the coin several weeks earlier."

"Exactly when was that, Mr. Mavrakis?"

Aris shrugged. "I'm not sure. Soon after Thanksgiving, I believe."

Detective Fallon stuck his tongue into his cheek and rooted around as though he were mining for a little leftover lunch. He raised one eyebrow eloquently, never taking his gaze from Aris Mavrakis, switched off the tape recorder and rose from the table. "Excuse me, please. I'll be back in a minute."

After Fallon left the room, Aris turned to the attorney and smiled. He was as cool as a cocktail shrimp, and his story smelled just about as fishy. Nevertheless, so far there were no cracks in it. It was going to be very difficult to prove that he had been any more than a pawn for Eva Paradissis. Beside me, Nick's worry beads were clicking aggressively. His jaws were so tight I was afraid he might crack his teeth. Miss Alma took hold of my hand and squeezed it like a lemon on a ninety-degree day. Even Spiros, who could have understood only a fraction of what was happening, was as rigidly immovable as a pillar of Hercules.

Detective Fallon was gone for about fifteen minutes. When he came back to the room, he carried a second folder, this one a darker brown color. He closed the door softly and took his seat across the table from Aris again and started the tape recorder.

"Mr. Mavrakis, the coin arrived in the United States on the seventeenth of December. Eva Paradissis could not possibly have given it to you at Thanksgiving. Are you still claiming that you did not receive the coin covertly at the New Year's Eve party at the *Mediterraneo* hotel?

"Eva gave me the coin some time prior to the party—I'm sorry, I cannot remember the exact date. She claimed to need money and I agreed to try to find a buyer for her. I did not know that it was not hers to sell."

"I see." Detective Fallon opened the darker folder and withdrew some photocopies, handing several across the table to Aris and his attorney. "Mr. Mavrakis, do you recognize these?"

Aris looked them over carefully, as if he were puzzled by them. In a minute, he passed them back to Detective Fallon. "They look like property appraisals."

"Exactly. Appraisals that you picked up at the office of Dunston and Associates in Panama City in the late afternoon of Monday, January third—four days ago. Either your memory is very short or you're trying to stonewall me, Mr. Mavrakis. Which is it?"

"May I see them again?"

"Certainly."

Aris played out his charade of once again examining the documents. His posture scarcely changed, but his foot—in its neat, ox-blood loafer—began to twitch nervously in the air. He wiped the palm of his right hand on his pants leg and handed the papers back to Fallon.

"Now that I look at them more closely, I believe you are correct," he said.

"These papers were found in Eva Paradissis's briefcase. Ms. Paradissis worked in her office until after eleven o'clock Monday night. According to the desk clerk, she had no visitors. She had dinner sent down from the kitchen and did not leave the office all evening. Dunston and Associates has confirmed that other than their own copies of these appraisals, all copies were in your possession late Monday afternoon. Which, as I'm sure you now understand, places you in contact with Ms. Paradissis no more than one to one and a half hours before she died."

Fallon squared the brown folder neatly on top of the other file and clasped his hands on top. He leaned toward Mavrakis until his nose was no more than two inches from the other man's face. "Mister, you're facing a first-degree murder charge. If I were you, I'd start talking."

*Chapter Thirty*

Aris's attorney cut off the exchange before his client could answer. "I would like a consultation with my client, Fallon." The detective nodded and started to rise. "Not here," the lawyer said with a quick glance toward the window. "In a secure room, please?"

After the two men were shown out of the examining room, Detective Fallon joined us in the observation room. "Well?"

"I think you've got him," I said.

Fallon smiled thinly. "It's pretty weak. No prints on the wine bottle or the glass. Nothing on the prescription box. No other physical evidence that he was even in the apartment. We're not going to be able to make a murder charge stick unless you people know something you're not telling me."

Oh, I wished we did. We knew things, all right. Or we suspected them, at any rate. We were pretty sure that Manolis had been right all along—that Aris Mavrakis was trying to undermine his business. And we were almost positive that he'd received the coin in the *vasilopita*. And none of us believed that he didn't know the Helios belonged to Christos Kyriakidis. But a quick inventory of the facts as we knew them disclosed that we could do nothing to advance Fallon's case. He wasn't happy.

"Then why the hell did I let you in here?"

The blond uniformed officer poked her head in the door. "They're ready for you, sir."

Fallon ran his big hand down his face, sighed deeply and turned away, materializing seconds later on the other side of the window. He turned on the tape recorder and fell back into his chair as Aris Mavrakis and his attorney were escorted back into the room. When they had taken their seats, the attorney leaned forward.

"My client," he said, "would like to make a statement."

"The coin was in the *vasilopita*, as you said. Alex had made it clear to Eva that we were no longer business associates." If Aris's tongue had been dipped in vinegar, his words could not have been more sour.

"She didn't want to be seen with me—the pariah—for fear of losing her job. Our Eva was a very ambitious woman. She couldn't afford to offend Kyriakidis at this stage in her plan."

"So she put the coin in the bread and passed it to you."

Aris agreed. "She slipped the coin into the bread just before she put it at my place. I had another in my pocket. I just exchanged them."

"Then you did know that the coin was stolen."

Aris glanced over at his attorney. "I would advise you not to answer that question," the lawyer said.

"All right, we'll skip it for now," Fallon said. "Go on with your story, Mavrakis."

Dark circles were spreading under the sleeves of Aris's shirt. He tugged the collar away from his neck and leaned forward to elbow the table, his hands folded in front of his mouth. Inside his loafers, his feet of clay were crumbling to dust.

"Eva had plans," he said. "She had always expected that Alex would work for his father in the Athens office. She thought that Christos intended for Alex to learn about contracts, appraisals—well, the business—from her, and then go back to Greece. But you see, that was before Alex met Kate. Once Kate was in the picture, everything changed. Alex didn't want to go back to Athens. He wanted to take over the American operation and stay here in Florida. Eva thought that if she could break up Alex's engagement, he would go back to Greece."

"And once Alex was in Greece, she figured she could do things the way she pleased, is that it?" Fallon asked.

Aris shifted in his seat, raised his leg to cross it over his knee, changed his mind and placed his foot back on the floor. "Eva was opposed to building in the big resort areas. She thought their prospects were better if they built in developing areas, where land was cheaper. And she knew I could work deals for her. I had managed to get them prime land on the bayou for the *Mediterraneo*, after all."

"Not to mention the fact that you would have been happy to kick a little of your fee back, if the deal was lucrative enough," Fallon added. Aris's attorney met the remark with a silent shake of the head.

Aris took out a handkerchief and mopped the back of his neck. "She had tried a few tricks on the old woman, but they didn't work. I guess she figured that if Christos's talisman disappeared, it might be the last straw."

"And if not?"

Aris folded the handkerchief into a perfect square and tucked it back in his pocket. "She was creating as much chaos as possible. While Alex and his father were falling apart, our very capable Eva would be holding down the fort. She was determined to prove to him that she could take over the operation—no problem."

"And what else did this chaos consist of, exactly?"

"Problems for Manolis, problems between Kate and Alex. I think she was still hoping Pagona would break them up."

*"To katharma!"* It seemed for a moment that Spiros might go through the glass to get to Aris. He gripped the windowsill until the wood popped and cracked under his hands. His nostrils flared and the veins in his neck bulged like blue ropes. I had seen him angry. I had never seen him enraged. Miss Alma sat forward in her chair to put a restraining hand on his arm as Nick quietly moved around behind him.

"Problems such as?" Fallon asked.

Aris's hand came up, palm over his heart. "You must understand that I had nothing to do with this."

"Go ahead, Mr. Mavrakis."

"She had made plans of some kind to make trouble for Alex—serious trouble, she said. She could almost guarantee that Alex would be on his way back to Greece, if not before the wedding, then as soon as he got back from his honeymoon."

"And how was she planning to do that?"

Aris rubbed his brow and eyes with his hand. "That, I do not know."

Once again, Aris Mavrakis was lying.


"Let's move on to the night of January third, Mr. Mavrakis."

Aris's glance darted to the attorney and back to Fallon. The handkerchief came out of the pocket again, this time to be fingered much as he had handled the matchbook at the party. "Yes. Well, I went to Panama City that afternoon to pick up the appraisals. Eva wanted to be prepared to move quickly once things fell apart. Christos would be at his most vulnerable then and she could have gotten him to agree to the deal."

"I see. So you made sure that the appraisals and aerial photographs were all ready for him."

Aris's complexion turned a waxy yellow as fear began to take an insidious hold on him. The reality of a murder charge had him in its cold grasp. "She was working in her office, as you said. I couldn't take the reports to her there, for fear of being seen by Alex or Christos. She called me when she got to her apartment, and I went right over."

"Did you go in by the main entrance?"

Aris shook his head. "Too risky. I slipped around the back of the hotel and went in by her private entrance—the French doors to the terrace—or rather, I went up to them. I never set foot in her apartment."

"You didn't have a glass of wine with her, to 'celebrate' the occasion?"

Aris looked Fallon directly in the eye. "No, I did not. We were business partners, and we were each holding up our end of the deal. I had no reason to kill Eva."

I glanced over at Nick. He was by then standing so close to the glass that mist from his breath was forming on the window. But the rest of us seemed to have stopped breathing, so hushed was it in the little room, with only the relentless clicking of Nick's worry beads. I reached over to still his hand.

"I still say he killed her," I argued with Nick as he poured the wine into my glass.

"Why would he do that? He had everything to lose."

"Not if Eva changed her mind. I'll bet there's another real-estate broker somewhere out there who thought he or she was working a deal with Eva—maybe was going to get a bigger cut of the action."

"After all the trouble she'd gone to setting it up with Mavrakis? Come on, Julia. It doesn't flush."

"Wash," I said automatically.

We were at the Epiphany ball at Innisbrook, a hotel and convention center on the outskirts of town. I'd been looking forward to it. The Grecian Keys were playing, and I had swallowed a cold, hard lump of pride and vowed that clumsy or not, I would spend as much time on the dance floor as Rula that night. Fortunately, she was mercifully absent.

"I'm afraid I have to agree with Nick," Miss Alma put in. "It doesn't make much sense for him to kill her. Don't forget, he had the coin and as long as he had that, he had her in the palm of his hand."

Too true. Fallon had booked Aris Mavrakis for receiving stolen property and sent him on his way to Clearwater. Aris had not yet been charged with murder. Fallon's investigation was still pending.

Aris claimed that he'd had no part in Eva's scheme, except to fence the coin. We were fairly sure that this was a lie, but as far as I could tell, there was no way to tie him to the rest of it. I doubted that Eva had sabotaged Manolis's business without Aris's willing help and participation, but I couldn't see any way to prove it, and Theo had said all he was going to say.

"But it's time for us to let the police do their job. They'll get it straightened out. The wedding is on and everything's fine, so let's just forget about it and have a good time," Nick said. He turned to Miss Alma. "Do you remember this dance? It's a *kalamatiano*."

"I'll remember it once I get out there," she said, rising. "Let's go."

I watched the two of them catch on to the end of the line. Spiros was already on the floor, leading the line as it wove among the tables. I knew Nick wanted me to join them, but he wanted me to do it of my own volition and I wasn't quite ready. Whatever confidence I'd had in my ability to dance had been eroding over the past week, along with my self-esteem. I picked up the wine bottle on the table, rejected it and signaled the waiter for a very stiff drink, hoping to bolster my courage.

"I have asked the band to play '*Al Di La,*' " a voice behind me said. I didn't have to turn around. I recognized the cologne. "I have such pleasant memories of New Year's Eve."

"Oh, I don't know," I said as Lucky dropped into the seat beside me. "I think Greek music fits the occasion better. I know Nick's enjoying it."

"Yes, well, some men are never able to throw off their ethnic identity," Lucky said. "Perhaps you need a man with more worldly experience." He took the bottle off the table and studied the label while I tried to think of a comeback, but since none sprang to mind, the silence grew a little long.

"Do you like *Mavrodaphne?*" he asked.

I shrugged. "It's all right, I suppose. Nick likes it. I guess I prefer something a little lighter, a little drier."

"We Greek men do tend to satisfy our own needs first, I'm afraid. A character imperfection cultivated by our very attentive mothers."

"But Nick isn't like that."

"Ah," he said, handing the bottle back to me and glancing across the room toward the dance floor. "Not yet. A few years of marriage sometimes changes things. But as to the wine, I have a small stock of Lazaridi *Amethystos 1992* in my office that you might prefer. It is made with several grapes, including the ancient Limnio variety, known even to Aristotle. If you like, we could—"

"I think I'll just stick it out here for a while," I said. "Maybe another time."

"Of course," he said gently, eyes dark, his expression sad. "Remember, Julia, that when things change—and they will—I'll still be here."

He stood up and made a little bow, taking my hand to brush my palm with his lips—a butterfly kiss that fluttered around in my stomach for another five minutes. "I'll be waiting for you."

## Chapter Thirty-One

"Well, at least you'll get the Helios back," I said to Christos the next morning. We had met him for brunch, at his invitation, in the hotel dining room. Manolis and Georgia, Kate and Alex were also in attendance. Spiros and Miss Alma joined us a few minutes later.

Although Detective Fallon had kept Christos more or less informed on the progress of his investigation into the coin, he had not been entirely forthcoming about Eva's murder. The case wasn't closed yet, and any one of us could end up as a suspect if Nick and Miss Alma were right that Aris had not had any reason to kill Eva. Even I had come to decide that they probably were.

I wanted the whole thing over, but I wanted the right murderer caught. None of us were sure that the man behind bars in Clearwater was anything but greedy and, in the cooler light of the next day, faintly ridiculous. After all, Eva had duped him into helping her with no real promise of a return. She couldn't have been sure that Christos would go for her plan. He might have rejected it, and left Aris with nothing for his trouble. Now he had been exposed and would be publicly humiliated, which seemed like perfect justice to me. It did not, however, solve the murder of Eva Paradissis.

Down deep, although I did not want to admit it, I knew we were sitting over eggs Benedict and Belgian waffles with five of the most probable suspects in the case. If Manolis or Georgia had known anything about Eva's plan to undermine *O Kritikos* and the wedding, either one of them could have decided to stop her. Manolis had a bad temper—in fact, we had seen it erupt all too often in the last week. And he was from Crete, where vendettas are not unknown, even today. Left on his own, he might well have murdered Aris that afternoon at *Mykonos*. And Georgia, gentle and practical though she was, would not have sat by and watched her daughter's future being destroyed. I began to feel sick. I pushed my plate away and sipped at my coffee, studying Kate and Alex over the rim of my cup.

Kate seemed to be the least likely suspect. She'd had little contact with Eva and no apparent reason to suspect that she was behind the *maya* and the needle. Even if she had, I didn't think she would resort to murder, especially not on the eve of her wedding. Of them all, Alex was the least-known quantity. He seemed like such a nice young man on the surface, but I'd had little contact with him, and then only in social situations. Ted Bundy had seemed like a nice young man, too. And Aris had said that Eva planned to make more trouble for Alex—a statement that had bothered me ever since. What kind of trouble had she planned? Could Alex have learned about it and decided to stop her permanently?

"I have apologized to Miss Saros," Christos said. "I regret that I ever suspected her in the first place. She has been very good with my mother. She has agreed to stay on in my employ."

"Yes, I know," I said. "She seems very happy to be back."

Although why, I couldn't begin to understand. Tending to Pagona required a bottomless well of patience and an inexhaustible desire to please. Christos Kyriakidis expected a lot of his employees—intelligence, patience, loyalty. An icy hand gripped my heart. Loyalty was the one attribute Eva had lacked. I wondered if it had gotten her killed.

Christos had turned to Miss Alma and was heaping laurels upon her head for her courage in taking on Aris Mavrakis. I studied him covertly as he went on to exclaim over her youthful vigor. Could Manolis have been right? He'd had Aris pegged all along, after all. Christos was a man who exuded power and was utterly confident in himself. Could he have already learned about Eva? He had taken the copy of the UPS packing slip, saying he would turn it over to his own security personnel. What if they had learned the truth quicker than we had? What if they had gotten the story out of Theo before we ever found him? What if Eva's game had been exposed before she died? Christos was the one man who would have had easy access to her apartment. She would not have refused a drink with him, even if it was a wine she detested.

And she did detest *Mavrodaphne*, I realized suddenly. She had commented on it at *O Kritikos*, saying that she hated sweet wine. Why would she drink it, unless compelled to do so by someone who had authority over her? Someone like Christos. I reached for Nick's hand under the table and gave it a squeeze.

"I have to talk to you," I whispered. "Let's get out of here as soon as we can."

It was another thirty minutes before we were able to gracefully excuse ourselves and hop onto the elevator. "What's going on?" Nick asked. I shook my head and nodded toward a security camera in the corner.

"Let's go back to our room, honey," I said, kissing him passionately for the benefit of the camera.

Nick yanked me off the elevator at a trot. "What is going on with you?"

I told him what I had been thinking—about the fact that Eva didn't like sweet wines. "She wouldn't have taken that drink unless someone insisted on it. Probably someone she couldn't refuse."

"Like her boss," Nick filled in. His face was grave as he thought about the possibility. Neither of us had any loyalty to Christos Kyriakidis, but we did have a loyalty to Kate, and disclosing her future father-in-law as a murderer the day before her wedding would not be doing her any favor.

"I hate this, Julia," Nick said. "But it makes a lot of sense. For one thing, *Mavrodaphne* is Christos's favorite wine. He could have easily brought it to her apartment and insisted she have a drink with him. It's so sweet that even if he loaded it with roofies, she probably wouldn't have tasted them."

We gazed at each other despondently. If Christos had gone to Eva's apartment that night—if he'd used the front door—he might have been seen. But that was a private hall. The only people likely to have noticed him were Alex and Pagona, and they probably wouldn't mention it. There was absolutely no way, that I could think of, to prove it. And I wasn't sure I wanted to anyway. We were now only hours from the rehearsal. Although we were not members of the wedding party, we had been invited to the rehearsal and the rehearsal dinner, which was to be held at *Dino's*. I wondered how either of us would face them all without giving our suspicions away.

"It's not our job, Julia," Nick said. "It's up to the cops now. We've done everything we can."

He was right, of course. I told myself that as I slipped into my bathing suit and walked beside him to the pool. I told myself again as I studied the statue of Venus and was reminded once more of Eileen Reilly. Eva's plans had hurt so many people—innocent and not so innocent. She had jeopardized Xanthe's job and future without so much as a blink of conscience. She had drawn her own brother into a scheme that had made him a murderer, and she had taken Aris Mavrakis for a ride that had terminated in the Pinellas county jail. If Eva Paradissis had not already been murdered, I could think of several people who might be gunning for her now. But she was dead—murdered before any of us had known what she was up to. Why?

Aris had said that Eva's plans included serious trouble for Alex. What kind of trouble? We knew that Eva had wanted to drive a wedge between the two families so that Alex would call off the wedding and go back to Greece. Toward that end, she had sent the gypsy and the *maya*, put the needle in the bread and stolen the coin. Her brother had drugged Eileen Reilly and jeopardized Manolis's business. But Aris had said she also had a back-up plan. What? We had the answers to a lot of questions, but there were still plenty of them unanswered, and *Who killed Eva Paradissis?* was at the top of the list.

I blew a handful of bubbles across the tub at Nick. "We're missing something, and I have a feeling it has to do with Eva's plans for Alex."

"You'd better hope not," he said, pulling himself up out of the tub. "Because if it involves Alex, then Christos—"

"—becomes suspect number one. Yeah, I know. Hand me another towel, will you?"

I wrapped one around my wet hair and another one around my body—a luxury I would never have allowed myself at home. I stood at the sink, putting on my makeup, conscious of the soft flokati under my toes. I was going to miss life at the *Mediterraneo*.

Nick's face was half covered with lather. He poked his tongue into one side of his lower lip and eased the razor over his face, rinsed it under running water and moved his tongue to the other side. "We're just going to have to forget about it, Julia."

I pulled the towel off my head, brushed through my hair and fluffed it with my hands. "But what about Kate? What if Christos really did kill Eva? Worse yet, what if Alex is the—" I couldn't bring myself to say it. Christos, maybe. But not Alex. Surely not Alex.

I took my dress out of the wardrobe and glanced at my watch. "We'd better hurry. Miss Alma and Spiros are due here in five minutes."

Nick was pulling on his pants with a cautious eye on Jack while I struggled with the zipper to my dress. He gave it a good tug, then went to the mirror to tie his tie. "Let's make a pact, Julia. We won't say anything about—"

"Niko, *anixe tin porta. Grigora!*" Spiros pounded on the door so hard the walls were shaking. I flung it open to find him standing with Miss Alma and, between them, Father Charles. The priest was clutching a box under his arm as they half-dragged, half-walked him into the room.

"Get him on the bed," Miss Alma said.

"What on earth?"

"He's intoxicated, my dear. We've got to try to get him sober for the rehearsal."

Father Charles pulled away from them, struggling back toward the door. He laughed maniacally when Spiros finally managed to wrestle him onto the bed.

"Your point," he said. "Round two!" He jumped up, fighting Spiros off with astonishing energy for a man of his years. At length, and with Nick's help, they got him back down on the bed. His energy dissipated, he lay quietly humming to himself.

"Where did you find him?" I asked Miss Alma.

"He was in the gift shop. He was singing and dancing. He's very keyed up about the wedding."

"How much do you think he's had to drink?"

"I have no idea, my dear, but I suggest we start a pot of coffee immediately. He simply can't go to the rehearsal like this."

I had to agree with her. He couldn't possibly conduct a wedding rehearsal in his present condition. At the moment, he was singing a little ditty in Greek—something about the bride and her mother-in-law. I headed straight for the coffeemaker.

"What was he doing in the gift shop, anyway?"

"Buying cigars."

Father Charles leaned up on his elbow. *"Poura, neh."* He swung his legs over the side of the bed. "For the dinner— for the father of the bride, and for the groom. A lit-tle gift."

"Not now, Father. We'll get them later," Nick said, gently pushing him back on the bed.

"He already got them," Miss Alma said, pointing to the box on the bed.

"What in the world are we going to do?" I said to Nick. "He's supposed to be at the rehearsal in a few minutes. We've got to get him sobered up right away."

"Niko," Spiros said, drawing Nick aside. *"Ella."*

They talked together softly for a minute before Nick followed Spiros over to the bed and sat down next to the priest. "Father?" he said, leaning close to the old man's face.

"Eh?"

"Father Charles, have you been drinking?"

*"Ohee!* Before I go to church? Never." Miss Alma and I exchanged skeptical glances.

"We're going to have to leave for the wedding rehearsal soon," Nick reminded him. "Are you up to going?"

Father Charles raised up on an elbow, peering at Nick through unnaturally bright, feverish eyes. *"Neh, neh.* Need *to poura."* He fell back on the bed and rolled onto his side. He slapped at his pocket and brought out a cigar, struggling with the plastic wrapper until finally he had it off. It took four tries before he managed to light it. He pulled himself up and sat propped against the headboard, his head thrown back, eyes closed as he puffed on his precious cigar.

"Nick, look at that."

Jack crept toward him, vaulted onto the bed and closed in on the priest. He gave a yelp and immediately began chasing his tail.

"He's doing it again—like the other time."

Nick swept the dog off the bed but he was right back, his paws resting firmly on the priest's chest, panting in his face. Father Charles giggled, but a low growl rumbled in Jack's throat. Nick went to the bed and picked up the box of cigars. He stripped off the plastic and pulled one out, holding it under Jack's nose. Jack gave it a cursory sniff. Not interested.

But Father Charles's cigar was another matter. No matter how often we pulled him down, Jack would not be kept off the bed, away from Father Charles and his cigar. "What's going on?" I asked. "He's never acted this way before— except that night when Eva was here."

Nick stared at me across the room, but I knew he wasn't really looking at me. He was looking backward, at that night when Eva had come to our room about Jack. Or was it about Jack? Come to think of it, she'd gotten here too quickly—right after Jack had started behaving so oddly, which had begun as soon as I started drawing a bubble bath.

"Nick, I wonder why—"

He wasn't listening to me. He was lighting one of the cigars from the new box. As we watched, he puffed on it a couple of times, then pried the cigar out of Father

Charles's hand and replaced it with the new one. We all followed him over to the sink, watching as he stubbed out the stogie and broke it open. Inside, nestled among the tobacco leaves, were tiny white granules. They looked like bubble bath, but somehow I didn't think they were.

"There," he said. "That's what this is all about." He turned to Spiros. "You got a Greek Key basket, didn't you?"

He had. By the time Spiros got back with his basket, Father Charles had eased off to sleep. Nick took the cigar from his hand, stubbed it out and broke it open. "This one's from the gift shop," he said. And inside, there was nothing but tobacco.

He took Spiros's basket, examining its contents carefully. "Didn't you get bubble bath?"

Spiros had given his to Miss Alma. She had put the bottle away to save it for a special occasion. At Nick's request, she fetched it. Nick dumped a little of its contents under running water at the sink. No bubbles. He handed the bottle back to Miss Alma. "Put this somewhere in a safe place," he said. Miss Alma handed it to me and I locked it in my suitcase.

"This is it, isn't it?" I asked. "This is the trouble Eva was going to make for Alex."

Nick held the broken cigar in his hand, staring at it thoughtfully. "Not just trouble for Alex, Julia. Trouble for someone else. Where did this come from?"

I swallowed hard. "I guess you could say I gave it to him."

## Chapter Thirty-Two

In all our years together, I don't think I'd ever seen Nick so angry. His olive complexion isn't given to ruddiness, except in the nastiest of situations. His face was crimson with rage. He slammed his fist against a wall so hard that one of the pictures jolted off its hook and crashed to the floor. Miss Alma and I stood frozen in our tracks.

"I'm going over there," Nick said. "Spiro, *ella!*"

I sprinted for the door, blocking it with my back. "Nick, why not just call Fallon?"

"And have him arrest Father Charles? I don't think so."

"Oh, surely he wouldn't. The old man didn't even know!"

"Are you prepared to take that chance, Julia? Suppose he does. What happens to the wedding? What about Kate and Alex? Now move please, before I have to pick you up and move you myself."

"Okay, Nick, maybe you're right about not calling Fallon. But we've got to have some kind of evidence. If you go in there and make trouble, I guarantee you there won't be a shred of proof when Fallon gets there in the morning. Then what have you accomplished? What you have to do is get some of the evidence in hand, take it to Fallon and let him get a warrant. And you're not going to accomplish that by storming in there. Don't you think that's going to arouse suspicion?"

Finally, I had scored a point with him. "Okay, supposing you're right, how am I going to get in?"

"I've already been invited."


We left Miss Alma and Spiros walking the floor with Father Charles and pouring coffee down his throat. Miss Alma had called the church and told them that he was running late for the rehearsal. She said he'd had a minor accident in his Jeep—a thoroughly credible excuse to anyone who'd ever ridden with him. The wedding party agreed to go back to *O Kritikos* and wait until they heard from her.

"I don't like this, Julia," Nick said as we pulled out of the hotel parking lot. "It's too dangerous."

"Not for me," I said with supreme confidence. "Just make sure you don't make any noise. I'll be able to keep him busy. As soon as you get some cigars, come storming in after me. I promise I'll go quietly."

"Busy doing what?"

"Talking, of course. He's very easy to talk to. He won't hurt me, Nick. He likes me—a lot."

At length, he said, "I wish there was some other way."

"There's not. I can do this, Nick."

He blew out a long sigh. "All right, but you be careful. Now tell me exactly what you're going to do."

"Okay. Do you have a matchbook?"

Nick patted around in his pockets and pulled out a book of matches he'd taken from our room. I gazed at the logo on the front—"*The Mediterraneo Hotel*"—bordered by the blue Greek key. I explained my plan to get Nick into the warehouse. It was simple, and the trick to it was composure. I swallowed hard. Self-confidence was the one attribute I seemed to have left behind in Delphi.

"What if he's not there?" I asked.

"We go to Plan B."

"Okay, what's Plan B?"

"I don't know yet."

We pulled into the parking lot and took the speed bumps at five miles an hour. The place looked deserted. I couldn't see any lights in the warehouse, but then, I couldn't remember any outside windows either, which probably took care of Plan B.

"It doesn't look like he's here," Nick said. "It would be better if—"

"He's here." I pointed to the Lotus, black and shiny, crouched down in the dark near the door. For our purposes, it was just perfect.

"Julia, I really don't—"

"Nick, we agreed. I know you don't like it. I don't either. But I don't see any other way. Now let's just get on with it. As soon as you've got what you need, break in and do the angry-husband routine." I got out of the car and began to walk toward the door, but abruptly turned back.

"There's something I want you to know," I said. "No matter what I say in there, you—you, Nick—are the only man I will ever love."

He took me in his arms. I could feel a pulse in his neck beating against my cheek. "Please," he whispered, "be very, very careful."

I left him crouched behind the Lotus, walked to the door, rang the bell and waited. Inside, I could hear footsteps on the concrete floor and my heart leaped into my throat.

What if Mr. Universe was still there? But the only car in the lot was the Lotus. Surely it would be all right. I felt better as soon as Lucky answered the door.

"Julia? What a nice surprise! What are you doing here?"

"I'm sorry I didn't call first. I was just so upset. Is this a bad time? You did say to come by at any time . . ."

"Of course. I'm just surprised."

He wore soft, loosely pleated, navy-blue slacks and a silky pale-blue shirt. The sleeves were rolled up above his elbows, exposing muscular forearms and the suggestive bulge of solid biceps. Once again my gaze went to his hands—broad, with strong, square fingers. Lucky held the door open. "Please, come in."

Now this was the tricky part. I stepped inside, hesitating on the threshold. "Really, I could come back," I said.

"Absolutely not. I've been chilling a bottle of *Amethystos* all day—"

I set my hand on his arm. "Your phone. I think I hear your phone ringing." Lucky took a step in the direction of his office, then shifted back. "No, go ahead," I urged him. "I can find my way."

He took off at a run, and I began following. As soon as he turned the end of the aisle, I tiptoed back and slipped the matchbook in the door, raced ahead and met him as he returned to the main aisle.

"They must have hung up," he said. "Whoever it was will call back, I suppose."

"I'm sure they will. Do you have a lot of customers in this area?"

"I'm working on it. The hotel, of course, is the main one. But there are many Greek restaurants—not just here, but also in Tampa and St. Pete. All over Florida." He showed me into his office, to a seat in front of his desk, and went to the small refrigerator in the corner of the room.

"Do you prefer *Amethystos*, or perhaps something else? I have *Metaxa* three-star."

"It doesn't matter," I said, settling into the chair. "Whatever you like." The warehouse was chilly—the temperature kept cool because of the wines, I supposed. I rubbed my arms briskly.

He studied me for a minute, cocking his head one way and then the other. "I think tonight the brandy. It will warm you up quickly." Gulp.

He closed the fridge and dug into one of his desk drawers, bringing out a bottle and a leather case. Inside the case, two crystal snifters snuggled in deep-blue velvet. Lucky poured us each two fingers of *Metaxa*, handing me one as he took his place in the other visitor's chair.

"So," he said, studying me over the top of his glass, "is it Rula again?"

I nodded and took a sip of my brandy. "She was at the rehearsal, and all over Nick. As usual."

"And your husband?"

I shrugged. "He just doesn't seem to understand."

Lucky set down his glass and stood up, crouched at my feet and began removing my shoes.

"What are you doing?"

He leaned against the desk, lifted my feet to his knees and began massaging them. "It will relax you. Now tell me, what doesn't he understand?"

I sighed, let his hands work gently on my toes and stared into my glass. "It's the thrill of the conquest for her," I said, remembering Nick's characterization of Lucky. "Although why it should amuse her to beat me out of my husband, I really don't know. I'm not much of a contender."

Lucky smiled gently. "You do not give yourself enough credit, Julia. To a woman like Rula, you are the most formidable type of rival." Was he speaking from experience, as Rula's male counterpart?

I felt a blush rising to my cheeks, which seemed to make him smile all the more. "Why? I can't compete with her. She's younger, prettier, more graceful."

"Because you have a natural dignity—"

I almost choked on my brandy at that one. "Dignity! I'm afraid you don't know me very well."

Lucky had worked his way up to my instep. No doubt about it, I was relaxed. "There is great dignity in accepting yourself for who you are. Women like Rula trade on their looks, their sensuality. If those things were stripped away from them, they'd have no idea of who they are—what they believe in, what their inner strengths are. They can't bear to come up against a woman who reminds them of how empty they are inside. A woman like Rula can take another woman like herself down in a flash. She knows how to fight her—hit her 'where she lives' is your American expression, I think. But she doesn't understand a woman like you at all. Believe me, I know how Rula thinks."

I swirled the brandy in my glass and thought about what he was saying. I knew that Nick was probably right about Lucky Plemenos, but down deep, I wanted him to be wrong. When I glanced up, Lucky was watching me with an enigmatic expression.

"I seem to have run into a lot of women like Rula on this trip. Eva Paradissis, for example," I said.

"Eva? Oh, no. Eva was not like Rula. Eva was far more ambitious. For Rula, business is a sideline. Her great ambition is to prove to herself that she is lovable, and the only way she knows to do that is to conquer men. In the end, they're all empty conquests. Now Eva," he said, leaning back against the desk to stare at the ceiling. "Eva was different. Eva was also insecure. I didn't know her well, but I suspect that Eva had an obsession with power."

His hands had reached my ankles, his fingers kneading

my flesh like it was fine pastry. I wondered what I was going to do when he got to my calves. "There may have been a traumatic event in her early life," he said. "Something frightening that was not within her control. As an adult, she had a great need to take control of her life."

It was a thoughtful analysis. I wondered how much Lucky actually knew about Eva Paradissis's background and how much was just supposition. "Do you think that's what got her killed?"

His eyes met mine in a direct and unwavering gaze. "Without a doubt. But now," he continued, setting my feet back onto the cold concrete, "I am wondering why you've come here. I don't think you're a woman who gives up easily, are you?"

I slipped my feet back into my shoes—glad to have one more layer between his fingers and my too-weak flesh. Another sip of brandy gave me the encouragement I needed. "Can I be honest with you?"

"By all means." He picked up his glass, swirled his brandy and raised it to his lips.

"You're easy to talk to, and you make me feel good about myself. I haven't had much self-esteem lately."

"Ah," Lucky said. "And Niko is not helping?"

"No, Nick is not helping."

Lucky set his glass down on the desk and took mine out of my hand, setting it next to his. Then he pulled me up and kissed me—deeply. I pulled away. "I can't—"

"Isn't that what you wanted?" he whispered in my ear.

"No, I—" Where was Nick? I let Lucky hold me while I tried to collect myself. *Play along,* I told myself, growing more uncomfortable by the second. *Nick will come.*

"It makes me very sad," Lucky went on, nuzzling my hair. "Women like you do not come into my life very often. I wish it had been different."

I nodded my head, resting it against his broad shoulder, letting his arms tighten around me. "I wish," he continued, "that I was not going to have to kill you."

I didn't try to move. It took a moment for his words to penetrate, and then I laughed it off as though it were a joke. "I think that's a bit much, don't you? To kill me just because you can't have me?"

Lucky lifted my face to gaze into my eyes. "I wish it were that simple," he said. "We both know I could have had you, don't we?"

I nodded as if he were right, too frozen by fear to think of a snappy rejoinder. "Then why would you—?"

He pushed my head back against his shoulder. "I don't know what shampoo you use, but I like it. It is very clean-smelling."

His grip on me was tight, but no longer the loving embrace of a man smitten by my all-American, girl-next-door qualities. My heartbeat pummeled the base of my throat so that I could scarcely swallow. He put a gentle finger over my lips.

"You asked me if I thought ambition was what got Eva killed. You didn't ask if it caused her suicide, Julia. There has been nothing about murder in the papers."

"But it was just a figure of speech."

"No, I'm afraid it was not. I wondered why you had really come here. I don't think infidelity is your style. In fact, I would be disappointed if it were. I prefer to remember you as that rare kind of woman—a woman above reproach."

He stroked my hair, his fingers gently fluttering through my curls. "You were looking for information, weren't you?"

"No, I—"

"Sit down," he said, leading me back to my seat. He

produced a small, snubnosed gun from the pocket of his trousers and effortlessly pointed it at me. I fell into the chair, my knees too weak to hold me up any longer. He walked over to the door and closed and locked it. So much for Nick.

"I would like to ask you a few questions. Then you may ask me yours and satisfy your curiosity."

I couldn't answer him. I could only stare at the gun. The man had a gun, and he was going to use it on me.

"Don't be afraid. I'm not going to hurt you."

Last I knew, bullets hurt. He glanced down at the weapon in his hand. "Oh, no, I won't use this. Whatever I do, it will be easy. I would never hurt you, Julia. I'm too fond of you." What a relief.

"Now," he said. He sat back down, crossing his legs as though we were just going to have a chat. "First of all, where is Niko right now?"

"I don't know," I said truthfully. Lucky watched me through narrowed eyes as I elaborated. "I left him at the rehearsal dinner with Rula. They were dancing. Again."

"How soon before he comes looking for you?"

"If he were coming, he would have been here by now. Look," I said, leaning forward. "I don't know why you're doing this. I don't know what you've done, or not done, and I don't want to know. I didn't like Eva."

"You could live with her death, eh?"

"Live" was the operative word here. "Yes," I said slowly. "I think I could."

Lucky shook his head sadly. "No, *agapi mou*. You might be able to live with her death, but you wouldn't be able to live with what I do for a living."

"Imports? There's nothing wrong with importing olives."

"No, indeed. But I suspect you know better than that."

He wasn't giving me an inch. There was no way I could bluff my way out of this situation. He might regret having to do it, as he claimed, but Lucky Plemenos really was going to kill me. I tried to swallow a lump of fear as hard and cold as Rula's heart, but like her, the fear just wouldn't go away.

"Julia, what did you think you were doing?" he scolded me. *Scolded*, like I was a child. Suddenly, irrationally, I felt the anger I should have felt when he pulled out his gun.

"How could you? How could you lead me into trusting you? Believing in you?"

Lucky seemed taken aback, even embarrassed. "I didn't lead you. You came to me. It was your idea."

I shook my head. "I really am a fool."

"That's your problem, Julia. You let people think you're a fool. You and I both know that you're not. Now, if you have questions, this is the time to ask them."

I sat back in my chair and thought about it. Why not? Why go to my death as ignorant as I had been in life? I might as well get some payoff for dying. "All right. I suppose all this means that you killed Eva. Why?"

"She tried to blackmail me. It was a very foolish thing to do."

"Because of the cigars?"

Lucky polished the barrel of the gun on his pants leg. "Yes. And no. She came here one day to pick up a case of wine and saw something she shouldn't have seen. We were busy that day, distilling cocaine into crack. She'd been looking for a way to cause trouble for Alex. He'd just started this club—"

"The baskets for special guests. The Greek Key Club."

"Yes. She wanted me to supply her with cocaine. She had some crazy idea of setting Alex up to look like he was dealing drugs through the hotel. It would never have worked, and worse yet, it might have led back to me. I couldn't afford that."

"But you did give her the cocaine, didn't you?"

Lucky leaned back and stared up at the ceiling. "One shipment, because she threatened to expose my operation if I didn't."

One shipment of coke. Enough for Eva to fill a few bubble-bath bottles and replace them in the baskets. She had already started to put her plan in motion when she discovered that Alex had sent some baskets to his friends. That was why she had shown up at our door that night. And that was what was wrong with Jack. He was as high as a kite from the coke I'd poured in the tub.

"So you led her on, went to her apartment to deliver more . . ."

"Suggested that we drink to the occasion—our new partnership. I'd already put the roofies in the bottle, resealed it and replaced the collar. She watched me open the bottle there in her apartment. She didn't notice that I never drank mine."

"So she had no reason to think there was anything wrong with the wine. Why didn't you kill her when she first discovered what you were doing?"

Lucky laughed, apparently at my naïveté. "These things take time to set up, Julia. To do it right, one must plan very carefully. Unfortunately, I will not have that luxury tonight."

I ignored his point, preferring to think that I still might be able to change his mind. "I guess I don't understand why you had to kill her."

He narrowed his eyes, gazing at me over the gun barrel. "I don't like to be threatened."

"But you could have exposed her just as easily."

Lucky shrugged. "Maybe. But it was simpler just to get rid of her. Any other questions?"

Well, yes. I had hundreds of them. I wanted to keep

him talking long enough for Nick to act. Nick was out there in the warehouse somewhere, getting evidence. It was only a matter of time until he showed up.

Actually, it was only a matter of seconds. There was a knock on the office door. Lucky kept the gun pointed at me, rose and confidently unlocked it. On the other side of it stood Nick. And Lucky's muscle-bound minion.

## Chapter Thirty-Three

"I found this guy out in the warehouse going through the exports," said Mr. Universe. He shoved Nick through the door and into the chair Lucky had just vacated. Nick gazed at me, his dark eyes filled with apology. Lucky walked past him and rested the gun against my neck.

"Should we be expecting anyone else?"

"Yes." Nick lied, looking him frankly in the eye. Lucky shoved the gun harder up under my jaw, but Nick didn't flinch. "I called the cops before we left. They'll be here any minute."

Would that it were so, I thought sadly. We hadn't called the cops. We hadn't even explained everything to Spiros and Miss Alma. Lucky must have read the truth on my face. He pulled the gun away, leaned back against the desk and smirked at Nick. "No, I don't think so."

His gaze hardened to a glare. "You should have treated her better than this," he said, gesturing at me. "You should never have let her come here."

Nick flushed angrily and started back up off his chair. I blinked, and the gun was back under my chin. "Don't make me do it," Lucky said. "She deserves better."

"It wasn't his fault. He didn't want me to come. I insisted." I reached for Nick's hand, squeezing it in silent apology.

Nick shook his head sadly. "He's right. I'm sorry, baby."

"Now, what shall we do with the two of you?" Lucky said. He glanced at Mr. Universe, who shrugged. Lucky turned back to us. "Drunk driving is always good. And an accidental drowning in one of the bayous. I'll need a bottle of *Mavrodaphne*. That's your favorite wine, isn't it?" he said to Nick. So we would go the way Eileen Reilly had gone, slowly drifting to the bottom of those dark waters. But at least we would go together.

Mr. Universe disappeared into the warehouse, returning shortly with a bottle of the wine and two large plastic cups from McDonald's. Ronald McDonald smiled at us dementedly as Lucky uncorked the wine and emptied the bottle into the two tumblers.

Fallon had remarked that suicides and accidents didn't mix their drugs in their drinks. Apparently Lucky knew that too, although it hadn't stopped him from killing Eva that way. "The way to do this now is for you to drink about half first," he said, passing us the cups. He laid the gun back under my jaw and gazed at Nick. "Drink it."

Nick swallowed the wine in a couple of gulps. Lucky stuck the gun under his jaw and gestured for me to do likewise. It was supposed to be a sweet wine, but it left a bitter aftertaste in my mouth. Or maybe that was just Lucky.

When we'd each drunk half the wine, Lucky opened his desk drawer and brought out an aluminum strip of blister-packed pills, punching a handful out of the packet. "Roofies. They're so easy to get in Europe, it's almost criminal." He passed the empty pill packet to Mr. Universe.

"Hang onto that. Wipe it down for prints. It'll have to be found in the car. And get another bottle of the *Mavro-*

*daphne*. Make sure you don't leave any prints on it either. Open it, pour it around inside the car——"

Lucky stretched his hand out to Nick. Nick fished around in his pockets and brought out his car keys, dropping them into Lucky's palm. Lucky in turn passed them to Mr. Universe, who snagged the ring gently between his fingers.

"——cork the rest of it and leave it lying on the floorboards. Go ahead and get the car started," he added. "We'll be out in a minute."

Maybe the drug wouldn't affect us the way it affected other people, I reasoned. At least, I thought, we might have a chance this way. There would be no chance against a bullet shot at close range, but shooting us would leave evidence that would be messy to clean up. Lucky wanted our death to look like an accident—cleaner, but riskier. However, Lucky Plemenos was not a man to shy away from risk. I knew now why they called him Lucky.

He turned back to us. "We'll give him a few minutes. Roofies react quickly. I don't want a couple of drunks on my hands when I show you out." He pushed the pills around on the top of his desk like shells in a con game.

"You know, I don't like this date-rape stuff. Most of the kids just use them to boost their high, but every now and then you get one who's got to try the rape thing—some loser who can't get a woman any other way. I hate that," he said. "That's why I don't bring them into the U.S. for sale."

Nick sat forward. "You want to tell us about the cigars?"

"Blunts. That's what they're called in the business. I buy them here, fill them with crack and export them to Greece. Crack's practically an open market over there, and the narcotics boys are so busy watching the imports from Turkey, South America, and the Middle East that they can't be bothered with me. The big cartels have created a neat little diversion."

"Let me guess," Nick said. "The top layer is just plain, everyday cigars. That's why Father Charles didn't notice the crack. He'd just gotten to the second layer. When the cigars arrive in Greece, someone in your organization re-packs them and—"

"We distribute the clean ones to legitimate tobacco deal-ers, and the others—well, you know what happens to them. That's right, exactly, Niko, my friend. You might have a talent for the business."

"The talent, maybe," Nick said, "but not the stomach."

Lucky glanced down at his watch and pushed himself away from his desk. "Okay," he said. "The car ought to be ready by now."

He picked up the pills from his desk and tendered them in his palm. "Who's first?"

I knew what I had to do. I wasn't looking forward to it, but I couldn't see any other way. I couldn't fake it, either. Lucky would not be fooled. I hoped that Nick had some-thing in mind. All I could do was try to make things easier for him.

"Couldn't we do it together, Lucky?" I pleaded.

He weighed the pros and cons of this and apparently couldn't see where it would hurt anything. "All right, but no games." He pointed the gun at Nick's chest. "I don't really want the mess, but if I have to use a bullet, I will." He handed each of us our McDonald's tumbler. "Put out your hands."

We did as told, watching as he dropped several small white tablets into each palm. "Take a sip and swallow the pills," he said, pointing the gun at Nick's forehead for added encouragement.

*Be calm. Just do it.* I glanced over at Nick, who met my gaze with surreptitious wink before popping the tablets in his mouth. I lifted my hand and dropped the pills onto my tongue. My other hand seemed disengaged from the rest of me as it brought the cup to my lips. *Do it,* I coaxed myself. *Do it!* I took a deep gasp of breath and aspirated the wine, sucking it toward my lungs.

My body kicked into protection mode—coughing and spraying wine and pills across the room as I doubled over, trying to dislodge the liquid from my lungs. Lucky leaped toward me reflexively, giving Nick only a fraction of a second. It was all he needed. He spat a stream of wine and pills across the desk, snagged the empty wine bottle and brought it crashing down against the desk. Before the shards could land, he lashed up the inside of Lucky's arm, digging into the flesh above the elbow. Lucky dropped the gun with a howl. It discharged when it hit the cement floor, the concussion echoing across the warehouse in a wave. I was still coughing—gasping and wheezing for air.

Blood spurted from the inside of Lucky's arm, spraying me as he pivoted toward Nick. Nick slashed again viciously, this time slicing at the neck. He missed, grazing Lucky at the jawline, but apparently his previous swipe had sliced the brachial artery. Blood still spurted from Lucky's arm. His blue-silk shirt, now slick and red, stuck to him like a wet suit. He lunged toward Nick in a blind stagger. I pushed myself out of the chair, still doubled over, and scrambled for the gun. Nick pushed Lucky back, slamming his head against the cinder-block wall of the office.

"The other one," I sputtered at Nick. "The shot. He'll be back."

Nick nodded and shoved Lucky into a chair. "Keep the gun on him," he whispered and tiptoed out the office door, the broken bottle still in his hand.

Lucky was breathing, but the blood was still coming fast. His complexion had drained to grayish white. Even the color in his hair seemed to be dissipating. His hands lay limp over the arms of the chair. His eyes were open and his face frozen into a glazed expression of surprise. I thought he must be going into shock and might bleed to death unless we did something fast. For all he had put us through, I couldn't let that happen. I reached for the phone and dialed 911.

By the time the connection was made, Nick was back. He prodded Mr. Universe along with the broken glass aimed at his kidney. Light flashed off the wicked green edge of the bottle—as good as, if not better than, a knife. Nick shoved him into the other visitor's chair and pried the gun out of my hand while I identified myself to the operator.

"We have a seriously wounded man here. We need an ambulance right away," I said, and added as an afterthought, "Oh, and please send the police. Get in touch with Detective Michael Fallon."

George, the bouzouki player, tucked his cigarette under his pinkie and strummed the opening bars of a song. *"Kapote piga stin America, plousios matia mou na yino,"* he sang—"Some time ago I went to America, my love, to become rich." From plumbers and sponge divers to soccer players like Nick and hoteliers like Christos, it was an old story. Sometimes it just didn't come true. If Eva's father had succeeded, how different would things have been now?

Our waiter—a young man from Brooklyn—tipped a bottle of *Mavrodaphne* over my glass. "No, thank you," I said. "I believe I've had enough."

Once the ambulance had left with Lucky, Nick led Fallon through the warehouse of Plemenos Imports. After giving a statement to a uniformed officer and watching as they cuffed Mr. Universe and took him on his way, I'd called Miss Alma and Spiros, in our room at the hotel.

"He's much better," she reported of Father Charles. "In fact, other than being restless and slightly irritable, he's more or less back to normal. I've just called Georgia. We're on our way over to the church for the rehearsal."

"I don't think we'll make it to the church, but we'll meet you at *Dino's* later," I'd said. And so we had, arriving just as the wedding party was coming in.

"Eva planned to set Alex up—to frame him as a pusher, using his father's hotel as his base of operations," Nick said, spearing a chunk of *kalamari.* "I doubt if she planned to turn him in. I think she would have urged Christos to send him back to Greece to keep him out of trouble. Lucky was right about one thing—it would never have worked."

Kate shook her head. "It seems too incredible, really. All her plots—curses and gypsies—for a job."

"I think her ambition must have been insatiable," I said. "But you have to look at it this way—at least it wasn't personal." I glanced around at the startled expressions of my companions.

"Eva had no interest in preventing the marriage other than to advance her career. The threats to Alex and Kate had no basis in reality—they were just scare tactics. The physical danger to both of them was minimal. And the gypsy," I said, honing in on Pagona, "was a fraud."

Pagona fingered her *mati,* grumbled something inaudible and turned her back to me. I caught Xanthe's eye and winked. I had known from the beginning that I was never going to like that little old lady. That's why I was caught completely unaware when, as we were leaving, she stopped me, took my face in her hands and kissed me on both cheeks. She grabbed my hand and dropped something into my palm.

"For you," she said, very slowly and carefully in English.

I opened my palm. There, encased in its gold bezel, was the *mati.*

## Chapter Thirty-Four

". . . That He send down upon them love perfect and peaceful, and give them His protection; let us pray to the Lord . . ."

". . . That He may keep them in oneness of mind, and in steadfastness of the Faith . . ."

". . . That He may bless them in harmony and perfect trust . . ."

". . . That He may keep the course and manner of their life blameless . . ."

Father Charles stood before a table in front of the cathedral's Royal Gate, facing the bride and groom. Although I couldn't see it, I knew what the table contained—the wedding crowns, the book of the Gospel, two rings, two white candles, and a cup of wine.

Kate reached up to adjust the *flouria* at her throat and the coins tinkled softly. They must have felt very heavy against her slender neck. Among them was the Helios. Although it was evidence in a crime, Detective Fallon had received special permission to return it to the family for the wedding only. After the ceremony, the coin would be exchanged for the fake and returned to police custody. Michael Fallon himself was there to collect it.

Father Charles took the rings, blessed them and made the sign of the cross over Alex's head. "The servant of God, Alexandros, is betrothed to the servant of God, Katerina . . ."

He turned to Kate. "The servant of God, Katerina, is betrothed to the servant of God, Alexandros . . ."

At Manolis's insistence, we had been seated in the family section with Miss Alma. Spiros, as the *koumbaros*, stood at the altar with the couple. He was rigidly attentive and as dignified as Christos. At Father Charles's signal, he took the rings from the priest and exchanged them on the couple's fingers, signifying the complementary roles of husband and wife.

Nick and I had always worked together. From the time he opened the Oracle, I had been there to help. He had cared for me throughout my pregnancy and miscarriage. We were different. If I hadn't realized it before, our trip to Tarpon Springs certainly opened my eyes. No matter how much I embraced the culture, I would never be Greek, nor would Nick ever be fully American. But as I sat there in the cathedral, I realized that it was our differences that made us complements.

". . . Bless this marriage and grant unto these Your servants Katerina and Alexandros a peaceful life, length of days, chastity . . ." Nick took my hand and lifted it to his lips with a smile.

". . . Keep their wedlock safe against every hostile scheme . . ."

If any couple had been confronted with hostile schemes, it was Kate and Alex. Aris Mavrakis was in jail and very likely to stay there a while. Theo had agreed to testify to what he knew in exchange for a reduced sentence in the death of Eileen Reilly. I couldn't help but think about her, and about the wedding that would never happen. Only one question was left—why do miracles happen for some people and not for others? But I knew that no one on this earth would ever be able to answer that one.

Manolis had been right about Aris after all. Fortunately, he had been wrong about Christos. Still, his apology had not come easily.

Christos had slapped his back heartily. "We are Greeks, man! If you were not suspicious of me, I would think you a fool. Do you imagine I want a fool in my family?"

Lucky Plemenos was still in the hospital, under guard. He was said to be too weak to be moved to the jail in Clearwater, where Mr. Universe was already in residence. Detective Fallon had a lengthy list of charges against Lucky, beginning with first-degree murder.

"Will you be able to make it stick?" I asked.

"I don't know. That's the DA's job. We've got the wine bottle, which just happens to have a bar code on it. We should be able to trace it to one of Plemenos's shipments. That's a good start. And now that we know who we're dealing with, we should be able to piece together some of the other evidence—fibers at the scene, that kind of thing— to place him there. And if we're really lucky, his buddy will crack and give us all the information we need. Accessory to murder is not a nice charge. I'm willing to bet he'll be happy to plead to a lesser charge in exchange for information."

"The servant of God, Alexandros, is crowned for the servant of God, Katerina . . ." Father Charles set one of the crowns on Alex's head and turned to Kate, repeating the petition. He set the crown, slightly tilted, on top of her veil.

"O Lord, our God, crown them with glory and honor . . ."

Kate and Alex stood beside one another wearing the *stefana*, the white-flowered crowns linked by a long satin ribbon. They would keep their crowns to display in their home, just as Nick and I had kept ours—a symbol of the sovereignty of our home and our marriage. Neither Lucky Plemenos nor Rula Vassos could ever undermine that.

We stood for the Gospel—the miracle at Cana. "The world is full of miracles," Miss Alma had said, and I finally understood what she meant. Nick and I—our marriage—that was a miracle.

Father Charles offered the couple the cup of wine. "Bless also this common cup given to them that are joined in the community of marriage . . ." They each drank from the cup three times before handing it back to the priest. He set it on the table and reached for their hands.

Kate lifted the hem of her gown, setting the coins on her necklace to jingling merrily. Father Charles took her other hand, placed it in Alex's hand and drew them forward, leading them around the table three times in the dance of Isaiah—a symbol of the couple taking their first steps into the world together. The wedding was concluded and the time for rejoicing had come. Spiros followed the bride and groom, holding the crowns above their heads. A tear slid down his cheek and lodged in his mustache, but a smile wreathed his face.

"O Isaiah, dance your joy . . ."


Spiros rose from the head table and lifted a glass of champagne to offer a traditional toast. He had practiced it in English from the day the invitation arrived until this moment. The room grew quiet.

"Now seeng, and dahnce and shek the r-r-room, and weesh good luck to the bride and groom!"

The band struck the first notes of a familiar *pentozali* as the bridal couple took over the dance floor. Nick took our drink orders and headed for the bar. He hadn't gotten far when he was intercepted by Rula. She wore a bright red dress—thigh length and as tight as the skin on a grape. I swallowed hard and turned my attention to Miss Alma.

"You know," she said, "I've been thinking about the coin. I have always wanted to own something from the Hellenistic period. I wonder how I might go about finding a small artifact."

"You could ask Rula, I suppose." She'd followed Nick to the bar, was leaning against him, her hand lightly resting on his lower back. Despite all my resolutions to the contrary, the old anger flamed.

"That's a good idea. She told me she found some of the vases in Salonika. I wonder . . ."

Salonika. What was it about Salonika and vases? Something Aris had said about—"Excuse me, Miss Alma. I'll be back in a minute."

I slipped into the elevator and descended to the first floor. The lobby was deserted. I gave Lucy a wave and crossed to the glass display cases. Cypro–Geometric ca 600 B.C. Or possibly somewhat later.

Back at the reception, Nick had returned to the table, Rula right on his heels. She laughed at something he said, set her drink on our table and turned toward the ladies' room. I crossed the dance floor and pushed open the door following her in.

I was wearing a soft, navy-silk belted dress. I took off the belt and smiled. The dress looked just as good—maybe better—not cinched in at the waist. I fingered Pagona's *mati*, which I'd slipped onto a delicate gold chain around my neck. Envy, Father Charles had said, was the root of the evil eye. Rula envied me my husband. But I wasn't willing to wait for the *mati* to do its work. I wanted to take care of the problem myself.

Rula had entered the middle cubicle. I took the belt,

threaded it through the handle of her stall and stretched it across the third door, tying it to the handle in a tight square knot. When I was sure it was secure, I stepped into the first cubicle and clambered up on top of the toilet. She was in the act of adjusting the pads in her WonderBra.

"Hi, there!"

She narrowed her eyes. "What do you want?"

"Just some girl talk," I said.

"Not on your life." She grabbed the door and pulled. In the third stall, the door slammed against the frame. "Hey!"

"Think of yourself as a captive audience."

"Let me out of here," she demanded.

I shook my head. "Not until you and I reach an understanding."

Rula doubled her fists and planted them on her hips, glowering at me. "About what?"

I rested my elbow on the divider and my chin in my hand. "My husband."

Rula smiled slyly. "Worried?"

I shook my head. "Not a bit. Oh, we'll also have to come to an agreement about Christos Kyriakidis's pottery." The last three words wiped the smirk off her lips. I nodded, confirming her fears.

"I know they're fakes. And I know he paid big bucks for them. Andreas of Salonika is quite a craftsman. Now, here's the deal. Tomorrow you will call Christos and tell him that you've discovered that the pieces are copies and you're returning his money. Also, regrettably, that you won't be able to decorate any more of his hotels. You'll have to forgo the party for tonight, because you'll be leaving immediately. Oh, and don't bother to say good night to Nick. He'll be busy dancing with me."

Rula folded her arms and leaned back against the divider between the stalls, smiling—cool as the blood in her veins. "I don't know what you're talking about. If Christos was taken on that pottery, then so was I. Besides, he won't believe you. And as for Nick—let's face it, babe, you just can't compete."

"Okay," I said, climbing down from the toilet. "I was going to give you a break—strictly because I didn't want to embarrass Christos—but I'll just have to tell him about it myself. I wonder what the charge is for forgery of an art object. I'm sure it's a felony."

Rula rattled the door. "Hey, wait a minute."

"Sorry, I guess you need some time to think about it." I checked my lipstick and my hair in the mirror while Rula silently fumed in the stall. She was going to hold out. I shrugged, patted myself on the back and headed for the door.

"He won't believe you."

"Oh, I think he will," I said. "After everything else that's happened, I definitely think he will."

Out in the dining room, Nick waited for me at the table. His face broke into a warm smile when he saw me. "Julia, where have you been? I've been waiting to dance with you."

"Sounds good to me," I said, setting my bag on the table. "Let's go."

He led me across the room to the dance floor, his arm cinched tightly around my waist. The drums switched to a beat in seven-eighths time, introducing a *kalamatiano*.

"*Ella, pame,*" Nick said, taking my hand. "One, two three four . . ."